GRAVE NEW WORLD

The Decline of The West in the Fiction of JG Ballard

DOMINIKA ORAMUS

THE TERMINAL PRESS

Back Cover Portrait of Dominika Oramus by Berenika Oramus

CONTENTS

AUTHOR'S NOTES

Grave New World. The Decline of the West in the Fiction of J.G. Ballard—my attempt to chart J.G. Ballard's unique universe—was written mostly in 2004 and 2005 and edited a year later. The twentieth century was already gone and its memories were receding into the past. And yet that century when Ballard was born, grew up, and wrote most of his *oeuvre,* the century which he determinedly described and commented upon, was still very much with us. This was the right time to write a book aimed at presenting Ballard's ideas concerning the titular Decline of the West—that is, his chronicles of the twilight of Western civilization.

The initial idea to trust the tale and not the teller, and to analyze his fiction, non-fiction, and autobiographical semi-fiction on the same plane proved fruitful and intellectually gratifying. Having in my book's initial chapters defined the *Grave New World,* i.e., Ballard's vision of the West in the second half of the twentieth century, I then went on to look at this territory from different angles: the chapter *Battlefields* presents diverse real and made-up wars Ballard describes; *Cityscapes* highlights Ballard's urban narratives; *Mediascapes* showcases his critique of simulacra and mass culture. The *Mindscapes* chapter is devoted to Ballard's inner space narratives which portray the *Grave New World* as it is reflected in characters' psyche, and *Wastelands,* the last and the most important chapter, depicts the contemporary West as a post-apocalyptic setting where catastrophe has already struck, though its inhabitants seem unaware of the fact. After my book was ready Ballard published one more novel, *Kingdom Come,* which I discussed in the appendix to the first edition. Now, that analysis is integrated into the body of the book. I also corrected some minor mistakes, but apart from these instances I decided not to alter the text of the book.

Today, from the perspective of the middle of the 21st century's second decade, I can see that approaching Ballard as if he were a philosopher and theorist of history of Arnold Toynbee's kind—and not a great stylist and ingenious fabulist was limiting. *Grave New World* is clearly a book written by a very young scholar with only two books to her credit at that time (an unpublished PhD on Angela Carter included), and whose ideas were quite radical. Nonetheless, the book still reads well and by discussing all Ballard's texts synchronically it is quite different than other critical works on him published to date.

The first edition of *Grave New World* was published by my alma mater, the University of Warsaw, in a very limited number of copies and has never been available to the general public. In fact, apart from reviewers and a few J.G. Ballard enthusiasts who e-mailed me asking for a copy, few people have read the book. It is thanks to The Terminal Press that *Grave New World* has finally been published and made available. Thank you, Terminal Press!

The very title *Grave New World* is of course a pun on Aldous Huxley's *Brave New World*, and it is perhaps worth remembering that in writing the preface to the post-war edition of his novel Huxley was genuinely surprised that his dystopian prophesy from the 1930s was already coming true in the late 1940s. Ten years previously he had deemed the decline of the West inevitable, though he believed it would take millennia and not decades to happen. And yet he lived to see his grim predictions already coming true. I do not feel it apt to say the *Grave New World* prophesied by Ballard is similarly already around us in the countless suburbs of the Western world. Rather, I leave that determination to the readers of my book.

I must mention one new and important context to the theme of my book, one which appeared after it was written. Just before his death Ballard commented on his life and *oeuvre* in his autobiography entitled *Miracles of Life*: *Shanghai to Shepperton*. There he claims that nowadays "it's no longer possible to stir or outrage by aesthetic means alone... A psychological challenge is needed that threatens... our dearer delusions" (Ballard 2008: 240). Hence Ballard's artistic decision to adopt the malleable stylistics of science fiction in order to defamiliarize "the pathology that underlay the consumer society, the TV landscape and the nuclear arms race, a vast untouched continent of fictional possibility" (ibid: 167). This creed seems to confirm the validity of my approach to his *oeuvre*: whether in writing fiction and non-fiction, or in fantasizing and reporting Ballard strove to say something important about the world we live in: the post-capitalist society in its decline. Following his critics, Ballard says that his entire fiction is "the dissection of a deep pathology that I had witnessed in Shanghai and later in the post-war world, from the threat of nuclear war to the assassination of President Kennedy, from the death of my wife to the violence that underpinned the entertainment culture of the last decades of the century" (ibid: 145).

In the light of *Miracles of Life* one is tempted to discuss Ballard's writings in reference to trauma theory, his persistent comings-back to the war being a compulsive re-telling of the traumatic experience. Moreover, a comparative analysis of J.G. Ballard and Kurt Vonnegut is also waiting to be written by some inquisitive scholar: one, an American with German roots who saw war in Europe, and the other a Shanghai-born Briton who saw war in China—both of whom continued to write traumatized science fiction and went on creating scenarios for the death and dissolution of Western civilization. Such a comparative analysis, along with a number of other books inspired by J.G. Ballard's outstanding imagination, should and will be written. Numerous anthologies of Ballard's texts and the criticism devoted to them are being published every year, which fact proves his long-lasting influence. The *Grave New World* has clearly recognized its prophet.

Dominika Oramus
Zenonów-Warsaw 2015

GRAVE NEW WORLD

INTRODUCTION

DISASTER AND DEVASTATION

Are we living in the happy times of a social utopia where everyone can participate equally in the blessings of advanced technology, modern science and sophisticated communications systems? Are we witness to the true *Brave New World* the human race has dreamt of for generations? Or is our contemporary reality yet another *Grave New World*[1]—a dystopian land of social manipulation and hegemonic mass media? Is ours a world that denies free will, breeds psychopathologies and supplants first-hand experience with simulacra?

1. This phrase comes from an interview Ballard gave to David Gale: "Grave New World. Interview with J.G. Ballard", BBC Radio 3, 10 November 1998 (www.jgballard.com, on 20 August 2006).

In 1932 Aldous Huxley published his *Brave New World* as a warning against what the future might bring. And indeed, throughout the last century numerous philosophers, historians, sociologists, and fiction writers repeated similar concerns and fears. In that same year, 1932, the first one-volume English translation of Oswald Spengler's *The Decline of the West* was published, thereby introducing to English literary culture the idea of an inevitable end to every civilization, ours included. His study prompted Arnold Toynbee to begin work on his monumental opus *A Study of History*, wherein he discusses a host of past human civilizations and points to the causes of their fall, indirectly suggesting that our own Western culture is well advanced on its own way to disintegration. Arnold Toynbee writes:

> The self-inflicted wounds from which civilizations die are not these of a material order. In the past, at any rate, it has been the spiritual wounds that have proved incurable (Toynbee 1949: 135).

It seems appropriate to me to start the present study of J.G. Ballard by quoting the above passage from Toynbee's lecture "The International Outlook"; coming in the wake of World War II, it reveals the sad truth about civilizations in general: they are universally threatened with decline and demise. Whatever may precipitate the West's fall will involve external factors (waves of immigration, dangerous weapons in irresponsible foreign hands, terrorism, alien cultures and religions filling in the spiritual vacuum, etc.), but these matters will be allowed in only because of the internal spiritual damage that is already underway. In both his fiction and non-fiction Ballard describes the dire spiritual changes that have been taking place since the war and have transformed the West. Though Western civilization has apparently succeeded in perpetuating itself to the new millennium in having overcome communism and avoided the threat of a Third World War, nuclear catastrophe and internal collapse, for Ballard Huxley's vision remains uncanny in the way it is coming true. At least in some of its key aspects.[2]

In this book I read Ballard's fiction (and some of his non-fiction) as a record of the gradual internal degeneration of Western civilization in the second half of the twentieth century. In sundry ways and styles Ballard's ostensibly very heterogeneous *oeuvre* depicts the same intangible catastrophe that has happened to the world. Contemporary reality is thus presented in his late prose as "post-apocalyptic": though we are not literally living amidst the ruins, the golden age is far behind us and we are witnessing the twilight of the West. It is difficult to pinpoint the exact moment in the past when things went wrong,[3] but that fateful

2. As late as in 2004 in an appendix to his novel *Millennium People* J.G. Ballard gives Huxley's *Brave New World* at the very top of the list of books he recommends for those who have liked his novel (Ballard 2004: Appendix 16).

3. For Ballard the plausible candidate is the invention and use of the nuclear bomb. For the first time in history the human race acquired the means to realize its latent propensity for self-destruction. Men have always been violent creatures unconsciously dreaming of death and war, something which culture has tried to cover up for thousands of years. Once the true human nature was revealed, there is no turning back and human destiny—destruction for internal reasons—is

turn has undeniably taken place and wrought grave spiritual change. Thus do we hear the death knells of our civilization, one growing increasingly hostile to individuals and erecting a cult of violence.

I hope to achieve two aims in this book. Firstly, I hope to show *Grave New World*, the imaginary territory Ballard describes in his books, which is a combination of the turn-of-the-millennium world, intertextual allusions to both fiction and non-fiction, and Ballard's projections for the near future with its sociological idiosyncrasies. I would like to prove that irrespectively of the literary conventions Ballard applies in a given text (science fiction, speculative fiction, detective story, thriller, war novel or any other), he charts the very same territory and remains throughout primarily interested in the reaction of the human mind to the post-World War II reality which is the common denominator of his diverse obsessions. Secondly, I would like to shed some light on the spiritual condition and social problems of contemporary Western civilization as seen by its ever so inquisitive member.[4]

My technique in approaching Ballard is mostly that of textual analysis and close readings of passages of his texts that best show his exuberant stylistics; sometimes I also point out his references to literary and cultural theories. As far as said theories are concerned, I shall follow Ballard's own readings. He very often alludes to critical schools and makes his characters discuss fashionable notions and ideas. Therefore, I will refer to the same sources: mostly psychoanalysts (many Ballardian characters are psychiatrists), but also historians and recent cultural theorists.

There are two problems with discussing Ballard's fiction, and they need be dealt with at the very beginning. The first concerns the generic classification of his books—the second is posed by Ballard's continuous attempts at auto-creation. As far as classification goes, the critics in different decades have described Ballard as a science fiction writer, a mainstream writer, a surrealist, a representative of the avant-garde, and an author who defies any classifications. To portray these controversies, in the next part of this Introduction (*The Critical Response to J.G. Ballard*) I will briefly present the most important critical approaches to Ballard, at the same time showing how his *oeuvre* alludes to many different literary conventions. As for myself, I am not going to deal with this problem and give my opinion about, for example, the precise moment when Ballard left science fiction behind and started writing *serious* books. Rather, I will discuss all his works on the same plane: moreover, I will not follow the chronology of Ballard's long and generically diverse literary career, opting instead to treat all of his work synchronically, as descriptions of different vistas of his *Grave New World*.

In the last part of this Introduction (*J.G. Ballard's Auto-creation*) I will deal with the second problem the Ballardian critic has to face. Over the fifty years of his career Ballard has continuously been creating his own image. His quasi-autobiographies, numerous articles and memories present a persona or rather a number of personas that he constructed in different moments of his life. Such

going to happen sooner or later.
4. In one of Freud's essays that Ballard often quotes, *Civilization and Its Discontents*, Freud calls human civilization a mistake. Ballard's fiction is devoted to the descriptions of this mistake.

a self-fashioning should not be mistaken with any kind of "historical truth"—
and in a study concerned with the intellectual history of the twentieth century
it is important not to take the fictitious "James Ballard" for a person who really
witnessed the war in Asia and the atomic bombing of Nagasaki. Therefore, I will
briefly discuss the images Ballard constructed in different decades of the last
century, and later—in the main body of my thesis—I will, to quote D.H. Lawrence,
"trust the tale not the teller" and try to avoid the auto-creation fallacies.

In my first chapter, before the focused discussion of Ballard's own works, I will
succinctly present those thinkers who are most important to the understanding
of his works. Such a spiritual map of the (mainly) twentieth century as sketched
by following Ballard's favourite philosophers and scientists will help to place his
fiction in the proper intellectual perspective, as his works are deeply informed
by theories that, from differing points of view, discuss the alarming state of our
civilization. This chapter does not aim to present on its but few pages a grand
critique of the century and the path our world is taking—as that, of course,
lies far beyond the scope of the present study. Rather, I will confine myself to
pointing out those books and essays that Ballard directly refers to. This chapter
will therefore give a theoretical frame to the subsequent discussion and will
allow me to avoid repetitive summaries of cultural theories in the rest of the
study. Thus, in the subsequent chapters I will refer back to this theoretical frame
numerous times, owing to the fact that Ballard often alludes to the very same set
of critical essays and enters into intertextual discussions with their authors from
changing vantage points.

As far as my own approach to his fiction is concerned, I will start by discussing,
in Chapter Two, the war narratives *Empire of the Sun, The Kindness of Women*
and some short stories devoted to both World War II and imaginary military
conflicts of the future. These texts describe events which for Ballard are the very
beginning of cultural decline, as it is after the war that Western civilization turned
into *Grave New World*. Though these books play with the reader by giving the
origins of events from Ballard's other fictional works and might be treated as a
conscious mythologizing of his life and career, they nevertheless do reveal the
crux of Ballard's historiosophy.

In the next chapters I try to map *Grave New World* and chart its diverse
territories. In Chapter Three I show cityscapes in Ballard's books and discuss
contemporary urban civilization—the cause of psychological traumas. Chapter
Four is devoted to mediascapes and the influence of modern communication
technology on the way people live, think and dream. Life in a world full of
highly developed technologies makes people indulge in escapist fantasies and
thus Chapter Five describes the mindscapes of contemporary Man: the end
of the world fantasies, death-drive utopias, and wish-fulfilment catastrophic
scenarios. Chapter Six, the final one, deals with the plexus of the contemporary
world and the near future, picturing the decadent decline of Western wastelands:
life in gated communities, secluded enclaves and luxurious resorts home to
psychopathologies, deviations and terminal boredom enlivened only by acts of
pointless violence.

The Critical Response to J.G. Ballard

J.G. Ballard's literary career started in the nineteen-fifties. His early stories were published in the popular magazines promoting a new, unique type of science fiction, one that differed from the pulp space fiction from America, which after the war flooded the British market. In the early sixties the need to reform the genre of science fiction and start a new thoroughly British artistic movement was all-pervasive. A small group of young writers, who later were dubbed the "New Wave", looked for a periodical that would publish intellectual SF, or "speculative fiction", as they insisted on calling it. Speculative fiction was to be a medium to discuss current social and cultural issues in an experimental, and often dramatic way.

The periodical they finally found was *New Worlds*, a magazine published since 1946, but which in its long history had many times changed publishing houses and its artistic profile. In 1967 the post of editor-in-chief was given to Michael Moorcock, an ambitious young writer and a friend of Ballard—together they prepared a number of artistic manifestos defining speculative fiction and setting the goals for British avant-garde science fiction. The term "speculative fiction" was soon abandoned, as the critics and columnists preferred to call the *New Worlds* group the "New Wave", which is a literal translation of the French *nouvelle vague*.[5] Christopher Priest, a writer and a journalist, and Judith Merril, an influential US-born anthologist and columnist, popularized the phrase "New Wave" among readers in Britain and the US.

Although the avant-garde tendencies in British science fiction are in fact older than the late-1960s term, and stories written by Ballard, Moorcock and Brian Aldiss a few years earlier are now subsumed under the "New Wave" label. Peter Nicholls writes in *The Encyclopedia of Science Fiction* (1993):

> By 1965, then, science fiction was ripe for change. In fact many of the so-called experiments of the period were not experiments at all, but merely an adoption of narrative strategies, and sometimes ironies that had long been familiar in the mainstream novel. In the event, some of the science fiction writers who felt they now had the freedom to experiment, especially Ballard, were to add something new to the protocols of prose fiction generally (Clute and Nicholls 1993: 866).

Therefore, from the very beginning of his literary career Ballard is considered an in-between writer oscillating between "low-brow" and "high-brow" literature Sometimes he is called a postmodernist, sometimes an avant-garde author.[6] The

5. An experimental artistic movement in the French cinema associated with the films of Jean-Luc Godard and François Truffaut.
6. It may be interesting to note that in 1993 Ballard wrote a review of this Encyclopedia. Published in the *Daily Telegraph*, that article was re-printed in Ballard's collection of journalism, *A User's Guide to the Millennium*. Ballard speaks in favour of the Encyclopedia and science fiction in general,

critic who as early as the nineteen-sixties writes about him passionately and is partly responsible for his being dubbed an experimental "New Wave" writer is Judith Merril. Merril is an author of a number of well-known disaster stories describing nuclear catastrophes, but only in the nineteen-fifties when she began editing anthologies did she become one of the most influential figures in American science fiction. Always experimental and eager to revise the cliché standards of American pulp magazines, she swiftly became an advocate of the "New Wave", and especially of Ballard. As a columnist in the *Magazine of Fantasy and Science Fiction* she presented speculative fiction to American readers and discussed the books of the *New Worlds* writers.

> *New Worlds* today is an altogether unique publication: and the astonishment of some of the stuffier intellectual circles in London when the Art Council announced an annual grant of 1800 pounds for a science fiction magazine... was probably no greater than the shock experienced by American fans attending the 1967 World Science Fiction Convention in New York when they had their first look at the transformed magazine of *Speculative Fiction*... The new magazine is quarto size, non-glossy... with cover art, interior illustrations and (increasingly) page design to match the most experimental of the fiction, and to suit the sophistication of Chris Finch's articles on avant-garde art and graphics (Merril 1968: 344-345).

In 1968 Merril edited an anthology of the "New Wave" writers: *England Swings SF. Stories of Speculative Fiction*. Apart from stories and poems Merril presents in this book her opinion on every writer in original fashion. *England Swings SF* tries to match the "New Wave" fiction in graphic experiments and narrative strategies. The very beginning of the anthology resembles an avant-garde poem:

> You have never read a book like this before, and the next time you read one anything like it, it won't be *much* like it at all.

> It's an action-photo, a record of process-in-change, a look through the perspex porthole at the momentarily stilled bodies in a scout ship boosting fast, and heading out of sight into the multiplex mystery of inner/outer space.

---

noticing that in the second part of the 20th century more and more mainstream writers (such as Angela Carter, Anthony Burgess, Doris Lessing and Kingsley Amis) turn to science fiction, which is the true folk literature of the century, with "folk literature's hotline to the unconscious" (Ballard 1997b: 193). Science fiction has the power to design the future, and to tell us what life might be like in some years' time. He also writes that in the mid-century, after the Moon Landing and during the space race, everybody was interested in the future and the conquest of space and in trying to imagine what the year 2000 would bring, while at the real end of the millennium people forget all about that. Certain crazy millenarian cults are treated in the same way, such as fitness fanatics, or animal-rights activists and New Agers—and they in fact deserve no better, which is a telling sign of our spiritual deterioration.

I can't tell you where they are going, but maybe that's why I keep wanting to read what they write. The next time someone assembles the work of the writers in this—well, 'school' is too formal and 'movement' sounds pretentious... (ibid.: 9-10).

The anthology contains works of over twenty young and ambitious writers— Ballard is the only one who has three of his stories reprinted: the other authors boast but one. Given the prominent position of "guru of British avant-garde", he is presented to American readers (the anthology was meant to introduce the new literary fashion in America) as an often misunderstood, intellectually challenging writer. Merril chooses the newest stories, ones which are written in the present tense and use the collage technique: images, bits and pieces of commercials, psychiatric studies and TV newsreels are juxtaposed to show the prevailing violence of the contemporary mediascape.

Merril also decides to characterize Ballard (and other writers) in collages. Her introductions to stories are combinations of different texts cut into pieces and glued together. According to Peter Bürger's *Theory of the Avant-Garde* (1974), the collage technique challenges the reader's expectation of a synthetic, singular meaning. Diverse passages, graphically rearranged quotes of interviews, reviews and Merril's own opinions do not give a unified picture but rather show, at least in the case of Ballard, discussions and quarrels concerning his person and his place in the British literary world.

One can only hope that for Ballard too the worst misunderstanding is over, so that he will be free to create in a more intelligent atmosphere.

And so it was—in England, where the earlier work had finally been digested.

Freud pointed out that one has to distinguish between the manifest content of the inner world of the psyche and its latent content; and I think in exactly the same way, today, when the fictional elements have overwhelmed reality, one has to distinguish between the manifest content of reality and its latent contents.

And his sponsorship of the *Ambit* contest for the best prose or poetry written under the influence of drugs (ibid: 104-105).

Though Merril's style is far from critical exactness[7] (she does not give the sources of the texts used in her collages, not all sentences are complete), but it

7. As one can see in the quote above, Merril's technique is to cut into pieces different texts and mix the cuttings irrespective of syntax, the only differentiation between them is in the shape of print (I preserve Merril's bolds and margins to show how difficult it is to read her).

very well reflects the atmosphere of the 1960s discussions of the "New Wave" and Ballard's place in it. Juxtaposed with other experimental writers he is discussed within the science fiction movement, with the strong suggestion that his literary goal was to uplift, renew and meliorate science fiction. Ballard at that time was praised not only by science fiction critics[8]—and the general tone of his reviewers is similar to Merril's: this writer is the best and the most interesting of the speculative fiction writers.

Gradually, speculative fiction writers were either absorbed by the literary mainstream or stopped writing experimental prose and turned to pulp fiction. Harlan Ellison, the editor of an influential American anthology of speculative fiction, *Dangerous Visions*, complains in his Introduction that: "despite the new interest in speculative fiction by the mainstream, despite the enlarged and variant styles of the new writers, despite the enormity and expansion of topics open to these writers, despite what is outwardly a booming, healthy market, there is a constricting narrowness of mind on the part of many editors in the field!" (Ellison 1983: XXIII). In his attempt to revive this ambitious kind of popular fiction, Ellison decided to create an anthology "intended as a canvas for new writing styles, bold departures, unpopular thoughts" (ibid., XXVIII). And although he did not manage to "save" speculative fiction, his *Dangerous Visions* remain an important book in the history of science fiction.

Ellison is a very intrusive anthologist: to each of the thirty-two stories in the book he writes a separate introduction and epilogue, wherein he gives his opinions, suggestions and remarks concerning both the meaning of the story and its author. It is interesting to see how he describes J.G. Ballard, whom he presents to his American readers as a leader of the young English writers. Indeed, it is Ballard's Englishness, his upper-middle-class origins and colonial past that appeal to Ellison the most, while he in fact cannot define Ballard's literary style:

> Yet in totality [Ballard's books] present a kind of enriched literacy, a darker yet somehow clearer—perhaps the word is "poignant"— approach to the materials of speculative writing. There is a flavour of surrealism to Ballard's writing. No, it's not that, either. It is, in some ways, serene, as oriental philosophy is serene. Resigned yet vital. There appears to be a superimposed reality that covers the underlying pure fantasy of Ballardian conception (ibid., 459).

I am quoting Ellison to show how Ballard was received in the United States, for the American market is the most important (if not hegemonic) as far as science

---

8. In 1973 Brian Aldiss published *Billion Year Spree*, a history of science fiction. In the last chapter, devoted to the newest phenomena in the field, Ballard is described in the following way: "His ferocious intelligence, his wit, his cantankerousness, and, in particular, his extraordinary rendering of the perverse pleasures of today's paranoia, make him one of the grand magicians of modern fiction. His is an uncertain spell, but it spreads... far beyond the stockades of ordinary science fiction" (Aldiss 1973: 343).

fiction goes. Ellison completed his anthology in the late 1960s, in the last days of the British "New Wave" in science fiction. James Gunn, the editor of probably the most important single anthology/history of science fiction ever written, the multi-volumed *The Road to Science Fiction*, produced his book in the following decade. At that time in the US nobody well remembered what the "New Wave" was about. So, while presenting Ballard and his story "The Terminal Beach" to his readers, Gunn had to lecture on this movement. He discusses it from the perspective of America in the late 1970s, treating it as a very remote phenomenon. He calls Ballard the leader and guru of the *New Worlds* group, compares his enigmatic symbolic style to James Joyce's *Finnegan's Wake* and John Dos Passos' *U.S.A.* and explains the nihilism of his writing by claiming that Ballard wrote against Americans in Vietnam, about drugs, the Beatles, pop-art, pop-music, political assassinations and terrorism. And this is probably how Ballard is read by fans of science fiction to this day.

Although Ballard's career stretched well beyond the "New Wave" movement, which ended by the early nineteen-seventies, his early fiction is often discussed in the context of "New Wave" poetics. The ambitious artistic programme of the movement and the fact that many of its representatives became well-known and important writers[9] attracted the attention of literary critics. One of the first scholars to study the output of the group was Colin Greenland, who in the late 1970s was a postgraduate student at Oxford. A great fan of *New Worlds* and science fiction in general, he dreamt of writing serious criticism about this literary genre, which at the time was considered too 'low-brow' to study.[10] Tom Shippey,[11] then Fellow of St John's College, Oxford, an author of criticism about J.R.R. Tolkien and a contributor to Patrick Parrinder's critical anthology *Science Fiction. A Critical Guide*, agreed to supervise Greenland's work.

Finally, in 1980 Greenland's thesis (entitled *The Entropy Exhibition. Michael Moorcock and the British 'New Wave' in Science Fiction*) was accepted for a doctorate in English Literature at the University of Oxford. Thanks to a grant from the Arts Council of Great Britain, Greenland reworked his thesis and in 1983 a book of the same title was published. *The Entropy Exhibition* is a superb criticism of science fiction, as Greenland shows the literary output of the "New Wave" in the context of cultural and artistic life in the nineteen-sixties. And

9. Ballard is the most prominent among them, but there are many others, for example: Michael Moorcock, Brian Aldiss, D.M. Thomas.
10. Greenland is now a prominent science fiction scholar and an author of highly regarded fantastic books.
11. Many years later Shippey remembers how science fiction critics were treated in the 1960s and 1970s by Academia: "A further way of putting this is to say that during my science fiction "lifetime" (1958 to now) being a science fiction reader was rather like being gay. In both cases, one could say, drawing out the similarities: *there was a definite pressure, especially in the 1950s and 1960s, not to admit the fact; *there were social penalties if you did; *you got used to hiding the fact" (Slusser and Westfall 2002: 8). Note: Volumes of criticism containing the essays, papers, and interviews which are quoted in the text of the present study are identified in the footnotes and then listed in the biography in alphabetic order under the name of the editor. The same is true for the prefaces and introductions which precede books written by some other author: in the footnotes the edition is identified and listed in the biography under the name of the author.

although only one chapter is devoted exclusively to Ballard, it remains to this day an important item in Ballardian criticism.

Greenland describes the social situation in the sixties, the emergence of youth culture, the influence of the Space Race[12] on popular imagination, the Vietnam War and the stormy history of *New Worlds*—a magazine that tried to reflect current cultural phenomena. Additionally, he inserts in his book three monographic essay-chapters presenting the works of Ballard, Brian Aldiss and Michael Moorcock.

As far as Ballard's output is concerned, Greenland discusses his early disaster novels and some of the stories he wrote in the fifties and sixties. The books *High-Rise* and *Concrete Island* (written in the seventies) are but mentioned, and Ballard's later works are of course absent from the study. His general approach to both Ballard and the "New Wave" is to read their output as a new kind of fiction growing out of traditional science fiction and characterized by its fascination with entropy: the universal and irreversible decline of energy into disorder. This fiction is in intimate connection with other cultural experiments of the epoch. Ballard, according to Greenland, is first of all a masterful stylist whose metaphors and allusions recreate the pessimistic attitude of the times and show a Universe doomed to death, one already frozen in its final stage. Ballard's early prose is described as pictorial and portrayed in the context of visual arts—Pablo Picasso, Paul Delvaux, Salvador Dali, René Magritte—Greenland points to colours, shades and figures borrowed by Ballard from concrete paintings.

Greenland also proves to what extent Ballard is indebted to Surrealism as far as his language is concerned, the poetic character of his early prose being an effect of a highly associative style:

> The Surrealist techniques that Ballard has used involve deliberate dissociations and mystifications. The object is taken from its usual context and dismantled, or put in a new context, or confused with other objects. But the result of the process is not mere nonsense, but a revaluation. The elements acquire new significance from the reorganisation, so that we sense more about the object than we knew or felt before. Surrealism can thus be said to have both a synthetic and an analytic aspect; it consists not only of inspiration, but also of inquiry. This duality Ballard has inherited (Greenland 1983: 104).

Such a characterization of Ballard's early style strikes as being very apt, as it accounts for Ballard's fascinations with Lautréamont, Alfred Jarry and André Breton, numerous visual intertextual allusions in his stories, as well as for Ballard's obsessive returns to the same or similar figures of speech. What Ballard and the Surrealists surely have in common is the belief that an apocalypse had

---

12. Disappointed by the space programme and disinterested in conquering the Universe, the "New Wave" writers produced anti-space fiction and were much more interested in the inner space of the human psyche.

already taken place, both in the intellectual sphere and in daily life. Ballard's prose shows the contemporary world abundant in fictions whose only connotations are the fantasies of their authors. Our environment is fragmented and coded, the popular imagery of posters and commercials needs deciphering—hence, Ballard's indebtedness to semiology and Roland Barthes. In other words, we live in the nightmarish world of the Surrealists.

Greenland describes Ballard's style and his specific figures of speech in an attempt to show why Ballardian prose is immediately recognizable and "unmistakable". He analyzes Ballard's habit of introducing a story with a stylized tableau and his conscious use of what he calls "pseudo-simile, one in which there is no discoverable parity between the terms. Ballard's version of it employs a literary sleight commonly used by ironists: he keeps the relation but blurs the distinction, so that the two halves of the simile, the actual and the virtual, can be swapped over" (ibid.: 103).

Greenland's book is still, after over twenty years, the best critical analysis of the "New Wave" movement, for among other reasons because it allows us to look at Ballard's early works from the perspective of the literary life in England at that time. It shows Ballard's involvement in the editing of *New Worlds*, his views on art and civilization in the 1960s, and his ambiguous position on the literary scene. Greenland (just like Merril) is very much interested in categories such as science fiction, mainstream literature, modernist writing, and the avant-garde. He shows the difficulties in pigeonholing Ballard and presents diverse opinions about how to classify his works. His major achievement as far as critical appraisal of Ballard's fiction goes is the discussion of his style in the context of the Surrealists: painters and poets alike.

In the nineteen-seventies many writers and critics discovered Ballard and came to highly prize his unique style and remarkable literary achievements. Among them were Kingsley Amis (a great advocate of "New Wave" prose), Graham Greene, Anthony Burgess, Susan Sontag and William S. Burroughs. They wrote reviews and introductions, but no monograph was published till the end of the decade.[13] Ultimately, David Pringle decided to work on a serious study of Ballard and in 1979 he published *Earth is the Alien Planet. J.G. Ballard's Four-Dimensional Nightmare*, a brief (61-page) but important monograph. His ambition in the book is to present Ballard's literary output to both science fiction fans and to the general reading public. Moreover, Pringle offers them a key to Ballard: he defines the place Ballard has on the market, divides his career into periods and classifies Ballardian characters and motifs.

Pringle starts by comparing Ballard to Ray Bradbury and Kurt Vonnegut, who also started their careers as science fiction writers, but subsequently transcended that category. Pringle describes Ballard as being less acclaimed, but equally worthy of being published "without the SF label" (Pringle 1979: 3). He pins

13. In 1973 David Pringle, a scholar specializing in writers associated with the field of science fiction, together with James Goddard edited *J.G. Ballard—the First Twenty Years*, a book which is not a monograph but a collection of texts consisting almost entirely of previously-published material by notable figures.

Ballard's lack of popularity on the fact that, unlike Bradbury and Vonnegut, he does not write for big and glossy magazines such as *Playboy*, but for the ambitious low-circulation press. This "courting of the avant-garde" (ibid.: 3) wins him a new but limited audience. Nevertheless, Pringle is sure that in the future Ballard will be fully appreciated and the book ends in a prophesy:

> Nevertheless, Ballard's reputation will grow in the decades to come, and he is likely to become recognized as by far and away the most important literary figure associated with the field of science fiction. More than that: he will be seen as one of the major imaginative writers of the second half of the 20th century—an author for our times, and for the future (ibid.: 61).

The division of Ballard's career into periods is also based on the genre of criticism. Here Pringle distinguished an early "romantic" stage, when Ballard published in the science fiction press stories concerned with the inner landscapes of characters' minds, and the post-science fiction period. It was then that Ballard shifted his interests to outer landscapes, abandoned science fiction conventions and embraced the avant-garde and literary periodicals. This is a "dark" period of formal experiments and of bitter criticism of the violence intrinsic to contemporary life. Pringle also suggests that Ballard is at the beginning of yet another period, one of writing present-oriented fiction describing technological environments: "he has also made larger concession to social realism... he is trying to become more of a *novelist*" (ibid.: 50).

Pringle explains that last statement by saying that Ballard is trying to construct rounded characters, while in his early prose his characters are symbolic "figures in an inner landscape" (ibid.: 51). He classifies these symbolic figures according to Jungian archetypes as the lamia, the jester and the king—and most Ballardian characters are demonstrated to belong to one of the categories. A similar symbolic key is used to deal with Ballardian themes (the categories are: Imprisonment,[14] Flight, Time Must Have A Stop, and Superannuation) and to classify his obsessively recurrent images.[15] Ballardian mythology is four-fold: Pringle distinguishes four groups of symbols representing mythical meanings of water, sand, concrete and crystal. Water stands for the past and the return to previous stages of evolution, sand and dryness are in the future of the human

14. Pringle is the first to explain Ballard's obsession with imprisonment by his personal experience of the three years spent in the Japanese prison camp. Such explanations in the nineteen-eighties became critical cliché.

15. Pringle enumerates typically "Ballardian" images: "concrete weapon-ranges, dead fish, abandoned airfields, radio telescopes, crashed space-capsules, sand-dunes, empty cities, sand reefs, half-submerged buildings, helicopters, crocodiles, open-air cinema screens, jewelled insects, advertising hoardings, white hotels, beaches, fossils, broken juke-boxes, crystals, lizards, multi-storey car-parks, dry lake-beds, medical laboratories, drained swamps, motorway flyovers, stranded ships, broken Coke bottles, vegetation, high-rise buildings, predatory birds and low-flying aircraft" (Pringle 1979: 16). This list is highly insightful; indeed, Pringle succeeds in pinpointing what the critics all vaguely describe as Ballard's unmistakable style.

race when only the exhausted shell of the planet will remain. Further, concrete is the world of the present day—the urban culture, while crystal, like a Jungian mandala, represents oneness with the Universe.

Generally speaking, Pringle's book represents Jungian criticism (though once he very rightly remarks, albeit in passing, that Ballard's references to Jung and Freud are mixed), and as such is it usually quoted. Pringle is also the first critic to mention Ballard's biography in the context of his fiction and to announce Ballard's affiliation to the avant-garde. In the following years Pringle remained Ballard's major critic, but more and more scholars interested in both science fiction and mainstream literature began to approach Ballard's books, often trying to ascribe his writing to some larger cultural frame. In *The Hidden Script* (1985), for example, David Punter discusses Ballard's fiction in the section "Narratives and the Unconscious", showing (in reference to psychoanalytic theories) the interrelation of the internal and the external spheres in his fiction.

The short chapter "J.G. Ballard: alone among the murder machines" is an excellent analysis of the metaphoric space Ballardian characters inhabit (e.g., in *The Atrocity Exhibition, High Rise, Concrete Island, Hello America* and *The Unlimited Dream Company*). This territory is nightmarish and ruled by man-made machines, "the lurking engines of destruction which keep us pinned down" (Punter 1985: 11), and people strive to regain a spiritual hold on objects, but they are in fact helpless victims of their own psychopathologies. Surrounded by technology and advanced communication systems, Man loses the ability of expression: "the areas of language already colonised by the public media too developed to allow for more than the slightest insertion of a discourse of individual desire" (ibid.: 10). Punter goes on to define Ballard's *oeuvre* in relation to contemporary culture and, although his analysis was written a quarter of a century ago, it is still very illuminating:

> Where character is concerned, Ballard is one of the few writers who can be sensibly termed post-structuralist: the long tradition of enclosed and unitary subjectivity comes to mean less and less to him as he explores the ways in which a person is increasingly controlled by landscape and machine; increasingly becomes a point of intersection for overloaded scripts and processes which have effectively concealed their distant origins in human agency (ibid.: 9).

In *Twentieth Century Science Fiction Writers* (1981), edited by Curtis C. Smith, a lexicon of those authors whose work goes beyond realism (even if they usually are not referred to as science fiction writers), the entry "J.G. Ballard" presents him as an original and distinctive writer whose style is described as idiosyncratic "as a signature" and shaped by the painter's eye of the author.[16] The stress falls on

16. The entry is written by George W. Barlow and in its bibliography all critical essays are by David Pringle. Pringle has also completed a new edition of *J.G. Ballard: A Primary and Secondary Bibliography*, which is very important to every Ballard scholar.

Ballard's intellectual fascinations: "masterpieces of literature (from Homer and the Bible through Shakespeare to Coleridge and Melville) and the arts (from Bosch to Dali and Leonor Fini)" (Smith 1981: 31). His early fiction is called romantic and exuberant science fiction rich in intertextual allusions, where bizarre landscapes "reflect and amplify the inner and mutual conflicts of... glamorous lamias and their suicidal wooers, in a baroque symphony of art, love, and death" (ibid.: 31). 1966 is given as the turning point after which Ballard abandons science fiction and starts to describe the contemporary world and to criticize its technology, violence and perverted entertainment. Such a present is just a fossil of the future, and his interest in science fiction gives Ballard an ability to look at social life in a detached, scientific way. Beyond that, Ballard's style changes abruptly: all exuberance is gone and instead we read about people like us, with popular names, living in real cities and made to cope with an inhuman urban existence.

It is interesting to juxtapose this entry with a later one hailing from the prestigious *The Encyclopedia of Science Fiction* (1993, revised 1999), edited by John Clute and Peter Nicholls. "J.G. Ballard" by David Pringle is a long entry and, for the first time, the author is presented not primarily as a science fiction writer (despite the very character of this *Encyclopedia*). Indeed, stress falls on those aspects of Ballard's output which transgress the standards of the genre. Even the earliest stories are shown as eschewing traditional science fiction themes and instead concentrating on "near-future decadence and disaster". We learn that Ballard was severely criticized by fans as a pessimist and a life-hater, that the science fiction world wrote him off, and that he never won a single science fiction award. Pringle also describes the hostility with which editors treated his later prose (the entire Doubleday edition of *The Atrocity Exhibition* was printed only to be pulped just before publication) because he used people such as Ronald Reagan, the Kennedys and Marilyn Monroe as characters. Pringle ends by presenting Ballard's psychological war novels and by briefly characterizing his biography— these are the beginnings of the legend of J.G. Ballard, his war and the impact it had on his imagination. Pringle concludes:

> Although most of his longer work of the past decade has been outside the field, the originality and appropriateness of his vision continue to ensure JGB's standing as one of the most important writers ever to have emerged from sf (Clute and Nicholls 1993: 85).

When in 1994 *Simulacra and Simulations* (1981) by Jean Baudrillard was translated into English, the prose of J.G. Ballard found a new and influential advocate. In a chapter devoted to Ballard's *Crash* (which had previously been translated and reprinted in *Science Fiction Studies*) Baudrillard calls Ballard's book one of the masterpieces of contemporary literature, one which shows the world of today as it really is, the simulated, unreal projection of mass culture and sophisticated hi-tech. Science fictionalizes reality, the world of cyber-technology is by nature fictitious and Ballard's prose is a rare example of the conscious exposure of the simulacra-ridden mediascape.

Generally, in the late nineteen-eighties[17] the status of ambitious science fiction changed. On the one hand some of the very good science fiction writers elevated the genre to the status of intellectually provoking, erudite reading, yet on the other hand many postmodernist writers began to apply science fiction conventions. Used as sophisticated literary trope, science fiction was no longer associated solely with an adolescent male audience and acquired the ambiguous status of "a game with the reader" or "a play with a convention". *'The Angle Between Two Walls'. The Fiction of J.G. Ballard* (1997) by Roger Luckhurst, the best critical book on Ballard to 2007, is devoted to the role Ballard's output plays in contemporary discussions about literary genres. Luckhurst's major thesis is that Ballard evades any and all classifications and that, moreover, his writing produces an effect of unease just because it exposes the binary, opposition-based categories we apply when reading. Ballard's books (especially *Crash* and *The Atrocity Exhibition*—other works are either but mentioned or discussed in brief subchapters) are for Luckhurst a pretext to expose contemporary reading protocols defining what is post-modern, what is modern, what is science fiction and what is avant-garde.

Luckhurst begins by showing Ballard as a fringe writer living literally in the suburbs of London and figuratively outside literary London and outside the Academia of English studies (a little like Ian Sinclair and, once, Angela Carter). His key to Ballard is the notion of *la brisure* (according to deconstruction, this is the point in any structural system that makes the working of the system at once possible and impossible), and in his analyses he most often refers to Derrida.[18] The choice of deconstruction as his approach is dictated by Ballard's paradoxical proliferation in recent criticism:

> The mainstream post-war novelist of increasing import; the aberrant foreign body within science fiction; the belated voice of a science fiction modernism; the anticipatory or timely voice of a paradigmatic postmodernism; the avant-garde writer of extreme experimental fictions; the prophet of the perversity of the contemporary world (Luckhurst 1997: xii).

Deconstruction exposes binary oppositions we constantly use while thinking and thus allows Luckhurst to subvert generic codes and frames of recognition that allow readability, and to "speak from a structurally similar space of the

17. In 1983 Ballard was contacted by V. Vale and the rest of RE/Search group, avant-garde publishers from San Francisco who became advocates of Ballard in the USA. In 1984 a special Ballard issue of their magazine RE/Search was published. In the following years they also re-published other of Ballard's works in America. For instance, RE/Search published an annotated version of *The Atrocity Exhibition*. Ballard wrote commentaries to each chapter of this difficult but very important book. In recent years they published two important Ballardiana: *J.G. Ballard Quotes* and *J.G. Ballard Conversations*. The first is a collection of one-line aphorisms taken from Ballard's books, the latter is a compilation of interviews given by him to different journalists (mostly from the RE/Search group).
18. Jacques Derrida has the largest number of references (of course after Ballard) in the index and the bibliography.

between" (ibid.: xiii). Such a critical standpoint sometimes makes his text a little enigmatic and focused not on Ballard's output but on the reader's (and critic's) response to it. Nevertheless, Luckhurst's study is very erudite, well grounded and full of insights into Ballard, the most valuable of which is the observation that Ballard's text anticipates its interpretations. "His work at once constantly activates theoretical models, but it is also awkward, didactic, and overtheorized, tending to evade or supersede the theories meant to 'explain' it" (ibid.: xvii).

Luckhurst proves his thesis on Ballard's fiction as exposing reading conventions by discussing in subsequent chapters the disaster story convention, surrealist writing, postcolonial writing, and theories of avant-garde and of contemporary reality as simulation. In each case Ballard's books are shown as both transgressing genres and subverting the oppositions they are based on. The conclusion is, expectedly, that Ballard's "*oeuvre* will not give up its irreducible core" (ibid.: xix), which very well sums up over forty years of critical discussion of Ballard's place on the twentieth-century literary map.

Currently a number of theses devoted to Ballard are being written at English universities by doctorate students, some of whom, like Sam Francis from the University of Leeds, publish their papers in international reviews of science fiction. A good example of critical evaluation of Ballard is a monograph published in the prestigious British Council-sponsored series *Writers and Their Work*, which is meant to briefly present the most important British authors to the reading public. *J.G. Ballard* (1998) by Michel Delville is a very good, concise account of all his most important works. Arranged in chronological order, it retraces subsequent stages in Ballard's career and attempts to show this diverse oeuvre as an example of artistic evolution. Delville is aware that critical assessment of Ballard is very heterogeneous:

> At least three J.G. Ballards have so far been championed in critical studies and literary histories: the science fiction writer, famous for his disaster novels and stories of entropic dissolution; and admirer of William S. Burroughs and author of scandalous tales remarkable for their sexual frankness and eccentric violence; and the Booker Prize nominee, whose account of a boy's life in Japanese-occupied wartime Shanghai in *Empire of the Sun* was published to great acclaim in 1984 (Delville 1998: 1).

Delville is aware of the temptation to draw a clear-cut line between Ballard's ambitious popular fiction and his mainstream novels. He is also careful not to reduce Ballard to a case of the prolonged artistic maturation of a science fiction writer who finally manages to disentangle himself from the immature genre. Instead he treats Ballard's obsessive and imaginary writing as a means to reflect the violent paradoxes of life in the twentieth century that escape less anxious discourses.

In 2005 another monograph under the same title, *J.G. Ballard*, was published in the new series "Contemporary British Novelists" by the Manchester University

Press. Written by Andrzej Gasiorek, this book (second in the series, after Aaron Kelly's *Irvine Welsh*) is a presentation of Ballard's oeuvre and a critical response to it. Like the whole series, it aims at disclosing controversies in contemporary literary life and theory. Just like Luckhurst, he reads Ballard in the context of surrealism, Pop Art and science fiction. Gasiorek's book marks the growing critical interest in Ballard's writing. He shows Ballard's output as "a symbolic rejection of the familiar heritage" (Gasiorek 2005: 2), writing against the tradition, against "Englishness", against "a socially rooted fiction based on psychological realism" (ibid.: 3), and against legitimate traditional literary genres.

The way the above critics approach Ballard seems to me very fair and it is quite similar to my own critical standpoint (I side especially with David Punter and Michel Delville). But as there have been so many exhaustive studies devoted to assimilating Ballard to generic categories (or abolishing the notion of genre fiction), I would rather refrain from repeating their arguments, and discuss what to my knowledge has not yet been discussed—the picture of the decline of the West seen from the perspective of both his fiction as a whole and that of theorists of civilization. Before embarking on that intellectual voyage, we need first look at the way Ballard constructs his own persona.

J.G. Ballard's Auto-Creation[19]

Many critics describe the surprising proliferation of "Ballards" in recent years, numerous doubles of the author, ones who people pages of other critics' studies and who seem to be quite different persons: an avant-gardist, a science fiction reformer and a mainstream writer of post-war classics. To me, this uncanny multiplication seems to result not only from the diverse criticism of essayists representing separate literary groups (the science fiction field, London's literary establishment, French postmodernists, American theorists of science fiction etc.), but also from Ballard's own journalism. In each stage of his long career Ballard was explicitly defining his artistic aims and describing the art of the writers, painters and filmmakers who influence him most, thus defining the context of his own output. During those years Ballard's ideas and likes have continuously evolved.

Ballard wrote essays and reviews for various literary magazines and daily newspapers; his journalism, collected in the 1996 volume entitled *A User's Guide to the Millennium*, reflects changes in his artistic fascinations and literary style. Initially he wrote for the ambitious counter-cultural SF magazine *New Worlds*, in the seventies he moved to *Ink, Vogue* and *Drive*; after the success of *Empire of the Sun* he started to collaborate with the *Guardian* and the *Daily Telegraph* and, occasionally, to contribute to thematic anthologies of essays. Read chronologically, his essays and reviews show both his development as a writer and the way in which he creates his own image, for example, by choosing and presenting his gurus—ones such as Salvador Dali or William Burroughs.

19. This sub-chapter is based on my article "From the Avant-Garde to the Autobiography: The Journalism of J.G. Ballard", in *Anglica* 2005, pp. 39-52.

Ballard's journalistic debut took place in *New Worlds*, a magazine intending to educate its readers. Apart from experimental fiction, Moorcock insisted on publishing Guest Editorials, reviews and articles that were meant to introduce to SF the artistic manifesto of the "New Wave". J.G. Ballard soon became his major essayist, and Moorcock called him "the Voice" of the movement. From 1964 to 1970 Ballard wrote numerous articles in which he described all the factors he saw as shaping contemporary artistic sensibility. His choice of subjects reveals his own fascinations, while the exuberant, metaphorical style of these articles imparts them with the unique character of revolutionary manifestos.

In these articles Ballard chooses his masters: the books and albums he reviews are by authors he admires and wants to be included into artistic canons. In the article "Myth Maker of the Twentieth Century" (1964)[20] he speaks strongly in favour of William Burroughs, whom he considered the second most important writer of the century, next to James Joyce. What he admires is Burroughs' ability to describe the "inner landscape of the post-war world", as we subjectively perceive it. The "man-made wilderness" of contemporary cities, the ugliness of civilization and paranoid perception of people surrounded by numerous fictions are for Ballard the true literary subject which Burroughs describes in the appropriate technique: his text is full of opposites, juxtapositions, chaotic imagery. Ballard enjoys the apparent contrast between organized, decent society and the psychopathic world of dropouts and, most of all, the way in which the differences between the two blur. Paranoia, fictionalization of media landscapes and hallucinations are characteristic for the contemporary psyche. Fictional elements derived from SF belong in our shared cultural competence and are incorporated into our inner landscape:

> What appear to be the science fictional elements… in fact play a metaphorical role… The sad poetry of… the whole apocalyptic landscape of Burroughs's world closes in upon itself, now and then flaring briefly like a dying volcano, is on a par with Anna Livia Plurabelle's requiem for her river-husband in *Finnegan's Wake*. (Ballard 1997b: 128-129)

Ballard admires Burroughs for his presentation of SF as a part of the general consciousness long ago absorbed into the mainstream of culture. His books are given as an example of the late 20th-century fiction that reflects the contemporary human mind and is not afraid of taboos and the truthful presentation of chaos. Ballard's tone is didactic; he instructs the readers of *New Worlds* in a very authoritarian way.[21]

20. Re-printed in *A User's Guide to the Millennium* (1997). All quotes of Ballard's articles (unless stated otherwise) come from this edition of his journalism.
21. His tone changes over the years, but his admiration for Burroughs remains intact. Nearly thirty years later he reviewed Burroughs' biography and the collection of his letters for the *Independent on Sunday* and the *Guardian*. Though these do not read like enthusiastic manifestos, Ballard still compares Burroughs to Joyce.

His even greater early fascination is surrealism: visual art, but also poetry. He strongly advises the readers to incorporate this esthetics into SF. "The images of surrealism are the iconography of inner space" (ibid.: 84). With this sentence he opens his famous early article "The Coming of the Unconscious" (1966). Admiring surrealism for its ability to appeal to our innermost often-subliminal feelings and advocating its "landscapes of the soul, the collage of the strange and familiar, and all the techniques of violent impact" (ibid.: 84), he indirectly postulates what literature, SF included, should be like.

Trying to persuade his readers that surrealism is the key to the 20th century experience he goes on to present its sources. He starts by describing the Dada movement and its protests against war, society and art and then goes back in time to the symbolists and expressionists of the nineteen-century. Sade, Lautréamont, Jarry and Apollinaire are able to reflect the whole human experience—sciences, physiology, even dreams and subliminal longings.[22] Ballard considers them the harbingers of psychoanalysis and compares their art to Rorschach tests, "with [their] emphasis on the irrational and the perverse, on the significance of apparently random associations" (ibid.: 85). Writing about André Breton and the *First Surrealist Manifesto* he implies similarities between the surrealist movement and the "New Wave" in imagery, language and attempts to reach to the deeper levels of the human mind.

The major part of Ballard's article is devoted to various surrealist paintings that for him are the best presentations of states of mind. A good example of his exuberant style is the paragraph on one of the very famous paintings by Salvador Dali:

> Dali: 'The Persistence of Memory' The empty beach with its fused sand is a symbol of utter psychic alienation. Clock time is no longer valid, the watches have begun to melt and drip. Even the embryo, symbol of secret growth and possibility, is drained and limp. These are the residues of a remembered moment of time. The most remarkable elements are the two rectilinear objects, formalizations of sections of the beach and sea. The displacement of these two images through time, and their marriage with our own four-dimensional continuum, has warped them into the rigid and unyielding structures of our own consciousness (ibid.: 87).

It is in the language of psychoanalysis that Ballard talks about thoughts and perceptions. Surrealism, the artistic movement that developed partly in response to Freud, is for him the ultimate 20th-century art. Three years later, in his article exclusively on Dali "The Innocent as Paranoid" (1969),[23] he divides the output of

22. Ballard's admiration for Jarry at the time can also be seen in his short stories from the 1960s, first and foremost "The Assassination of John Fitzgerald Kennedy Considered as a Downhill Motor Race", which is an intertextual echo of Alfred Jarry's "The Crucifixion Consider as an Uphill Bicycle Race".

23. In 1994 this article was revised and reprinted as "Introduction" in Salvador's Dali's *Diary of a Genius*.

this painter into periods on the basis of references to different cultural phenomena (psychoanalysis tops the list). He maintains that Dali, "with Max Ernst and William Burroughs ... forms a trinity of the only living men of genius" whose "paintings constitute a body of prophesy about ourselves unequalled in accuracy since Freud's *Civilization and Its Discontents*" (ibid.: 91).

The prevailing references to Freud and psychoanalysis may seem strange in a SF periodical such as *New Worlds*, but according to Ballard only science fiction and surrealism are presently able to give an imaginative response to science. Psychoanalysis together with other schools describing the human mind are becoming one of the most important contemporary sciences.[24] He continues this line of reasoning in his most famous Guest Editorial in *New Worlds*, "Which Way to Inner Space" (1962), considered to be the fullest artistic manifesto of the "New Wave". In that text he postulates a rejuvenation of SF: replacement of outer space exploration and technological detail with interest in the inner space of the human mind. He sites Ray Bradbury as an example of the very few authors who are able to "transform even so hackneyed a subject as Mars into an enthralling private world" (ibid.: 195), but criticizes lesser writers who have made SF synonymous with fantastic stories for small boys. Nevertheless, because of the inherent lack of limits and restrictions:

> SF has a continuing and expanding role as an imaginative interpreter of the future... The biggest developments of the immediate future will take place, not on the Moon or Mars, but on Earth, and it is inner space, not outer, that needs to be explored. The only truly alien planet is Earth. In the past the scientific bias of SF has been towards the physical sciences—rocketry, electronics, cybernetics—and the emphasis should switch to the biological sciences (ibid.: 197).

Ballard goes on to postulate abstract science fiction, uninterested in dramatic stories, but rather in the oblique presentation of phenomena such as the human experience of time, genetic memories, subliminal drives, and archaeopsychic time. Science fiction should develop a vocabulary to deal with the social and psychological problems of tomorrow and, Ballard fervently claims, it has chances to become the intellectual and artistic avant-garde.

In the second half of the decade, long after the decline of the "New Wave", Ballard was slowly recognized as one of the theorists of contemporary society and postmodernist culture. Always placed on the margins of the mainstream and associated with scandal and artistic provocation, he was nevertheless often asked his opinions on SF, futurology and different aspects of contemporary life. No longer restricted to avant-garde magazines, he published his essays and reviews in a wide range of titles. His most interesting journalism of this decade

24. His analyses of psychopathology in this magazine even include a review of Hitler's *Mein Kampf*, in which he compares Hitler to Oswald and, surprisingly to Leopold Bloom—a self-educated man in the streets who tries to control the cross-referential knowledge he acquired.

is concerned with the status of art in a world dominated by mass media and the numerous fictions of urban landscape such as commercials, billboards and ever-present TV screens. Leitmotifs of these essays include the latent artistic potential of science fiction, the regrettable decline of this genre, the prospects of future life in postmodernist society and the new kind of imagination shaped by the late 20th century: the Moon landing, Vietnam and the assassination of J.F. Kennedy.

Aware of the rapid changes in culture he formulated a whole new artistic program for the future SF writer. Our reality is now full of people filling the environment with all kinds of fictions, therefore a writer cannot just produce fictitious stories, but has to "out-imagine everyone else", analyze the minds of contemporary men, and create situations and images able to move, excite and reach to the unconscious. Such an artistic plan soon proved too idealistic. In subsequent years Ballard witnessed the rapid decline of intellectual SF, the commercialization of the genre and the dominance of visual media.

In his review of *Star Wars*, "Hobbits in Space?" (1977), his criticism of this film ("totally unoriginal, feebly plotted, instantly forgettable, and an acoustic nightmare") is only a pretext to examine the condition of science fiction: a genre, which is becoming *passé* as its intellectual values resist translation into cinema:

> Although slightly biased, I firmly believe that science fiction is the true literature of the twentieth century, and probably the last literary form to exist before the death of the written word and the domination of the visual image. SF has been one of the very few forms of modern fiction explicitly concerned with change—social, technological and environmental—and certainly the only fiction to invent society's myths, dreams and utopias. Why, then, has it translated so uneasily into the cinema? (ibid.: 14).

The commercialization of culture maims both SF film and SF literature. Ballard is aware that in the 1970s there is no place for ambitious writing of the "New Wave" kind. In "The Cosmic Cabaret" (1974), a review of Brian Aldiss' *Billion Year Spree*, he announces that modern SF has come to an end. "Anything that happened five minutes ago is already the centre of a cult, embedded in Lucite and put on a display shelf. Modern SF… has already become a victim of this nostalgia" (ibid.: 203). There is no interesting new movement and the tendency of more ambitious writers is to come back to stylized 'retro' poetics. The authors who ten years earlier had been the "New Wave" abandoned SF and their postmodernist experiments are being misunderstood,

> One of the most inaccurate jibes leveled at the so-called "New Wave" is that its writers suffered from delusions of literary grandeur, that they took themselves far too seriously. In fact in my own personal experience, it is the absolute reverse that is true (ibid: 203).

Such a decline in science fiction is for him the result of a huge civilizational change that is taking place in America, the centre of the world's science fiction. Concepts for the future no longer cause excitement, stress falls on the present day and, moreover, the huge moral and imaginative reserves possessed by the USA in the first part of the century are exhausted. In times of pessimism, distraction and social entropy there is no place for a literature exploring the excitements of tomorrow. The post-Vietnam world abandoned the future and then SF. This process gained momentum over the decade, and, at the beginning of the 80s, Ballard's voice sounded even more pessimistic. In "New Means Worse" (1981), published in the *Guardian*, he wrote:

> In fact, science fiction today... is entering the most commercial phase it has ever known. The "New Wave", along with almost all the more intelligent magazines and anthologies, has long since been inundated by a tsunami of planet fiction, sword-and-sorcery sensationalism... What science fiction needs now is a clear, hard and positive voice (ibid.: 190).

Nostalgia and dissatisfaction with the contemporary world and its stupid escapist fables made Ballard concentrate on the history of SF rather than its present state. The ability to probe deep down into our psyche is the ultimate goal of literature. Nevertheless, in the 1970s something wrong happened to SF and culture at large. For some years Ballard kept toying with SF ideas in a playful and less serious way. A good example of this kind of journalism is his cooperation with *Vogue*, where in the late 1970s he published several impressions on the future. Easy and nice to read, they described a make-believe 21st century. In "The Future of the Future" (1977) he talks about a world dominated by TV. Each one of us lives in a room full of TV screens that report on our daily life and bodily functions. People spend their evenings editing the material recorded by cameras—their own talks and interactions with the family and friends. They live keeping in mind the film they are continuously making. Gradually they step back into their rooms and perform their work and family life via the TV screen, unable to cope with unmediated reality.

This article is interesting for several reasons. Firstly, soon thereafter Ballard used this idea to write two short stories—"The Intensive Care Unit" (1977) and "Motel Architecture" (1978), both picturing a society in which people live separately in screen-filled studios. Secondly, it is worth noticing that 1977 is long before the creation of virtual reality, and that Ballard quite rightly anticipated the development of media. Thirdly, compared with earlier texts on SF—engaged artistic manifestos teaching how to write, read and think—this article shows his disappointment in SF, which he now treats as only a plaything. Lastly, we can see here Ballard's growing obsession with TV screens and media culture, something so very characteristic of his fiction (and journalism[25]) at the time.

25. Compare: "The Kennedy assassination alone, it seems to me, makes 1963 the most important year since the war. Kennedy's murder, the greatest mystery of the twentieth century, was the crime for which television was waiting, just as Vietnam was the war that TV needed. Together they freed

In the second *Vogue* text, "The Diary of A Mad Space-wife" (1979), he describes life in one of the hundreds of satellite cities in Earth orbit. The future's life, entertainment and abortive work lead people to depression and space-madness. The article combines science fiction-like ideas and descriptions with bits and pieces of real-life astronauts' memories and recorded dialogues. The atmosphere is sad and nostalgic, and the article shows that the Space Age is really over, no one dreams of space conquests, and what we are left with is TV. The beginning of the eighties is for Ballard the end of artistic involvement with science fiction (he never abandons the genre as a writer of fiction, but ceases to see it as means of social education and artistic experiments) and he turns to quasi-autobiographical writing.

The tremendous artistic success of *Empire of the Sun* marked a sudden breakthrough in Ballard's literary career. After nearly thirty years of continuously writing and publishing both fiction and non-fiction he was finally recognized as a modern classicist for writing an autobiography and World War II novel. Set in pre-war Shanghai and the Lunghua camp, where the Japanese interned British civilians during the war, the novel was generally received as a confession of the real-life sources of Ballard's literary fascinations and obsessions[26] and was often confused for a factual account of his early years. His popular image as an orientalist (enhanced by the acclaimed Steven Spielberg film *Empire*) prompted the numerous essays and reviews having to do with China and Japan that he was asked to write in subsequent years.

Some of this non-fiction is explicitly autobiographical. For example "Unlocking the Past" (1991), written for the *Daily Telegraph*, is a report on Ballard's visit to Shanghai, which took place during the making of the Spielberg film. Ballard writes this text for readers who know his novel: there are implied comparisons of Shanghai at the end of the 20th century and the city described in *Empire*. Ballard visits the places important for Jim, his fictitious persona (without referring to the book or summarizing it), and the suspense works only if we wait for him to locate his prison room. At the same time the article has certain features of a travelogue:

> The first day I moved around Shanghai in a daze. Memories jostled me like the Chinese crowds who surrounded the film crew. Watching as the Belgian lad cycled past the Cathay Hotel, where Noël Coward had written *Private Lives*, I remembered the Shanghai of gangsters and beggar-kings, prostitutes and pickpockets. I had opened a door and stepped into a perfectly preserved past, though a past equipped with a number of unattractive reflexes of my

the medium from the airless, studio-bound realm of stilted news announcers and staid game shows, transforming the screen into a global media landscape that soon became a direct competitor with reality itself, and may even have supplanted it" (ibid.: 243), he wrote in his memories for the year 1963 in "The Overlit Carousel" for the *Guardian*.

26. Such as the recurrent imagery of disaster and desolation in his prose, the leitmotif of finding dead pilots in crashed aircraft and an abundance of violence.

own—walking along the Nanking Road, I caught myself expecting the Chinese pedestrians to step out of my way (ibid.: 175).

Ballard creates his own image here; partly an elderly English sentimental tourist, partly a boy from half a century earlier with the imperial ways of a colony dweller and describes the modern, exotic city from such a perspective. We read about his walks throughout the city, the visit to the former Ballard house, and a trip to Lunghua, his search and the final retrieval of memories of his younger self. All of these adventures are described in such a way as to emphasize the real life details which he had incorporated into *Empire of the Sun*. This article is in itself a piece of fiction, a footnote to this novel, in which Ballard presents his half-literary persona: the writer of *Empire of the Sun*, an English intellectual with the vivid though naïve memories of a rich European boy in colonial China.[27]

This persona is used in numerous other journalistic texts that Ballard wrote in the nineties: from this perspective he judged Chinese books, discussed the history of Asia, the Second World War and recent political changes. A good sample of this style is the beginning of "Survival Instincts" (1992), a review of *Wild Swans*, a Chinese woman's memoir,[28] published in the *Sunday Times*;

I can remember the bad-tempered amahs of my childhood, ruthless and hard-fisted little women darting about on their bound feet. At the other end of the social scale were the dragon ladies—tycoons' wives or successful businesswomen—in their long fur coats and immaculate make-up, who could petrify a small boy at fifty paces with their baleful stares.

Returning to China last summer, I was startled to find an advance guard of dragon ladies apparently waiting for me in the Cathy Pacific lounge at Heathrow. But there were none in the streets of Shanghai, and, fortunately, their places were taken by thousands of relaxed and cheerful young women (ibid.: 36).

A similar procedure can be found in a group of texts that deal with the powerful Asiatic politicians and royals.[29] In "Lipstick and High Heels" (1993),

27. Ballard is nevertheless very careful to avoid political commitments. He turned down a prestigious offer of membership in the Royal Society of Literature (because he did not like the adjective "Royal"). Offered a "Commander of the British Empire" medal he also turned it down. Thus he builds his public image in a consequent way, he wants to be seen as somebody "on the outside", a keen and intelligent but non-committed observer.
28. *Wild Swans: Three Daughters of China* by Jung Chang, a Chinese woman who after years of life under the Mao regime managed to emigrate to the UK, describes the atrocities of Chinese governments from the point of view of a person who, just like Ballard, knows both the Far East and the affluent West. The great success of this book in England in the early 1990s is perhaps partly due to the general interest people had in China after the publication of *Empire of the Sun* in the mid-1980s.
29. Or other celebrities: see for example "The Samurai of the Epic" (1991), his text on Akira Kurosawa

written for the *Daily Telegraph*, it is Ballard's recent visit to China compared with the mental picture of pre-war Shanghai that gives him a background to talk about political issues. Reviewing Richard Evans' *Deng Xiaoping and the making of Modern China* Ballard juxtaposes references to *Empire of the Sun* and the making of the film with the revolutionary changes described by Evans. His comments on Hirohito in "Last of the Great Royals" (1989), published in the *Observer*, discuss the emperor's policy line during the war from the perspective of China, not Japan.

Therefore, the readers of Ballard's fiction and non-fiction in the early 1990s grapple with a small mountain of autobiography material encompassing *Empire of the Sun*, its 1991 sequel *The Kindness of Women* and a body of journalism. The resulting confusion of facts and fiction made Ballard write in "The End of My War" (1995), in the *Sunday Times*, an exact account of what happened to him (and not to Jim, the protagonist of *Empire of the Sun*) in Shanghai in the 1940s.

The end of the war is viewed here from the perspective of the Lunghua Camp (a place described in detail in *Empire of the Sun*). This time instead of Jim (the war-name adopted by the protagonist of the novel when he is separated from his parents and left to his own devices in the middle of the war) we have Jamie, who spent the three years of internment with his parents.

> Then at last it was all over. The day after Hirohito's broadcast, we heard from the Swiss Red Cross that the war had ended. The Japanese armies had agreed to lay down their arms. We were told of the atomic bombs dropped on Hiroshima and Nagasaki, which had vaporized both cities and brought the war to a sudden halt.
> 'Is the war over?' I asked my father. 'Really, really over?'
> 'Yes, it's really over.' My father stared at me somberly. 'Jamie, you'll miss Lunghua' (ibid.: 284).

In a similar way the events described in *Empire of the Sun* are here briefly narrated from Jamie Ballard's point of view, thus demonstrating artistic distortions in the novel. Camp life, the English school in Shanghai before the war, the small boy's memories of colonial times—this autobiography encompasses all aspects of *Empire of the Sun*. The very fact of being in Asia during the war gives Ballard the moral right to judge the American decision to drop the bomb:

> As a nation the Japanese have never faced up to the atrocities they committed, and are unlikely to do so as long as we bend our heads is shame before the memories of Hiroshima and Nagasaki.
> The argument that atomic weapons, by virtue of the genetic damage they cause to the future generations, belong to a special

---

in the *Guardian*. Moreover, he is an unquestionable authority on Shanghai, its history and its present day, which he discusses on many occasions. A good sample of his style might be found in "A City of Excess" (1991). This text written for *Daily Telegraph* juxtaposed the review of Harriet Sergeant's Shanghai with the account of the 1941 evacuation of the Ballards' house.

category of evil, seems to me to be equally misguided. The genetic consequences of a rifle bullet are even more catastrophic, for the victim's genes go nowhere except the grave and his descendants are not even born (ibid.: 293).

His scandalous works from the 1960s and 1970s forgotten, Ballard started to enjoy the privileged position of an authority on literary and moral issues. The success of *Empire of the Sun* made Ballard write its 1991 sequel, *The Kindness of Women*, in which he describes Jim after the war: a young man who does not fit into the world of post-war Britain. He thus created the next chapters of his autobiography. In his journalism he refers to them from time to time; all this writing, regardless of the chronology of its publication dates, forms one intertextual whole.

The cultural shock of leaving Asia for Britain is best reflected in numerous articles about the books he read as an adolescent. The sharp comparison of dull English life and the Far East he found in Greene, as he remembers in "Memories of Greeneland" (1978), was written for *Magazine Littéraire*:

> I first began to read Graham Greene in the mid-1950s, and will never forget the sense of liberation his novels gave me… whether serious or 'entertainments' as Greene likes to call them, [they] had the tonic effect of stepping from an aircraft on to the airport tarmac of a strange country (ibid.: 138).

"Memories of James Joyce" (1990) is concerned with the same period, the 1950s, and describes the young Ballard who was then studying medicine, but wanted to be a writer, just like the protagonist of *The Kindness of Women*:

> James Joyce's *Ulysses* had an immense influence on me—almost entirely for the bad. I read Joyce's masterpiece as an eighteen-year-old medical student dissecting cadavers at Cambridge, then a bastion of academic provincialism and self-congratulation…
> *Ulysses* convinced me to give up medicine and become a writer, but it was the wrong example for me, an old-fashioned storyteller at heart, and it wasn't until I discovered the surrealists that I found the right model (ibid.: 145).

The most revealing in this context is the piece "The Pleasures of Reading" (1992), written for the anthology edited by Antonia Fraser entitled *The Pleasure of Reading*. Here Ballard juxtaposed each phase of his life with the books he remembers enjoying at that time. In the pre-war polyglot Shanghai he read the Victorian children's classics and American comics together with the *Latin Primer*, described in *Empire*, just like the books and magazines which circulated among the prisoners of the Lunghua Camp.

Arriving in England in 1946, I was faced with the incomprehensible strangeness of English life, for which my childhood reading had prepared me in more ways than I realized. Fortunately, I soon discovered that the whole of late nineteenth- and early twentieth-century literature lay waiting for me, a vast compendium of human case histories that stemmed from a similar source (ibid: 181).

He finishes the article with a list of his favourites and his own characterization of a reader of other people's books.

In recent years his fiction and non-fiction together influence his image: his preferences, ideas and opinions are often made public. Sometimes an interesting intertextual links join his novels and essays, like in the case of his descriptions of Shepperton,[30] the Great London village where he lives:

Shepperton, like most Thames Valley towns, is now a suburb not of London but of London airport, and one can see the influence of Heathrow in the office buildings that resemble control towers and the huge shopping malls whose floors remind the visitor of a terminal concourse... we live in the TV suburbs, among the video shops, take-aways and police speed-check cameras, and might as well make the most of them, since there is nowhere else to go (ibid.: 183-84).

This quote comes from "Shepperton Past and Present" (1994), published in the *Guardian*, and is a good example of his journalism in the nineteen-nineties. The impressions and descriptions of the contemporary world and post-modernist culture mingle with personal memories and ciphered allusions to his books. The devoted reader of Ballard is now faced with a maze of cross-referential allusions and remarks, which together form his imaginary autobiography.

---

30. The town of Shepperton has a very special place in Ballard's fiction: the protagonists of *Crash* and *The Kindness of Women* live there, the action of *The Unlimited Dream Company* takes place there. Ballard is very fond of talking and writing about Shepperton, it seems that he purposefully wants to be associated with this town and by notoriously describing it in his novels he blurs the reality/fiction dichotomy and seems to be saying: "these books are about me".

CHAPTER ONE:
GRAVE NEW WORLD

The *oeuvre* of J.G. Ballard reflects the social, cultural and, to a certain extent, also the political history of the 20th century. Though some of his stories describe the near future of affluent, Western societies, it is always current events that provide inspiration for his prophesies of what life in ten or twenty years time is going to be like. In his texts Ballard describes what I call in this book *Grave New World*, a realm which although it is fictitious, is dependent on contemporary reality and heavily influenced by theories dealing with current social and cultural phenomena. *Grave New World* is set not in the future but, as Ballard put it in one of his interviews, in "the visionary present",[1] an alternate 'now' of the affluent countries. Therefore one should read Ballard with an awareness of the theoretical sources that influence him. The 20th century, with its traumas, revolutions and new technologies that

1. Ballard was in fact talking about one of his books, *Vermilion Sands*, but this remark seems appropriate in relation to his whole oeuvre.

have completely altered life on Earth, is Ballard's point of departure. What has happened since he was born in 1930 is recurrently referred to in his prose. The life span of over seventy years gives him a broad perspective to look at today's social reality and, moreover, this perspective is not limited to the UK.

Born in Shanghai, Ballard grew up in Asia and in a huge Americanized metropolis. Shanghai in the 1930s was an international city of commerce and show-business. The little boys living in the rich International Settlement read comic-strips, listened to American radio shows and watched Hollywood films. For Ballard America has always been the true modern empire, the source of the 20th century's culture and lifestyle: even after sixty years of life in a London suburb he has not become fully British at heart. In his interviews he ever repeats that at the moment he first saw Britain he was already sixteen, and thus too mature to acquire national cultural identity.[2] Therefore, in comparison to other British writers who started publishing in the 1950s, the end of the British empire impacted his understanding of history to a lesser extent. Even in his early stories depicting the gloomy future of Western civilization he looks "beyond Little England for the source of what interest[s him] as a writer" (Self 1995: 332).

This broad perspective provided by a childhood spent on the Pacific coast, in a milieu encompassing the cultures of Europe, Asia and America, allows Ballard to judge the modern history of the West from both the inside and the outside of Western culture. His prose very often alludes to historical events from the last seventy years, but his choice of such references is highly subjective. What for Ballard is crucial for understanding the way our culture has evolved might well be neglected by orthodox historians. Ballard does not try to recreate a linear textbook-like version of modern history. Instead, he obsessively returns to a set of facts and moments that for him have shaped the present cultural standing of the West.

In order to understand Ballard's growing disaffection with Western civilization it will be useful to chart the Ballardian map of 20th-century history and to point to the events he considers prominent. As I already stated in the Introduction, though Ballard is not chronological in describing the century's traumas (rather, he compulsively, repeatedly narrates the same situations), the chronological enumeration of those events would allow us to see his own 20th century. In such an endeavour one should start with Pearl Harbour. For Ballard the Japanese attack and the beginning of World War II in the Far East mark the end of the carnival-like years of life in the affluent colonial setting of inter-war Shanghai.[3]

Pearl Harbour in Ballard's prose signifies the abrupt change in the world—the pre-war life of the privileged, white, upper middle-class minority was luxurious,

2. For example an interview given to Will Self and reprinted in the collection *Junk Mail* (Self 1995: 332).
3. For Ballard World War II is significant not only as a historical event but as a psychological breakthrough, a moment when the irrational fears and desires kept repressed during more rational times were set free. Compare Ballard's interview with V. Vale, where he claims that the war marked the end of the Age of Reason in Europe: "People like Mussolini and Hitler tapped psychological forces that came straight out of the abyss. Forces deep down in the core of the human psyche were certainly empowering Hitler, the Nazis and Mussolini to a large extent, and, I would guess, Stalin and the Soviet regime" (Vale 2005: 128).

full of parties and popular entertainment, while fear and humiliation marked the subsequent years of the Japanese internment. Pearl Harbour is the end of childhood and the moment when grown-ups—all the British in Asia—panic and their worldview based on trust in the imperial military proves invalid. After over four decades Ballard remembers that day in one of his articles:

> Over their drinks at the Country Club people boasted that the war against Japan would be over in weeks, or a month at the outside.
>
> These arrogant assumptions were put to the test on December 7, 1941, when the Japanese carrier planes attacked Pearl Harbour. In Shanghai, across the International Date Line, it was already Monday, December 8... I heard tanks clanking down the Amherst Avenue as the Japanese began their seizure of the International Settlement.
>
> My father and mother raced around the house in a panic, followed by the chattering and exited servants Ballard 1997b: 289).[4]

The next important event according to Ballard, perhaps the most important single moment in the history of the 20th century, is that of the nuclear attacks of 1945. The invention and use of atomic weapons signify in his writings the moment when aggression and the self-destructive drives latent in Western man become apparent and Western civilization enters the path leading to annihilation. The Cold War brought about the invention of even more dangerous technology: weapons as well as fast cars and various machines causing the deaths of millions of users. The nuclear bombardment of Nagasaki is a recurrent motif in Ballard's stories (his characters on the Chinese coast are too far away to see Hiroshima burning), and the deadly pearl blaze in the sky, far stronger that the sunshine, has metaphysical meaning. It is the moment human civilization dies spiritually. What follows is but a nightmarish simulacrum of life.

The end of the war: Hirohito's surrender speech, the arrival of the American soldiers to Eastern Asia and the first days of peace are far less significant. Europe after the war is barely described at all (but for the feelings of claustrophobia that Ballardian characters have in England in the forties, along with the oppressive feeling of World War III inevitably approaching). All the decades of the Cold War are referred to only via two aspects of the period: the nuclear tests and the space race. First of all, Ballard is keenly interested in the side effects of ever-advancing nuclear technology—people's reaction to constant threat, the consciousness of deadly experiments that transform faraway islands or deserts into fragments of the future's post-atomic landscape. The Pacific island of Eniwetok, where

---

4. "The End of My War", an article written in 1995 and reprinted in *A User's Guide to the Millennium*.

nuclear and then thermonuclear tests were conducted in the late 40s and early 50s, represents in Ballard's prose the idea of what the future Earth is going to look like. The artificial landscape of the island—contaminated concrete blocks covered with rubbish and the desert inhabited only by tiny mutated organisms— is probably a glimpse of the future of the whole planet.[5]

The second important aspect of the Cold War referred to very many times in Ballard's fiction and non-fiction is the space race. The initial fascination with space technology and the possibility of exploration it promises is very soon replaced by the feeling of disappointment and the opinion that Western civilization has lost its chance to develop and grow in new directions. The West replaced the dream of space flight with TV shows, and now we are eternally grounded with our eyes cast down to the soil.

> One of the most surprising but barely noticed events of the period since the Second World War has been the life and death of the space age. Almost twenty years ago to the day, 4 October 1957, I switched on the *BBC* news and heard for the first time the radio call-sign of *Sputnik I* as it circled the Earth above our heads. Its urgent tocsin seemed to warn us of the arrival of a new epoch...
>
> I took for granted that the spin off of the US and Russian space programmes would transform everything in our lives... In fact nothing remotely like this occurred (ibid: 224).[6]

Though Ballard even in the fifties was never a romantic advocate of outer space exploration (he in fact was far more interested as a writer in the inner space of the human mind), the transience of the space age was for him unbelievable. In spite of the unprecedented publicity that surrounded the American astronauts in the sixties, in but a few years time nobody wanted to watch the flights. "Now that the space age is over—or at least its heroic phase—it seems surprising that it lasted for barely fifteen years, from Yuri Gagarin's orbital flight in 1961 to the last *Skylab* mission in 1974" (ibid.: 273),[7] writes Ballard in the late seventies. Western civilization has chosen to stay forever on our planet and instead of conquering, it spends its time and money on entertainment and consumerism.

After the brief space age the TV age followed and the West has become a culture of spectacle overwhelmed by advertisements, live shows and violent games. In 1963 the assassination of John Fitzgerald Kennedy became the first murder shown on TV. Vietnam was for Ballard a TV war spreading images of

---

5. The controversies concerning the tests are described in numerous historical documents from the epoch, for example the warning letter of Nikita Khrushchev to Harold Macmillan. As far as the situation on Eniwetok after the tests (the fallout and contamination) is concerned see: Kopaliński 1999: 108. Or, for exact data concerning the geology and zoology of the island after the tests see Dirk H.R. Spennemann, *Marshall Islands Bikini Atoll Eclectic Bibliography*, (http://www.microworks.net/ pacific www.microworks.net/pacific, on 20 Jan. 2006).
6. "The Future of the Future", an article written in 1977 and reprinted in *A User's Guide to the Millennium*
7. "Kings of Infinite Space", an article written in 1979 and reprinted in *A User's Guide to the Millennium*.

atrocities and making people immune to horrors on the screen. The importance of images and mediated reality within Western culture causes human life to grow unreal. People spend their time in front of TV sets and computer screens, and the post-modern architecture transforms the countryside into a concrete labyrinth of highways, malls and parking lots car-friendly and hostile to pedestrians. Affluent families move to gated communities full of security cameras and their contact with the world is limited to images on screens and views through the windscreens of fast cars. In the south of Europe and the US "sun cities" inhabited by rich retired people are built. Yet the life of these estates is far from active; the inhabitants mostly doze off in front of their cable TVs. The invention of virtual reality and the new kinds of entertainment that probably will very soon be available are the final resignation from unmediated real life. Therefore, Western culture has chosen a zombie-like existence—the apparently utopian happiness of the affluent becomes life on an insufferable spiritual desert and the West slowly approaches its cultural and emotional twilight.

Therefore, whatever is going on in the world during the last two decades of the 20th century is (at least in the West) heavily influenced by the way it is reported on and shown in the media. Belonging in society means consuming the same images and thus sharing a vision of the world that replaces first hand experience of reality. This process of turning the world into images and the consequent emergence of totally new types of both society and the individual personality is the most important subject of Ballard's late novels. The political and economic issues in these novels are rather confined to the background[8]—or in the case of some shorter fictions—are discussed in satirical manner.[9]

It is worth noticing that in Ballard's fiction the Western world/Soviet Union antagonism and its miraculous end in the days of perestroika has very little importance. Quite opposite to the authors of classic disaster stories, who are terrified by Russia's sinister power (and Ballard did start his career writing disaster fiction), he mentions Russia rarely and mostly in the context of the space race.[10] Such a significant omission of one of the key factors in the recent history of Europe makes his picture of the turn of the millennium in Europe rather incomplete—for him the far-reaching social and cultural consequences of political changes are of sole importance.[11] The dividing line he draws goes across society, not between

8. See Appendix I and the description of *Kingdom Come*, a novel published after the completion of my paper. In this novel the way Western society is presented is different.
9. In "The Largest Theme Park in the World" Europe is dwarfed and depends on rich American and Japanese tourists, its institutions and traditions degenerate and the UK loses all its international importance—in some other stories the UK becomes an overseas territory of the US.
10. Even in the early eighties when the Soviet empire was already on the verge of economic catastrophe the space industry was still flourishing thanks to the special attention paid to it by apparatchiks proud to be as good as the Americans in at least this one area: see for example Archie Brown *The Gorbachev Factor* (Brown 1997: 63).
11. Some sociologists tend to obliterate this Western Europe/Russia post-Cold War division. Compare, for example, the beginning of the list of arguments for such an obliteration given by Wojciech Kostecki: "*The post-Cold War East and West are of geopolitical nature; they were established by the Yalta-Potsdam order into two spheres of influence; at present, the Yalta-Potsdam order having collapsed, there is no reason for the existence of these notions. *The post-Cold War

societies or nation-states and their territories. The new Europe is divided into the unreal enclaves of gated communities, post-modern business parks and white Mediterranean resorts with their computers, CCTV, clubs and psychopaths on shooting sprees—and the pariahs' world outside: immigrants, servants and poor national TV viewers. What Ballard is mostly interested in are the enclaves and the way such milieux influence human perceptions, while the outside world is only the context and the scenery where, for example, hidden aggression is vented during racist[12] assaults.

Western civilization as he describes it is thus heading for a spiritual death such as Arnold Toynbee defined in the passage I quoted at the beginning of the Introduction. The death of the soul of a civilization, according to his theories, is going to provoke outsiders to attack and destroy otherwise mighty civilizations. Toynbee claimed that there was still time to reawaken the West and save its civilization. Ballard half a century later is not that optimistic anymore. Of course, nowadays it is difficult to say who is going to play the part of barbarians destroying the old empire, and the prophecy will likely come true in a more figurative sense. As Francis Fukuyama notes in his *The End of History and the Last Man*, a new type of society is being born, a society deprived of thymos (Fukuyama borrows a term coined by Plato)—that is, virtue, ambition and pride.

Ballard's fiction across his career describes the slow process of spiritual degeneration in the West. In his works he alludes to numerous theories created in the 20th century that try to understand and analyze the status of Western civilization from the point of view of different sciences. Before approaching his own oeuvre, let us briefly discuss the theories that have the greatest impact on his works.

"The Lamps are going out all over Europe"[13]
—Edward Gibbon, Oswald Spengler, Arnold Toynbee

I started this book by referring to Aldous Huxley and thus to the tradition of literary dystopia. Ballard is very much indebted to this esthetics and his dystopian texts are also influenced by the disaster story tradition that flourished

East and West cannot be perceived as monolithic system; divergent national interests stand revealed, power criteria are differentiated, the balance-of-power logic is revived. *The European security complex is, in fact, dividing into a number of subcomplexes of variable and mutually penetrating borders; some of the states belong to more than one of them". (Kostecki 1996: 108). The second point is very much relevant for the understanding of Ballard's late narratives as it seems to reflect his opinion.

12. Therefore, in those narratives we are dealing with a 'multiple' and divided Europe—"a complete dismembering of Europe, an outbursts of national and ethnic conflicts and local feuds" (Stefanowicz 1995: 82), which some social scientist predict to be born soon. But the local antagonisms and outburst of violence—mostly against the immigrants—will be, according to Ballard, happening within one unified media culture of pan-European consumer society.

13. The famous remark of Edward Grey, Viscount of Fallodon, "The lamps are going out all over Europe", dates from 1914, when German forces crossed the borders of neutral Belgium. For Grey it meant the end of European diplomacy and civilized standards.

in Britain in the late fifties. Pessimistic attitudes toward the future of the world and the direction modern societies are taking are characteristic for mid-20th century writers and can be seen in fiction and non-fiction alike. Though Ballard is an author well read as far as literary classics are concerned, it is non-fiction writers who have the greatest impact on his stories. With the passing decades, his own books, in turn, influence the end of the millennium theorists of culture who refer to his fiction as a prediction of what the Western world is going to soon look like.

Huxley seems a good starting point for the discussion of Ballard's readings concerning civilizations—Western included—because not only is Huxley one of Ballard's favourite authors, but also because the gloomy future he predicts involves affluent society. In contrast to the other great dystopia of the mid-20th century, George Orwell's *1984*, the society depicted in *Brave New World* seems happy. Its members are provided with wealth and entertainment, they are not prosecuted or spied on, they do not feel underprivileged or used[14]. In short, they are quite similar to the members of consumer societies of the type that are emerging in contemporary liberal democracies that value hedonism, the human right to feel good and whose economy is based on oversell and advertising. At first it is difficult to say what is wrong in such a society and why the world so described might be called a dystopia and not the final realization of the dreams of happiness people have always harboured.

In 1946, just after the second of the great wars of the century, Huxley wrote a foreword to a new edition of *Brave New World*. In this short essay he discusses his novel as both a warning and a prognosis for the future of the West. Ballard's novels written over fifty years thereafter portray a world that is a gloomy realization of Huxley's worst dreams.

> As political and economic freedom diminishes, sexual freedom tends compensatingly to increase. And the dictator (unless he needs cannon fodder and families with which to colonize empty or conquered territories) will do well to encourage that freedom. In conjunction with the freedom to daydream under the influence of dope and movies and the radio, it will help to reconcile his subjects to the servitude that is their fate.

> All things considered, it looks as though Utopia were far closer to us than anyone, only fifteen years ago, could have imagined. Then, I projected it six hundred years into the future. Today it seems quite possible that the horror may be upon us within a single century. That is if we refrain from blowing ourselves to smithereens in the interval (Huxley 1946: 14).

In that same year, 1946, Ballard set foot on British soil for the first time

---

14. For the discussion of the differences between *1984* and *Brave New World* in the context of modern sociology and futuristic visions of the development of the West see Francis Fukuyama *Our Posthuman Future*, (Fukuyama 2002b: 3-10).

in his life. During his first years in Britain (if we believe his autobiographical articles) he read very widely in getting to know the European canon and felt sure that World War III is waiting in the wings. The pessimistic attitudes of English intellectuals who discussed the end of Western civilization and the twilight of European culture were prevailing. The first wave of pessimism was felt as early as during World War I. After World War II it came back twofold.

The theorist of civilization whose ideas influence early Ballard the most is Arnold Toynbee. It is via his writings—*A Study of History* and numerous essays and addresses—that he got to know the works of other thinkers. In his attempts to understand the mechanics of civilizations, the factors impacting their development and transformation, Toynbee analyzes the theses of many historians and anthropologists who linked historical and political changes to the spiritual life of nations. He criticizes those who, like James Frazer, see Oriental religions (first and foremost Christianity) as the cause of the decline of classical civilization. Religions which teach that the soul's eternal salvation is the only object people should live for make, according to Frazer, "the prosperity and even the existence of the state sink into insignificance" (Frazer 1914: 300). Similar remarks may be found in the monumental work of Edward Gibbon *The History of the Decline and Fall of the Roman Empire*, where Christianity is one of the factors leading to the destruction of the ancient world. Toynbee disagrees: "Christianity was not the destroyer of the ancient Greek civilization, because that civilization had decayed from inherent defects of its own before Christianity arose" (Toynbee 1949: 230).

Gibbon's work is here a necessary point of reference to understand the 20th-century discussions concerning cultures, states and the spiritual life of nations. Gibbon is the great classicist who was not afraid of using a very large canvass to describe long-term processes. One may argue that the dystopias of writers such as H.G. Wells, Aldous Huxley and, indirectly, some of the disaster stories authors, belong in the tradition Gibbon commenced, as their narratives discuss generations-long processes transforming whole nations.

Ballard's fiction also springs from this literary tradition, though he by no means copies the stylistics of his predecessors.. The hypothesis Gibbon makes—that the fall of nations and civilizations depends upon changes in the spiritual life of people—is a very prominent question in Ballard's *oeuvre*. Gibbon, as his biographers stress, was biased against religions after "[a] boyish freak led him at the age of sixteen to turn Roman Catholic" (Gibbon 1905:v),[15] very much to the distress of his father, who reacted in a very authoritarian manner. This early experience and his love for classical pagan ideals made him rather hostile to religious subjects.

> He narrates [the rise and early struggles of Christianity] with his habitual honesty and completeness. But his sceptical and somewhat cynical prepossessions colour his judgement, and he does not

---

15. The quote comes from Sidney Lee's "Edward Gibbon", a note in the 1905 edition of *The History of the Decline and Fall of the Roman Empire*.

always conceal a polemical intention of challenging the religious views of orthodox contemporaries (ibid.: ix).

In Gibbon's narrative of how the ancient world faced the challenge of alien peoples and their non-Greek value systems and social structures, the main difference between civilizations concerns not metaphysics but earthly attitudes to state and civil duties. Roman culture represents the love of reason, loyalty to the state and good sense.

> The magistrates could not be actuated by a blind though honest bigotry, since the magistrates were themselves philosophers; and the schools of Athens had given laws to the senate. Ambition or avarice could not impel them, as the temporal and ecclesiastical powers were united in the same hands. The pontiffs were chosen among the most illustrious of the senators... They knew and valued the advantages of religion, as it connected with civil government. They encouraged the public festivals that humanize the manners of the people (ibid.: 31).

This noble and civilized culture that values religion as a useful device to "humanize" citizens and is far from religious zeal and metaphysical follies is contrasted with the barbarian nations. In Gibbon's account barbarians are deprived of any intellectual values and interested only in "the animal gratifications of sleep and food" (ibid.: 221). They manage to undertake any action at all only thanks to their inborn restlessness. Wars, campaigns and conquests are presented as side effects of their blind, unconscious need of violence and immoderately fierce temper. "The languid soul, oppressed with its own weight, anxiously required some new and powerful sensation; and war and danger were [its] only amusements" (ibid.: 221). Barbarians are a potentially dangerous, although brainless mass "agitated by various and often hostile intentions" (ibid.: 233), and one wonders how they could in fact challenge the empire. Therefore, in Gibbon's views concerning the dynamics of civilizations spirituality is replaced by the inborn psychological characteristic of nations, and religions play a subsidiary role. If any of them, like Christianity, is strong enough to remodel the mentality of people it serves as a debilitating force that makes the nation neglect earthly ideals in a vain attempt to reach communion with the absolute.

Another theorist whose works have great impact on Ballard is Oswald Spengler. The characters of early disaster stories Ballard wrote in the late fifties and early sixties read Spengler's *The Decline of the West* and are fascinated by his determinism in describing the inevitable end of every social structure. Such a biological view implies that civilizations behave like living organisms or species and their life span is pre-determined: at the moment the last days come, nothing can done to save them from extinction. History is but a blind force and despite what people may do, they cannot overcome the inevitability of historical processes. The technological progress Western civilization has made and all the inventions and discoveries of science will most definitely not save the West from the fate of earlier great civilizations. Indeed, the opposite is true: material welfare and technological marvels are part of the great historical design and will "help" the West reach its end. "Machines, [Spengler] argued, simply proliferated, whether or not they actually benefited those whose lives they ostensibly enriched; they made servants of those who had once been their masters" (Spengler 1991: xii), writes one of Spengler's commentators.[16]

According to Spengler, the moment a civilization turns into empire marks the beginning of the extinction of this culture, closes the period of expansion and growth and introduces rigidity to its social and intellectual life. People in Spengler's view are but a boundless mass that brainlessly flows in a stream of history "upstream, a dark past... downstream, a future even so dark and timeless" (ibid.: 73). Following the example of Gibbon, Spengler analyzes the decline of classical culture and concludes that a similar destiny awaits the West, and very soon indeed.

> [A]nother decline, entirely comparable to it in course and duration, which will occupy the first centuries of the coming millennium but is heralded already and sensible in and around us today—the decline of the West. Every Culture passes through the age-phases of the individual man. Each has its childhood, manhood and old age (ibid.: 74).

Civilization understood as the final stage of a culture is the period when the soul of a people dies. Religions are replaced by atheism, and highly developed intellectual and spiritual life becomes rigid and then dies. It is inevitable that civilizations should arise, as smaller expanding states always form empires and empires are always prone to seeing themselves as the last and the most advanced social structures ever created. Every civilization once it feels grand and safe heralds its own "end of historical change" and this is precisely the moment when its decline commences.[17]

Arnold Toynbee calls this level of cultural development a "universal state"—a civilization that conquers and/or outshines all rival political organisms and has a dominant role in the whole known world—just like Rome in antiquity or the West in the 20th century. What Toynbee opposes is precisely Spengler's major thesis, namely, that following the highest developmental stage come disasters and declines. Instead (and in stark distinction to Spengler) he shows how one

16. H. Stuart Hughes' "Introduction" to the 1991 English edition of Oswald Spengler's *The Decline of the West*. It is rather too far-fetched to call Spengler a proto-environmentalist or a prophet warning against the application of nuclear power long before it was discovered. Nevertheless, it is precisely after World War II, in the period of anxiety and anti-war movements, that Spengler was re-discovered and widely read—precisely for his pessimism and the thesis that technological progress may prompt disaster.
17. By "the end of history" Fukuyama means the everlastingness of liberal democracy and the end of historical change leading to this happy moment. Similarly, each civilization at some point announces that it has reached such an end and now it is going to last forever in its shape. No one is aware that the decline has already started

civilization morphs into another, something he calls "apparenting". In composing a narrative that embraces twenty-six examples drawn from the past millennia and from all over world, Toynbee conducts his analysis of the dynamics of civilizational growth searching for universals, yet maintaining a phenomenological approach. Thus at the moment, from a Spenglerian perspective, the time comes for the final and pessimistic conclusion that our Western civilization has attained the status of a "universal state" and is now steadily heading for self-annihilation, Toynbee withdraws and offers counter-arguments. Those attempts to save the West are rather feeble[18] in comparison with Toynbee's ever so robust discussion of how one civilization after another has risen from the debris of a "parent" civilization, in time only to suffer spiritual crisis and fall, though often spawning a civilizational heir. Indeed, Toynbee's hopeful case for our civilization begs the question: Why should Western civilization differ? Let us compare two passages describing the future of the West.

High history also lays itself down weary to sleep. Man becomes a plant again, adhering to the soil, dumb and enduring... Only with the end of grand History does holy, still Being reappear. It is a drama noble in its aimlessness, noble and aimless as the course of the stars, the rotation of the earth, and alternance of land and sea, of ice and virgin forest upon its face. We may marvel at it or we may lament it—but so it is (ibid.: 381).

If we are to try to look into our future, we may begin by reminding ourselves that, though all the other civilizations whose history is known to us may be either dead or dying, a civilization is not like an animal organism, condemned by an inexorable destiny to die after traversing a predetermined life curve. Even if all other civilizations that have come into existence so far were to prove in fact to have followed this path, there is no known law of historical determinism that compels us to leap out of the intolerable frying-pan of our time of troubles into the slow and steady fire of a universal state where we shall in due course be reduced to dust and ashes (Toynbee 1987: 553).

Thus, concerning Western civilization, *A Study of History* is in fact a jeremiad, something more than a scholarly attempt to persuade Westerners that decline and transformation into another kind of civilization need not come, however probable that may look. Toynbee worked on his book (and the abbreviated

18. At least for Ballard who, as it will be clear in the following chapters, tends to conflate Toynbee's theses with those of Spengler. Both thinkers are for him theorists of disaster whose works point out the inevitability of the decline of every system—political and social ones included. In one of his short stories, "The Voices of Time", the protagonist, aware of the approaching end of life on Earth, says: "That's the last thing I want to do. I want to forget Toynbee and Spengler, not try to remember them" (Ballard 2002b: 170).

version that is now in use) for several decades in the first half of the last century. Conceived just after World War I and re-edited in the forties, the book has to incorporate the experience of World War II and the indisputable failure of the British Empire. Toynbee bravely tries to overcome the prevailing pessimism in calling for spiritual renewal, but his descriptions of falls are more gripping and ominous than is his summons to rejuvenate Western civilization inspiring.

In his narrative Toynbee relies amply upon similes and parables. His historical discourse is figurative and depicts social and political mechanisms as if they were adventure stories. He starts by comparing the growth of civilization to the alternance of Yin and Yang—with periods of peace and stillness interrupted by outbursts of energy, to wit, rapid growth, conquests and development. Societies grow and develop, but they may often become "arrested", which means that they petrify and freeze on a certain stage of their development. The examples he gives in his work as a whole derive not only from the historical past, but also from literature. This kind of discourse makes his narrative a rich source of inspiration for writers of the disaster story—Ballard included.

The widest range of comparisons is applied to render the causes and mechanisms of the breakdowns of civilizations:

> They are failures in an audacious attempt to ascend from the level of a primitive humanity to the height of some superhuman kind of living, and we have described the casualties in this great enterprise by the use of various similes. We have, for example, compared them to climbers who fall to their death, or to an ignominious state of life-in-death, upon the ledge from which they have last started, before completing the 'pitch' and reaching a new resting-place on the ledge above. We have also described the nature of these breakdowns in non-material terms as a loss of creative power in the souls of creative individuals or minorities, a loss which divests them of their magic power to influence the souls of the uncreative masses (ibid.: 245).

It is the said spiritual element of social life that makes Toynbee's thesis attractive to mid-century young readers who, like Ballard himself, are interested in the future of their world. Toynbee analyzes contemporary life in the West and points to social phenomena that in the cases of declining civilizations in the past marked the approaching end and merger with a "younger" foreign culture. Contempt for the past and traditional values, the emergence of new experimental artistic styles and schools ridiculing old masters, easy import of barbarian fashion, the music and religion of conquered peoples and the overwhelming feeling of depression and impotence in both social life and individual souls—these for him are portentous signs. In his attempt to discover why civilizations fall, Toynbee rules out answers traditionally given by historians, ones concerning biological laws that determine life-spans, the running down of some cosmic clockwork or the deterioration of races grown too old. His own answer points to the spiritual suicide of a civilization and, despite his attempts to give hope to Western readers, *A Study of History* implies that the West is dangerously near such a situation.

A Study of History poses several questions concerning historiosophy and the "ways" of civilizations. In numerous essays and addresses[19] Toynbee, a very prominent scholar in his epoch, discusses them in detail. One such question is "Does History Repeat Itself?", which Toynbee analyzes in an eponymous article first published in 1947. Starting with a simple observation that most Western people feel they are somewhat different than representatives of societies from the past, he tries to establish whether we have any right to think we are the crown of creation and the final global civilization. His conclusion is far from optimistic: "history has repeated itself about twenty times in producing human societies of the species to which our Western society belongs, and ... with the possible exception of our own, all these representatives of the species called civilizations are already dead or moribund" (Toynbee 1949: 38). What Toynbee is afraid of (and so is Ballard) is the consequences of the global character of Western dominance. In "The Unification of the World and the Change in Historical Perspective", a very "Ballardian" lecture delivered in 1947, he depicts the illusory character of Western superiority and tries to imagine the moment our own culture will collapse under the weight of too many imported styles and values.

What Ballard finds fascinating in Toynbee's works (judging from the remarks made by characters in his stories) is the very wide perspective and the ability to look at the world from a great distance. The feeling that the future is going to be much different than the past and that nowadays we are witnessing one of the greatest shifts of power in the history of the world can be equally felt in Toynbee and in much younger fiction writers who in the times of the Cold War tried to imagine the future. Toynbee writes his essays in the late forties, when the twilight of the British Empire is indisputable. Though only ten years earlier England seemed invincible, the global balance of power has shifted and the UK has lost its dominant position. In "The International Outlook" (1947) Toynbee discusses the situation of Europe after World War II and his conclusions are again pessimistic—the European continent is a battle ground fought over by two non-European powers: Soviet Russia and the US.

Once an older civilization loses its importance, alien powers come. However, Toynbee argues, those powers are not the reason of the civilization's downfall: they are merely attracted by the vacuum. The reasons empires and civilizations fall are always internal, or "spiritual", as Toynbee labels them. He states that in history up to the present moment "it has been the spiritual wounds that have proved incurable" (Toynbee ibid.: 135). This conclusion and Spengler's thesis concerning the innate suicidal character of every civilization are at the crux of Ballard's beliefs, as seen in his early stories. He finds Toynbee's works attractive because their mood reflects his own mid-century pessimism, and also because of the cosmic perspective Toynbee is capable of adopting:

19. Some of them are collected in the 1948 volume *Civilization on Trial,* London: Oxford University Press—all quotes from Toynbee's articles in the below discussion are to this edition.

In space, our Western field of vision has expanded to take in the whole of mankind over all the habitable and traversable surface of the planet, and the whole stellar universe in which this planet is an infinitesimally small speck of dust. In time our Western field of vision has expanded to take in all the civilizations that have risen and fallen during these last 6000 years; the previous history of the human race back to its genesis between 600,000 and a million years ago; the history of life on this planet back to perhaps 800 million years ago (ibid.: 151).

This quote comes from a lecture Toynbee delivered, during which he looks at the present situation of the West from a number of points of view—starting with post-war England and moving on in space and time. He guesses at the opinions of how future historians will describe the 20th century from the distance of tens and then hundreds of years and even wonders at the reaction of an alien intelligence (for example, that of an ant civilization) if it were to study our history. Such mental experiments allow him to see the spiritual and intellectual crisis of post-war Europe in the way fiction writers see it—as one episode in the vastness of time reflecting some general truths concerning the nature of civilizations.

The Keys to Mindscapes
—Sigmund Freud, C.G. Jung, R.D. Laing, and the Surrealists

One of the most important themes recurring in Ballard's fiction is the way the human mind reacts to the traumas of the 20th century—both to historical events, and also the cognitive stress of life in the contemporary mediascape. Psychological concepts and often very famous psychological essays resound in Ballard's prose. The single most important intertextual influence on him (generally, not only as far as psychology goes) is Sigmund Freud. Ballard's characters quote Freud, argue with him, develop his concepts, and laugh at him—but never ignore him. Ballard does not treat Freud uniformly; his own attitude towards the father of psychoanalysis changes just as the general attitude changed in the last century. In the fifties Freud was considered a genius and a universal point of reference in all the humanities—towards the end of the nineties he was remembered rather as a thinker or a philosopher.

Ballard alludes to Freud very many times and seems to accept his theories concerning the death instinct, the way civilization breeds neuroses and the repetition-compulsion mechanisms, but he cannot be called an orthodox Freudian even in the first period of his career when he was under the spell of psychoanalysis. Freudian references are mingled in his books with allusions to Freud's archenemy C.G. Jung, and they do not form any unified theory. Moreover, Ballard is aware of later trends within psychology: hence, he makes his characters allude to anti-psychiatry and to one of its most prominent representatives, R.D. Laing, though he is far from accepting Laing's theories. Rather, he enters an intertextual dialogue with his cult books. Beyond that, Ballard's unquestionable love of the Surrealists (whom he himself calls his main intellectual and artistic fascination) is not only esthetic in nature. He treats surrealist paintings on a more cerebral level, as exercises in psychoanalysis allowing spectators to glimpse the unconscious.

Freud's *Civilization and Its Discontents* (1929) is for Ballard a work of sheer genius defining in philosophical terms the reasons for the mid-century's traumas. He often alludes to this paper in both his fiction and non-fiction. Freud manages to answer a seemingly simple question: why do most people feel unhappy most of the time if in the nineteenth century the enormous progress of science and technology made human life (at least in Europe) much easier than before? Instead of feeling lords of creation, people suffer numerous neuroses. The sources of human unhappiness are numerous: the body, other members of society, and the outside world cause continuous distress. Human nature makes people seek pleasure and avoid discomforts, therefore it is quite surprising that one of the most powerful sources of pain is the very civilization that people have created. In order to function within society we have to renounce most of our drives and wants and accept unpleasant feelings of shame, deprivation and humiliation.

The ostensible blessings of civilized life—art, science, religion, intellectual pleasures and the like—are, according to Freud, substitutes of gratification invented to ease the pain of participating in society. Nevertheless, there is something in the mental constitution of man that makes it impossible for us to be happy within the constraints of civilization, for in response to the degree of privation imposed by society (in virtue of its cultural ideas) man develops neuroses. In the late twenties it was obvious enough that "power over nature is not the only condition of human happiness" (Freud 1994: 777), and that most modern inventions answer the needs created by previous inventions.[20] Privation is not a side effect of civilization, but its very heart, as civilization is built upon renunciation of instincts. Moreover, in order to hide this unpleasant truth, numerous myths about humanity's gentleness and noble nature are created and the primary hostility between men (who by nature hate strangers and outsiders) has to be internalized.

> Men are not gentle, friendly creatures wishing for love, who simply defend themselves if they are attacked, but a powerful measure of desire for aggression has to be reckoned as part of their instinctual endowment (ibid.: 787).

Every human being repeats in his development the process of renunciation the human race underwent at the dawn of civilization. Sacrificing needs and drives in exchange for a place in social structure makes people neglect an important part of their psyche. Internalized aggression in the moment of stress "is sent back where it came from, i.e., directed against the ego" (ibid.: 792), and thence neuroses. Towards the end of the paper Freud defines one of the major causes of contemporary anxiety:

---

20. For example, if there were no railways and no long distance travel there would be no need for telephones, people would live in one place and communicate easily.

Men have brought their powers of subduing the forces of nature to such a pitch that by using them they would now easily exterminate one another to the last man. They know this—hence arises a great part of their current unrest, their dejection, their mood of apprehension (ibid.: 802).

Freud is able to predict the causes of the mid-century traumas, he links psychic discomforts to what happened thousands of years ago when the first human societies developed and, what is the most important for Ballard, he identifies the past of the human race with the mysterious depths of the contemporary psyche. In his other late essay (one Ballard also very often refers to), *Beyond the Pleasure Principle* (1920), Freud renounces his earlier claims that sexuality and self-preservation are basic and the most primordial of the instincts. He admits that the theory of the pleasure principle and the reality principle, which co-operate in order to give us maximum satisfaction while protecting us from the pitiful consequences of immediate gratification, fails to explain human behaviour. He also admits that the drives of love, to perpetuate and to survive are superficial and evolutionally new: underneath there lies something far more archaic.

Beyond the Pleasure Principle was written just after World War I. In this text, Freud is very much influenced by pessimism and disbelief in progress. He studies cases of post-traumatic neuroses among soldiers who cannot stop re-enacting fear and the behaviour of frustrated children. Traumatic dreams and nightmares tend to have a similar pattern: "the dream at night takes them back to the situation which has caused the trouble... perhaps the expedient left us is of supposing that in this condition the dream function suffers dislocation" (Freud 1967: 641). "These dreams are attempts at restoring control of the stimuli by developing apprehension, the pretermission of what caused the traumatic neurosis" (ibid.: 30). Freud notices that the need to repeat, to come back, even to unpleasant things, is stronger and older than the narcissistic pleasure principle. All life tends "to repeat as a current experience what is repressed, instead of, as the physician would prefer to see him do, recollecting it as a fragment of the past" (ibid: 27).

Re-living the past is the oldest and the most rudimentary of mechanisms. The very embryo of every animal is obliged in its development to repeat structures of all ancestral forms without the possibility of taking any short-cuts. Our evolutional descent is imprinted on every cell of our organisms: they all "remember" previous conditions. The repetition-compulsion state lies at the bottom of all systems, and this causes Freud to re-define the notion of an instinct: "an instinct would be a tendency innate in living organic matter impelling it towards the reinstatement of an earlier condition" (ibid.: 68).

All organic life has to endure pain and, as such, its existence is traumatic and full of suffering. As all living cells remember the long-distant past, they also remember the most beautiful and the oldest of states: the painlessness of inanimate matter. Deep inside our cells, time does not exist:

The Kantian preposition that time and space are necessary modes of thought may be submitted to discussion today in the light of certain knowledge reached through psycho-analysis... unconscious mental processes are in themselves timeless. That is to say, they are not arranged chronologically, time alters nothing in them, nor can be the idea of time applied to them (ibid.: 54).

Thus, we unconsciously still remember being inorganic; on a certain level of microbiological or molecular make-up, we still are. In this blessed state without pain, we have no desire and no frustration. In moments of prolonged stress, we try to repeat the past in a vague hope to return to this inanimate nirvana. Freud concludes in the utmost pessimistic manner that all life is a mistake. Unhappily, life did arise—and hence tension and pain. The Earth is contaminated with life, which perpetuates itself eternally. Such mechanisms as self-preservation, narcissism or desire are secondary and serve to make us forget about our most primordial will to die:

If we may assume as an experience admitting no exception that everything living dies from causes within itself and returns to the inorganic, we can only say the goal of all life is death, and casting back, The inanimate was there before the animate.
At one time or another, by some operation of force, which still completely baffles conjecture, the properties of life were awakened in lifeless matter. Perhaps the process was a prototype resembling that other one which later in a certain stratum of living matter strove to attain an equilibrium; the first instinct was present, that to return to lifelessness (ibid.: 70-71).

The idea that within the psychic apparatus striving for pleasure there exists a tendency towards self-annihilation renders the search for one's true self suicidal. In their descent into their inner space Ballardian characters often choose death or mutilation. For the outsider this is auto-destruction, but for said characters it means finding peace of mind and fulfilling innermost desires.

Apart from the discord between a psychic apparatus spontaneously striving for pleasure and the demand of society that imposes stressful restrictions on one's drives, there is one more enemy to the psyche's well-being. The introduction of "beyond the pleasure principle" forces in the psyche implies the existence of a "death drive", a foreign entity which renders final bliss impossible.[21] In many essays Freud analyzes the paradoxical tendencies

21. Slavoy Žižek links the Lacanian interpretation of Freud's death drive with the perverse "pleasure in pain"—the pleasure which comes from beyond the pleasure principle because it originates in tension and frustration re-claimed by pleasure later: "the intruder which disturbs the harmonious circuit of the psychic apparatus run by the 'pleasure principle' is not something external to it but strictly inherent to it: there is something in the very immanent functioning of the psyche, notwithstanding the pressure of 'external reality' which resists full satisfaction... The Lacanian name for this "pleasure in pain" is of course enjoyment—*jouissance,* and the circular movement which finds satisfaction in failing again and again to attain the object... is the Freudian drive" (Žižek 1992: 48).

inherent in the psychic apparatus and the human propensity for contraries: fear and pleasure, death and sexuality, the known and the unknown are often depicted as two sides of the same psychic phenomenon. Gregory Zilborg, the American editor of *Beyond the Pleasure Principle*, claims that Freud started working on this paper in the same month that he was completing his famous essay "The Uncanny" (1919).

In "The Uncanny" he tries to identify the origins of human fears and his conclusion is that the feeling of horror is born when we face an embodiment of contradiction: for example our own double or a walking dead. The uncertainty as to whether a given object belongs to the realm of life or death is the essence of all horror stories (about ingenious dolls coming to life, wax figures, zombies, ghosts, etc.). Rosemary Jackson in *Fantasy. The Literature of Subversion* connects this uncanny feeling with the deepest levels of human consciousness as formed eons ago in the times of animistic beliefs when all—magic included—seemed possible. Facing such an embodiment of contradiction touches residues of animist activity in our minds and provokes an inexplicable anxiety associated with the return of repressed unconscious material to consciousness, especially when this repressed material includes vestiges of the magical mode of thinking. As another critic of fantasy literature, Sam Francis puts it; "the indistinction between animate and inanimate, real and imaginary, is uncanny because it evokes repressed memories of a stage of individual or cultural development at which these distinctions were not made" (Francis 2006: 77).

The human propensity for projecting their inner feelings and fears onto inanimate objects or landscapes and then considering those outer phenomena to be actual sources of emotions that in fact come from within the human soul is one of Freud's very important discoveries. Ballard never questions the existence of this mechanism, in his fiction this is one of the major principles ruling the relationship between a human being and the world he or she perceives. A careful reading of Ballard's oeuvre allows us to see more Freudian assumptions underlying the way characters behave. This Freudian heritage is so immanent in mid-century Western culture that it functions as a set of universal rules—just like the discoveries of Newton. In fact, the discoveries of Freud mark the end of the Age of Reason initiated, among others, by Newton. Ballard says in an interview:

> We ran from Voltaire to Freud. Freud ended his life on a very pessimistic note. If you read *Civilization and Its Discontents*... he was more or less saying that human beings now have the power to destroy themselves utterly if they wanted to.
>
> The death instinct seems to be in the ascendant. If you think of the Enlightenment (roughly speaking) as running from the birth of modern science up to 1933 and the arrival of Hitler, obviously its influence continued on to the Second World War and beyond that. One senses that the Age of Reason has now begun to fade (Vale 2005: 53).

Ballard borrows from Freud the essential distinction between the latent and the patent. Whether Ballard talks about dreams, human behaviour, metaphors used in a literary text or the contents of a novel the distinction is always valid and we can distinguish the surface, apparent meaning from the hidden, latent meaning generated by the unconscious. In Ballard's texts landscapes, allusions, the geometry of rooms, the haphazard juxtaposition of photographs or other items very often reveal a supplementary meaning that is far more important than the obvious one. The same is true on many other levels of his texts—sometimes character's actions, travels or wanderings seemingly "real" in the world described in the book turn out to be symbolic renderings of his mental processes. Reading Ballard's books (especially those written before the nineteen-eighties) very often involves an act of translation between two languages similar to the act of dream interpretation described by Freud:

> The dream-thoughts and the dream-content present themselves as two descriptions of the same content in two different languages; or, to put it more clearly, the dream-content appears to us as a translation of the dream-thoughts into another mode of expression, whose symbols and laws of composition we must learn by comparing the origin with the translation. The dream-thought we can understand without further trouble the moment we have ascertained them (Freud 1938: 319).

This passage written by Freud at the turn of the 19th century introduces to Western culture a set of assumptions that underlay much of the 20th century's understanding of the way the human mind works. The idea that we hide our true thoughts and feelings even from ourselves and that every text is in fact a cipher is essential to understanding Ballard's fiction. The necessary procedure of deciphering his meanings involves Freudian techniques of pursuing associations and symbols. To quote Freud again:

> By pursuing these associations further we obtain knowledge of thoughts which coincide entirely with the dream but which can be recognized—up to a certain point—as genuine and completely intelligible portions of waking mental activity. Thus the recollected dream emerges as the manifest dream-content, in contrast to latent dream-thoughts discovered by interpretation. The process which has transformed the latter into the former, that is to say into 'the dream', and which is undone by the work of interpretation, may be called the 'dream-work' (Freud 1986: 137-138).

This concise rendering of Freud's major early discovery should be kept in mind while we read Ballard. His prose is structured following the psychoanalytical pattern of the latent\patent distinction and therefore Freud should be enumerated among Ballard's masters.[22] Nevertheless, one should remember that his fiction is not a precise and faithful realization of Freud's postulates, although he agrees with Freudian ideas concerning the unconscious and the relationship between the personal and social life of an individual, he mixes allusions to Freud with allusions to Jung.

Some critics even call Ballard a Jungian writer[23] and it is certainly true that in Ballard's prose separate ideas from Jung function as intertextual echoes—indeed, Ballard engages his readers in an intellectual game of guessing. We are led to realize that Ballard's characters and situations are supposed to make us think about very precise essays or concepts. Such a Jungian idea that Ballard finds very attractive is the theory of the Self. Instead of following the Freudian model of a triple psychic apparatus id-ego-superego that is necessary from the evolutionary and structural point of view, Jung postulates the existence of one united Self. Due to some unhappy incident in the evolution of the human race the Self was split into its conscious and unconscious parts, but this division may and should be overcome.

In *Man and His Symbols* Jung and a group of his associates describe the major achievements of Jungian psychoanalysis, whose principal goal is to teach people to regain the Self. The Self, in their understanding, should encompass all parts of the mind and, indirectly, absorb the whole heritage of humankind. Ballard takes the Jungian theory of archetypes and applies it to literature—in his stories characters are often compared to figures from the literary canon because this very canon represents recognizable types of personages that we collectively know. Similarly, myths, dreams, collective imagination, and genetic memory from the times of "fossil men" (as Jung calls them) form one united body of references and ideas. Symbols recurrent in different artistic styles, ideas appealing to members of alien civilizations, cultural universals are all in accordance with hidden parts of our minds.

> Man has developed consciousness slowly and laboriously, in a process that took untold ages to reach the civilized state (which is arbitrarily dated from the invention of script in about 4000 B.C.). And this evolution is far from complete, for large areas of the human mind are still shrouded in darkness. What we call the "psyche" is by no means identical with our consciousness and its contents (Jung 1978: 6).

Jung is not afraid of describing humankind's standing in a very wide context of thousands of years of history, nor does he hesitate to juxtapose scientific facts with theories that sound half-fantastic. The mythical dawn of the human race,

---

22. David Pringle puts it thus in an interview with V. Vale: "A certain understanding or knowledge of Freud is definitely helpful in understanding Ballard, because I think he was deeply, deeply influenced by Freud. He talks about Freud being a great novelist, which might not be literally true but symbolically—!" (Vale 2005: 220).
23. Compare the discussion of David Pringle's criticism in "Introduction".

palaeontology and the character of our ancestors are for him handy points of reference. By history he means not the conscious description of the past known through language and old scripts, but 'the biological, prehistoric, and unconscious development of the mind in archaic man" (ibid.: 57), which, he holds, is preserved in the modern psyche. Ballard seems fascinated by linking the inner space with the past and in some of his stories he follows the Jungian path of descending deeper and deeper into the mind in order to study human prehistory.

> This immensely old psyche forms the basis of our mind, just as much as the structure of our body is based on the general anatomical pattern of the mammal... the experienced investigator of the mind can similarly see the analogies between the dream pictures of modern man and the products of the primitive mind, its "collective images", and its mythological motifs (ibid.: 57).

Jung argues that more attention should be paid to the individual human being. Nowadays modern science, which is based on abstraction and generalization, tends to ignore individual differences between people in trying to define objective rules and types. In so doing, most of the characteristics of human nature are lost and instead of understanding the world we lose contact with our own internal life. Ballard in his early stories investigates this mysterious inner space of the contemporary mind showing that it contains both the past and future of our species and that deep inside we are aware of cosmic rhythms which rule all life.

The Jungian psychoanalysis maintains that the Self is the first and the most archaic psychic entity. The "fossil man" and members of primitive tribes are in contact with this power, considered to be magical and to come from their ancestors. They have numerous names for the embodiment of the collective unconscious and wisdom of the whole society, while contemporary people have lost contact with their heritage and only sometimes in dreams can they catch a glimpse of the Great Man or other personification of the psychic wholeness. Nowadays, the stress falls on a separate person as our culture values individuality and clearly defines what is real and what is imagined. In order to function within the sphere of contemporary reality we have to develop the ego.

> It even seems as if the ego has not been produced by nature to follow its own arbitrary impulses to an unlimited extent, but to help to make real the totality—the whole psyche. It is the ego that serves to light up the entire system, allowing it to become conscious and thus to be realized (ibid.: 163).

The dominance of the ego maims people and cuts them off from their heritage and potential. Yet Jung can imagine a type of civilization that allows the Self not to be sacrificed for the good of progress. Ballard, who often writes his own critiques of contemporary culture and the ways Western civilization mutilates human identity, likes to encode in his texts allusions to Jung's theory.

Many of his characters set out on a journey to discover the true identity that is hidden in their minds and in the past of the human race,[24] and on their way they sometimes encounter persons embodying Jungian archetypes. His favourite one is the anima—in Ballard's stories we encounter numerous lamias and *femmes fatales* that combine predatory sexuality with sinister powers.

As far as post-Freudian and post-Jungian psychology is concerned, Ballard is aware that numerous schools in the 20th century attempt to find their own key to inner space, but he remains rather sceptical. The late 60s gurus who look for illumination in drugs and eastern mysticism are for him funny or dangerous figures and the only fashion he acknowledges in his stories is anti-psychiatry. R.D. Laing, whose books were cultic for the hippie generation, is sometimes alluded to in Ballard's text. One of his protagonists is actually called Laing, and in the case of his late novel *Millennium People* (2004) a character, himself a psychologist, remembers the 1960s when his irresponsible mother used to go drinking in Soho with R.D. Laing, the LSD fanatic.

Despite his irony, Ballard seems to accept some of Laing's theses. Laing's popularity dates from the moment he published *The Divided Self* (1965), a book about schizophrenics in which he claims that in the contemporary sick society the only healthy response to the overwhelming paranoia is mental withdrawal. Schizophrenics are much more honest than their doctors are and there is no worse ailment than the acceptance of social demands on oneself.[25] Laing argues for regaining the lost wholeness of the human psyche at any cost, social ostracism included, and the Jungian ideal of finding the Self is for him and his acolytes not a metaphor but a matter of free will and perseverance.

In *The Politics of Experience* (1966), a book that although written by a psychiatrist reads like a strange mixture of philosophy, sociology and "New Wave" fiction, Laing formulates his manifesto. He starts by defining the relationship of the inner and the outer worlds, experience and behaviour. He stresses the fact that inner experience is not enclosed in one's head but "happens' in the outside world. It is interesting to notice the similarities to the "New Wave" artistic program. Laing, just like his fiction-writing colleagues, would like to see people exploring both the world around and the contents of their brains that are projected onto reality. He repeats the Jungian thesis that while growing up we lose the innate ability to communicate with the realm of dreams and imagination and are unhealthily conditioned to tell the real from the fantastic.

From the moment of birth, when the stone-age baby confronts the

24. In some cases the hints that characters are in fact involved in Jungian enterprise are cryptic, in some obvious. For example in *The Crystal World* a protagonist searching for his true inner self finds himself in a petrified forest where all living creatures are slowly turning into crystal. Compare Jung: "In many dreams the nuclear centre, the Self, also appears as a crystal. The mathematically precise arrangement of a crystal evokes in us the intuitive feeling that even in so-called "dead" matter, there is a spiritual ordering principle at work". (Jung 1978: 221).

25. Once they decide to abandon social restrictions and set out on a journey to discover their true inner personality, Ballard's protagonists can hardly be considered mentally healthy. For any outsider, the characters of "Terminal Beach", *Concrete Island* or *High-Rise* behave like psychos.

twentieth-century mother, the baby is subjected to these forces of violence, called love, as its mother and father have been, and their parents and their parents before them. These forces are mainly concerned with destroying most of its potentialities. This enterprise is on the whole successful. By the time the new human being is fifteen or so, we are left with a being like ourselves. A half-crazed creature, more or less adjusted to a modern world (Laing 1990: 50).

Our society is sick and the norms that it imposes on individuals are harmful. This society values "normality" and only "normal" people are its rightful members, but at the same time the very definition of this "normality" is abnormal. Normal people have killed 100,000,000 other normal people in the previous fifty years. To conform and to become like all the other people is an act of self-annihilation. This civilization is already doomed and is heading for a disaster—Laing quotes Heidegger's famous phrase, the Dreadful has already happened, to emphasize the failure of Western culture. For him in the nineteen-sixties the global catastrophe is waiting in the wings, Western civilization has chosen the wrong track and now swiftly approaches Armageddon.[26] It is high time to abandon its norms and concentrate on one's own psychic life, as that can offer fulfilment and revelation.

> We all live under constant threat of our total annihilation. We seem to seek death and destruction as much as life and happiness. We are as driven to kill and be killed as we are to live and let live. Only by the most outrageous violation of ourselves have we achieved our capacity to live in relative adjustment to a civilization apparently driven to its own destruction. Perhaps to a limited extent we can undo what has been done to us, and what we have done to ourselves (ibid.: 64).

By "undoing" the harms caused by civilization Laing means unifying human perceptions of the Self and the surrounding reality and liquidating "the split of our existence into what seems to be two worlds, inner and outer" (ibid.: 103). In explaining his ideas concerning how to re-unite the two worlds Laing uses the language of the "New Wave" writers, but his point markedly differs from that of the artistic aims of the group. He claims that the distinction between mentally healthy people and the deranged (drug addicts, social dropouts and mental

---

26. This last opinion sounds similar to Ballard's rendering of the cultural meaning of Hiroshima and Nagasaki—the final proof that humans are violent creatures subliminally dreaming of aggression and annihilation. The implications are nevertheless different. Laing calls for a kind of passive social revolution—the abandonment of values and norms and undertaking Jungian journeys towards the Self. For Ballard the certainty of disaster gives people an existential freedom of doing whatever they like—the catastrophe should be embraced happily because it is what we have really wanted for thousands of years of repression. In other words, for Laing civilization is a bad thing, for Ballard it has been a feeble attempt of the human race not to annihilate itself. But this attempt has proven futile.

patients) is artificial—people are just undergoing different phases of their journey towards a profound understanding of their psyche.

> Some people wittingly, some people unwittingly, enter or are thrown into more or less total inner space and time. We are socially conditioned to regard total immersion in outer space and time as normal and healthy. Immersion in inner space and time tends to be regarded as anti-social withdrawal, a deviancy, invalid, pathological per se, in some sense discreditable (ibid.: 103).

Laing sees the re-discovery of the inner space as a kind of social therapy and means to increase individual freedom. Ballard, and other "New Wave'" writers, are more interested in the artistic qualities of the inner landscape. Laing uses Jung and his theories of the Self in political debates and his psychoanalysis is subjected to the needs of his revolutionary manifestos. Ballard is interested in psychoanalysis because it gives insight into the ways contemporary people behave within the constraints of modern Western civilization and, additionally, because it opens a new territory for artistic exploration. The Surrealists, who were the first artists to use Freud as a guide to the realm of dreams, fears and obsessions, are among his favourite painters and poets.

He told Lynne Fox in an interview:

> I began to get interested in modern fiction—by which I mean modern classics, Kafka, Thomas Mann, Hemingway—and in psychoanalysis, so I was reading a great deal of Freud, and Surrealists abutted all these writers and thinkers. (Vale 2005: 162) I felt an instant recognition—Dali in particular, Max Ernst: oh, this was home. I understood all these landscapes completely. I never had any doubt that this was my imagination; these paintings were like newsreels of the inside of my head. I thought that these were the real landscapes of the 20th century; and of course they were rather similar in some respects to the landscapes I'd known in the Far East during the war (ibid. 165).

Although he is primarily interested in the visual art of the Surrealists— the paintings of Salvador Dali, Yves Tanguy, Max Ernst and Rene Magritte are described in his stories and sometimes his literary landscapes are modelled upon some of them. Moreover, he also accepts the theory behind the art. Psychoanalysis is for the Surrealists akin to avant-garde art because it allows an exploration of the forbidden sphere of human sexuality and the innermost, often shameless, feelings. Such introspection is quite revealing and quite shocking for traditionally minded spectators. The Surrealists absorbed other artistic schools, for example the Dada movement (Ballard has always been a great admirer of Alfred Jarry), and moreover they reclaimed as their spiritual fathers the nineteen-century symbolist poets. Reread with the knowledge of Freud, their poems yield new interpretations and their figurative language is often echoed in Ballard's style.[27] Arthur Rimbaud, Charles Baudelaire and principally Comte de Lautréamont[28] are the poets he admires the most, with the possible exception of Samuel Taylor Coleridge, whom, by the way, the Surrealists also liked.

Of course the Surrealists were not faithful followers of Freud in the clinical application of psychoanalysis. They were interested in the productive imagination of dreams and Freud, mainly in their therapeutic potential. Nevertheless, psychoanalysis allowed the poets to penetrate previously unknown areas, and this gives their poems a new quality. André Breton makes this point in *What is Surrealism* (1934). "The question was no longer essentially to produce works of art, but to light up the unrevealed and yet revealable part of our being in which all the beauty, all the love and all the virtue with which we scarcely credit ourselves are shining intensely" (Breton 1978: 81). The rediscovery of the Surrealists in the sixties and the seventies (Ballard's fiction partly inscribes into this renaissance) was due to the fact that they tried to integrate the high and the low, the psychic life of ordinary people and sophisticated artistic fashions.[29]

Andreas Huyssen comments on this renaissance:

> However, the original impetus to merge high art and popular culture—for example, say in Pop Art in the early 60s—... was indebted to the historical avant-garde—art movements such as Dada, constructivism, and surrealism—which had aimed, unsuccessfully, at freeing art from its estheticist ghetto and reintegrating art and life (Huyssen 1986: 60).

> What is the meaning of this energetic come-back, in the age of postmodernism, of Dada, constructivism, surrealism, and the new Objectivity of the Weimar Republic? Exhibits of the classical avant-garde in France, Germany, England and the United States turned into major cultural events. Substantial studies of avant-garde were published in the United States and in West Germany

27. In the early period of his literary career Ballard's style is very exuberant, his trade mark is that of a long complicated simile abundant in symbolic connotations. Critics usually claim that Ballard is influenced by the poetic diction of Lautréamont.
28. Lautréamont is the favourite poet of the early 20th-century avant-garde. He "simultaneously challenges the literary tradition of comparison, the standard definitions of beauty, the acceptance of codes, and the belief in fixed and, even more, lasting measures or laws. As he parodies description, he implicitly supplies a more dynamic, daring, and flexible criterion for beauty and he forces us to reassess its value. Breton's famous conclusion to Nadja can be construed as the ultimate summation of this new esthetics, partially derived from Lautréamont: Beauty will be convulsive or it will not be" (Hubert 1987: 190).
29. Although, as Peter Bürger notes in his *Theory of the Avant-garde*, surrealist poetry examines only isolated subjects, a human mind in this poetry is separated from fellow men and every psychic life seems solipsist, which in fact is contrary to the avant-garde postulate that art and life should merge.

initiating lively debates. Conferences were held on various aspects of modernism and the avant-garde (ibid.: 162).

This fashion is an important context in understanding Ballard's *The Atrocity Exhibition, Crash* and his short stories written in the sixties and early seventies. His keen interest in psychoanalysis is influenced by the ways it was used by early 20th-century artistic movements in order to highlight the meanders of human thought. What Ballard has in common with Breton or Paul Eluard is his fascination with mental derangement. Madness, neurosis and paranoia allow us to see the rough psychic mechanisms at work. "Naturally the Surrealists are on the side of the self, the madman... reason itself being defective, reason must be overcome; it is the world which must submit" (Breton and Eluard 1990: 12), writes Anthony Melville, the English editor of Breton's and Eluard's *The Immaculate Conception*. In the "Insert" written for the original edition of this book by Salvador Dali this point is discussed in detail:

> The original wish to make simulations of deliria, categorised or otherwise, will have not only the appreciable advantage of bringing to light unforeseen and totally new poetic forms, but also the transcendent effect of sanctioning in an exemplarily didactic manner, the free categories of thought which culminate in mental derangement.
>
> *The Immaculate Conception* will be the experimental source to which one will have to return in order to recognise the power thought has of adopting successively all the modes of madness; to recognise this power is equivalent to admitting the reality of this madness and affirming its latent existence in the human mind (ibid.: 25).

Salvador Dali is for Ballard one of the very few artists who could show on canvas the confusion of the human mind in the midst of "the media landscape with its emphasis on the glossy, lurid and bizarre, its hunger for the irrational and sensational" (Ballard 1997b: 5). Ballard wrote numerous articles about Dali and he always claims that Dali's surrealism, owing mostly to Freudian influences, allows the viewer to enter a modern mind. Dali can juxtapose the most bizarre and haphazard elements of contemporary life: the H-bomb, the religious iconography we remember from our childhood, the images of atomic physics, the commercial landscapes, the fear about the future and the like. It is thanks to psychoanalysis that Dali's paintings look like some modern "newsreel filmed inside our head":

> This reflects Dali's total involvement in Freud's view of the unconscious as a narrative stage. Elements from the margins of one's mind—the gestures of minor domestic traffic, movements

through doors, a glance across a balcony—become transformed into the materials of a bizarre and overlit drama. The Oedipal conflicts we have carried with us from childhood fuse with the polymorphic landscapes of the present to create a strange and ambiguous future (ibid.: 8).

This passage comes[30] from an "Introduction" to Dali's *Diary of a Genius*, but also in many other texts does Ballard emphasize the fact that Dali's paintings are akin to Rorschach tests in that they can be used for the exploration of the inner reality of human lives. Moreover, he considers the techniques of surrealism especially relevant in recent times, "when the fictional elements in the world around us are multiplying to the point where it is almost impossible to distinguish between the real and the false—the terms no longer have any meaning" (ibid.: 88). Ballard goes on to explain that popular culture and the media change the world into one big show: politicians and public figures are comedians, and giant advertisement hoardings are more convincing than any relevant message. Life is but isolating the few elements of reality from the ocean of fictions appealing to our unconscious and surrealism offers contemporary people the tool for this task— Giorgio de Chirico, Salvador Dali and Max Ernst are for him "the iconographers of inner space" (ibid.: 200).

It is interesting to note that Ballard raises the problem of numerous fictions blurring our notion of what is real as early as the mid-sixties. The cultural theories of the end of the century discuss the same phenomenon and work out a whole critical apparatus to define simulacra and the ways it maims human personality. Ballard was there first and in the last decades of the century he both read these theorists and, by his own fiction, influenced their ideas.

Understanding Simulacra:
Marshall McLuhan, Guy Debord, Jean Baudrillard

Mass culture is one of Ballard's recurrent themes. He describes popular entertainment in the Americanized Shanghai of the nineteen-thirties, the development of communication techniques in the sixties and the paradoxes of the electronic information age. The multiplication of messages and fictions produced for the sake of entertainment and commerce alters the whole shape of Western civilization and marks the beginning of a new era when life mostly revolves about consuming images.

As early as the nineteen-sixties, when the hegemonic role of the media (primarily television) started to be felt, Marshall McLuhan coined his famous phrase "global village" and tried to study the rapid changes information technology was introducing to human life in the West. In *Understanding Media* (1964), a book subtitled "The extensions of man", McLuhan discusses not only the

---

30. The text was a reworking of Ballard's article "The Innocent as Paranoid", written in 1968 for *New Worlds* and in 1997 re-printed for the third time in *A User's Guide to the Millennium*, (Ballard 1997b: 91-98).

media, but also other "extensions" such as cars, architecture and fashions—all the modern inventions that allow man to extend his power over the world and to see more, hear more, notice more and get faster to more places. McLuhan describes the birth of the contemporary mediascape, this half-unreal territory Western people populate. He links the development of new information technologies with the growth of commodity culture: late capitalism cannot perpetuate itself without the means of persuasion, and vice-versa—the media need advertisements.

> In the new electric Age of Information and programmed production, commodities themselves assume more and more the character of information, although this trend appears mainly in the increasing advertising budget. Significantly, it is those commodities that are most used in social communication... that bear much of the burden of the upkeep of the media in general. As electric information levels rise, almost any kind of material will serve any kind of need or function, forcing the intellectual more and more into the role of social command and into the service of production (McLuhan 2003: 40).

Economy, communication and entertainment merge. The arrival of electric technology alters relationships between people and the world around. Technology for McLuhan is an extension of man's senses: with the help of modern devices we remodel our central nervous system in "sending" its endings to numerous places on Earth. A human self sits in the middle of this spider-web absorbing more and more data concerning things necessary, as well as redundant bits and pieces of information and, moreover, being the recipient of persuasive messages often geared at his unconscious. The new communication era is therefore a time when a new definition of the self must be formed, as the role of man within the social and economic structure changes and, additionally, human perceptions and innermost thoughts are heavily influenced by civilization. We become more passive, less independent and prone to manipulation.

> Thus the age of anxiety and of electric media is also the age of the unconscious and of apathy. But it is strikingly the age of consciousness of the unconscious, in addition. With our central nervous system strategically numbed, the task of conscious awareness and order are transferred to the physical life of man, so that for the first time he has become aware of technology as an extension of his physical body (ibid.: 52).

Thus the new era is also an era of cyborgization, as man becomes a partly mechanical being heavily dependent on his technological inventions. McLuhan attempts to discuss the present stage of civilization in reference to previous revolutions and the history of progress. He thinks in terms of landscapes, trying to define subsequent kinds of the environment man inhabits and analyzing the ways in which the physical conditions of life influence human culture. From our nomadic ancestors who roamed the countryside and lived in isolation and hostility towards each other we moved to cities. The city culture made people communicate far more and develop a shared culture that required the first remodelling of the individual's mind. Nowadays, with the increase of communication techniques we share more and more of our psychic life with other members of society and the result might be a translation of our entire lives into the spiritual network encompassing the entire globe.

This process is prompted by the invention and lavish use of motorcars that devastated the countryside and created a new landscape of motorways, parking lots and plazas. The city as a shared territory inhabited by families living in tightly connected neighbourhoods has ended. The streets and sidewalks are no longer a casual environment where children play and parents gossip. The city is now inhabited by mobile strangers and city architecture suits the needs of car owners. Psychologically, such a situation is bound to reshape man's attitude towards machines and fellow citizens. "The machine world reciprocates man's love by expanding his wishes and desires... one of the merits of motivation research has been the revelation of man's sex relation to the motorcar" (ibid.: 51).

This last remark is important to any Ballard reader, as in his stories, especially these collected in *The Atrocity Exhibition*, the relation of man to technology (principally the motorcar) plays a prominent role. Ballard quotes "research" on the psychic consequences of cohabitation with modern technology, and he studies the subliminal dependence on cars we have developed. In his examination of contemporary culture Ballard is indebted to McLuhan in one more aspect—television and crime. Both writers consider the Kennedy murder, the first assassination on screen, to be the turning point in the history of media. From this moment on violence entered entertainment and newsreels became a kind of violent entertainment spreading the images of atrocities we have grown to ignore.

McLuhan's famous sentence that nowadays "the medium is the message" fascinated nineteen-sixties avant-garde artists and theorists all over the Western world. The French Situationists are no exception, their leader Guy Debord in his famous manifesto *Society of the Spectacle* (1967) rephrases it to say "the spectacle's form and content are identically the total justification of the existing system's conditions and goals" (Debord 1967: § 6). Debord's book, with its unnumbered pages and numbered paragraphs, describes contemporary social life as an "immense accumulation of spectacles" and he claims that whatever used to belong to directly lived social experience has now moved away into pure representation. Life in the modern conditions of production is contemplating an image of reality, a pseudo-world given to us for contemplation.

> In the spectacle, one part of the world represents itself to the world and is superior to it. The spectacle is nothing more than the common language of this separation. What binds the spectators together is no more than an irreversible relation at the very

centre which maintains their isolation. The spectacle reunites the separate, but reunites it as separate (ibid.: § 29).

Society is thus a number of isolated subjects who consume spectacles prepared for them in separation. The spectacles are the same and, therefore, society seems homogeneous, although there is no direct communication between its members as everybody is linked to the source of spectacles only. The power structure of such a society depends on the circulation of images as all aspects of human life: politics, economy, culture, etc., are presented as spectacles and aimed at manipulating the individual.

The Situationists in their attempt to discuss the society of the spectacle from the outside of the network of cross-cutting spectacles had to cut themselves off from all capitalist institutions. First of all television (Debord's slogan was "revolution will not be on TV"), but also the publishing business,[31] and for a long time they walked the streets expressing themselves via graffiti. Utopian as these efforts were, the Situationists protested not only against the overwhelming power of the agencies producing spectacles and thus producing the reality shared by the spectators, but also against the rapid reduction of human life. "The more he contemplates the less he lives" (ibid.: § 30), writes Debord about each spectator. Watching and absorbing spectacles we accept dominant images and identify with the needs and desires projected on us, which finally leads to the situation of total alienation—we no longer understand our existence and 'real' desires.

This spectacle guarantees the undisturbed development of modern capitalism, and becomes an apologetic catalogue of commodities we are made to believe we need. The abundance of objects and images encloses the consumer who can directly touch only fragments of this commodity happiness and thus is never satisfied, always dreaming of the utopian consumption of the whole.[32] Debord's final conclusion is that by obliterating the difference between the individual self and its environment (both are images produced by successive spectacles) the society of spectacles liquidates the distinction between true and false, fiction and non-fiction. What is left is only ideology perpetuating itself endlessly.

> The spectacle is ideology par excellence, because it exposes and manifests in its fullness the essence of all ideological systems: the impoverishment, servitude and negation of real life (ibid.: § 215).

Defining the society of the spectacle and showing that it is the dominant power structure encompassing the whole of Western civilization Debord announced the end of culture and the destruction of urban life, adding to the list

31. My English edition of *Society of the Spectacle* does have an ISBN, but also a caption "No copyright, No rights reserved", and neither the name of its translator nor the date the translation was published are stated.
32. The vicious circle of consumption within the conditions of modern capitalism and the spectacles it produces is the subject of some of Ballard's stories, the most drastic case being "The Subliminal Man".

of ends and exhaustions widely discussed in the second half of the 20th century. The circulation of images replaces genuine artistic production and culture changes into a repetition of already existent images. People living in separation are connected to the media and their motor cars, but are devoid of any direct contact with each other and the countryside, too. Space is reshaped according to the whims of architecture, which also borrows from older styles.

Frederic Jameson in his essay "Postmodernism and Consumer Society" (the later, expanded version is entitled "Postmodernism, or the Cultural Logic of Late Capitalism") calls this state of culture postmodernism and defines the postmodern condition by the terms "schizophrenic temporality" and "spatial pastiche". Schizophrenia is for him (like for Jacques Lacan) a breakdown between signifiers and the failure of access to the symbolic—things surrounding the subject cease to have any meanings as seem separate and disconnected. Devoid of any signification, images dispersed by spectacles form a never-ending "now", a world without time and sequential order where the subject is enclosed and has no possibility of relating the images to any stable point of reference. "Time" becomes an abstract term and as far as space is concerned civilization changes it into a pastiche—architecture imitates dead styles, our cities and motorways are but a mixture of esthetic quotations that are not even funny: shopping centres, multiplexes and business plazas look grotesque. "It is in the realm of architecture... that modifications in esthetic productions are most dramatically visible, and that their theoretical problems have been most centrally raised and articulated" (Jameson 1984: 54).[33]

The human subject is reduced, and people lose their identities and no longer can explore the outside world, as the "reality" they live in is growing unreal. Scott Bukatman in his essay "Who Programs You? The Science Fiction of the Spectacle"[34] discusses late capitalism (which, following Jean Baudrillard, he calls the age of *Simulacra and Simulations*) with the help of cybernetics:

> Exploration outward has been superseded by the inward spiral of orbital circulation—in cybernetic terms, the feedback loop. The world has been reconstituted as a simulation within the mega-computer banks of the Information Society, the terminal identity exists as the mode of engagement with the imploded culture (Kuhn 2003: 196).

Science fiction and computer studies provide terms to discuss contemporary culture and society. Jean Baudrillard in his essays trying to define the culture of simulacra employs the discourse that apparently is very far from reality and rather fits the discussion of imagined universes (Baudrillard does write science fiction criticism and the language he uses in both cases is the same). Acknowledging

33. Jameson's point that architecture may serve as an indicator of the state of culture is taken by Ballard in his late novels *Super-Cannes* and *Cocaine Nights* where the landscape of southern Europe is described as pastiche.
34. In *Alien Zone. Cultural Theory and Contemporary Science Fiction Cinema* edited by Anette Kuhn.

McLuhan's "the medium is the message", he goes further and announces not only the implosion of the message but also of the medium and of the real. Instead of a reality (that might be shown as images and mediated) we live "in a sort of nebulous hyperreality" where the world is transformed into circles of watching and we can no longer distinguish media from things mediated.

Television is responsible for producing the greatest amount of simulacra, and TV networks penetrate deep into social structures, infiltrating all spheres of life and shaping mass culture. Contemporary society reflects TV (not the other way round): the postmodern subject, "the citizen", is constituted by watching TV, which provides him with a socially shared vision of reality. In the conditions of late capitalism television apparently gives an abundance of promise—it presents the wide range of commodities to choose from, the "stars" who use these commodities and a superficially endless choice of channels. At a glance an ocean of cross-cutting narratives, images and stories is offered and the spectator (the postmodern subject) has only to choose. This power of choice vanishes at the moment any spectacle is actually chosen, as the very act of watching enslaves. The human mind becomes an ultimate medium reflecting numerous TV screens.

Jean Baudrillard in *Simulacra and Simulationss* (1981) discusses Ballard's *Crash* as the best example of the culture of simulacra described in contemporary fiction, a paradoxical book of "no more fiction or reality; it is hyperreality that abolishes both" (Baudrillard 2003: 118). *Crash* and other products of postmodern culture (like Disneyland, Hollywood, Watergate etc., *Crash* is the only work of literature Baudrillard discusses in detail) provide him with material to define hyperreality and show his readers the way it shapes our world. We live in the days of simulation—"the generation by models of a real without origin or reality: a hyperreal" (ibid.: 1). The world as we know it is produced by constructing and spreading its images: we deal with a "precession" of simulacra".

> The real is produced from miniaturized cells, matrices, and memory banks, models of control—and it can be reproduced an infinite number of times from these. It no longer needs to be rational, because it no longer measures itself against either an ideal or negative instance. It is no longer anything but operational. In fact, it is no longer really the real, because no imaginary envelops it anymore. It is a hyperreal, produced from a radiating synthesis of combinatory models in a hyperspace without atmosphere (ibid.: 2).

What is lost in the Western world is the difference between fact and fiction, metaphysics and reality. Postmodern society lives within the frames of a spectacle it continuously produces and nothing outside the propagation of images exists.[35] As the

35. Compare Ballard's interviews: "I see a future of deepening boredom interspersed with random acts of violence. I think, going back to what you're saying: people do feel that there is some sort of core identity which they haven't quite been able to get hold of. As I was saying to Vale a few months ago, we're living in an era when nothing is true and nothing is untrue" (Vale 2005: 46). And: "It

notions of sign and medium cease to have any meaning, according to Baudrillard, we no longer live in the society of the spectacle of the Situationists. Television is no longer a spectacular medium (it watches you far more than you watch it) and the relation spectator/spectacle becomes dubious. "There is no longer a medium in the literal sense: it is now intangible, diffused, and diffracted in the real, and one can no longer even say that the medium is altered by it" (ibid.: 30).

Baudrillard goes on to describe the hyperreal mediascape with gigantic billboards that preside over the countryside and observe citizens. This mediascape is very much like the setting of Ballard's novels from the nineteen-seventies: it consists of hypermarkets, highways, factories and parking lots that are interconnected and constitute postmodern space:

> The hypermarket cannot be separated from the highways that surround and feed it, from the parking lots blanketed in automobiles, from the computer terminal—further still, in concentric circles—from the whole town as a total functioning screen of activities (ibid.: 76).

> And the automobile, the magnetic sphere of the automobile, which ends by investing the entire universe with its tunnels, highways, toboggans, exchangers, its mobile dwelling as universal prototype, is nothing but the immense metaphor of life (ibid.: 113).

The space is de-humanized and fit for cyborgs only, the people-cars that defy nature. In the contemporary mediascape the reality principle disappears and people cannot function as biological beings because the conditions are lethal to life. They also cease to be social beings as no interpersonal communication is possible any longer. Instead of communication we have acts of staging communication: numerous shows and programmes with listeners who call in and participate telling everybody "you are the event, you are concerned".

The U.S. is for both Ballard and Baudrillard the harbinger of the future of the West, the land of the beginning, where cultural phenomena are born and may be studied. In *Hello America* (1980) Ballard described the eponymous continent as a cradle of mass-culture and a pilgrimage site of the future generations living in the post-apocalyptic times of the regress of Western civilization. In *America* (1986) Baudrillard describes his impressions from a stay in the US in such a way as to show the Europeans what hyperreality is and what future awaits all of us. His America is in love with senseless and endless repetition: you watch it travelling by car across the desert where the views in the windscreen are monotonous like old films. In order to fight the feeling of a catastrophe, of being in the devilish, post-apocalyptic wasteland you drive faster and faster. "Speed is simply the rite that initiates us into emptiness: a nostalgic desire for

---

seems we almost live inside of an enormous novel, thanks to the media landscape which has now locked itself around our planet" (ibid.: 274).

forms to revert to immobility, concealed beneath the very intensification of their mobility" (Baudrillard 1994: 7).

America is infested with screens, images and billboards. The towns look taken from the movies, city streets have stepped right out from the screen. In order to do some sightseeing one should begin with the movies and move outwards to the city. The screen idols embody stereotypes of life and love, dreams and fascinations are prefabricated and sold. Movie stars are the dream come true, they are the quintessence of "the passion for images" that in America replaces dreaming. America is nothing but Simulacra and Simulations.

> Everything is destined to reappear as simulation. Landscapes as photography, women as the sexual scenario, thoughts as writing, terrorism as fashion and the media, events as television. Things seem only to exist by virtue of this strange destiny. You wonder whether the world itself isn't just here to serve as advertising copy in some other world (ibid.: 32).

Things do not come in sequences, the feeling of chronology is lost and instead we are surrounded by hosts of simultaneous images, something which results in the dissociation of any feeling of predestined order. Everything is transient, haphazard, and unnecessary. The last real thing that ever happened in America was the Kennedy murder—it was real because it was filmed and its energy still radiates. America, the land of the future, is the desert of simulacra—its inhabitants are watchers who participate in the hyperreal culture because they consume images. Their produced reality is what the rest of the world is rapidly becoming. Baudrillard predicts that this process will soon be completed.

Civilization on Trial:
Alvin Toffler, Francis Fukuyama, Samuel Huntington

Contemporary Western society lives within a media culture that values speed and glamour but is devoid of depth. Nowadays Western people spend a lot of their time passively watching rapidly changing images and consequently they grow to expect things to be altogether fleeting. This new kind of culture, which Alvin Toffler in *The Third Wave* (1981) labelled "blip culture", produces a great amount of modular "blips" of information—ephemeral, electronically sent bits and pieces of mostly irrelevant data that attack our nervous systems. New electronic technologies have changed the human environment and human perception enormously, to the extent that in the late 20th century members of affluent societies lead lives that are totally different than those of all the previous generations.

> For we have not merely extended the scope and scale of change, we have radically altered its pace. We have in our time released a totally new social force—a stream of change so accelerated

that it influences our sense of time, revolutionizes the tempo of daily life, and affects the very way we "feel" the world around us. We no longer "feel" life as men did in the past. And this is the ultimate difference, the distinction that separates the truly contemporary man from all others. For this acceleration lies behind the impermanence—the transience—that penetrates and tinctures our consciousness, radically affecting the way we relate to other people, to things, to the entire universe of ideas, art and values (Toffler 1980: 17).

This passage comes from Toffler's *Future Shock* (1970) and since it was written the changes have accelerated and the human environment has become even more transient. Toffler and many other critics in the last decades of the 20th century tried to record and study the new social and cultural phenomena that have been emerging so rapidly. The early century's discussion about the definition of civilization and the future of the West was rekindled.

Future Shock was written at the moment when the change started to be generally felt. The book became a bestseller, which is rare for a sociological study, and this success shows that people at the time wanted to understand more about what was going on around them. In this early book Toffler is still very optimistic (not to say naïve) about the future. He believes in progress, in a new epoch that is just beginning and teaches how to embrace the changes and become people of the future. The basic distinction he makes is between three kinds of social groups: one lives in the past (agricultural communities whose life is slow), the biggest one in the industrial present and a chosen few already in the future. These mostly American "trendmakers without knowing it" (ibid.: 37) have already adopted the speed of life of next generations.

Toffler believes that the future will be above all fast—people will move endlessly and hate to stop (of course some people hate to rush, but they prove ill fitted to the present conditions of life). The pace of life is the principal American export and the way the US Americanizes the rest of the world. People who live faster are accustomed to changes of environment, friends, houses, and to the turnover of things and ideas, but their lifestyle might seem for those who still inhabit the present psychologically too demanding. The danger is overstimulation— nowadays people receive too many messages that are not redundant enough to make them feel comfortable. Faced with an abundance of informationally compact data they get lost and start to miss the good old times and talk about the world changing for the worse.

Trying to depict the social life of the imagined future West Toffler guesses that an important branch of the entertainment industry will be the creation of virtual adventures to be sold to those who cope with the desire to escape from the stress of modern life. This guess is interesting to us not only because Toffler does anticipate VR (virtual reality) parlours and, to some extent, computer and role-playing games, but also because Ballard in his fiction and non-fiction often describes the future culture as escapist.

One important class of experimental products will be based on simulated environments that offer the customer a taste of adventure, danger, sexual titillation or other pleasure without risk to his real life or reputation. Thus computer experts, roboteers, designers, historians, and museum specialists will join to create experimental enclaves that reproduce, as skilfully as sophisticated technology will permit, the splendour of ancient Rome... and the like (ibid.: 228).

People will seek escape to find a psychological vent to the cognitive tension of future life. Toffler points to two psychic dangers that will together produce the trauma that he nicknames "future shock". Firstly, the overstimulation through the abundance of messages attacking us from everywhere via every possible channel causes the state of disorientation. Secondly, in order to defend our nervous system against this stress, the human mind tends to plunge into the coma-like state of sensory depravation, where data cannot get through to our consciousness. Therefore, in the near future the Western world according to Toffler will be divided into those who live in the future and are happy to accelerate their pace of life, and the rest who will suffer future shock.

The maladaptation to the conditions of life in late capitalism will express itself in many ways, depending on individual features of personality. Some people will reject the changes and the modern world by denying progress and trying to find safe enclaves for themselves; escapist ideologies, life in communes, strange cults or even psychic derangement. Others will specialize—i.e. they will keep up with the changes and the progress, but only in the very narrow field of their professional life. The development of civilization outside this field will sooner or later surprise them and probably push them towards future shock. Though both reactions might be found in Ballard's fiction set in the near future, the most important for Ballard's reader is the third—violence.

Violence, too, offers a "simple" way out of burgeoning complexity of choice and general overstimulation. For the older generation and the political establishment, police truncheons and military bayonets loom as attractive remedies, a way to end dissent once and for all... For those who lack an intelligent comprehensible program, who cannot cope with the novelties and complexities of blinding change, terrorism substitutes for thought (ibid.: 362).

Despite its warnings, *Future Shock* is rather an optimistic vision of the future. In 1970 Toffler believes that though some people will lag behind social changes and suffer, most of the population of the West will embrace modernity willingly. In the early 1990s he had to revise his prognosis. First of all, the changes have proven to be much faster than he had anticipated and secondly, the social and cultural situation has deteriorated. In *Power Shift* (1990) Toffler describes not an imagined future, but the future which is already happening around us and the way he chooses to describe it is via shifting power structures. He believes that the very last decade of the 20th century is the time when the global power structure (the post World War II political, economical and industrial systems) collapses, but also "all the rules of the power game change at once" (Toffler 1991: 7). In many apparently disconnected spheres of life we face the end of traditional authoritarian power systems and the birth of new, mobile structures of constantly shifting power.

Power at the turn of the millennium is connected to knowledge and "info-politics". Those who know and those who decide which pieces of information to distribute rule, especially if they can influence the choice of programmes on TV channels. Toffler analyzes the impact TV has on all spheres of human life in detail and finds out that apparently irrelevant background scenery in TV dramas such as landscape, cars, street scenes, architecture, telephones, answering machines and barely noticed everyday behaviour do matter. People subliminally notice all and their life—current fads and fashions, popular attitudes toward sex, religion, money and politics—is modelled by the media. This kind of power should not be mistaken with political propaganda, as it does not come from a single authoritarian centre. "High-tech governments face a future in which multiple, conflicting, custom-tailored commercial, cultural, and political messages will bombard their people, rather than a single message repeated in unison by a few giant media outlets" (ibid.: 335).

A similar mechanism is at work in the sphere of economics. On the one hand, factory mass production of goods results in the unification of the market and consequently of the choices customers make. On the other hand though, producers send different images, ideas and symbols to closely targeted population segments and differentiation is maintained. Toffler attempts to define future society and the mechanisms ruling it by presenting such dichotomies: old monopolies and multiple power-centres replacing them. According to Toffler, diverse 'power shifts' are taking place in the last years of the millennium and in the future most power in the society of the affluent West will be delegated to numerous multiple agencies operating on a low level of social structure. The times of monopolies and tyrannies are over and we face a truly free and diverse civilization, but we have to learn to live in it and take advantage of the choice it offers because members of future society have to be active customers, not passive users of things.

Toffler's books (principally his definitions of "future shock" and "the third wave") were very influential and often referred to in the last decades of the 20th century. And so are the books of another theorist of civilization, Francis Fukuyama. In *The End of History and the Last Man* (1992) Fukuyama announces that after the collapse of the communist bloc, and thus of the post-World War II balance of power, a new epoch begins. The final victory of liberal democracy is the end of the West's history of social and political progress. In the past, events such as wars, battles, inventions and spells of regress formed one narrative of the civilization struggling towards a better and more just political system. Once the ideal of democracy is achieved, the events and changes going on in the world do not form a single narrative with a political moral to it, but happen randomly.

For Ballard Fukuyama's book is important for a number of reasons. On a superficial level some of his stories mock the idea of the end of history and political struggle, showing how in the post-historical future human communes are psychologically bound to re-start old conflicts. More profoundly, in many of Ballard's texts written in the last decades of the 20th century we find societies that lead a post-mortem, nightmarish life. In these books the history of humankind logically leads to the voluntary act of self-annihilation by people who have created a violent, aggressive and suicidal civilization. Once their true selves are discovered during the atrocious wars of the 20th century the final Armageddon should have taken place, and it is a bitter irony that it did not actually happen—which fact sentences humans to an existence with no sense of direction and no future. Finally, the most interesting correspondence between the ideas of Ballard and Fukuyama becomes apparent only when we carefully read into *The End of History and the Last Man*.

This book is very often quoted, but also misquoted—the "end of history" does not imply the end of events happening in the world nor does it suggest that Western society is going to become a utopia overnight. In the second part of the book, the much less famous *The Last Man*, Fukuyama asks a number of very Ballardian questions concerning the psychology and sociology of the post-historical civilization. He begins by discussing the unfolding of modern natural science. The marvellous development of technology results in a practically limitless accumulation of wealth and military safety. Not threatened with wars and offered the satisfaction of an ever-expanding set of material desires, societies in affluent countries become homogeneous as a uniform horizon of economic possibilities makes them resemble each other. In a uniform satiation world tensions and conflicts weaken, people feel happy with representative democracy and gradually lose interest in politics and other kinds of rivalry.

What kind of people will populate our brave new Western world? Won't they lose their humanness? In order to answer these questions Fukuyama refers to philosophers who have analyzed the social consequences of utopian political happiness, principally Friedrich Nietzsche:

> The typical citizen of a liberal democracy was a "last man" who, schooled by the founders of modern liberalism, gave up prideful belief in his or her own superior worth in favour of comfortable self-preservation. Liberal democracy produced "men without chests", composed of desire and reason but lacking *thymos*, clever at finding new ways to satisfy a host of petty wants through the calculation of long-term self-interest. The last man had no desire to be recognized as greater than others, and without such desire no excellence or achievement was possible. Content with his happiness and unable to feel any sense of shame for being unable to rise above those wants, the last man ceased to be human (Fukuyama 2002a: xxii).

Following Nietzsche's line of thought, Fukuyama tries to depict a near-future Western man with neither aspiration nor striving. And he asks a fundamental question about human nature: "does not the desire for unequal recognition constitute the basis of a livable life, not only just for bygone aristocratic societies, but also in modern liberal democracies?" (ibid.: xxiii). Do we need to feel better than others and to strive to prove our superiority or can we be satisfied by peace and prosperity? According to Nietzsche, the last man is a slave: although happy, he deserves our contempt. With no pride, manliness or righteous anger he will satisfy his needs through economic activity, but never risk his life in battle. In other words, last men would slowly become animals with none of the aspirations that once made human beings conquerors of the planet.

For Fukuyama Nietzsche's theory is a starting point to discuss the future of the West. Firstly, he pictures possible catastrophes that would restart history and change the face of human civilization. In science fiction-like scenarios of disasters recommencing a new Middle Ages he presents resurrections of earlier forms of social organization, but in conclusion he claims that sooner or later the present state of affairs would be restored anew. The basis of our civilization—modern natural science and its offspring technology—guarantees a constant progress towards an affluent safe society and liberal democracy. Fukuyama does not believe that technology and science might ever be lost, for unlike in the past, societies today are too inter-connected to forget the benefits of material welfare. "There are, in other words, no true barbarians at the gates, unaware of the power of modern natural science" (ibid.: 88).

Therefore, it seems that Western civilization cannot escape its post-historical future and the inevitable revolution in morals and psychology. Referring to great philosophers of the Western world, Fukuyama notes that they define the humanness of *homo sapiens* precisely by describing the features Nietzsche's last man lacks. Plato spoke of *thymos* (the "spiritedness" of noble men), Jean Jacques Rousseau of *amour-propre*, Niccolo Machiavelli of desire for glory, Thomas Hobbes of vainglory and Georg Hegel of recognition. Usually, in order to understand man within society philosophers discuss his value system and the ambition to prove himself superior to fellow citizens, at least in his own eyes. So what will we do in a system that equally distributes privileges and wealth and discourages competition? Fukuyama ends with an open question:

> The life of the last man is one of physical security and material plenty, precisely what western politicians are fond of promising their electorates. Is this really what the human story has been "all about" these past few millennia? Or is the danger that we will be happy on one level, but still dissatisfied with ourselves on another, and hence ready to drag the world back into history with all its wars, injustice, and revolution? (ibid.: 312).

The answer is quite shocking and unexpected. In 2002, seeing that his prophecies are far from being right, Fukuyama publishes *Our Posthuman Future*, a book which describes the future that is already around us with all its moral and sociological dangers. The parallels between his concerns and the social phenomena described in Ballard's late novels are striking.

Fukuyama abandons geo-political discussions and concentrates on the impact of the biotechnology revolution on human life claiming that it is going to be the major factor influencing Western civilization in the beginning of the new millennium.[36] As I have already mentioned in my Introduction, he starts his book by referring to two mid-twentieth century dystopias: Orwell's *1984*, which as we can see after the collapse of the communist bloc has clearly not come true, and Huxley's *Brave New World*, which has proven disturbingly prophetic. Huxley depicts the spiritual death of affluent humankind and nowadays biotechnology is bringing about similar moral dilemmas. Fukuyama sketches three scenarios of science fiction-like transformation of the Western society into Huxley's dystopia (a Ballardian "Grave New World"), and the striking thing is that they in fact are technologically quite probable. They are: drugs altering human perception and self-esteem, genetic modification of future generations and rejuvenation techniques that will result in the ageing of our civilization. Working in conjunction, these three dangers are going to recommence history and open a new epoch in the life of the West.

Fukuyama (just like Ballard in his latest novels) contrasts the early 20th-century belief in Freud and his premise that mental illness is primarily psychological in nature with the rise of psychotropic drugs. Modern neuroscience is based on knowledge of the biochemical nature of the brain and allows us to alter its workings. Doctors no longer try to locate and bring about the repressed memories and thus to heel the unconscious, they prefer to ordain Prozac.

> For Prozac is said to affect that most central of political emotions, the feeling of self-worth, or self-esteem.

> Self-esteem is of course a trendy psychological concept, something Americans are constantly being told they need more of. But it refers to a critical aspect of human psychology, the desire all people have for recognition...

> The normal, and morally acceptable, way of overcoming low self esteem was to struggle with oneself and with others, to work hard to endure sometimes painful sacrifices, and finally to rise

36. One should mention here the end-of-the-millennium fears and the socio-cultural phenomenon of millenarianism. Books such as *The Late Great Planet Earth* by Hal Lindsey or *Left Behind* by Tim LaHaye and Jerry Jenkins, which describe the end of the world based on Biblical prophecies coming true literally (the virtuous ones are taken alive to Heaven before Armageddon, and thus some people disappear in airplanes, football matches or from the middle of supermarkets) sell in millions of copies. Ballard has always been very critical towards millenarian sects and their teaching, but the very popularity of these theories are telling for him as far as the intellectual and spiritual condition of Western civilization goes.

and be seen as having done so. The problem with self-esteem as it is understood in American pop psychology is that it becomes an entitlement, something everybody needs to have whether it is deserved or not. This devalues self-esteem and makes the quest for it self-defeating (Fukuyama 2002b: 46).

Just like Huxley's *soma*, drugs such as Prozac alter social life and make the individual strive for an individualist, escapist satisfaction felt subjectively instead of fighting and struggling in the real world. Social life in a civilization of Prozac-addicts will be null as everybody would close themselves in a virtual space of make-believe successes and pleasures—a disquieting Ballardian vision. Drugs altering human abilities to judge reality are especially dangerous within liberal democracy where every citizen has the power to choose, vote and decide about the future of the world. Not only might the choice be blurred by drug-induced states of consciousness, but also the well-wishing majority might decide to pharmacologically "help" maladjusted people. Fukuyama is far from horror-like visions of tyrants doping their subjects, but he fears the situation when a too protective system tames the unhappy members of society into oblivion, thus eliminating all outstanding traits of personality and unifying people.

The prolongation of human life and the consequent ageing of affluent societies will also be a potential danger to the *thymos* of future society. An elderly population (and a feminized one, because old women live longer than their male peers), will force politicians to take a new line in international politics. Valuing safety, affluence and non-engagement elderly societies will also produce a new kind of culture with, probably, distinctive anti-ageism traits. The cult of youth will be replaced by new fashions, most products will be targeted at much older buyers and young people will find it very difficult to start their professional careers in a world ruled by seniors. Moreover, the growing possibilities of genetic engineering will make it possible to alter future generations and a new kind of society will emerge. It is indeed difficult to guess what these last men will be like and what kind of world they will inhabit.

One more author has to be added to this list of thinkers important to understanding Ballard's *oeuvre*. Though Samuel Huntington wrote his *The Clash of Civilizations and the Remaking of the World Order* in 1996, which makes it too late to directly influence most of Ballard's writing, his book reflects similar concerns about the future of the world. In the interview he gave to V. Vale, Ballard quotes Huntington and describes the social situation in England after the terrorist attacks in reference to the "Clash of Civilizations" theory (Vale 2005: 13 and 97). Huntington prophesies the beginning of a spell of chaos when, after the end of the old world divided between the Eastern and the Western blocs, a new kind of balance has to be worked out. In this period we might witness the breakdown of governmental authority, the break-up of states, the emergence of international mafias, the spread of terrorism and the proliferation of nuclear weapons.

In this new world, local politics is the politics of ethnicity; global politics is the politics of civilizations. The rivalry of superpowers is replaced by the clash of civilizations.

In this new world the most pervasive, important and dangerous conflicts will not be between social classes, rich and poor, or other economically defined groups, but between peoples belonging to different cultural entities. Tribal wars and ethnic conflicts will occur within civilizations (Huntington 1996: 28).

Thus Huntington sees the near future as the time of a disruption of the seemingly monolithic world. In contrast to the theorists describing "global villages" or "ends of history" he perceives the contemporary world as heterogeneous and ready to explode. Though he agrees the Western media are a very powerful tool of unification, he sees them as the last stronghold of Western hegemony.

Huntington believes in the inevitable decline of the West: referring to the theories from the beginning of the 20th century he comes back to the age-old theses of Spengler and proves that the process of the decline is already advanced. According to him (and according to Ballard) "the end of history" so loudly discussed in the early 1990s is the end of the Western Universal state (to use Toynbee's term). Each civilization in sensing its own approaching and inevitable termination preaches the end of the World and the end of history for humankind.

J.G. Ballard in his fiction and non-fiction pictures a rather pessimist vision of humanity's perspectives. The *Grave New World* in which his stories are set (and which is so uncannily similar to our own world) is the land of decadence. Though Ballard has never taken seriously the irrational millenarian fears,[37] there is a prevailing feeling of no future in his books. The portentous sense of the end is overwhelming, rational behaviour and the progress of societies belong to the past only. Western societies are reaching the state of stasis, a point of no movement when only random acts can occur granted they are motivated by unconscious, irrational impulses.[38]

In his output Ballard describes the decadent phase of Western culture from different perspectives. Depicting *Grave New World* he enters an intertextual dialogue with diverse theorists, signalling that his attitude towards our reality is the well-grounded opinion of a person who has read voraciously in many disciplines. The major influence on Ballard is that of the theorists of civilization: from Gibbon and Spengler to Toynbee, Fukuyama and Huntington. The fact of

---

37. Compare his article "Back to the Heady Future" reprinted in *A User's Guide to the Millennium* (Ballard 1997b: 192-194).

38. "Masochistic societies are the pattern of future societies, where because of immense potency of psychopathic behavior, it may become the command structure that links people's unconscious minds to the government of the day" (Vale 2005: 101) says Ballard. In the same interview he describes the future of the West as a marriage of Disney and Microsoft, a corporation-governed post-capitalist state whose inhabitants are force-fed with infantile pulp entertainment wrapped in high-tech parcels.

the fall of the Roman Empire and the demise of the British Empire (which he witnessed from the perspective of a POW camp during World War II) inclines Ballard to believe in the organic character of civilizations, that they have a "life-span" with birth, growth, decline, and death as necessary phases. Moreover, civilizations, just like biological life-forms, are subject to some higher cosmic order, and what is more, unconsciously every human being senses when the end is coming. Theories of Freud and his followers Jung and Laing give Ballard an access to the latent parts of the human mind and thus to the death instinct theory, which claims that irrationally we long for the peace of an inorganic, post-biological Nirvana. The art of the Surrealists depicts a similar attitude and allows Ballard to actually see the mindscapes of contemporary people.

The decadence of the West is characterized by the dominance of the media, which invades our psyche and structures the way we perceive reality. Thinkers such as McLuhan, Baudrillard, Debord and Toffler allow Ballard to analyze the mediascape of *Grave New World* and to guess what its future might be like. In order to understand how previous epochs—the Age of Reason in the West—got transformed into *Grave New World* one has to return to World War II and its huge psychological consequences. For Ballard the war ushers in the beginning of today's culture and is the crux of Western civilization: the way he describes the world at war in his fiction with all certainty helps to understand the way he describes today and tomorrow.

CHAPTER TWO:
BATTLEFIELDS

J.G. Ballard is principally known as an English writer who was born in Shanghai and was interned in a Japanese prison camp during the Second World War. Every short biographical note—on book jackets, in the Internet or in promotional coverage for his new novels—repeat these few snippets of information. Now, over twenty years after the success of his quasi-autobiographical war novel, *Empire of the Sun* (1984), it is cliché to treat Ballard's childhood experiences with wartime atrocities as a key to all his fiction: whether his science fiction, disaster stories or surrealist avant-garde writing. The autobiographical explanation of the obsessive recurrence of certain images and situations in his fiction (deserted landscapes, drained swimming-pools, empty cities full of abandoned cars, etc.) is partly of Ballard's own making, as he has referred to his personal past in the context of his literary career in numerous interviews.[1]

---

1. A good example is the paperback edition of Ballard's novel, *Millennium People* (it has nothing to do with the Second World War), which has a short appendix about the author. In the interview quoted there Ballard is asked about the impact of his childhood experience of internment. He answers: "Shanghai during World War Two, and my period interned in a Japanese camp, was a very extreme version of ordinary life. I experienced so many things that my children, for example, will never experience. Living in a camp for nearly three years was like living in a huge slum. I was living in effect, the kind of life that refugees live today in Africa and the Middle East: very short of food, very cramped. I saw adults around me in a state of great stress, and that's something that most children today never see. Also I saw an occupied city, enemy soldiers on the street and tanks rumbling around, bombing and all the rest of it. It was a very extreme world. I think that feeds into the imagination" (Ballard 2004, appendix 2).

Ballard is keen on saying that World War II is the true intellectual and spiritual beginning of his output. "I have often thought writers don't necessarily write their books in their real order. *Empire of the Sun* may well be my first novel, which I just happened to write when I was fifty-four" (Self 1995: 360). This quote is typical for him, as he both comments on his fiction (suggesting that it should be read as springing from the personal experience described in *Empire of the Sun*) and, at the same time, he self-fashions his literary persona. Thus he creates a meta-narrative of his life as a story starting with the war and the internment, matters which have a huge impact on his imagination and result in the type of fiction he writes in post-war times. Moreover, the war in Ballard's fiction, in being his own artistic beginning, is also a source of *Grave New World* with its post-traumatic and violent culture.

The war terminated what Ballard calls "the Age of Reason",[2] the post-18th century Western world which believed in science, the soundness of reason and solid bourgeois decency. Colonial empires, primarily Britain's, fell and America took over and began to envelope the world with its mass-culture and media network. Pre-war times in Ballard's fiction seem film-like and unreal, they fade away in juxtaposition with the experience of WWII, whose core is that of blatant violence—the outburst of which is almost liberating. The latent aggression and drive to self-destruction that had been kept at bay were set free during the war and, after its conclusion, are not re-internalized. On the contrary, they become the essential feature of the *Grave New World* we live in.

Empire of the Sun and its sequel, *The Kindness of Women* (1991)—an account of his life after the war, where the autobiographical origins of many of his stories is suggested—depict the war as a collection of images, situations and props. In remembering the war Ballard mixes up half-forgotten memories with quasi-cinematic scenes as if taken from a film seen many years earlier. The war is a myth that feeds a range of the narratives created after its end. The outburst of aggression and violence that took place in the forties cannot ever be forgotten as it awoke a taste for violent entertainment and transformed Western culture.

Empire of the Sun and *The Kindness of Women* are at the beginning of my discussion of Ballard's career because they are the intellectual starting points of his ideas. Here he describes the very moment when the aggression that for generations had been buried deep in the social unconscious broke through to the surface. The fear of nuclear Armageddon, the feeling of remorse caused by the war and the strange fascination with disaster and post-apocalyptic times that are recurrent in post-war culture can be traced back to the events of August 1945. Contemporary entertainment cherishes images of violence and, as we live in the culture of simulacra, it is able to turn history into fiction. War becomes a myth and a simulacrum. Thus *The Kindness of Women* ends with the filming of *Empire of the Sun* and Ballard's story is completed. In the last scenes of his quasi-autobiography we see Ballard coming to Los Angeles and staring at gigantic billboards with his name on them—commercials for the premiere of Steven

2. In the interview I discuss in the previous chapter.

Spielberg's film *Empire of the Sun*. Stepping into the mediascape of *The Atrocity Exhibition* and *Crash* makes Ballard become a character of his own fiction and signifies the final merger of fact and fiction.

Waiting for World War III

Though Ballard waited until his fifties to describe his experience of the Second World War in China, from time to time before 1984 he alludes to war in Asia: sometimes he created allusive, impressionistic texts loosely connected with his experiences, sometimes stories set in deserted paddy fields around Shanghai. He wrote the first such texts in the period of his collaboration with *New Worlds*. These texts juxtapose the human mind with the challenges of the contemporary world: the mediascape, the A-bomb, the threat of World War III, the coming of the space age, the growing violence of public life. In "The Terminal Beach" (1964), a short story about a man who finds psychological fulfilment in the deserted landscape of Eniwetok, the nuclear test island, with its empty, concrete barracks, abandoned military bases and the prevailing deadness that recall both World War II and herald World War III. As the H-bomb tested on the island is an echo of the bombs of Hiroshima and Nagasaki, Eniwetok is presented as a harbinger of humanity's future—an empty, desolate and mutated place of death. In the final sections of the story the protagonist finds and guards the corpse of a Japanese soldier and in their long discussions the future of the human race is described.

The style of this story is under the influence of the poetics of *New Worlds*,[3] i.e., it is characterized by a consistent use of the present tense, a fascination with entropy and concentration on the inner space of the protagonist. At the same time, however, the story is unmistakably Ballardian and anticipates his war narratives. "The Terminal Beach", although narrated mostly in the past tense, is in one sense the most extreme case of the "New Wave" writers' concentration on the present. The abolishment of the past-present-future chain is here completed: the past blurs in the half-amnesiac mind of the narrator and the future is destroyed by Eniwetok's nuclear tests. The order of narration is again spatial. The text is divided into numerous very short chapters whose titles recreate either the geography of Eniwetok ("The Blocks", "The Synthetic Landscape", "Third Beach", "The Terminal Bunker") or objects ("The Corpses", "The Marooned Japanese", "The Fly"). Only a few refer to events (e.g., "Traven lost within the blocks", "The Naval Party"), and even these events are rather more images and scenes than actions.

Traven formulates his theory of "The Pre-Third", the eternal 'now' of a civilization doomed to die and waiting for this to happen. Eniwetok is the example of what the whole Earth will soon be:

---

3. In the influential American history of science fiction *The Road to Science Fiction* by James Gunn, which I discuss in the Introduction, this story is presented as the most typical and the best "New Wave" story, mostly because of its avant-garde form and depiction of the entropic inner landscape.

The series of weapons tests had fused the sand in layers, and the pseudo-geological strata condensed the brief epochs, micro-seconds in duration, of thermonuclear time... This island was a fossil of time future, its bunkers and blockhouses illustrating the principle that the fossil record of life was one of armour and the exoskeleton (Ballard 1979: 139-140).

This island is for Traven a harbinger of the post-World War III reality and in its absolute deadness he can find his Nirvana, a feeling of equilibrium between what is inside and what is outside. People unconsciously long for the zero world where nothing happens, because such a wasteland is the final destination of our species and on some deep-down cellular level we know it. These stressful contemporary times, *Grave New World*, is just a period post-Second World War and pre-Third World War and the total destruction it will bring about. Traven, the post-apocalyptic man, learns to live in non-time without the divisions people are used to:

All sense of time soon vanished, and his life became completely existential, an absolute break separating one moment from the next like two quantal events (ibid.: 142).

Time had become quantal. For hours it would be noon, the shadows contained within the blocks, the heat reflected off the concrete floor. Abruptly, he would find that it was early afternoon or evening, the shadows everywhere like pointing fingers (Ballard 1964a: 132).

This island is an ontological Eden, why seek to expel yourself into a world of quantal flux? (ibid.: 136).

The adjective "existential" is the keyword in this passage, as Traven's life is no longer a linear progress from the past to the future, but a pure existence in the everlasting moment "now". Reduced to the very core of his personality he has no expectations, no desires, no plans—and thus he is liberated in the way the Existentialists describe. In his "ontological Eden" all that may be is pure being with no possibility of joining "quantal" moments in one linear narrative of a "then...and then..." order. The word "quantal" additionally alludes to Max Planck and the history of modern physics, which resulted in the creation of the A-bomb and the H-bomb.

Ironically perhaps, there is some peace in this vision of a post-human world of no time, no people rushing around, no media, no continuous flux of white noise. For entropy will give us rest. The only things to remain will be deserted, surreal landscapes. Traven refuses to leave the island, as to die here is to be true to the logic of the Universe. He has insight into the order of things and he is the one to bid civilization farewell.

Life after August 1945 is only a nightmarish illusion. These years before the terminal war join the datable past (the previous war) with the inevitable future. Eniwetok is deserted and deprived of virtually any fauna: labyrinths of concrete blocks, barracks full of old magazines, a few meagre palms, rubbish left by the soldiers and a merciless sun form a minimalist entourage. The landscape is man-made, fully artificial. For Traven the island has been magically transported from the future to the present day, and it shows what the entire world is going to be like. All life ends, and human beings (who also are part of the biological kingdom) subliminally search for the reversed Eden, the place of the end of creation.

This is the place where one is already half-dead and thus may communicate with the dead. Thus, Traven watches the ghosts of his wife and his son (both killed in a car crash) as they approach him. After he escapes from a rescue expedition that tries to take him away from the island, his only companion is the body of a Japanese doctor with whom he conducts long philosophical debates. They talk about Hiroshima and the fatal car crash. And the Japanese gives Traven the ultimate moral lesson: one has to have humility and accept all. This is precisely what the people who tried to help Traven failed to understand. They thought about him as a martyr who, with the sacrifice of his life, tries to make amends for his past as a military pilot (the name of Earthly, the pilot of "Enola Gay" is recalled), while Traven tries to explain that the opposite is true. [4] For him the time is zero, the wheel has completed its turn and thus he feels sustained like a Buddhist yogi may feel.

The story juxtaposes references to World War II (shadows of manikins imprinted on the walls by a nuclear blast, Traven's memories from the 1940s, the uniformed Japanese marooned on the island) and the allusions to post-war reality. The most important event is the Cold War and the nuclear tests, the manifestations of contemporary violence. His stay on Eniwetok is for Traven the chance to bid farewell not only to his personal life, but also to the whole of civilization and, indirectly, to the whole universe.

'Goodbye, Eniwetok...Goodbye Los Alamos...Goodbye Hiroshima. Goodbye, Almagordo. Goodbye Moscow, London, Paris, New York...'

Shuttles flickered, a ripple of lost integers. He stopped, realising the futility of this megathlon farewell. Such a leave-taking required him to fix his signature upon every one of the particles in the universe (ibid.: 152-153).

4. As Colin Greenland claims in *The Entropy Exhibition*, from the standpoint of existential philosophy the bomb (and thus the certainty of disaster) gives people an absolute freedom. Traven is not making amends and people are not sorry that the bomb has been invented, as self-destruction is what the human race has always unconsciously longed for. Man is in complicity with a catastrophe of his own making.

The end of one particular civilization, the affluent West, turns out to be only a part of the universal decline: a gigantic cosmic clock unwinds itself, the human race ends together with life on Earth and the Universe itself. Whatever begins also ends, and people, who because of the anti-metaphysical character of our civilization are estranged from the rest of creation and unaware of its rules, suffer their traumas—ones which will end when we complete the cycle and dissolve painlessly.

Though Armageddon in physical terms has not happened, *Grave New World* is portrayed as a post-apocalyptic era. The media rule our lives and disfigure our perception of the world; show business makes use of psychopathologies, and entropy invades all spheres of human activity. Writing his stories devoted to the portrayal of the contemporary Western world, Ballard alludes to World War II in a psychoanalytical manner. His characters, for example the protagonist of *The Atrocity Exhibition*, are often troubled by memories of the war, but it is difficult to say whether they actually remember or have imagined the traumatic events that haunt their unconscious.

In the story-chapters of *The Atrocity Exhibition* personages such as American pilots in old uniforms, girls with radiation wounds, and victims of the coming World War III recur. They are probably figments of the protagonist's mind, agitated as it is by violent images of Vietnam and the Kennedy assassination on TV screens. In one of the chapters, in a section entitled "Too Bad", the protagonist[5] explicitly describes his war memories—this is the first of Ballard's Shanghai narratives.

> Of this early period of his life, Travers wrote: 'Two weeks after the end of World War II my parents and I left Lunghua internment camp and returned to our house in Shanghai, which had been occupied by the Japanese gendarmerie. The four servants and ourselves were still without any food. Soon after, the house opposite was taken over by two senior American officers, who gave us canned food and medicines. I struck up a friendship with their driver, Corporal Tulloch, who often took me around with him (Ballard 2001: 112).

What follows is a description of the boy and the American's planned plane trip to Osaka, which was never to take place. The abandoned suburbia of Shanghai is full of corpses. After the capitulation of Hirohito the Japanese are waiting to be killed, buildings and aircraft burn. What is interesting, the boy in Lunghua spends the war with his parents and is rather a passive recipient of whatever the war and peace bring. Fascination with Americans, who represent the real power in being able to challenge the invincible Japanese army, is already important in the boy's life. America turns out to be the new plebeian empire

5. His name is uncannily similar to Traven's and moreover, it changes in nearly every chapter of *The Atrocity Exhibition* (however, it always starts with T- and has two syllables), suggesting a total dissolution of the subject.

that is going to suppress not only the Empire of the Rising Sun, but also the British Empire that has been unable to defend its citizens against the Asians. The landscape which used to belong to the British crown—English cotton mills, paddy fields which produced its raw material—now become a desolated, post-apocalyptic countryside.

In this short chapter Ballard suggests that war memories are food for imagination and a reservoir of metaphors describing the late twentieth-century world. We do not know whether these memories are "real", i.e., whether or not the protagonist of *The Atrocity Exhibition* really spent the war in Shanghai and made friends with Corporal Tulloch. The beginning of the paragraph "of this early period of his life, Travers wrote…" is rather ambiguous as Travers is not able to tell imagination from facts. But this ambiguity only emphasizes Ballard's point: the war is inscribed in our unconscious, and it is the true spiritual beginning of all contemporary atrocities.

One further return to the very same time and the very same place is "The Dead Time" (1982).[6] The story starts with the description of the world just after the end of the war—one epoch has ended, the new has failed to begin and the world is suspended in an uncanny in-between period. The story abounds in dead bodies and pictures of decay; the suggestion is that the world has already ended and the characters are but hallucinating in the moment of their own death.

> Without warning, as if trying to confuse us, the Japanese guarding our camp had vanished. I stood by the open gates of the camp with a group of fellow-internees, staring in an almost mesmerized way at the deserted road and at the untended canals and paddy-fields that stretched on all sides to the horizon. The guard-house had been abandoned (Ballard 1982: 141).

The image of the first days after the victory is an image of confusion: American planes cross the sky, but the Japanese are still there. Not knowing what to do, the Japanese are violent and unpredictable—they kill and torture, or let their captives go free. Their life has ended with the capitulation—they have no idea of what their world will now be like. Neither are the British, our protagonist included, able to cope with the situation. Ransacking empty villages for bottles of rice wine, they fall victims to wayward Chinese communists and Kuomintang deserters. The atmosphere in the Shanghai area in the story is surreal and nightmarish—it is of a life after death with no sense of purpose or direction. The protagonist, an early avatar of Jim from *Empire of the Sun*, is twenty on the day he leaves the camp where he had spent his late teens. Isolated but safe within its gates, the protagonist knows very little about life outside Lunghua. All the gossip he hears seems unreal and his new freedom is uncertain, if not uninvited:

6. The analysis of the presentation of war in J.G. Ballard's "The Dead Time", *Empire of the Sun* and *The Kindness of Women* is partly based on my article "In the pearl light of Nagasaki: J.G. Ballard's War Narratives", in *Anglica* 2006, pp. 11-22.

In spite of everything I had heard on the radio broadcasts, I was still not certain that the war was over... We had heard detailed accounts of the atom-bomb attacks—Nagasaki was little more than 500 miles from us—and of the Emperor's call for capitulation immediately after. But at our camp, eight miles from Shanghai at the mouth of the Yangtse, little had changed (ibid: 142-143).

The protagonist spent his internment alone—his parents and young sister[7] were kept in another camp, and the attempt to find them is the only purpose he can think of. Nevertheless, he is unable to undertake any effective action. Immediately captured by the Japanese after an attempted escape he does not get killed on the spot thanks to sheer luck alone. Instead he is given a horror-like task—he is to transport a lorry load of dead bodies to one of the Protestant cemeteries outside Shanghai. Though he tries to abandon the bodies on the way, he cannot get rid of his nightmarish load: dumped into the river, the bodies block the bridge he has to cross and the Japanese soldiers make him reload them. Finally, only hiding among the dead saves him from bandits. Slowly and gradually, the story changes from a realist account into a hallucinatory phantasmagoria. Days go by and the protagonist is still in the labyrinth of small roads, lost among deserted fields. The dead are now his family, and he cannot part from them.

The story depicts the end of the war in Southeast Asia as a stylized Armageddon. In the chaos after the withdrawal of the Japanese forces and the rumours about the annihilation of Hiroshima and Nagasaki life and death converge. Those who have survived in the deserted landscape of open graves and rotting corpses should join the legions of the dead. All life after the moment history and time stopped is an illusion, merely the dreams dreamt in the moment of dying. Lost in the Shanghai area the protagonist is haunted by the dead and gradually he starts to feel united with them in a strange marriage. His own death becomes an act of sacrifice and it opens the gates of "the commonwealth of the living" to the victims of the war.

Shanghai after the war is the realm of death, and the living seem strangely misplaced here. The protagonist from time to time suffers from "a sudden presentiment of death". His newly met companions, an old man and a little girl whom he feeds his own bleeding flesh, might be dead as well. The landscape they cross is full of images of death:

Untended canals and drowned paddies stretched away on all narrow causeways. The vanished peasants had built their burial mounds into the shoulders of the road, and the ends of the cheap coffins protruded like drawers from the rain washed earth, lockers ransacked by the passing war (ibid.: 151).

7. A permutation of the same motif—Jim in *Empire of the Sun* lost his parents in the confusion after Pearl Harbour, while the sister comes straight from Ballard's biography, and this is the only place she ever makes an appearance in his fiction.

This very image—of coffins compared to chests of drawers—recurs throughout Ballard's entire *oeuvre*, each time signifying the supremacy of the dead over the living. In "The Dead Time" the war and the landscape it created make any change impossible—the world is frozen in an outburst of violence. There is no conceivable future, the living can do nothing but join the dead. The only vague plan the protagonist has for the future is nothing other than a return to his pre-war childhood in the world the war destroyed once and forever. "We would move back to our house in the French concession. My father would re-open his brokerage business... After years of war and privation, Shanghai would be a boom city again..." (ibid.: 153). The world before Pearl Harbour, the A-bomb and the twilight of the British Empire is nothing but nostalgic memories. With no chance for development and transformation the world is immobile as if frozen in the flash of Nagasaki. Death is no longer only a metaphor—it becomes material and overwhelming, the whole Earth is a huge cemetery. The story fades away into the prevailing image of the dead claiming their command over the living—our protagonist included:

> I felt that presentiment of death I had sensed so many times, surrounding me on all sides, in the canal beside the road, in the drone of an American aircraft crossing far overhead (ibid.: 157). From this time onwards, during the confused days of my journey... I was completely identified with my companions (ibid.: 160).

The final epiphany of the narrator's death bringing the dead back to life emphasizes the fluidity of the borders between "the commonwealth of the living" and the realm of death. Only after the unification of the two does the narrator exclaim that the war is over: it ended together with human civilization and the world.

The Sun Weapon

The next time Ballard returned to the theme of wartime Shanghai was in his masterpiece *Empire of the Sun* (1984), the book about the end of a certain civilization—the British colony in China. *Empire of the Sun* is concerned with the war, but in fact the story takes place in moments of change; before the war, in the confusion following Pearl Harbour and after it, and in the confusion following the Japanese capitulation. This novel set in the turning point of history—the end of the colonial era—and in a place where different civilizations (Chinese, Japanese, British and American) clash, is an epic and in that sense is similar to the nostalgic movie all Shanghai watches: *Gone with the Wind*. Gigantic billboards advertising the film preside over the city at war; this omnipresent Hollywood production with Chinese subtitles announces that the era of show business has come.

Pre-war Shanghai, the city of Jim's childhood, is described in an equally nostalgic mood, as if already from memories, and the gigantic success of the novel and the film seem to support Ballard's thesis that people do miss the war, especially in England (which then lost its empire) and especially in the times of Margaret Thatcher. The charm of a glorious past is appealing both in the case of the American South and the British Isles. Ballard waited forty years to describe the war, and then wrote a book that is not a report of what happened in Shanghai, but a nostalgic account of bygone days. Ballard told his American friend and editor in an interview:

> People here are in the middle of a huge nostalgia boom; they love anything connected with the Second World War. And I wrote a book that seemed to have an eye-witness account about a virtually unknown theatre of World War II, taking the lid off British behaviour and all that sort of thing. If I'd planned it myself, I couldn't have hit the target more exactly (Vale 2005: 138).

War in *Empire of the Sun* possesses a theatrical quality: despite the numerous dead bodies and all the atrocities described, it seems to be a fiction straight from a huge cinematic screen. The beginning of the war for Jim is similar to the beginning of a party. He waits for it and is afraid to miss the show. He imagines the war to be a newsreel come true with a lot of beautiful aircraft in the sky. In the day just before Pearl Harbour he and his parents go to a costume party: dressed up as a *pierrot* actor and a pirate his parents seem as childish and unprepared for the traumas to come as Jim in his silk costume and with a model plane in his hands. The last moments before the war are a farewell to the colonial past: the sleek, luxurious life of endless bridge parties and cricket matches. Though the first outbursts of violence in Shanghai took place in 1937, the English colony was only too eager to ignore the fighting as an internal Asian affair. As a result, their happy, affluent life was set in a landscape of death and destruction, something they nonetheless felt immune to. Their parties and balls seemed surreal because they took place in the fresh battlefields. Little Jim, dressed in his costume, wanders out to the field in the corner of the estate of the people giving the party:

> A burial tumulus rose from the wild sugar-cane at its centre, and the rotting coffins projected from the loose earth like a chest of drawers.
>
> ... Once again Jim was struck by the contrast between the impersonal bodies of the newly dead, whom he saw every day in Shanghai, and these sun-warmed skeletons, every one an individual (Ballard 1985c: 17).

The recurring image of coffins protruding from the field[8] is far less shocking for the boy than for the adult protagonist of "The Dead Time". Jim grows up in a

8. This is going to appear once more in Ballard's fiction in 1991 in *The Kindness of Women*.

cruel city full of violence in the streets, and he considers death and mutilation to be a kind of street festival. The costume party ends abruptly because of the ominous news and Jim goes with his parents to spend the night in a hotel for safety reasons. The next day, in the confusion after the beginning of the war, the Europeans intending to leave the hotel in a hurry dress in hats and overcoats and pack their suitcases "as if deciding to take the next steamer to Hong Kong" (ibid.: 29). All look confused and unprepared, like under-rehearsed actors forced on stage. Japanese marines capture British and American ships and shoot at the soldiers who try to swim to the shore. Violence and elegance are juxtaposed as the Shanghai Britons dressed up in business suits try to help them. Jim looks at the silk glove his father carries as he steps out of water with the body of a petty officer: "Looking at the glove, Jim realized that it was the complete skin from one of the petty officer's hands, boiled off the flesh in an engine-room fire" (ibid.: 32).

Costumes, screens and mirrors often appear in the first, pre-war part of the novel. Jim's childhood ends abruptly when he is separated from his parents and is left alone in the empty European district of the city among the deserted villas of the interned clerks and businessmen. He finds his way to his father's house and there, in the empty, looted bedroom of his mother he is forced to accept the fact that his world has come to an end. He looks at the broken dressing-table mirror:

> Jim sat on the bed, facing the star-like image of himself that radiated from the centre of the mirror. A heavy object had been driven into the full-length glass, and pieces of himself seemed to fly across the room, scattered through the empty house (ibid.: 45).

The end of the colonial era in Shanghai and of Jim's childhood is presented here as the destruction of a mirror reflection,[9] as if the affluent life in the security of his father's house was a dream and a fiction. Jim has to adopt a new personality, that of a boy on his own, prepared to fight and determined to survive—without parents, nannies, coolies and servants. The beginning of this new life takes place in the ruins of the world he used to know. Jim rides his bike along empty streets, spends his days in abandoned villas which he loots for food, looks through other people's photos, clothes and possessions. He does not panic: this careful examination of the underside of the world of his childhood satisfies the intellectual curiosity of an eleven-year-old. Things reveal their hidden dimensions and unknown properties. For example, Jim is fascinated by a drained swimming pool:

> Jim had never seen the tank empty, and he gazed with interest at the inclined floor. The once mysterious world of wavering blue lines, glimpsed through a cascade of bubbles, now lay exposed to the morning light... Around the brass vent at the deep end lay

---

9. For Michel Delville, the author of *J.G. Ballard*, the destruction of the mirror represents the disembodiment of Jim's self (Delville 1998: 69).

a small museum of past summers—a pair of his mother's sun-glasses, Vera's hair clip, a wine glass, and an English half-crown which his father tossed into the pool for him (ibid.: 49).

Mysteries of childhood turn out to be dull and unreal, just like the fantastic underwater world of the pool that changes into a thin layer of residue. Driven by hunger, Jim has to leave the International Settlement, the district of his childhood, and go to the other part of Shanghai, a port city at war, with dead bodies in the drinking water, Japanese patrols, and runaway American soldiers hiding. Here the atrocities of war, though still picturesque for him, cease to be abstract. Jim used to listen to accounts of torpedoed British soldiers in the Atlantic taking to cannibalism and Japanese cruelty, but now he finds himself in the very middle of such unspeakable horror. Given "a new name for a new life" (an American ex-steward makes him abandon his baby-name Jamie and calls him Jim), he faces the Apocalypse and finds emotional balance.

Jim enjoys the war in an amoral enthusiasm for aircraft, Japanese bravery and American self-sufficiency; he is proud to be coping on his own and bored by the scenes of death and mutilation, ones simply too numerous to impress. His immunity to the abundant horrors in the camp resemble "the death of affect" phenomenon described in *The Atrocity Exhibition* (Ballard 2001: 116). In the inhuman mediascape of the twentieth century, the self-preservation instinct makes the mind take the world around to be abstract and impersonal. Just as we fail to emotionally react to all the images of violence in the media, so do we slowly start to ignore the pain and anguish around us. In a sense we believe we live in a gigantic film production. Jim in *Empire of the Sun* lives in the inhuman rigor of prison camp life, with daily violence, death and starvation. And here we witness the same attitude of taking part in something unreal—his real self was perhaps the one fragmented in his mother's mirror. Michel Delville makes an interesting observation when he describes Jim's friendships in the Lunghua camp, where the Japanese finally intern him:

> The theme of the divided self is once again re-enacted in Jim's interaction with two other major characters in the novel, who embody two basic attitudes to life: one amoral and ruthlessly optimistic (Basie) and one which is, instead, based on compassion and self-sacrifice (Dr Ransom). Basie, an American ... teaches [Jim] basic survival skills... Dr Ransom represents the moral and cultural authority that had shaped his former self until the war began (Delville 1998: 69-70).

Dr Ransom (with all the symbolic connotations of his name) is British and represents traditional Victorian values above all—he is a missionary and Jim's self-appointed foster parent. Though he cares for the boy far more than Basie (who tried to sell him to the Japanese and abandons the boy at the moment he considered him worthless), Jim is under the influence of the American.

Basie knows how to care for himself, he sells other prisoners' possessions to the Japanese and Chinese and is never hungry. Jim happily runs errands for him and is deeply awed by the power of America. The planes that appear in the sky in the mid-1940s are American, and the Americans are the ones who know how to survive.

In comparing and contrasting the British and the Americans, *Empire of the Sun* follows the tradition of World War II novels such as James Clavell's *Rat King* and Pierre Boulle's *Le Pont de la Rivière Kwai*, whose action takes place in the prison camps of the Far East. The British are idealistic and reserved and the Americans plebeian but efficient. Jim fails to notice any merits of British cultural heritage: in his childhood he was fed stories about England and he disliked the country immensely. Closed in a confined space with tens of grown-up Englishmen, civilians unable to cope with the war, he despises their nostalgic moods and conversations about home.

> [Mrs Vincent] stared at the whitewashed wall... as if watching an invisible film projected on to a screen. Jim worried that Mrs Vincent spent too much of her time watching these films. As he peered at her through the cracks in his cubicle he tried to guess what she saw—a home-made cine film, perhaps, of herself in England before she was married, sitting on one of those sunlit lawns that seemed to cover the entire country (Ballard 1985c: 139).

The British way of life proves inefficient, as the adults could not defend their luxurious little enclave against the war. The empire fell and it is very unwise to hold to its spent glory. Jim adores Japanese kamikaze pilots for their courage, the Japanese soldiers in the camp who defend the prisoners against hungry coolies outside the gates and, to a lesser extent, the self-sufficient Americans. He is aware how much the war has changed him when he thinks about his parents and his pre-Pearl Harbour life. "He felt a strange lightness in his head, not because his parents had rejected him, but because he expected them to do so, and no longer cared" (ibid.: 123).

Free to do whatever he wants for the first time in his life, Jim does not have to worry about the consequences of his misbehaviour, nor about the violation of standards people like his parents respect. Though alone and often threatened by death, he feels strangely happy in the camp, in fact 1943, the year when the war is still moving in the Japanese favour, is the happiest in his life. Preoccupied with thousands of little tasks, he cherished the life in the camp and knows his way round. He lives among the dying and the dead, immune to the surrounding horror:

> The heavy rains of the monsoon months softened the mounds, so that they formed outlines of the bodies within them, as if this small cemetery beside the military airfield was doing its best to

resurrect a few of the millions who had died in the war. Here and there an arm or a foot protruded from the graves, the limbs of restless sleepers struggling beneath their brown quilts. Rats had burrowed deep into the grave of Mrs Hug (ibid.: 166).

People at Lunghua die so often that Jim gets accustomed to their disappearance and is not afraid of the bodies at the least. The routine of war has a certain theatrical quality for him. For instance, when he is first arrested the Japanese keep him in an abandoned open-air cinema. Also, the internees have their own theatre society and they stage plays performed in impromptu costumes. In their attempted mental escapes the internees organize lectures and discussions on many abstract subjects and Jim, who participates in all of them, treats this kind of entertainment on the same plane as the numerous deaths of the lecturers and actors. Nothing quite seems real, especially now that his fellow British prisoners strike him as highly irresponsible. Even at the moments when they are forced to leave Lunghua after the Japanese capitulation and go off in unknown direction (perhaps to meet their deaths) they carry the most bizarre possessions: tennis racquets, cricket bats, fishing rods and pierrot costumes. Jim assumes that:

> Recreation had clearly come high on the prisoner's list of priorities while they packed their suitcases before being interned. Having spent the years of peace on the tennis courts and cricket fields of the Far East, they confidently expected to pass the years of war in the same way (ibid.: 197).

Jim is a child of the prison camp, his knowledge about life and death makes him feel patronizing towards his fellow prisoners, Britons who still partly live in the colonial past. The world around is coming to its end, even the relatively safe Lunghua camp can no longer protect the Westerners. After the Japanese capitulation they have to face the post-apocalyptic reality of Asian battlefields. Hungry coolies, renegade Kuomintang soldiers, desperate Japanese guards, escapee European prisoners, and American troops loot the deserted villages while the fields are full of corpses and rusting military equipment. For Jim, leaving the camp means entering the surreal realm of pre-war scenery juxtaposed with the cruelty of war.

The prisoners are finally taken to the Nantao stadium full of old American cars—Buicks, Packards, Lincoln Zephyrs and Cadillacs—parked there before the war. In the first moment Jim looks for the Asian chauffeurs who should have been waiting by their cars, as they always did in his childhood. Only later does he realize that the cars have been here for years, caked with dirt and looted by the Japanese. The exhausted prisoners are left on the damp grass of the stadium among the cars and other trophies seized from the houses and nightclubs of Shanghai. The stadium was used by the Japanese as a transit camp, but now no one seems to bother about the former inmates of Lunghua, who start hallucinating about their pre-war existence. Numerous people die during the night, and the next day is the ninth of August 1945, when at 11:02 in the morning, on the other side of the sea dividing the Chinese mainland from Japan, the Nagasaki bomb lights up the atmosphere. Though some 500 hundred miles away, the Shanghai suburbia is filled with the unreal pearl light. Hardly anybody is still conscious, but Jim and a Japanese sentry actually see the deadly light which marks the end of the world. In the book's climax, the chapter entitled "Empire of the Sun", there is a strong suggestion, that all life after the explosion is nothing but waiting for the inescapable death of a civilization that is already doomed.

> They were sitting on the floor of a furnace heated by a second sun. Jim stared at his white hands and knees, and at the pinched face of the Japanese soldier, who seemed disconcerted by the light. Both of them were waiting for the rumble of sound that followed the bomb-flashes, but an unbroken silence lay over the stadium and the surrounding land, as if the sun had blinked, losing heart for a few seconds. Jim smiled at the Japanese, wishing that he could tell him that the light was a premonition of his death, the sight of his small soul joining the larger soul of the dying world (ibid.: 218).

From this moment on Jim is changed and his life is centred around notions such as apocalypse, World War III, and death coming from the air. But he is not killed at the stadium. He manages to reach Shanghai, find his parents and go back to England, but this world seems to him illusory, like the day-dream of a mind "joining the larger soul of the dying world". It is as if in the moment the a-bomb was dropped the world ended[10] and what we believe we experience is only an illusion.

The pearl light of Nagasaki in the air is his bane, following him for years. Immediately after the explosion he thought of it in metaphysical terms, and was afraid that his soul had died at the stadium. Then one renegade Eurasian explained to him that: "Uncle Sam threw a piece of the sun at Nagasaki and Hiroshima...One great big flash" (ibid.: 226). The sun motif is very important in the post-Nagasaki part of *Empire of the Sun*: Jim dreams about flying to the sun with a young kamikaze pilot he found dead in the fields. Japan—the Empire of the Rising Sun—is defeated by America, the true *Empire of the Sun*, one that had built the sun weapons to destroy the world.

Jim is sent to the "strange small country on the other side of the world" (ibid.: 290), but he feels that only a part of himself goes there, while the rest is to remain forever in Shanghai, "returning on the tide like the coffins launched from the funeral piers at Nantao" (ibid.: 290). The post-war world seems to Jim equally as abstract and unreal as his pre-war film-like memories of Shanghai. In a sense the pearl light of Nagasaki is the only true thing that ever happened

10. In fact the scientists in Los Alamos had feared that a nuclear explosion could set the Earth's atmosphere on fire or provoke via a chain reaction the annihilation of all matter in the Universe

to him and his knowledge of the inevitable end is for him the most important outcome of the world. Lost among people who did not experience the war in Asia he feels wiser and more resigned.

> Yet he knew that that he had seen the flash of the atomic bomb at Nagasaki even across the four hundred miles of the China Sea. More important, he had seen the start of World War III, and realized that it was taking place around him. The crowds watching newsreels on the Bund had failed to grasp that these were the trailers for a war that had already started. One day there will be no more newsreels (ibid.: 288).

Empire of the Sun closes with an image of Shanghai as a harbinger of a coming war, the Doomsday city bathed in the lights of an atomic bomb. Shanghai saw the end of the British era, the rise and the fall of Japanese imperialism and, finally, the emergence of globe-spanning American culture. The crowds gathered in Bund watch American newsreels: the era of the image, of simulacra and the media dawns.

Memories and Films

In 1987 Steven Spielberg filmed *Empire of the Sun*, a Hollywood epic production whose success made Ballard known the world over. The first Western film made in communist China, it tried to re-create Shanghai in the colonial era and at war. With the screenplay by Tom Stoppard,[11] consulted with Ballard himself, the film holds very close to the novel. Nevertheless, despite the fictional character of the novel, it was marketed as an autobiography—Spielberg wanted it to appear to be a real survivor's story, a piece of the past brought back to the screen. This attitude seems to heavily influence the way both the novel and its adaptation are now perceived.

In fact what we are confronted with is a mass-cultural phenomenon that might be labelled "*Empire of the Sun*, a story of Ballard's life", this being a mixture of fact and fiction created by a number of texts: the autobiographical press articles I discussed in the Introduction, interviews, the novel, its sequel *The Kindness of Women* (which describes the making of the movie), the movie and *The China Odyssey: Empire of the Sun by Steven Spielberg* (a report about the making of the movie filmed simultaneously and starring Ballard among others). Nothing is real or false any longer: we are in a world of mass culture similar to Baudrillard's hyperreality, where "the real is produced" (Baudrillard 2003: 2).

These texts influence each other, thereby adding to the confusion: in the novel *Empire of the Sun* Jim's family name is not given. In *Empire of the Sun* the movie it is Graham (J.G. Ballard in the real world is James Graham Ballard),

---

11. Stoppard also spent a part of World War II in the Far East, but he was younger than Ballard and his own memories are those of a very small child (Stoppard, in a private conversation).

and in *The Kindness of Women* it is openly "Ballard" (just like the name of his other protagonist in the novel *Crash*). Moreover, *Empire of the Sun* is a third person narrative: focalization is nearly exclusively Jim's, but sometimes we read the opinions of somebody older and more experienced, probably the narrator, who tells the story from a perspective of many years. *The Kindness of Women*, in turn, is narrated in the first person by "Ballard", who is asked to participate in *The China Odyssey: Empire of the Sun by Steven Spielberg* and to appear as an extra in the movie proper, from time to time inserting in the texts several titles of his other books via phrases such as "the atrocity exhibition" or "the drowned world", spelt without the inverted commas.

The final closure of the war is thus filming the war, turning it into images and artefacts: the filmed war looks larger than life, better and truer, and makes it possible to come to terms with memories, which in comparison seem blurred and unconvincing. *The Kindness of Women*, which is the story of Jim in the years after the war, shows his gradual adaptation to the post-war reality. Haunted by his memories of wartime atrocities, he finds himself in England and has to learn to live in peace-time among people who do not share his past and whose knowledge about the war in the Far East is very limited.

On the surface, *The Kindness of Women* narrates the adult life of Jim, his attempt to study medicine, his years of pilot training, marriage, bereavement, his literary career—but it is not just a life story. Artistically, the book is a conscious discussion with *Empire of the Sun*, and it combines permutations of the same motifs and images. Just as over the years Jim gradually comes to terms with his traumas, the war described in this story ceases to be realistic and becomes an image. The book ends with the filming of *Empire of the Sun* and Ballard's visit to Los Angeles, the capital of the world of make-believe, to see the first night. Turned into celluloid, the events of the 1940s become acceptable and only half-real. "Ballard" in the novel feels that perhaps the original experience was nothing but a rehearsal for the Spielberg film.

The beginning of *The Kindness of Women* takes the reader back to pre-war Shanghai, to the year 1937, when the war between China and Japan started. The seven-year-old Jim plays with his toy soldiers, re-arranging their positions each time he hears the news. War is fiction and a game which he "[keeps] alive single-handedly" (Ballard 1994: 9). Shanghai's residents are in love with violent entertainment such as the shows of American dare-devil drivers, and war seems just one more figment of the creators of pop culture. Nearly everything Jim remembers about the city has something to do with entertainment. The first outburst of the violence in 1937 is shown from the perspective of the Amusement Park, a favourite place for European and American children in Shanghai, who are taken there by their chauffeurs and amahs. The rich and care-free international population is preoccupied with having fun, and the Chinese were gladly amusing them when a bomb, dropped in error by a Chinese pilot sent to fight the Japanese, massacres the people at the fun fair. One of Jim's earliest memories is the image of the Amusement House turned into a nightmare:

An office clerk without his arms sat against the rear wheel of a gutted bus. Everywhere hands and feet lay among the debris of the Amusement Park—fragments of joss sticks and playing cards, gramophone records and dragon masks, parts of the head of a stuffed whale, all blanched by the dust. A bolt of silk had unravelled across the street, a white bandage that wound around the lumps of masonry and the mislaid hands (ibid.: 25).

These images of war are described from a time perspective, and in their surreal appeal they might be partly fictionalized. Indeed, the narrator himself confesses that in his mind the events of the year 1937 have got confused with newsreels. The scenes of the Spanish civil war and the filmed manoeuvres of the French and British armies mingle with the memories of the hospital where he was taken after the explosion in the Park. In his mind the bloody events "had been little more than a peripheral entertainment of a particularly brutal kind" (ibid.: 28) in a city in love with violence. The pre-war past in the book is stylized to look like one huge theatrical happening, the unconscious preparation for the traumas to come—the garden parties and picnics of the colonial elite are often held in the fields, which have recently seen the Chinese-Japanese war. Ballard describes both atrocities and balls with similar detachment. *The Kindness of Women* enters intertextual dialogue with *Empire of the Sun*, often referring to the same situations, but giving their different "versions". The narrator's past seems to be the 'rough material' for *Empire of the Sun*, a theatrical rehearsal of what is to get its artistic shape only when narrated—by Ballard or by Spielberg. The image of the protruding coffins 'like a chest of drawers' is one such Ballardian trademarks—*The Kindness of Women* shows the 'original' event, Jim's trip to the countryside in the late 1930s, later artistically disfigured in Ballard's adult fiction.

I remember the battlefield under the silent sky... Hundreds of spent rifle cartridges lay at our feet. Abandoned trenchworks ran between the burial mounds, from the open coffins protruding like drawers in a ransacked wardrobe...

Together we gazed at this scene, the ladies fanning away the flies, their husbands murmuring to each other, like a group of investors visiting the stage-set of an uncompleted war film (ibid.: 29).

The way this simile works is significant for the narration of *The Kindness of Women*, a novel which takes phrases and situations from Ballard's earlier fiction and presents them once again in an attempt to connect Ballard's literary style with the version of his life that it narrates. At the same time though, the life-story is described in such a way as to cast doubt on its truthfulness: the war, which is the seeming source of his fiction and one of its final meanings, is "like... the stage-set of an uncompleted war film". Simulacra: films, newsreels, reports etc. showing the war all over again influence the memory of the narrator to such an extent that the very notion of autobiography is subverted: facts reflect fiction.

In *The Kindness of Women* we again do not see the war itself. After the 1937 episode we are taken already to the mid-1940s—the end of the war. The prevailing feeling of the narrator is nostalgia—in the very beginning of the novel we read about the fall of Imperial Russia (Jim's governess is a White Russian). Now a similar process touches Imperial Britain, the luxurious enclave of the International Settlement in Shanghai and the orderly pre-war world at large. "The Japanese attack on Pearl Harbour had marked the first revolt by the colonized nations of the east against the imperial west" (ibid.: 53), one of the Lunghua internees was wont to say.[12] The change in the world is the change of civilizations: stepping outside Lunghua Jim has to face a new kind of reality, and again, his first impression is that what he sees is unreal and theatrical.

> The wild rice growing by the roadside, the blades of sugar cane and the yellow mud of the abandoned paddy fields were touched by the same eerie light, as if they had been irradiated by the bomb dropped on Nagasaki. The drowned canals and the grave-mounds, the forgotten ceramics works by the river, looked like an elaborate stage-set (ibid.: 52).

For a second Jim feels he is the last man alive and that the war has ended because there is no one left to fight, and thus he is doomed to a ghost-like existence amidst the post-apocalyptic ruins. There is no return to his childhood self, and Jim feels rejected by Shanghai the dream-city that easily absorbed the occupation period into its rich history. Setting out for England, he looks at the Asian coast with nostalgia. What he leaves behind is a beautiful and cruel fantasy, one which he would wish to continue on, but he has to exchange it for an unknown 'truth' of Europe.

Jim's painful adaptation to the world after the war is depicted in a series of images: his studies, his decision to become a pilot and his literary career seem to be a reaction to teenage traumas. For years he lives in constant expectation of World War III, whose coming he believes he had glimpsed. Instead of socializing with other students at Cambridge he compulsively visits American airbases and watches powerful air planes and huge cars driven by large men "with the confident eyes of an occupying power" (ibid.: 84). The displays of power make Jim think of an inevitable future, the A-bomb attacks that will bathe England in the eerie pearl light he had seen in Asia. Americans are the only people ready for the war to come.

> From their closely-guarded bases they were preparing England, still trapped by its memories of the Second World War, for the

12. Alas, his generalization slipped right into two major errors: 1) Japan of course was never colonized; and 2) Japan completely defeated in war an imperialist Western power (Tsarist Russia) three and a half decades before the attack on Pearl Harbour. On both scores Japan is unique among the countries of Asia.

third war yet to come. Then the atomic flash that I had seen over
Nagasaki would usher these drab fields and the crumbling gothic
of the university into the empire of light (ibid.: 84).

Jim is sure that his profound knowledge of death and disaster makes him
belong to the few who are aware of the coming end and isolates him from his
peers. Women who helped him during the post-war decades prompt his slow
integration into the world of the living. The first of the eponymous kind women
is the dead body of a woman doctor he is to work on in the dissecting room in his
first year of medical studies. Cutting her body and coming back to the corpse each
day, Jim is reminded of the dead Japanese and Chinese he saw daily in Lunghua.
He thinks about her as the queen of death, the pharaoh in her dream of death and
his only friend and teacher. When Dr Elizabeth is reduced to a bundle of bones
and gristle at the end of the semester he feels free to leave Cambridge and follows
his dreams of empires of light. Cambridge is for him excluded from the urgent
reality—from American bombers "readying themselves for the final global war"
(ibid.: 102), the Berlin Airlift, the Korean War and the re-arming of Europe.

A chain of girlfriends, prostitutes, along with his wife and daughters
accompany him in the coming years—he joins the RAF and, sent to Canada,
spends the Cold War preparing to fight. In his dreams he sees himself at the
controls of a nuclear Volcano "as it sped over the marshy forests of Byelorussia
armed with pieces of the sun" (ibid.: 100). Jim believes in global disaster, to
which most people are blind, and by flying he tries to enter "a realm [he] had
seen born over the paddy fields of the Yangtse estuary" (ibid.: 102).

Jim keeps self-analyzing his own motifs.[13] He concludes that his military
training helps the "real elements of his life" come together, and wakes him from
the dreams of Shanghai and the past. Reality waits for him in the skies of Central
Europe and has the form of Armageddon.

> A career as a military pilot offered an even more direct entry
> to the realm of violence for which we hungered... I was looking
> for a means of recreating the pearly light I had seen over the
> rice-fields of Lunghua beside the railway station, and which
> seemed to hover so promisingly over the American airbases near
> Cambridge (ibid.: 105).

Jim's prevailing feeling throughout the 1950s and 1960s is that of unreality,
dreaming, hallucinating, being surrounded by some make-believe simulacra. In
metaphors and similes he continuously speaks about his life after leaving the
RAF as being dreamt up and imagined, as if the true reality were somewhere else,
perhaps in the paddy fields near Shanghai, perhaps somewhere else. Shepperton,
the Thames Valley village where he moved with his young family, is described as

---

13. It is not accidental that the studies he abandoned were initially to prepare him for a psychiatric
career. Indirectly, the suggested intertext to his alleged autobiography are the works of Freud he
read at Cambridge—compare the discussion of Freud in Chapter One.

an unreal, sunny town with a gigantic factory of make-believe, e.g., TV studios. Jim calls Shepperton "a marine world that had invaded our minds", and dubs its inhabitants as "a new form of aquatic mammal" (ibid.: 123). The programmes all England was watching on TV were filmed there and the city streets stood for locations all over the country. Shepperton was colonizing the imagination of the nation and replacing reality with televized simulacra. Jim takes his children to the Magic World, a park adorned with props from numerous commercials: gigantic toothpaste tubes, bottles of shampoo etc.,—all known from TV—are displayed and left for children to play in.

The idyllic life in Shepperton (marred by the tragic death of Jim's young wife) seems far from real. Spent in the shadows of TV studios, it is presented as a preparation for the filming of *Empire of the Sun*, the real closure of the war. In his annotation of the 1990 edition of *The Atrocity Exhibition*, Ballard formulates this paradox:

> Spielberg returned to Shanghai for *Empire of the Sun*, an eerie sensation for me—even more so were the scenes shot near Shepperton, using extras recruited from among my neighbours, many of whom have part-time jobs at the studios. I can almost believe that I came to Shepperton thirty years ago knowing unconsciously that one day I would write a novel about my wartime experiences on Shanghai, and that it might well be filmed in these studios (Ballard 2001: 15).

The psychological closure of the war, the feeling that it had receded into the past, takes place in the chapter "After the War". It is significant that this chapter is set in the late seventies, while the previous thirty years go together with wartime memories. With his peace of mind at last regained, his children grown up and all the old debts paid, the protagonist feels free to retire, enjoy himself and visit old friends. During one such visit in the English countryside he and his friend David, an ex-RAF pilot also born in Shanghai and interned during the war, witness the unearthing of an old craft.[14] Sunk in the marshes the plane attracted the attention of a local air plane enthusiasts' club who decided to dig it up and renovate it. The picnic-like event of beer drinking and digging in the beautiful meadow is for the protagonist strangely disturbing. "It's like your bloody car exhibition" (Ballard 1994: 293), David says, alluding to the exhibition of wrecked cars Ballard organized in the 60s trying to show, via the reactions of spectators, how our culture relishes the images of violence.

14. The character of David is very enigmatic, he accompanies Jim in nearly every period of his life but from time to time they lose contact for some years. David shares all Jim's important experiences, but in his case they are slightly different, one more variation on the theme played out in *Empire of the Sun*. David spends the war in the camp together with his parents, does not find "the right girl" in the fifties and therefore is deprived of the idyllic Shepperton family life, does not leave the RAF so quickly and cannot forget the war even longer than Jim, compulsively re-living his traumas. In fact it seems justified to suggest that he is Jim's double in the Freudian meaning of the uncanny, the repressed part of Jim's unconscious coming to him from the outside in the disguise of somebody else.

At the moment the old Spitfire is unearthed, a macabre relic of World War II is discovered—a small bundle of bones proves to be the remains of a pilot who had not manage to leave the plane before the disaster.

> As he felt under the instrument panel and between the brake pedals, I imagined [the RAF friend] at the controls of this Spitfire, sitting on its grass airfield somewhere in the southern England in 1940. Had he or I been a few years older we would have returned to England to fight in the war, and our bones might well be brought to light by these weekend archaeologists. I thought of the crashed Japanese and Chinese planes at Hungjao aerodrome, and of how as a ten-year-old I had often climbed into the cockpit of a forgotten fighter lying in the long grass (ibid.: 297).

Buried in the earth the memories of trauma cannot be forgotten for good. The suppressed thoughts of violence and the consciousness of our inherent cruelty and aggression haunt Western civilization and compulsively return in films, TV and popular entertainment. The only way to "tame" them is to turn them into images and re-play them so very many times that they cease to shock. Nevertheless, from time to time an old wreck is unearthed and we see a dead body inside—a skeleton which is not an image, but a material relic of the war. When the two world wars ended the West entered a new phase in its development—a culture of violence and simulacra Ballard describes in his entire *oeuvre*.

In the world where image comes before the real thing, the truth can be found only in simulacra, "the super-real" as Jim calls it (probably under the influence of the theories of Baudrillard). The cathartic experience is watching Spielberg produce the real *Empire of the Sun*, where memories materialize "in a fusion of the real and the super real" (ibid.: 331). The technology of the media dismantles and reshuffles the past, present and future: the real thing is the image that looks real. Visiting the location Jim feels that designers are working to construct "a more convincing reality than the original I had known as a child" (ibid.: 333). Images are reflected in yet other images, the chain of simulacra multiplying itself is unstoppable. Jim is being filmed during this visit for a documentary about the production, "a film within a film that took its place in the corridor of mirrors" (ibid.: 334).

Ballard is keenly interested in the way in which television manipulates the reality of war and creates images 'more real than the real thing', the version of truth which enters the collective imagination of millions of viewers. [15] Twice he wrote stories which elaborated the same idea—what would happen if Britain proved the second Vietnam and the abstractness of violence from the TV screen became flesh and blood reality. In "The Killing Ground" (1969) and "The Theatre of War" (1977) we see Great Britain impoverished and divided into hostile camps: the ultraconservative loyalists and the militant left Liberation Front. In order to

15. I am going to elaborate his thought in Chapter Four, "Mediascapes".

pacify the situation, the United States decides to enter the Island with her own army and a new Vietnam starts.

In the first, shorter story we see an English officer—the forcefully recruited teacher—and a group of his soldiers, all hungry and in tatters, who have to fight with well-equipped, technologically advanced American troops. England in the story is shown as Europe's backwater, a God-forsaken, small state whose engineers are not even able to understand how the wristwatches of the captured Americans work. The minimal action of the story (a skirmish which ends in an unexpected victory for the British squad; the interrogation of the captured Americans; their execution prompted by a new American attack in which all the British are killed) lasts less than an hour. All happens around an American Kennedy Memorial erected near Magna Carta island, a place which proves important for the Americans, but for the English is totally meaningless. The memorial is covered with dirt and graffiti, but the American before his death manages to clean it sufficiently to decipher a decade-old slogan marked in engine grease: "Stop US Atrocities in Vietnam". The reference to Southeast Asia in the text points to the beginning of the conflict which evolved into a global war the US wages against a dozen national liberation armies in its effort to pacify the world.

"The Theatre of War" presents a similar war on the British Isles, but this time we see everything via TV. The story is a script of the *World in Action* live show—with the speaker in the studio, reporters in the battlefields, talking heads, rhetorical commentaries and interviews with ordinary people in the streets. The action is vivid, the montage of sequences of images from different places in the Isles takes us to the headquarters of the loyalist forces (Prince Charles and the puppet government of the Prime Minister collaborate with the US) and to battlefields all over Britain. We see bloody disturbances in London's streets, an economy based on the needs of American troops, shooting sprees (one of the journalists is killed on the screen), and the liberation front commune (journalists infiltrated their mountain camp). Attacks, executions, battles and the propaganda speeches of corrupted politicians are juxtaposed with the opinions of American G.I.s and bombastic commentaries from the studio. Ballard's ironic acknowledgements for all the dialogue at the end of the story are to General Westmoreland, President Thieu and Marshall Ky, which places the text in the right historical context. Television and its schemes of narration infiltrate our minds and dictate the way we respond to reality; televized atrocities are not shocking anymore. Moreover, violence on the screen is a necessary addition to any show—blood and dead bodies make the news.

One of Ballard's last short stories, "War Fever" (written in 1989 just before he abandoned writing short fiction), is a good summing up of his ideas concerning war, violence and human civilizations. The story is a return to the science fiction entourage, to a once-popular convention of sociological science fiction.[16] It first

16. In this type of fiction we see an usually small and isolated society whose members are being manipulated and kept in ignorance as far as the outside world is concerned. The truth about reality their propaganda diffuses is heavily ideological and false. One character from inside the system manages

appeared in *Fantasy and Science Fiction*, the strictly fantastic magazine where Ballard had previously published his fiction in 1967.

"War Fever" is about an experiment conducted by UN forces in Beirut, some time in the early 21st century, which is the utopian times of no war and no violence and a seeming Paradise on Earth. Societies and nations settle all disputes by negotiating and compromising and most fear the return of the barbarian, violent past. But as it turns out at the end of the story, there is massive and utterly amoral social engineering behind this idyllic existence. The enlightened and peace-loving future societies consider violence and war to be dangerous and virulent diseases which should be dealt with in the way they deal, for instance, with smallpox:

> The smallpox virus is constantly mutating. We have to make sure that our supplies of vaccine are up-to-date. So WHO was careful never to completely abolish the disease. It deliberately allowed smallpox to flourish in a remote corner of a third-world country, so that it could keep an eye on how the virus was evolving. Sadly a few people went on dying and are still dying to this day (Ballard 2002: 1157).

This example used by UN doctor Edwards in a talk with the story's adolescent protagonist, Ryan, perfectly describes the situation in Ryan's native Beirut, the only city at war in the whole globe, a scapegoat city which suffers for the sake of the rest of the world. There are continuous fights in Beirut, skillfully provoked conflicts of everybody with everybody whose goal is to isolate the virulent psychological war virus. Pretending to help the victims and never to intervene, the UN forces spread aggressive propaganda, secretly distribute weapons and provide orphaned infants from all over the world so that the war in Beirut goes on forever. Edwards explains:

> We have to see what makes people fight, what makes them hate each other enough to want to kill. We need to know how we can manipulate their emotions, how we can twist the news and trigger off their aggressive drives, how we can play on their religious feelings or political ideals (ibid.: 1158).

The inhabitants of the city are made to believe that the whole world is at

---

to learn what the situation is really like and either he leaves the confined space or meets its rulers, or sometimes starts a revolution. In the communist countries sociological science fiction was very often used to allegorically represent the political situation behind the Iron Curtain in a sort of game with the censors. Polish representatives are Janusz Zajdel, and Edmund Wnuk-Lipiński; some elements of this convention might be found in Stanislaw Lem's *Eden*. Sociological science fiction is often akin to dystopia, as in the case of Yevgeny Zamyatin's *We* and George Orwell's *1984*. An important English representative of this convention is Brian Aldiss, who introduced sociological fiction to the "New Wave" movement. His best known novel is *Non Stop*. Ballard did write some sociological fiction in the times of his cooperation with *New Worlds*, i.e., the story "Thirteen to Centaurus".

war and no one is going to help them and the best they can do is to resolve the conflicts themselves and hope no bigger country is going to invade and pacify them. In fact the whole city was designed and built by the UN architects to resemble a typical world city, the population isolated and the fake atrocities skillfully prepared. Ryan, a peace-loving and exceptionally intelligent boy, over the course of the story learns the truth and exposes the mechanisms of power at work in Beirut.

What strikes him first is the arbitrariness of political divisions in the city and the absurdity of the war: "the Royalists don't want the king, the Nationalists secretly hope for a partition, the Republicans want to do a deal with the Crown Prince of Monaco, the Christians are mostly atheists, and the Fundamentalists can't agree on a single fundamental" (ibid. 1150). And then step by step Ryan discovers that he is a part of a gigantic experiment and his exceptional skills make him an interesting object of observation "at a significant junction of a maze" (ibid.: 1155) in this urban laboratory. It is his attempts to bring a cease-fire (by persuading all the fractions that there is really no point in fighting) that made the UN forces evacuate him from the city and let him see the truth, which is meant to be a reward for his performance in the experiment.

The way aggression is presented in "War Fever" exposes some universal psychological laws concerning the human propensity for violence. Apparently the city's suffering is justified and helps to perpetuate social utopia on Earth, but the moral stance of the world's powers represented by the UN is very ambiguous. Ryan cannot stop wondering how very easy it is to prompt "a war spirit", even against common sense, just by exposing people to media images, seeing newsreels of enemy atrocities he himself killed with a vengeance.

Apart from showing the destructive power of the media, the story also proves that humans do need war—and ever will, as drives to destruction (self-destruction included) are their immanent feature. The seemingly humanitarian Dr Edwards (who abandoned his comfortable practice to help in Beirut) is in fact the opposite of Dr Ransom from *Empire of the Sun*: the latter tries to save his fellow internees though he did not choose to be with them, the former willingly helps to kill his charge. "He had become curiously addicted to the violence and death, as if tending the wounded and dying satisfied some defeatist strain in his character" (ibid.: 1146) Ryan notices. Given such psychic make-up people are organically unable to live in peace and the war virus will always have them in the end, and therefore, expectedly, the story ends in a frenzy of the uncontrolled explosion of violence: the people in Beirut killing the UN personnel and preparing themselves to attack the world beyond Beirut, "that far larger laboratory waiting to be tested, with its millions of docile specimens unprepared for the most virulent virus of them all" (ibid.: 1180).

War (and in more general terms, the human predilection for unnecessary violence) is one of the most important motifs in J.G. Ballard's *oeuvre*, and surrender to aggression and the death drive are basic characteristics of his vision of contemporary culture: *Grave New World*. World War II is for him *The War*, the most important event of the last century, something responsible for the type of civilization we are now living in. From that war everything starts: both culturally speaking, and as far as his own life/writing career/ autobiographies go. Ballard returns to describing it numerous times: in quasi-historical novels, in speculative fictions set in the near future, and in fantastic stories. Other wars he depicts or mentions: Korea, Vietnam, the American occupation in Europe, and fictional conflicts in the 21st century are off-springs and alternate versions of the one he participated in as a child.

World War II has always been food for documentary-makers and fiction-makers and the abundance of war images spread by the media makes it a half-fictitious event. Therefore Ballard's "autobiographies" are in fact not first-hand reports, but intertextual games and self-subverting texts which openly claim to be partial re-workings of other fictions. Ballard describes, and his protagonists cherish, the spectacular aspect of war. "[I]t is the spectacle of violence that haunts his mind and compels his imagination. The fictive worlds produced by that imagination are then expressions of a particular psychology, which creates its pictures of reality from a specific angle of vision" (Gasiorek 2005: 151).

The result of such a concentration on the spectacle of war, its epic quality and vast panoramas full of trauma and mutilation is "the death of affect", a psychological state in which contemporary people do not respond emotionally to atrocities and view images of war with an intellectual curiosity as abstract artefacts. Moreover, the spectacular character of war, which after having seen so many films and newsreels seems unreal to the contemporary subject, results in a blurring of the real/false distinction. Memories of what really happened are for Ballard's narrators vague mirror-reflections of simulacra, and it is in the theories of Jean Baudrillard that they can find the way to describe these cognitive phenomena.

In his descriptions of war Ballard intertextually alludes to Freud as well, whose essays (primarily *Beyond the Pleasure Principle*, written just after World War I and *Civilization and its Discontents*, written during World War II) present the human mind as conditioned to violence and self-destruction. Any civilization formed by million of such minds must be heading for self-destruction once it is technically possible. Hiroshima and Nagasaki are therefore the turning point of history, thereafter there is only waiting for the end, whether of the whole planet, or at least Western civilization. This thesis is in accordance with theorists of civilizational dynamics, first of all Spengler, whose views Ballard's characters readily accept. After World War II we entered the last period of the decline of the West: *Grave New World*.

CHAPTER THREE:
CITYSCAPES

The affluent, turn-of-the-millennium Western culture, the *Grave New World* of the books by J.G. Ballard, is primarily an urban phenomenon. Available space is transformed into a maze oaf car-friendly highways, malls and concourses. Nature and rural landscapes are conquered and colonized into a chain of continent-covering cityscapes. This is a man-made, media-controlled space which affects people's conscious and unconscious and where there seems to be nothing real or unreal any longer, as all is simulated, produced and constructed.

The motif of cities and cityscapes is so important to understanding the *Grave New World* civilization that it deserves a separate discussion. Ruined and deserted towns in Ballard's catastrophic fiction symbolize the end of the world as we know it; their empty or submerged streets and parks are but the surreal scenery of the last humans, who grow to accept their fate. In *The Drowned World* London is under the water of new seas and its humid lagoons cover once famous places. In *Hello America* the American continent, long after its inhabitants departed, remains full of empty cities with intact cars, along with tons of rubble and the remnants of twentieth century mass-culture. In such texts Ballard depicts once-proud cities, the quintessence of our contemporary way of life and social structure; their ruins show our world in dregs, a surreal[1] collage of cultural artefacts.

In novels such as *Crash, The Atrocity Exhibition, High-Rise* or *Concrete Island* cities are something more than a scenery abundant in symbols and psychoanalytical innuendos. They are the only conceivable world for deranged citizens, a model of the contemporary mind and the site of the struggle to survive, which is very often shown as unstoppable violence: death on highways, crimes, paranoia, reversed evolution and the degeneration of culture. In some of his writings, i.e., *Vermilion Sands, Cocaine Nights* and *Super-Cannes* the cityscape is transformed further: we do not see a huge agglomeration, but rather a chain of villages, resorts and business parks linked by numerous highways, the Internet, CCTV, media networks, etc. Luxurious enclaves, gated communities and densely peopled poorer districts form one gigantic overwhelming city, the urban *Grave New World* of the near future.

In his descriptions of cityscapes Ballard often refers to Freud, Jung and Laing, as one of his major goals is to survey the influence of urban areas on the human mind. References to Baudrillard and Debord allow him to grasp the spectacle contemporary culture has become[2] and the hyperreal space cityscapes form. Frederic Jameson's famous essay "Postmodernism, or The Cultural Logic of Late Capitalism" is also a very important intertextual source, especially as far as Ballardian descriptions of urban architecture are concerned.[3]

1. "Surreal" because, just like in case of surreal poetry and painting, by random juxtapositions of separate elements torn from their original context Ballard tries to externalize states of mind and unconscious fears and drives: his surreal style is (just like André Breton advises in his writings) influenced by psychoanalysis.
2. Media culture and the way it shapes human lives are the subject of my next chapter, so in the present discussion I will refer to this aspect of urban life only briefly.
3. The first sentence of this essay is worth quoting here in the discussion of life in Ballardian cities: "The last few years have been marked by an inverted millenarianism, in such premonitions of the future, catastrophic or redemptive, have been replaced by senses of the end of this and that (the end of ideology, art… or the welfare state, etc.): taken together, all these perhaps constitute what is increasingly called postmodernism" (Jameson 1984: 53). In this attempt to describe what is meant by the catch word "postmodernism" Jameson refers to an intangible but overwhelming "sense of the end". In such an understanding of this term *Grave New World* is postmodernism incarnate.

Urban Architecture

The first of Ballard's urban dystopias, a Malthusian vision of an overpopulated future society, can be found in "The Concentration City" (1957). This early story depicts a planet-wide city without limits in space and time, stretching in all dimensions and deprived of sky, space, trees, parks etc.—all is living units, transportation and factories. What is important for the discussion of Ballard's views on civilization is the way the inhabitants of the city are subliminally aware of the fact they live in an unnatural way. Though none of them knows any other reality, they dream of flying, of empty space and the representations of trees and birds seem for them strangely appealing.[4] The plague of pyromania and the attempts to destroy parts of the city make it plain that for some their world is an aberration of some long-forgotten norm, while allusions to Kafka place the story within the modernist symbolic tradition.

People built cities and somehow managed to make the world suit their inner selves: in Ballard's fiction urban civilization is a mirror reflection of human psychopathologies. The man-made artificial environment is equally as aggressive as its creators, and the way to survive and even enjoy the sadistic traits of human culture is to revert to the primordial savagery of our nature—even if generations of civilized forefathers tried to pretend it does not exist. *High-Rise* (1975) discusses this thesis in detail. It starts as a realist account of the contemporary urban life of London high-rise dwellers, but it soon changes into an allegoric tale about the latent barbarism in even the most civilized people. Ballard tells a shocking story about a luxurious multi-storey building erected near the Thames in an attempt to create a civilized urban dwelling designed to house a perfect community of educated and well-bred middle-class professionals. Despite their refined veneer of good style, once closed up together, the inhabitants slowly give in to their hidden instincts and lusts. In less than a year they revert to the level of primitive nomads from the times of the last Ice Age: they cut themselves off the outside world and organize themselves in a clan system. In loose communes grouped around the strongest leaders they raid one another, kill and eat pets, and compete for space and womenfolk.

Ballard's book might be read as an exercise in cultural regression showing that in playing human history backwards he exposes the mechanism of social progress and the illusions we have about ourselves. What is interesting is the fact that his conclusions, just like the theses of Sigmund Freud and R.D. Laing, are that only by giving in to our instincts can we become full and complete beings. Described from such a point of view civilization seems a mistake and what we call 'progress' involves repression of the greater part of the human soul.

Ballard's intellectual starting point is Freud's essay of 1929 *Civilization and Its*

---

4. David Pringle comments in his discussion of this early story: "Claustrophobia is a key to Ballard's view of the present world. There is a continuous sense of being hemmed in and enclosed by a universe of concrete" (Pringle 1979: 26). Pringle goes on to explain how the claustrophobia felt already in this story is also present in other of Ballard's narratives set in cities.

Discontents.[5] Written after the Great War this paper gives an utterly pessimistic view of human nature. *High-Rise* attempts a description of happy barbarians, people who do what Freud deemed impossible: namely transgress the division of the psyche and attain a state of psychic completeness. In this respect Ballard evokes theories of Freud's major opponent, C.G. Jung, as he alludes to the utopian concept of the Self—with no borders between id, ego or super-ego, but with full access of the consciousness to all mental processes.[6] The high-rise dwellers (of course these few who survive) manage to unite their conscious and unconscious selves and thus achieve perverse but complete happiness.[7]

High-Rise juxtaposes different kinds of utopias: first we see the late 20th-century equivalent of Corbusier's radiant city—"a vertical city" peopled by the happy, and which is designed to serve, albeit as an enclave, as a uniform and happy society. Later in the book we are faced with the Jungian ideal of the complete Self. The latter utopia is heavily ironic; happy barbarians, heeding the back-to-nature manifestos of many gurus from the 1960s, regress to the state of social animals cherishing violence and wayward sexuality.

Corbusier's utopia embodies the old myth that social progress should produce in some distant future an angelic-like population of profoundly intellectual humans, much too refined for violence or prejudice, dwelling in happy cities proudly reaching the skies. The high-rise with its over-priced apartments, luxurious facilities and the atmosphere of "peace, quiet and anonymity" (Ballard 1975: 7) initially is presented as this dream come true. Situated on a bend of the Thames, it gives its inhabitants space, light and the emptiness of the vast air, and isolates them from crowded streets, traffic hold-ups, poverty, dirt and noise. With its storeys of shops, restaurant, cinemas, and sport facilities it is nearly self-sufficient. The inhabitants feel as if they had travelled fifty years forward in time and that the massive scale architecture of concrete and glass is simply destined to take over.[8]

5. Ballard considers this essay a work of sheer genius in terms of its sagacity and verisimilitude.. Compare "The Innocent as Paranoid (Ballard 1997b: 91).
6. Compare the discussion of *High-Rise* in Michel Delville's *J.G. Ballard*, pp. 48-51. Especially illuminating is Delville's conclusion that: "Implicit in Ballard's dystopian fable is the way in which the new man-made environment panders to a number of archetypal anxieties and perversities, some of which may lead to the final disintegration of the 'social contract' that binds the characters to each other. One of the underlying 'theses' of the novel is indeed that the structures and mechanisms which regulate our late-twentieth century societies deny our deepest unconscious needs in the name of security and order" (Delville 1998: 50).
7. The recently altered subliminal meaning of urban space is described by Jameson in the following words: "I am proposing the motion that we are here in the presence of something like a mutation built in space itself. My implication is that we ourselves, the human subjects who happen into this new space, have not kept pace with that evolution; there has been a mutation in the object, unaccompanied as yet by an equivalent mutation in the subject; we do not yet possess the perceptual equipment to match this new hyperspace, as I will call it, in part because our perceptual habits were formed in that older kind of space… The newer architecture therefore—stands as something like an imperative to grow new organs, to expand our sensorium and our body to some new, as yet unimaginable, perhaps impossible, dimensions" (Jameson 1984: 80).
8. Compare Jameson's discussion of how urban architecture, especially the International Style (Ballard's high-rise seems to be created by an architect following this style) changes the look of

Nevertheless, Dr Laing, one of the protagonists of the novel, at the very beginning; "found something alienating about the concrete landscape of the project—an architecture designed for war, on the unconscious level if no other" (ibid.: 10). Laing, who as a person living in the middle of the block (the high-rise's social hierarchy is reflected in the ascension of storeys) represents an average inhabitant, soon forgets this impression and cherishes his life in the high-rise. But the point he initially makes is worth analyzing. It introduces the personage of the architect and suggests that this creator figure is not uniform but, as the ego of the psychoanalysts, is prone to the manipulations of the latent part of his mind. In *Civilization and Its Discontents* Freud describes human cultural achievements as a sublimation of the instincts people have repressed: here architecture is a give-away of what its creators would like to forget.

We are soon introduced to the architect himself—Anthony Royal is quite appropriately living in the penthouse apartment at the very top of the building. As his name suggests he represents the sublime aspect of humanity, he dreams of "coloniz[ing] the sky" (ibid.: 22) and represents ambition, skill and elegance. He designed the high-rise's concourses, the roof with its children's sculpture-garden, the furnishings and elevator lobbies—even if his colleagues from the architectural team contributed more to the very construction of the building, Royal monopolized its esthetics. Therefore, the rapid devastation of all the surfaces and the décor is an insult to him and to the higher values he represents. Royal is identified with the building's architecture and, on a more general level, with humanity's intellectual achievements. But upon a closer inspection his designs respond to something in the inhabitants' minds which is far from noble:

> Laing [was] aware of his ambivalent feelings for this concrete
> landscape. Part of its appeal lay all too clearly in the fact this was
> an environment built, not for man, but for man's absence... less a
> habitable architecture, he reflected, than the unconscious diagram
> of a mysterious psychic event (ibid.: 29).

What later happened in the high-rise seems encoded in its very structure, even in the initial civilized grandeur the building stands for the psyche conditioned to react in a certain manner.[(9)] Though first it looks like a quiet block inhabited by "a

---

cities: "More decisively than in the other arts or media, postmodernist positions in architecture have been inseparable from an implacable critique of architectural high modernism and of the so-called International Style (Frank Lloyd Wright, Le Corbusier, Mies), where formal criticism and analysis (of the high-modernist transformation of the building into a virtual sculpture, or monumental "duck", as Robert Venture puts it) are at one with reconsiderations on the level of urbanism and of the esthetic institution. High modernism is thus credited with the destruction of the fabric of the traditional city and of its older neighbourhood culture (by way of the radical disjunction of the new Utopian high-modernist building from its surrounding context); while the prophetic elitism and authoritarianism of the modern movement are remorselessly denounced in the imperious gesture of the charismatic Master (Jameson 1984: 54).

9. In *Simulacra and Simulations* Baudrillard analyzes modern urban architecture, where the abundance of security destroys the very system it should serve: "What is produced in reality is that

virtually homogeneous collection of well-to-do professional people" (ibid.: 11), differences soon assert themselves. Laing, who is a middle-class everyman, merges invisibly into the background. Everybody here is educated—lawyers, doctors, tax consultants, senior academics, pilots, film-industry technicians etc.: everybody has similar taste, culture and the shared proclivity to isolate themselves. Their life is as far away from the natural habitat of *Homo sapiens* as possible. Life in the high-rise is civilized to the point of being unreal; people forget the physicality of things. Laing, the physician, for reasons he resents, teaches medicine instead of practicing it. A famous gynecologist from the top floor belongs "to the new generation of gynecologists who never touched their patients, let alone delivered a child" (ibid.: 99). He analyzes birth-cries instead. People in the building lose contact with the material world and their own half-animal selves.

> A new social type was being created by the apartment building, a cool, unemotional personality impervious to the psychological pressures of high-rise life (ibid.: 42).

With the slow and incremental disintegration of the artificial facade of life, hidden emotions take over and the first healthy reaction (on the part of the lower storey lodgers) is hatred of the architect. The creator of "our hanging paradise" (ibid.: 17) becomes "the fallen angel" (ibid.: 17), the enemy lodged in his penthouse apartment, who spends his days watching them from above. Ballard's narrative technique emphasizes the growing antagonisms between the lower and upper storeys of the high-rise. We see three points of view among the different lodgers, people who know and meet one another: first socially, then during combat. The interwoven narratives of Wilder, a TV journalist living on the first floor, Laing from the 25th, and Royal from the very top, comment on the situation in the building and show the attitudes of the three very different men to other inhabitants.

The choice of these protagonists is telling and heavily symbolic: Wilder with his imposing body, physical aptitude, vulgarity and propensity for violence stands for the animal part of human psyche—the id. His numerous love affairs, instinctual behaviour and low position in the social hierarchy (already signalled by his very name) impel him to abandon culture and civilized ways very quickly. In fact he commits the very first offence in the building—the provocative drowning of the dog of his upper class (and upper storey) lover, which initiates outbursts of violence. Another allusion to psychoanalysis may be found in the kind of death he dies after the high-rise falls into barbarism. Ascending the building in an imperative to gain control over the whole block he falls victim to a tribe of mothers—cannibalistic women kill him in what seems an Oedipal dream of the id come true.

---

the institutions implode of themselves, by dint of ramifications, feedback, overdeveloped control circuits. Power implodes, this is its current mode of disappearance. Such is the case for the city. Fires, war, plague, revolutions, criminal marginality, catastrophes: the whole problematic of the anticity, of the negativity internal or external to the city, has some archaic relation to its true mode of annihilation (Baudrillard 2003: 70-71).

In their bloodied hands they carried knives with narrow blades. Shy but happy now, Wilder tottered across the roof to meet his new mothers (ibid.: 198).

Another of the three narrators, Royal, stands for the noble art of architecture and the consciously refined part of the mind—ego. He planned and built the high-rise with its masked social hierarchy and he presides over the whole construction, as his name suggests. Narcissistic and self-conscious he suppresses all baser instincts in his attempts to subjugate the unruly lower storeys. He is often seen with animals: there is his Alsatian and the birds he tries to tame that nest in the roof. Moreover, in his thoughts he refers to the high-rise as "his private zoo".

In between Wilder and Royal, the id and the ego, there is Laing, the third narrator, who symbolically embodies the Jungian ideal of the united Self. The Self is the wholly conscious psyche aware of all its parts and instincts, able to unite the base and the refined, not ashamed of being what it is. Laing, a doctor, who at the beginning is afraid of practicing and chooses a quiet medical school and theoretical lectures, ends as a quasi-Neanderthal savage. In the process of 'devolution' he rediscovers the physical nature of man: his biological body, bodily functions and latent instincts. Finally he is restored to the traditional successful male position: he has his territory, his womenfolk and his pride. Significantly, at the end, camping in ruined apartments and cooking Royal's Alsatian over an open fire, Laing thinks about starting a doctor's practice—he has grown up and is ready to face the realities of adult life.

The ideal of the whole, united Self derives from the writings of C.G. Jung and in England it became popular in the 1960s, when the cultural avant-garde was fascinated by the idea of rediscovering hidden parts of the human psyche. The hippie culture, the LSD cult and new trends in psychiatry changed the dominant attitude towards natural instincts and social conventions. Interestingly, one of the most prominent gurus of the period was R.D. Laing, a psychiatrist and the author of the influential books *The Divided Self* (1965) and *The Politics of Experience* (1967).[10] Ballard's protagonist is his namesake for two reasons: his story shows that the distinction between madness and normality is very fluid, and he manages to reconcile the animalistic instinct with intellectual abilities.

The case of Ballard's Laing seems to prove one of the most important of R.D. Laing's theses: that in contemporary, affluent times we live in alienation from our inner world of fantasies and drives to the point of not knowing our own psyches. Ballard's Laing, a man hardly aware of what he is and what he needs, used to live in the way described in the above quote from *The Politics of Experience*. His stay in the high-rise and his regress there allows him to rediscover his physicality and reconcile it with his mind. Only when we are aware and unashamed of the whole range of the stimuli we receive can we get rid of the artificial distinction between reality and fantasy imposed by civilization.

10. See Chapter One for a detailed discussion of Laing's output.

Ballard's protagonist manages to side-step artificial distinctions and to become a whole being—one able to survive inside the high-rise by means of force and cunning and, perhaps, capable of maintaining a "doctor practice". The latter would mean introducing to the barbarian life of the inhabitants an element of education and culture, i.e., true medicine (as contrasted to the dehumanized theory Laing used to teach at school).[11]

Ballard systematically refers to psychology and psychiatry: the writings of Freud, Jung and Laing seem to be his most important inspiration for *High-Rise*. I would argue that the book may be read as an intellectual exercise—an attempt to use these theories as a narrative starting point. Ballard creates a story in which mechanisms theoretically described by great psychologists are applied to an actual situation—a high-rise in central London. The characters and their fate function in the book as allegories, with readers having to guess their intertextual source. In the last paragraph of *High-Rise* Laing, the only survivor of the three narrators, watches the light of the neighbouring high-rise go out. Guessing that its inhabitants are going to face a similar regress of civilized values and illusions, Laing wishes them well in their "first confused attempts to discover where they were" (ibid.: 204). This phrase acquires in context far more metaphorical meaning—our whole 'discontented' civilization should ask itself the same question.

One of the inhabitants of the high-rise, a passive effeminate friend of Laing, is actually a psychiatrist. Often beaten up and unable to cope with his new environment, he is capable of diagnosing the psychic motivation behind seemingly haphazard acts of vandalism and violence. Hiding in a devastated apartment with graffiti on the walls "like the priapic figures drawn by cave-dwellers" (ibid.: 128), he shares with Laing his professional opinion, not only about the building, but in a much broader sense about contemporary urban society at large.

> This building must have been a powerhouse of resentment—everyone's working off the most extraordinary backlog of infantile aggressions...

> It's a mistake to imagine that we're all moving towards a state of happy primitivism. The model here seems to be less the noble savage than our un-innocent post-Freudian selves, outraged by all that over-indulgent toilet-training, dedicated breast-feeding and parental affection—obviously a more dangerous mix than anything our Victorian forebears had to cope with. Our neighbours... resent never having had a chance to become perverse (ibid.: 129).

Ballard's characters interpret their own case and refer to theories of education and human development—in the post-Freudian age we are aware of psychoanalytical thought, something which has infiltrated middle class

---

11. Yet another link between the fictitious and the historical Laing are drugs: Ballard's protagonist gives his wives morphine in order to make them happy and obedient while R.D. Laing was (in)famous for his thesis that LSD allows us to find our real selves.

culture[12]. The most significant observation is the parallelism between individual development—the way we are introduced into culture and a system of dos and don'ts—and the long-forgotten historic process of how our forefathers discovered culture, that is, they created it by repressing instinct. There is no Margaret Mead-like past of happy barbarians and there is no idyllic childhood of angelic creatures à la Rousseau. Both processes of entering culture from the outer realm of biology are painful and breed aggression. In travelling backwards in time the high-rise dwellers have a chance to enact their repressed traumas—some of them rediscover their Jungian "true Selves", but this means indulging in unacceptable behaviour.

Wilder, a less reflective person, has a much simpler interpretation of the symbolic meaning of the high-rise. His never-made documentary would portray this one building as a society in miniature—an apparently homogeneous collection of privileged people splitting into hostile camps. For Wilder, "The old social sub-divisions, based on power, capital and self-interest, had re-asserted themselves here as anywhere else" (ibid.: 62).[13] This down-to-earth interpretation proves wrong—despite his power and fitness Wilder does not survive when faced with psychopathological behaviour he could not predict. Royal with his Corbusier ideals of utopian architecture also fails, as he tends to treat the high-rise as his private enterprise and an experiment gone wrong.[14] From the roof of the building he looks down at the new social order he helped to create:

> Without knowing it, he had constructed a gigantic vertical zoo, its hundreds of cages stacked above each other. All the events of the past few months made sense if one realized that these brilliant and exotic creatures had learned to open the doors (ibid.: 159).

So Royal sees himself as a fallen zookeeper or even a god-like creator of a world stained with imperfection. Significantly, Wilder often unconsciously compares Royal to his own absent father (ibid.: 136), and rebels against the ideals represented by this paternal figure, thus proving Freud's basic theories right. At the end of the novel we see the ultimate picture of regress—a once famous

12. It is important to remember though, that the psychiatrist figure (who in the case of *High-Rise* voices out a psychoanalytical interpretation of what is going on) in the 1960s culture was very often despised and criticized. In R.D. Laing's famous book *The Divided Self* schizophrenics mock their psychiatrist and have much better insight into the psyche.

13. Guy Debord in *Society of Spectacle* discusses the way the capitalist system uses city space: "If all the technical forces of capitalism must be understood as tools for the making of separations, in the case of urbanism we are dealing with the equipment at the basis of these technical forces, with the treatment of the ground that suits their deployment, with the very technique of separation (Debord 1967: § 171).

14. A similar experiment is well described by Jameson: "[In the International Style] the act of disjunction was violent, visible, and had a very real symbolic significance—as in le Corbusier's great *pilotis* whose gesture radically separates the new Utopian Space of the modern from the degraded and fallen city fabric which it thereby explicitly repudiates (although the gamble of the modern was that this new Utopian space, in the virulence of its Novum, would fan out and transform that eventually by the very power of its new spatial language)" (Jameson 1984: 91).

gynecologist in a strange rite from before the stage when id and ego were divided:

> From his mouth came a series of peculiar whoops and cries, barely
> articulated grunts that sounded like some Neanderthal mating call
> but, in fact, were... renderings of the recorded birth-cries analyzed
> by his computer (ibid.: 165).

Birth-cries, the only human sound produced before infants enter culture and communication prove most appealing to the new barbarians living in the high-rise.

Laing is a surgeon who thinks within the boundaries of mechanics—the building, like a body, is a complicated system of many interacting parts. For him the situation in the high-rise is not a verification of theories of mind, but a social experiment where the inhabitants "were free to behave in any way they wished, explore the darkest corners they could find" (ibid.: 43). Advanced technology creates this luxurious enclave and has perversely enabled people to forget civilization and express their hidden instincts. Laing survives because he is able to understand and accept this mechanism and follow his own psychopathology wherever it takes him.

Laing, the reunited 'Self', is the book's most crucial character. It is around him the narration pivots, with the stories of Wilder and Royal serving only as points of reference to interpret Laing's narrative. The book starts with a scene of ultimate regression: most of the inhabitants are already dead, and in one of the ruined apartments Laing bakes Royal's Alsatian over an open fire, while his women wait for their portion of meat. Laing starts to remember the stages of the high-rise's gradual degeneration, and the sequence of his flashbacks forms the main plot of the book. His first memory is the first violation of civilized rules—a bottle from a party going on upstairs smashes on Laing's balcony.[15]

With his detachment and sardonic distance Laing observes the antagonisms between his neighbours—the quarrels between the upper floor owners of pets and lower floor parents over the roof gardens and the swimming pools and the first assaults during the power outage. The death of a dog drowned in the pool triggers minor wars, as the petty impulses of the civilized professionals take over—in a few months the building is transformed into a new wilderness, with staircases terrorized by military groups and 'the lake people' camping in the cabins around the swimming pool. Acts of provocation and outbursts of hatred divide the inmates of the building into tribes: the primordial division into 'us and them' is restored. Laing with his surgeon's perspective compares the disintegration of civilized structures to the physical destruction of the human body:

15. Compare David Pringle's analysis of focalization in *High-Rise* in his monograph about J.G. Ballard *Earth is the Alien Planet. J.G. Ballard's Four-Dimensional Nightmare*: "[Laing, Royal and Wilder] function as centres of awareness, and each is given approximately a third of the book. It soon becomes clear, however, that these three are in fact the familiar Ballardian characters in a new, and more intimate, guise. Laing is the hero, the man with whom the book begins and ends, the one who survives. He is the... sardonic observer with a weakness for giving in to his more obscure impulses, Wilder and Royal (their very names are a give-away!) turned out to be the jester and the king, a Caliban and a perverted Prospero". (Pringle 1979: 48)

He let himself into the dissecting rooms of the anatomy department and walked down the lines of glass-topped tables, staring at the partially dissected cadavers. The steady amputation of limbs and thorax, head and abdomen by teams of students, which would reduce each cadaver by term's end to a clutch of bones and a burial tag, exactly matched the erosion of the world around the high-rise (ibid.: 41).

The disintegration of structures and systems of values leaves people to do whatever they like: it sends them back to very early childhood. Once left to themselves they regress to the ultimate stage of devolution: in days of hunger less-skilled hunters are reduced to cannibalism and eat human corpses. Laing watches this with cold detachment, as a successful survivor and a clan leader he understands that one should not try to restore civilization. Civilization as such was a mistake, it is only in the pre-civilized state of competition and open rivalry that the human potential is free to express itself and each person can reunite their divided selves—granted they are not killed and eaten.

What we see is a regress and not a spectacular end of the world, the characters are tired with high-tech civilization and subliminally search for an enclave free from its constraints. In *The Hidden Script: Writing and the Unconscious* David Punter compares Ballard's urban dystopias: *High-Rise* and *Concrete Island* (1974) to American narratives of the end of civilization, i.e., Thomas Pynchon's famous "Entropy":

> The holocaust is less likely than a kind of seizing-up, the parts becoming frozen into an ironic metal grimace. There can be no vandalism here, for there is nothing to protect; there is instead the strange purity which is a cover-story for undifferentiation, a kind of reverse ecology in which all things are connected to each other through their unuseability. *Concrete Island* and *High-Rise* are thus not cosmic fictions of entropy, which remain an American "province", like interstellar space as a sub-department of the military/industrial complex; they are instead insistently suburban, the fiction of a (British) society which has already, through the abortive 'special relationship' , abandoned its right to protest, and whose only role now can be as a less than conscious harbinger of the terminal tedium of the over-consuming West" (Punter 1985: 19).

Punter sees an unconscious "harbinger" of the decline of the West in *Concrete Island*, where Ballard describes death within the confines of the urban environment. There death is psychologically fulfilling as in the last seconds of life the protagonists are at last able to reconcile with the latent parts of their psyches and become complete human beings.

Robert Maitland could remember little more of the crash than the sound of the exploding tyre, the swerving sunlight as the car emerged from the tunnel of an overpass, and the shattered windshield stinging his face. The sequence of violent events only micro-seconds in duration had opened and closed behind him like a vent of hell" (Ballard 1992a: 7).

This is the beginning of the book, whose protagonist Robert Maitland is marooned on a small traffic island in a suburb of London amidst three high-ways. After a tyre of his Jaguar blows-out, Maitland, who was driving fast along the M4 motorway, finds himself isolated in the middle of an industrial landscape. The novel recounts his attempts to escape, to attract someone's attention, and his exploration of the island and, finally, his quest for domination over its strange inhabitants.

Concrete Island depicts an artificial man-made wilderness, polluted industrial areas full of garbage and choked with exhaust fumes. In such a world everything deteriorates; people, relationships, mental health. Even stories, classic narratives deeply rooted in our culture, ones which are often alluded to in the text, get disfigured and degenerate: the enactment of William Shakespeare's *The Tempest*, Daniel Defoe's *Robinson Crusoe* and Edgar Rice Burroughs' Tarzan stories breeds nightmares.

Some critics[16] claim that the eponymous island is an allegory of the contemporary mind and that Maitland in fact explores his own psyche. My reading of *Concrete Island* continues this critical tradition, but the point I would like to make is more extreme. I will discuss the novel as a study of a disintegrating mind at the moment of its death: the "micro-seconds" in "the swerving sunlight in the tunnel" from the passage quoted above. Such a reading allows us to look at the events described in the novel as the projection of the contemporary psyche disintegrating, while the death of Maitland starts to signify the emotional decay of our life. Therefore, *Concrete Island* is not a horror story whose aim is to scare its readers with some 'life after life'[17] experience, but rather is a quasi-allegory of civilizational self-destruction.[18]

Superficially, what happens to Maitland resembles the adventures of Robinson Crusoe: "Maitland, poor man, you're marooned here like Crusoe— If you don't look out you'll be beached here for ever..." (ibid.: 25), Maitland says to himself at the very beginning of his imprisonment on the island. This intertextual dialogue with Defoe continues throughout the text: Maitland does what Crusoe did: explores the island, sends messages outside and finds footprints of the 'natives'. The comparison to Defoe emphasizes the fact that *Concrete Island*

16. For example, Roger Luckhurst in his *'The Angle Between Two Walls'. The Fiction of J. G. Ballard*.
17. It is interesting to notice that Ballard's *Concrete Island* was publish in 1974, and Raymond Moody's *Life after Life* in 1981.
18. In "The Organization of Territory", a chapter of *Society of Spectacle* consecrated to the way capitalism colonizes space, Guy Debord stresses that our high-tech civilization aims at isolating its members, not connecting them: "The society which eliminates geographical distance reproduces distance internally as spectacular separation" (Debord 1967: § 167).

depicts a decaying world—instead of oceans and wildlife there are motorways and a concrete wilderness. Looking around Maitland sees: "the evening corona of the city, the dark facades of the high-rise apartment blocks hung in the night air like rectangular planets" (ibid.: 19). The deserted island surrounded by over-populated Greater London becomes a symbol of contemporary alienation. Even Proctor, a contemporary man Friday, is degenerated: this model "other" is no longer an unspoilt child of nature and a native à la Rousseau, but a mentally deranged tramp, an ex-acrobat, who after an accident in a circus was rejected by society and found shelter on the island.

In the late 20th-century cityscape, the scrap-yard of industrial garbage, every narrative gets degraded. *Concrete Island* also evokes William Shakespeare's *The Tempest* and presents a grotesque contemporary version of this classic tale of subjugating a newly found land. In Ballard's book we find haphazard allusions to *The Tempest*, motifs and situations torn out of context, but persistently calling the old masterpiece to mind. The island is full of voices, there is a rapid storm and a downpour. Maitland bribes Proctor with wine and Proctor shows him the secrets of the island. All these elements are nevertheless only decorative, for according to Ballard it is no longer possible to enact the story itself. The deranged Proctor is Caliban and the role of Miranda is given to Jane, a twenty-year old dropout and a prostitute who has made her home in a deserted basement on the island. Jane knows how to handle Proctor. Some time before Maitland gets there she took the island from him and made him her slave. Now she defends her realm against Maitland. It is important to note that there is no Prospero on the island and no Ferdinand either—in the late-20th century there is no place for magicians and kings, wisdom and love. Maitland is given the role not of the Shakespearean Ferdinand, but of the usurper brother Antonio: his love affair with Jane is paid for. He has no right to take the island from its inhabitants, but he feels an urge to humiliate and dominate them.

There is also one more intertextual allusion in the novel—to Edgar Rice Burroughs' Tarzan[19] stories, popular culture and early 20th-century classics. Civilized and articulate Jane and her beast-like mute companion Proctor recall the famous pair of American pulp fiction heroes: Tarzan and Jane. Shakespeare, Defoe and Burroughs stand for three visions of nature and exotic wilderness: the Renaissance, the Enlightenment and the turn of the century. They, in turn, are contrasted with 'our' own exoticism, the concrete jungle of urban wasteland.

Concrete Island begins like a realist account of an unlucky ride adorned with descriptions of polluted industrial suburbs, but gradually the novel turns into a pure fantasy, a contemporary equivalent of well-known adventure fictions. This change of genre is rather dramatic: first the language and descriptions are exact,[20] the setting precise and the story probable. Then the exactness is gone, the island grows larger and more secretive; hallucinations replace report-like narrative, time

19. *Tarzan of the Apes* Chicago, McClurg, 1914; *The Return of Tarzan*, Chicago, McClurg 1915 and about twenty other Tarzan books published in the subsequent years.
20. Even time-obsessed, as in the first few pages Maitland keeps looking at his watch every two, three minutes.

changes into timelessness and the story (focalized exclusively by Maitland) loops. This gradual dissolution of the narrative reflects the growing disintegration of Maitland's mind. Trapped in his crashed car he is slowly dying,[21] and during the last few seconds of his life he hallucinates: apparently about the island, but in fact about the past. In these hallucinations personal memories mingle with history. The island is the I-land in between life and death—between the internal world of the psyche[22] and the external reality that this psyche is leaving.

Maitland, an architect, at the moment of his death thinks within the boundaries of geometry: remembering his wife and his mistress he recalls the architecture of the places they visited together, the thought of his childhood brings back to him memories of gardens, rooms and cinema buildings. Similarly, his exploration of the island (and indirectly his own psyche) consists of unearthing half-buried buildings. The ruins of a 1940s cinema, an Edwardian graveyard, traces of a late Victorian alley overgrown with grass and the half-erased borders of gardens represent his notions of the past receding into history. Places and shapes stand for feelings, while the enigmas and unresolved conflicts of his emotional life are symbolized by scenes of finding and interpreting strange relics. Maitland discovers many uncanny[23] objects that are simultaneously both unknown and familiar. A set of photographs in Jane's bag, letterpress blocks in a ruined printing shop, film posters in an underground shelter and

21. Perhaps it would be interesting to compare *Concrete Island* (1974) by Ballard and *Ubik* (1969) by Philip K. Dick. Dick, the American science fiction writer, is less refined stylistically, but his extraordinary imagination made him a guru among science fiction enthusiasts (and Ballard in the 1960s did write for science fiction magazines). *Ubik* pictures a group of people who survived an explosion in a lunar colony. They in fact died, but the narration presents their subjective point of view: the moment of agony is stretched out, they think they are coming back to the Earth to find the world slowly falling apart. Another possible "source" of Ballard's book is *Pincher Martin*, a World War II narrative by William Golding, in which the slow dying of a marooned soldier from a torpedoed ship is a pretext to examine morals in the contemporary world. Our culture praises the human ability to survive, to win, never to give up and to get what there is to be gotten. The shipwrecked soldier, Martin, is a model winner, a man whose lack of constraints makes him a Darwinian fittest. Despite some moments when Martin-the focalizer hallucinates, most of the book is a realist account of him struggling heroically to survive on a rock in the mid-Atlantic with the help of all his determination, strong will and physical resources which in the past he had used to cheat and use other people. As Martin understands what his real nature is, the novel turns into a psychological and spiritual examination of his self. "At the end it transpires that he had been drowned almost immediately, everything is illusion, the ordeal takes place not in time but in eternity, and the rock is Purgatory in which his courage and endurance are merely an obstinate refusal to accept God's existence and his offer of redemption" (Ford 1995: 429). It is also worth mentioning here an enigmatic life-after-death novella by Muriel Spark, *The Hothouse by the East River*. A small group of people who died in a railway bomb attack in 1944 live a hallucinatory after-life in mid-1970s America. The contrast between the memories of their heroic and passionate youth in wartime Europe and the contemporary empty and senseless existence shows the spiritual void of the declining West, which, like in Ballard's fiction, lost its spiritual dimension in the war.
22. In the early 1960s Ballard, a science fiction writer at that time, coined the term 'inner space' and claimed that contemporary fiction should portray precisely this realm of the human psyche. It is not the events, adventures, catastrophes etc. that are important, but our psychological reaction to them. *Concrete Island* seems to follow this artistic manifesto.
23. Compare the definition of "the uncanny" as given by Sigmund Freud in his famous 1919 essay "The Uncanny" and discussed in Chapter One of this book.

car parts around one of the graves have for him a haunting *déjà-vu* quality. Each of them recalls a period of his life and allows him to abandon one part of his self—anxieties disappear and only serenity remains.

> The image in his mind of a small boy playing endlessly by himself in a long suburban garden surrounded by a high fence seemed strangely comforting (ibid.: 22).

> ... He thought of his parents' divorce; the uncertainties of this period... seemed to be replicated in the negative image on the letterpress plate... (ibid.: 48).

Deep inside, Maitland is aware of the fact that he is surveying his memories, not the island, and reluctantly he has to admit that the exploration of this triangular plot of ground[24] is the reassessment of his Oedipal psychic life:

> More and more, the island was becoming an exact model of his head. His movement across this forgotten terrain was a journey not merely through the island's past but through his own. His infantile anger ... reminded him of how, as a child, he had once bellowed unwearyingly for his mother while she nursed his younger sister in the next room. For some reason, which he had always resented, she had never come to pacify him (ibid.: 51).

Childhood traumas and memories buried deep inside return in the last moments of life and Maitland is able to look at his own ego from the outside. "I am the island" (ibid.: 52), he finally claims. This act of identification allows us to interpret the past of the island—a one-time green Victorian suburb turned into an industrial wasteland—as a model of the contemporary self. A basement filled with Ché Guevara, Charles Manson and Black Power prints and inhabited by a hippie prostitute stands for the 1960s and early 1970s, while a post-war ruined cinema, a bomb shelter and a pre-war churchyard represent previous decades. This latter place, seemingly the most remote (and dating from before Maitland was born) is at the same time intimately known to him, and provokes uncanny feelings. It is there that Maitland finds a crypt with empty coffin chambers, one of which is adorned with "a collection of metal objects stripped from his car" (ibid.: 115): his own burial place.

Though his thoughts concern the island and the attempts to escape from it, he subconsciously knows he is dying. Moreover, on some still deeper subliminal level Maitland is aware he had wanted to die and "he had almost willfully devised the crash, perhaps as some bizarre kind of rationalization" (ibid.: 9). Thinking of his ostensibly comfortable way of life: his detachment and alienation, his lack of any real relationship, he feels "he had himself almost deliberately created this

---

24. Which some of the critics compare to a pubic triangle whose exploration is like the Freudian return to the womb. See for example David Pringle's *Earth is an Alien Planet*.

situation, as if preparing the ground for his crash..." (ibid.: 21).[25] By picturing Maitland, a successful and privileged member of society who subliminally wants only to dissolve into the peace of death, Ballard proffers commentary on contemporary Western civilization and its catastrophic influence on the position of humankind in a polluted and socially hostile world.

At the moment of the accident Maitland's personality splits: he is both the dying mind and its surveyor. He looks in the rear-view mirror and: "the eyes staring back at him from the mirror were blank and unresponsive, as if he were looking at a psychotic twin brother"(ibid.: 8). It is this uncanny 'twin brother', who is sent to explore the island and Maitland persistently looks at him from the outside: "Maitland stared at the distorted reflection of himself. His tall figure was warped like a grotesque scarecrow, and his white-skinned face bled away in the curving contours of the bodywork" (ibid.: 12). The tension between the two opposite movements—towards escape and towards death—results in a horror-like effect in the text: the motif of the return to the womb, strange recognitions, nightmarish feelings.

Maitland desperately tries to rationally explain his hallucinations: he blames his wounds, fever, carbon monoxide poisoning, and even a virulent plague in central London. Yet the process of disintegration increases:

> He knew that he was not merely exhausted, but behaving in a vaguely eccentric way, as if he had forgotten who he was. Parts of his mind seemed to be detaching themselves from the centre of his consciousness. (Ibid.: 46)

> He knew that he had begun to forget his wife and son, Helen Fairfax and his partners—together they moved back into the dimmer light at the rear of his mind (ibid.: 66).

Gradually the distant past replaces recent memories; the island is expanding and growing dim. In the back of his mind Maitland realizes that the end is approaching. His hallucinations compete with the awareness that he is hallucinating, and simultaneously with the apparent action—his interactions with Jane and Proctor, his fight for domination—we learn that his delusion is not complete:

> Was the entire island an extension of the Jaguar, its windshield and windows transformed by his delirium into these embankments ... as he lay forward on his crushed chest across the steering wheel? (ibid.: 49).

Though such reflections seem marginal and spread over numerous pages of descriptions and adventures, allusions to the classics and social and

---

25. "'You know, you could have got away from here, if you'd wanted to'" (Ballard 1992a: 82) says Jane, who is in fact a projection of Maitland's own unconscious.

civilizational commentary should not be overlooked. Traced and taken together they allow us to follow the process of Maitland's coming to terms with his own end. Initially deluded by wish-fulfilment dreams, he eventually grows ready to abandon his self. As he explains it to Jane, who offers to take him away from the island, he wants to "leave in [his] own way" (ibid.: 124). Only after his hallucinatory companions have departed and his memories re-enacted is he ready. *Concrete Island* is a report on terminal fantasies and the assessment of Maitland's psyche allows Ballard to show the degree of alienation and trauma inscribed in contemporary urban life.

Let me prove my point by quoting two extracts taken from the initial and the final part of the novel, ones which are as near to a direct presentation of death as Ballard risks:

> An elderly man approached the island, pushing [a] light motorcycle... As he watched this old man...Maitland was overcome by a sudden sense of fear that drove away all the awareness of his hunger and exhaustion. By some nightmare logic he was convinced that the old man was coming for him, perhaps not now but by some circuitous route through the labyrinth of motorways, and that he would eventually arrive to summon Maitland to the point where he crashed (ibid.: 44).
>
> For a brief moment he had seen the familiar white-haired figure of the old man with the light motorcycle... Maitland tried to find him again, but gave up as vehicles clogged all lanes of the motorway. He remembered his previous state of terror on first seeing the old man. This time, by contrast, he felt reassured (ibid.: 118).

Maitland is "reassured", and therefore one may risk the thesis that, after his stay on the island/I-land he managed to come to terms with his memories and traumas and find peace in the acceptance of his past life and the way he had lived it. This is a very ambiguous happy end to the age of psychoanalysis: given the chance to explore his unconscious, the hero re-discovers the Self in order to peacefully perish in a Godless universe. The mysterious white-haired person on the motorcycle may be Death and may be an incarnation of the Jungian Old Wise Man, but it would be rather difficult to interpret this figure as God, whose existence Maitland finally accepts and craves for after a purgatory-like period of readjustment. Inhabitants of *Grave New World* live in a spiritual void and in their cities there is no place for Salvation.

Autogeddon

The title of the present subchapter comes from the article "Autopia or Autogeddon", which Ballard wrote for the *Guardian* in 1984.[26] In this article,

---

26. It was re-printed in *A User's Guide to the Millennium*, pp. 232-234.

while discussing some books published to commemorate the hundredth birthday of the automobile, he asks a number of apparently naïve questions concerning men and cars. Why do people use such a dangerous machine, paying as they do a yearly tribute of millions of lives worldwide? Why have we allowed cars to change the entire surface of our globe and to cause so much pollution? Why has our civilization developed such a strong irrational attachment to this machine, even against our better judgement? The answer that "a large part of the car's appeal lies in its combination of comparatively primitive and static technology with a decorative shell capable of generating enthusiasms and obsessions of the most extravagant kind" (Ballard 1997b: 232) seems inadequate. Ballard quotes Marinetti's *The Founding and Manifesto of Futurism*: the famous phrase that a car is more beautiful than the Victory of Samothrace, but he also refers to some grim statistics and, eventually he leaves his questions unanswered. Similar ambiguity in the way cars are described prevails in all Ballard's books that take up the century-old discussion of motorization.

Not only his scandalous novel about the erotic appeal of car accidents, *Crash* (1973) and its predecessor, the "Crash!" chapter of *The Atrocity Exhibition*, but almost every other of Ballard's books at some point depicts cars: and not only crashes (*Concrete Island, High-Rise*, where Royal recovers from an accident, *Super-Cannes, The Kindness of Women*), but also admiration for them (*Hello America, Empire of the Sun, The Day of Creation* and many others). Automobiles are described in detail, sometimes endowed with symbolic meanings[27] and the characters develop strong, sometimes deviant attachments to them. In *The Atrocity Exhibition* mock-scientific accounts of the latent erotic meaning of the car are inter-woven with scenes of violent driving, and there is similar ambiguity in Ballard's non-fiction. Moreover, the Autopia/Autogeddon trait can be found in his autobiographical texts and journalism, as well.

Ballard's *oeuvre* is thus a part of a nearly century-old debate whose participants come from all over the modern West and discuss cars as status symbols, along with their subliminal meanings, esthetic beauty, erotic endowment—but also the way they alter the countryside, destroy societies and introduce violence to everyday life. As early as the beginnings of the last century Lewis Mumford, an American critic of urban architecture and the way it shapes human lives, started to investigate the role cars have in Western culture. His greatest achievement, *The City in History* (1961),[28] is a very pessimistic account of how car-friendly, modern urban planning destroys the traditional social fabric and alienates men from their living spaces. For Guy Debord its message is that urban design isolates people to keep them under control (Debord 1967: § 172).

In his less known, but crucial as far as motorization goes, *Technics and Civilization* (1934) Mumford shows two possible ways a civilization might approach technological inventions. Firstly, it might invest in diverse modes of technology

27. In *The Drought* a young boy manages to restore a limousine dating to before the end of civilization to symbolically turn back the clock, but it does not have any fuel and, ironically, is a hearse.
28. Mumford's biographer, Donald Miller in *Lewis Mumford: A Life*, calls this his most important book: Marshall McLuhan and Guy Debord often refer to it as to a classic of urban criticism.

and create a complex framework of technical devices and networks enabling each individual to find a unique solution to his or her problems, which is what he strongly advises. Unfortunately, our Western civilization (his book describes the United States in the 1930s, but it seems fair for me to generalize), has chosen "monotechnics", by which he means oppressive technology for technology's sake. The West has chosen to rely on cars and cars become an obstacle to other kinds of transportation, consuming vast amounts of space (roads, parking lots, driveways, garages, etc.) and creating a constant peril to human lives. Because of the pressures of urban life and professional careers, it gradually becomes less and less possible not to drive. Western society has willingly chosen to yearly pay what may be called a "ritual sacrifice" of millions of killed and injured victims of motorization.

Marshall McLuhan in *Understanding Media* describes another way in which motorization destroys the world: the changes wrought by the network of roads encompassing the countryside.

> Great improvements in roads brought the city more and more to the country. The road became a substitute for the country... With super-highways the road became a wall between man and the country. Then came the stage of the highway as city, a city stretching continuously across the continent, dissolving all earlier cities into the sprawling aggregates that desolate populations today (McLuhan 2003: 102).

People grow ever more alienated from the world outside the city and the city becomes omnipresent, covering all territory and making the "inurbane" reality disappear. Human perception changes to fit the frames of a windscreen, soon even the cityscape can only be viewed from inside an automobile, and finally a person in their car becomes a stranger everywhere and to everyone:

> The motorcar ended the countryside and substituted a new landscape in which the car was a sort of steeplechaser. At the same time, the motor destroyed the city as a casual environment in which families could be reared. Streets, and even sidewalks, became too intense a scene for the casual interplay of growing up. As the city filled with mobile strangers, even next-door neighbours became strangers (ibid.: 244).

Thus motorization uproots family networks, friendships, neighbourhoods and makes new generations of drivers estranged not only from other people, but also from the place they grow up and live in. As Alvin Toffler explains in his *Future Shock*, increasing social mobility does not allow for sentiments, nostalgia or a quiet life. Moreover, in time the repressed feeling of insecurity about modern technology has made the human attitude to rapid means of transport ambiguous. Drivers accept a huge amount of risk each time they get into their beloved cars, but subliminally they resent acknowledging it: in his non-fiction Ballard often mentions what a cultural shock the publication of *Unsafe at Any Speed* by Ralph Nader was. In the very first sentence, claiming that the car "has brought death, injury and the inestimable sorrow and deprivation to millions of people" (cit., Ballard 1997b: 260), Nader voices aloud the unspoken fears of modern people.

Jean Baudrillard in his *Simulacra and Simulations* makes an even more radical point showing that it is the very violence involved in driving and in the whole motor-based civilization that defines our culture. *Grave New World* is not rational and its acceptance of the commonplace of death shows the fundamental aberration which has permeated every aspect of life: perversion is not the opposite to the norm, "perversion" and "the norm" do not mean anything.

> The car is not the appendix of a domestic, immobile universe, there is no longer a private and domestic universe, there are only incessant figures of circulation, and the Accident is everywhere, the elementary, irreversible figure, the banality of the anomaly of death. It is no longer at the margin, it is at the heart. It is no longer the exception to a triumphal rationality, it has become the Rule, it has devoured the Rule... It is the Accident that gives form to life, it is the Accident, the insane, that is the sex of life. And the automobile, the magnetic sphere of the automobile, which ends by investing the entire universe with its tunnels, highways, toboggans, exchangers, its mobile dwelling as universal prototype, is nothing but the immense metaphor of life (Baudrillard 2003: 113).

Ballard has always been a keen observer and passionate investigator of attitudes toward cars: in interviews he often describes people at the site of car crashes in real life, the fascination people have looking at newsreels and feature films of car crashes and the "special magic" surrounding them which plays an important role in the contemporary imagination. For him (as he says in an interview with Maura Deveraux) the key thing is the car wreck, which symbolizes our ambivalent feelings to technology:

> At certain points in the technological world that we inhabit, there are fracture lines that somehow allow us to see through into the reality that lies beyond. And one of these fracture lines is represented by the car crash. It's a collapse in a technological system that has the same sort of revelatory power that, say, an earthquake in a major city has (Vale 2005: 201).

In the same collection of interviews Ballard recalls his crashed cars exhibition, which was to probe what the reaction to a display of wrecks would be. This project, realized after Ballard had written the "Crash!" chapter of *The Atrocity Exhibition* and before the novel of the same title,[(29)] sent him to many salvage

---

29. Compare Ballard's commentary in the annotations to this chapter in *The Atrocity Exhibition*

yards and was a source of numerous problems as everybody was hostile to the idea. The very event was successful, as far as it did prove that the materiality of motorized violence is more than people can take once it is shown in a gallery and publicly acknowledged to be a part of the deal we all agree on. Ballard has described this exhibition many times: in interviews, authorial comments to the Re/Search edition of *The Atrocity Exhibition* I have been quoting from, and in his novel *The Kindness of Women*, where the exhibits grow to the status of a symbol of violence we do not want to face. "[The exhibits] became the focus for nervous laughter and angry comment. Visitors who wandered into the gallery and found the cars unexpectedly in front of them began to titter to themselves or swear at the vehicles" (Ballard 1994: 227).

If we believe his autobiographical writings, this reaction showed Ballard that there is a very important point to be made about modern technology, the death drive and the erotic fascination that car crashes provoke in onlookers—and therefore he wrote *Crash*. Most of Ballard's critics consider that this novel together with *The Atrocity Exhibition* form the nucleus of his oeuvre, an avant-garde, Pop-Art manifesto of the psychopathologies of late twentieth-century life as preceded by disaster stories and subsequent memories of World War II. Such a megastory of his writing puts the two novels in the very centre of his work: they are preceded by a science fiction "prequel" and followed by a war "sequel"; the former discusses catastrophes of make-believe societies, the latter of British colonial society in the Far East. The two central novels have therefore provoked numerous critical essays and are probably the most "written about" of Ballard's books.

In Roger Luckhurst's excellent *'The Angle Between Two Walls'. The Fiction of J.G. Ballard* (the title is, by the way, a quote from *The Atrocity Exhibition*) nearly one-third of the text is devoted to *The Atrocity Exhibition* and *Crash*, though at the time Luckhurst wrote his paper Ballard was the author of over twenty books. Comparing these two novels Luckhurst juxtaposes the complex narrative techniques of *The Atrocity Exhibition*—collage, condensation, and multivocalism with the monologism of *Crash*, its intense single voice enumerating the ways in which cars and bodies merge, or rather how the body is incorporated in the

---

"This 1968 piece was written a year before my exhibition of crashed cars at the New Arts Laboratory, and in effect is the gene from which my novel *Crash* was to spring. The ambiguous role of the car crash needs no elaboration—apart from our own death, the car crash is probably the most dramatic event in our lives… Aside from the fact that we generally own or are at the controls of the crashing vehicle, the car crash differs from other disasters in that it involves the most powerfully advertised commercial product of this century, an iconic entity that combines elements of speed, power, dream and freedom within a highly stylized format that defuses any fears we may have of the inherent dangers of these violent and unstable machines" (Ballard 2001: 156). In another comment Ballard describes the exhibition's opening: "The reaction to the telescoped Pontiac, Mini and Austin Cambridge verged on nervous hysteria, though had the cars been parked in the street outside the gallery no one would have given them a glance or devoted a moment's thought to the injured occupants… The cars were exhibited without comment, but during the month-long show they were continually attacked by the visitors to the gallery who broke windows, tore off wing mirrors, splashed them with white paint. The overall reaction to the experiment convinced me to write *Crash*, in itself a considerable challenge to most notions of sanity" (Ibid.: 39).

inhuman traffic.[30] He points to the fact that Ballard in this novel is primarily concerned with the media and the way they penetrate the human mind, thus changing our notions of history, knowledge, and memory.

> There are no doubt new systems of information and accelerated cycles of capital that affect forms of knowledge, modes of representation, the archivization and narrativization of history— transformations that Ballard's texts repeatedly work over. Undoubtedly, too, *Crash* intersects with these shifts at the level of affect in a totality that plays undecidedly between performance and ironization (Luckhurst 1997: 128).

According to Michel Delville, the car crash in the novel is a metaphor which Ballard uses to examine "the latent and manifest meanings of our technological culture, as well as the relationship between violence and sexual fantasies" (Delville 1998: 35). He develops his psychoanalytical meaning of the book showing that motorized violence is for the characters not only an outlet of repressed sexuality and deviated religiosity, but that they seek to unite with the car. Violent mergers of bodies and technology follows, "a process… reflecting a Freudian displacement of affect and its subsequent annihilation into the inorganic" (ibid.: 40).

Andrzej Gasiorek notices that *Crash*, by describing violent accidents happening daily, shows the "structural-institutional parameters that permit this to happen" (Gasiorek 2005: 82), which means that the whole of contemporary society is subliminally empowered by the death drive: violent human characters and violent man-made technology conspire to realize latent destructive desires. He also makes an interesting point concerning the way Ballard enters the intertextual dialogue with psychoanalytical writings:

> In…reversal… of the influential psychoanalytic account of responses to trauma, the novel is peopled with characters who not only remember their traumas but also use their reminiscences as a means of confronting the inner significance of the logics that produced the trauma in the first place. Thus in *Crash*, far from leading to a repetition-compulsion attributable to repression of the unconscious, the trauma of a road accident is a stimulus to a conscious exploration of all their parameters (ibid.: 89).

These critics rightly show that Ballard does not follow psychoanalysis blindly, but uses theories to his own ends (moreover, he does the same with the text of his own *The Atrocity Exhibition* from which *Crash* borrows plots and characters). The novel anatomizes traumas and shows them in slow motion, but the usually latent processes are here made overt, i.e., the characters know they seek immolation

---

30. Writes Luckhurst: "There is only one transaction here mantrically asserted: between semen and engine coolant, body and car, the bruises of medallions, steering wheel and instrument binnacles flowering subcutaneously, as if the technology had been wholly incorporated" (Luckhurst 1997: 123).

and plan their crashes. One of the most important subplots of *Crash* is the story of Vaughan, a man obsessed with the auto-death of Elizabeth Taylor. His dream to die in a head-to-tail collision with the star unites violence, sexuality and the utopian idea of entering the image, the world of simulacra. In his notes to *The Atrocity Exhibition* Ballard recalls Taylor:

> Elizabeth Taylor, the last of the old-style Hollywood actresses, has retained her hold on the popular imagination... a unique collision of private and public fantasy took place in the 1960s, and may have to wait some years to be repeated, if ever... I can't imagine writing about Meryl Streep or Princess Di... Unlike Taylor, they radiate no light (Ballard 2001: 17).

Among the numerous characters who appear on the pages of *The Atrocity Exhibition* and who are mostly figments of the protagonist's mind, there is also a man called Vaughan, "who was later to appear as the 'hoodlum scientist' in *Crash*" (ibid: 124). His relationship with the protagonist of *The Atrocity Exhibition* anticipates the "Ballard"[31]-Vaughan pair in *Crash*. Met somewhere on the road, Vaughan, the strong, violent driver and a connoisseur of physical force, takes the protagonist on a strange journey. They escape in Kerouac-like fashion driving their car across a vast territory full of empty resorts with huge vacant parking lots, filling stations and motels. This is *Grave New World*, a car-dominated territory:

> Together they set off on a grotesque itinerary: a radio-observatory, stock car races, war graves, multi-storey car parks. Two teenage girls whom they picked up Vaughan had almost raped, grappling with them in a series of stylized holds. During this exercise in the back seat his morose eyes had stared at Travers through the driving mirror (ibid.: 106).

In *Crash* Vaughan takes "Ballard" on a similar journey, but this time the journey is mental, it leads towards an understanding of the new sensitivity based on simulacra and the world where the bodily and the mechanic merge.[32] After a crash in which he killed a man, "Ballard" falls victim to a number of compelling obsessions—he is determined to discover the real significance of the crash and

31. The protagonist of *Crash* is called 'James Ballard', which is thus yet another fact/fiction game Ballard plays. The interrelations of three texts: *The Atrocity Exhibition, Crash* and the twenty-years-later commentary to *The Atrocity Exhibition* render the border between fact and fiction still more problematic.
32. Gasiorek sees a parallel between this merger and the Vaughan-"Ballard" relationship: "The narrator's homo-erotic attachment to Vaughan is a doubled phenomenon, at once a form of male bonding in which the car functions as the object par excellence through which homo-sociality is mediated, and an expression of desire for the object itself, a displacement of libidinal energy from the human to the machine. Just as Vaughan wants to penetrate and thus merge with the car (in a process asserting his phallic masculinity) so "Ballard" in wanting to penetrate Vaughan is unsure what exactly is his real object of desire". (Gasiorek 2005: 95)

establish a new mode of contact with the outside world. During his experiments with motorized sex and road aggression he comes across Vaughan, who plans his self-immolating collision with Taylor. Delville notices:

> Vaughan's obsessive longing for the eroticized atrocities of car crash injuries invites comparison with the marquise de Sade, whose interest in discovering the seeds of the psychopathologies of his age and cataloguing all forms of erotic pleasure was equally unembarrassed by traditional moral considerations. To "Ballard", Vaughan and other characters in the novel, the car crash appears primarily as a means of triggering new sensations which would enable them to escape the burden of their psychic past and enliven a sexual life that has become sterile and perfunctory (Delville 1998: 36).

Though the characters drive ceaselessly and at high speed in fact they stay in a very limited area, London's southern suburbia. Descriptions of death-defying acceleration and dangerous manoeuvres are all the time set on the very same few streets: Western Avenue, the northern and western perimeters of the airport, the Northolt expressway, the road to Shepperton, and countless parking lots. The claustrophobic effect is immense. Despite the ostensible freedom of expressways and fast lines, it turns out that there is nowhere to go—the whole world is the same concrete and glass artificial architecture.

The landscape through which they drive is an industrial wasteland: access roads of abandoned petrochemical plants, deserted filling stations, terminals at the airport with their tactile geometric shapes, hotel mezzanine balconies and studio car-parks. Cars and planes seem to people to be these domains: the architecture is post-human, hostile to men. Even "Ballard"'s' home is in the middle of an artificial desert. The inhabitants of this estate never stop to look around, everybody rushes headlong, there is no feeling of belonging to the neighbourhood. During his convalescence "Ballard" for the first time actually looks at his environment:

> On the first afternoon I had barely recognised the endless landscape of concrete and structural steel that extended from the motorways to the south of the airport, across its vast runaways to the new apartment systems along Western Avenue... shielded from the distant bulk of London by an access spur of the northern circular motorway which flowed past us on its elegant concrete pillars. I gazed down at this immense motion sculpture, whose traffic deck seemed almost higher than the balcony against which I leaned (Ballard 1977: 40).

The offices and apartments described in the novel are always situated above car parks and airport infrastructure. Looking through the window the characters see a metallic lake of car roofs. The city is dirty and full of garbage. Sidewalks and traffic islands are covered with rusty car parts and rubbish dumped from the car windows. The major attractions of massive steel expressway constructions are places known as extremely dangerous. Repeated crashes transform them into modern shrines, places of special interest and quasi-mystical meaning, which in the landscape of simulacra stand for the sacred groves of bygone days.[33] The first place "Ballard" visits after his convalescence is the turn where he had crashed:

> At my feet lay a litter of dead leaves, cigarette cartons and glass crystals. These fragments of broken safety glass, brushed to one side by generations of ambulance attendants, lay in a small drift. I stared down at this dusty necklace, the debris of a thousand automobile accidents. Within fifty years as more and more cars collided here the glass fragments would form a sizable bar, within thirty years a beach of sharp crystal (ibid.: 47).

Broken glass transforms the garbage heaps of "cigarette butts, spent condoms and loose coins" into something special and nearly beautiful—future geologists will be able to study the layers of glass and get to know the past. Crystals of glass anticipate crystals of LSD, which at the climax of the novel give "Ballard" the mystical vision of the sacred union of men and cars.[34] Cars have infiltrated culture and altered our perception of reality and the architecture of our cities—if you want to move you may only drive, as nowhere is walking possible. The city is built for cars and can be appreciated only from speeding cars; Ballard does not describe any parks, gardens or greens, only a few half-dead trees along the access roads. The glass and concrete landscape is adorned with gigantic billboards, everybody drives in their car at high speed in a mechanical manner, as if slowly becoming androids themselves. No one knows the world outside the motorways.

In an interview in 1995 Ballard describes England in such a way: "Now we are a northern turn-off, a slip-road off the northern end of the great European motorway" (Self 1995: 340). This world of high speed and nowhere to go is essentially identical all over a globe peopled by millions of drivers pursuing their dreams of sex and aggression, the only means to assert their ability to feel. In the future the affluent countries will be:

> Not just a planetary suburbia, a future of utter boredom, lit by totally unpredictable acts of violence. The forces of social cohesion will ensure we get the drab city of plain again. These unpredictable acts of violence may take all sorts of forms, not necessarily physical

33. Crashes are metaphysical in that they allow to see beyond the mundane reality. Writes Gasiorek: "the crash is the traumatic event, the rent in the social fabric, that shatters habituated lives and uncovers a repressed social unconscious, displaying the individual's fantasy life as the conduit for a perverse technology that embodies a potent will-to-death (Gasiorek 2005: 88).

34. Compare Carl Jung's account of the psychoanalytic meaning of crystals: "In many dreams the nuclear centre, the Self, also appears as a crystal. The mathematically precise arrangement of a crystal evokes in us the intuitive feeling that even in so-called "dead" matter, there is a spiritual ordering principle at work. Thus the crystal often symbolically stands for the union of extreme opposites—of matter and spirit" (Jung 1978: 221).

violence. There could be weird consumer trends or bizarre vacation schemes, financial scams (ibid.: 367).

In the same interview Ballard calls *Crash* a psychopathic hymn, not a warning or a moral lesson, but a pure projection of consumer trends onto the near future. As Jean Baudrillard notes in *Simulacra and Simulations*, it is tempting to read the novel as perversion—which most reviewers in the 1970s did, calling Ballard an author beyond psychiatric help. The message is so nihilist that even Ballard himself in the introduction to the French edition of the book tried to weaken it by pointing to the didactic role of pessimistic visions, but soon he regretted that often quoted statement.[35] *Crash* shows a post-human world of no morals, where hardly any values are left and metaphysics shrinks to a mystical union with cars. For their survivors, crashes often are a sort of initiation or awakening to the real nature of reality. "Ballard" pursues his strange compulsions to explore the sexuality of car crashes because he senses that somewhere in the "nightmare marriage of sex and technology"[36] the new logic of the culture of simulacra can be found. The moment of illumination comes during his LSD trip:[37]

> An armada of angelic creatures, each surrounded by an immense corona of light, was landing on the motorway on either side of us, sweeping down in opposite directions. They soared past, a few feet above the ground, landing everywhere on these endless runaways that covered the landscape. I realised that all these roads and expressways had been built by us unknowingly for their reception (Ballard 1977: 171).

The magical transformation of speeding cars into angelic creatures makes "Ballard" understand that the times of men are over and some new post-human era is starting and that automobiles are its harbingers. In a world devoid of meaning and essence what counts is the momentary vertigo produced by speed and drugs, a moment of understanding the transitory nature of reality. Ballard's fiction shows

35. Ballard called *Crash*: "a warning against that brutal, erotic and overlit realm that beckons more and more persuasively to us from the margins of the technological landscape" (Vale and Juno 1984: 98).
36. V. Vale, Ballard's American friend and editor who published his avant-garde texts in RE/Search publications, always underlines Ballard's abilities to diagnose what is wrong in social life and to project these phenomena to the future. In a conversation with David Pringle, Vale shows how Ballard's prognoses from the early 1970s are coming true: "For me personally, when I first discovered Ballard, the key quotation was "Sex Times Technology Equals The Future"—that was around 1972. You can apply that quotation everywhere. For example, I've met a lot of Americans who lost their virginity in the automobile. And on the Internet, the first successful money-making usage was for sex—in fact it's estimated that 70% of Internet traffic involves sexual content. And with cell phone cameras, people are sending each other "live" nude footage of themselves—way more than you might think. Every time there is a technological innovation, it gets steered toward sex, if possible" (Vale 2005: 212-213).
37. In *The Kindness of Women*, a novel with strong autobiographical undertones, Ballard describes his own experimentations with LSD in a similar manner.

such a world filled with simulacra: the TV screens, billboards, the mechanical reproduction of gestures and rituals. In the following years these concepts entered cultural studies, especially the works of Jean Baudrillard, who tries to render this new stage of our civilization. In *America* (1986 tr. 1988) he writes:

> Speed is not a vegetal thing. It is nearer to the mineral, to refraction through a crystal, and it is already the site of a catastrophe, of a squandering of time... Speed is simply the rite that initiates us into emptiness: a nostalgic desire for forms to revert to immobility, concealed beneath the very intensification of their mobility (Baudrillard 1994: 7).

The manic love of cars and speed expresses this subliminal need to blend with technology in creating a macabre human-machine hybrid. All the numerous crashes in the novel exemplify this death drive—both in the Freudian and the literal meaning of the term. As Ballard's early disaster fiction showed people eagerly embracing global catastrophe and finding it psychologically fulfilling, *Crash* shows a psychopathic and suicidal civilization longing for the calmness of the inorganic world. Here the Freudian idea that all life forms subliminally long for the state from before the beginnings of life is made literal—the characters heed their psychopathologies and orchestrate the macabre marriage of body and car.

The merger of bodies and cars is made literal in Ballard's texts. We read about mixtures of blood, semen and engine coolant; a description of anatomy and technology intermingling, and both are done in the mock scientific style of a medical journal[38] or a technical manual. The narrator describes bodies and cars comparing one to another—"Ballard's" bruises change tone "like the color spectrum of automobile varnishes" (Ballard 1977: 22), and Vaughan's face has a metallic sheen. Moreover, his jeans are smeared with "a blend of semen and engine coolant" (ibid.: 86), and when he makes love to "Ballard's" wife, the headlamps "covered their bodies with a luminescent glow, like two semi-metallic human beings of the distant future making love in a chromium bower" (ibid.: 139). Vaughan identifies with cars to the extent of losing his humanness. "The equations between the styling of a motor-car and the organic elements of his body Vaughan mimed continually in his own behavior" (ibid.: 146).

In fact it is difficult today not to read *Crash* as an anticipation of Jameson and Baudrillard, who wrote their essays in the 1980s. Ballard describes the contemporary *Grave New World* in advance, simply by projecting into the future some trends he noticed in culture; they in their essays saw it coming in the car-ridden world around.

---

38. In his discussion of *Crash* Baudrillard writes: "[H]ere, all the erotic terms are technical. No ass, no dick, no cunt but: the anus, the rectum, the vulva, the penis, coitus. No slang, that is to say no intimacy of sexual violence, but a functional language: the adequation of chrome and mucous as of one form to another." (Baudrillard 2003:116)

Future Enclaves

What might the future of cityscapes be like? After centuries of growing bigger and higher, cities have already devoured most of the available space of *Grave New World* and changed the countryside forever. According to Ballard in the contemporary urban landscape one can find enclaves of the super-rich that can tell us what the cityscape in the near future will be like. Gated communities of the high-earning professional class, sun cities inhabited by retired millionaires and luxurious business parks whence international corporations are managed are presently suffering from social malaises which soon will bother all middle-class people (the underprivileged and the poor are lagging behind and still live in the past, we cannot yet see their future enclaves).

> Where is Vermilion Sands? I suppose its spiritual home lies somewhere between Arizona and Ipanema Beach, but in recent years I have been delighted to see it popping up elsewhere—above all in sections of the 3,000-mile-long linear city that stretches from Gibraltar to Glyfada Beach along the northern shores of the Mediterranean, and where each summer Europe lies on its back in the sun. That posture, of course, is the hallmark of Vermilion Sands and, I hope, of the future—not merely that no-one has to work, but that work is the ultimate play, and play the ultimate work (Ballard 2002b: 7-8).

This passage written by Ballard comes from the preface to the *Vermilion Sands* short story collection first published in 1971. The stories in this volume describe an imagined seaside resort in the near future. Peopled by tourists and bohemian artists the village is the homeland of an ultimate leisure society, where everybody is affluent and has to cope with ennui and its consequences: psychological trauma, deviations, decadent excess and crime. In the following years Ballard's gradually less and less fantastic books display similar concerns; they discuss contemporary culture and its possible development in the near future.

Consumerism, leisure and the mass media are going to create a new kind of civilization, the beginnings of which can already be seen. No need to work (or a decade or two of labour in the average life of more than ninety years), access to modern media and no goal in life result in a classless society of resort dwellers who withdraw from social interaction. Enclosed in gated estates of constant security surveillance, people are going to spend their days dozing in front of their TV screens and consuming handfuls of tranquillizers. As the affluence of this civilization will depend on constant spending and purchasing ever more commodities, potential buyers cannot live in a coma. In order to go shopping people have to be woken up: to break the spell of their apathy and the overwhelming feeling of sensory deprivation strong stimuli will have to be used—including crime and perversions of sundry kinds.

In his novels written at the close of the last century Ballard tries to imagine future leisure communities, taking as his example already existing luxury enclaves: gated estates, the Mediterranean villages of retired Europeans and high-tech Côte d'Azur business parks. Viewing them as samples of Europe's future he describes their settings and architecture: the man-made cityscape of replicas, models and stylization; the lifestyles of the inhabitants, the social problems which are going to arise. In *Cocaine Nights* and *Super-Cannes* the *Grave New World* is described in detail.

In 1977 in "The Future of the Future", an essay written for *Vogue*, Ballard describes life in a few decades time: houses full of screens and cameras filming our everyday life, electronic wallpaper on which this film about us is constantly shown. People spend their lives inside watching their own fantasies and even graphs of their bodily functions displayed and adorned with suitable music. No one cares about the outside world, to say nothing of outer-space and gigantic global undertakings like the conquest of space. Everybody encloses themselves in their inner space.

This essay was partly a joke, nevertheless in the following years Ballard kept coming back to the idea of this future society and its artificial world. The publication of Alvin Toffler's *Future Shock* in 1970 and Francis Fukuyama's *The End of History and the Last Man* in 1992 were both an important context for his subsequent books. As I have mentioned in Chapter One, Toffler claims that the future is already descending—a totally new type of society is replacing the one we know. People are going to work for much shorter periods and will spend most of their lives at leisure. Social mobility and the transitory character of interpersonal and professional bonds are going to eliminate permanency from our life. Fukuyama maintains that inasmuch as the "motor" of history is the tension or antagonism between thesis and antithesis—the sudden collapse of the West's antithesis (communism) severed the dialectic in that it left neither a new challenger in its wake, nor, hence, any need of synthesis. Thus, the end of wars, revolutions and breakthroughs. We live in the times 'post-': when traditional concerns: whether religious, political, patriotic etc., are no longer important. What Fukuyama does not describe is the psychological impact of the end of history on future generations, this being the theme Ballard finds fascinating.

As early as in 1989 Ballard wrote "The Largest Theme Park in the World", a short story for the *Guardian* with clear political undertones. Mocking ideas of the kind presented by Toffler, Fukuyama and the late 1980s enthusiasts of global unification, the abolition of borders, the dissolution of nation-states etc, he gives his own vision of the 'end of history' in Europe. The creation of a united Europe in Ballard's story results in the exodus of the European middle-class to the beaches of the Mediterranean. After their long holidays lawyers, architects, accountants, managers, etc., decide not to go back home:

> It became all too clear that in rejecting the old Europe of frontiers
> and national self-interest they had also rejected the bourgeois
> values that hid behind them. A demanding occupation, a high
> disposable income, a future mortgaged to the gods of social

and professional status, had all been abandoned (Ballard 2002b: 1140).

Europe is transformed into a theme park for American and Japanese tourists. The northern European authorities try to summon back their most educated and efficient citizens, but in vain. The end of national borders and the overwhelming victory of liberal democracy (earlier prophesied by Fukuyama) means precisely the end of this very system. In this short story Ballard does not yet seriously explore the far-reaching social consequences of the creation of a leisure society, he rather toys with ideas. His permanent holidaymakers indulge in body cults, fitness, fringe philosophies and new religions—they camp in Southern European villages, which connected with each other form one gigantic Mediterranean cityscape. Leading a loose hippie lifestyle they finally have to use violence to preserve their communities.

Crime and violence wake people from their leisure-induced stupor, national groups gather around charismatic leaders. Finally, the millions of tourists decide to march North and reclaim their native cities to "reinstate a forgotten Europe of nations, each jealous of its frontiers, happy to guard its history, tariff barriers and insularity" (ibid.: 1144). This but few pages-long story reads like a tongue-in-cheek commentary to the current political and cultural discussion in England, nevertheless it alludes to important themes: leisure society and violence as a necessary part of social life.[39]

Ballard describes the unreal cityscape of the near future in *Cocaine Nights*, a novel set in the fashionable corner of Spain inhabited by super-rich, retired Northern Europeans. What immediately strikes in the description of British settlements there is "an obsession with crime"—everything there is designed around perfect security. Moreover, there is something uncanny about the look of architectural designs; isolated and guarded the estates have a futuristic look:

> The future had come ashore here, lying down to rest among the pines. The white-walled pueblos reminded me of my visit to Arcosanti, Paolo Soleri's outpost of the day after tomorrow in the Arizona desert. The cubist apartments and terraced houses resembled Arcosanti's, their architecture dedicated to the abolition of time, as befitted the ageing population of the retirement havens and an even wider world waiting to be old (Ballard 1997a: 33-34).

The book's protagonist, Charles Prentice is a connoisseur of the bizarre and in his numerous voyages around the globe he has developed a taste for pastiche, as he once mentions his longstanding plan for a book on the architecture of

---

39. Ballard makes a similar point in his interview with Will Self when he talks about the future: "All sorts of strange diseases may well flare up, and they will be welcomed by the bored inhabitants of the super-Switzerland of the future... They will be welcomed in the way that people like reading about serial killers or rent videos about psychopaths" (Self 1995: 367).

brothels, the token postmodernist fantasy-place.[40] Nevertheless, in Costa del Sol even he feels apprehensive and his first impressions are rather gruesome: "Perhaps this was what a leisure-dominated future would resemble? Nothing could ever happen in this affectless realm, where entropic drift calmed the surfaces of a thousand swimming-pools?" (ibid.: 35). In his first days in Andalucia he still has the perception of a travel writer: looking around he notes the features of the countryside and already makes up catchy phrases: "the memory erasing white architecture; the enforced leisure that fossilised the nervous system" (ibid.: 34). Even at first glance he senses "the apparent absence of any social structure; the timelessness of a world beyond boredom, with no past, no future and a diminishing present" (ibid.: 35). The Andalucian architecture seems to him a patchwork collection of diverse styles: market gardens, villa projects, numerous golf courses, nightclubs, artificial hills and "a half completed Aquapark, its excavated lakes like lunar craters". Everything is disguised as something else, nostalgic pastiche is the dominant style:

> White-walled Andalucian pueblos presided over the greens and fairways, fortified villages guarding their pastures, but in fact these miniature townships were purpose-built villa complexes financed by Swiss and German property speculators, the winter homes not of local shepherds but of Düsseldorf ad-men and Zürich television executives (ibid.: 15).

People whose work consists of creating and spreading images and fictions—in TV, film or advertisements, opt for the countryside, which is in itself a sham and a mockery. They go for the mock-Roman columns and white porticos "apparently imported from Las Vegas" (ibid.: 16), dismantled Spanish monasteries, mock-Arab architecture. "Costa del Sol lacked even rudiments of scenic or architectural charm" (ibid.: 16), as Prentice sums up his first impressions.[41]

This eclectic architecture is what marks the difference between 'normal' Spain (along with the most of Europe) and the futuristic or post-modern realm of the enclaves. The enclaves are isolated spatially (by security systems), but also temporally: not only do they belong in the future of our culture, but their inhabitants have a different feel of time as well. Nobody wears wristwatches, there are no clocks. For Prentice, who has travelled in the Third World, this seems the fourth one: "the one waiting to take over everything", as one of his friends puts it. Before carefully applied crime and violence re-install reality, people in pueblos lead an unreal, futuristic "no-life":

40. Compare Frederic Jameson's "Postmodernism and Consumer Society" where he describes postmodern pastiches: "Pastiche is, like parody, the imitation of a peculiar or unique style, the wearing of a stylistic mask, speech in a dead language: but it is a neutral practice of such mimicry, without parody's ulterior motive, without the satirical impulse, without laughter, without that still latent feeling that there exists something normal compared to which what is being imitated is rather comic" (Jameson 1983: 114).
41. Compare Chapter One—the passage about architecture and nostalgia in Frederic Jameson's essay "Postmodernism, or the Cultural Logic of Late Capitalism".

[W]e were witnessing an immense inward immigration. The residents... had retreated to their shaded lounges, their bunkers with a view, needing only that part of the external world that was distilled from the sky by their satellite dishes. Standing empty in the sun, the sports club and the social centre, like the other amenities engineered into the complex by Swiss consultants, resembled the props of an abandoned film production (ibid.: 216)

Nowadays limited to resorts for the rich and retired middle-class, such architecture and lifestyle will probably soon spread all over the affluent countries. "Town-scapes are changing. The open-plan city belongs to the past" (ibid.: 219). Instead we are going to have security grills and defensible space. "As for living, our surveillance cameras can do that for us. People are locking their doors and switching off their nervous systems" (ibid.: 219). Gated communities resemble fortified medieval cities and, worse still, there is hardly anything going on inside. In the pastiche architecture and artificial nostalgic landscape people doze instead of live. Nothing happens—at least nothing we can comprehend by our traditional cause-and-effect logic. Even crime seems pastiche: "Kafka re-shot in the style of *Psycho*" (ibid.: 71).

Another look at the cityscape of the near future can be found in Ballard's descriptions of Eden-Olympia, the setting of *Super-Cannes*, which is a business park built at the very end of the twentieth century. This is not a place of enforced leisure, but of the most efficient work, which is the greatest privilege in the future society, where only the very best work for a decade or two. Indeed, the top executives of multinational corporations control the economy of half the planet from their post-modern offices.[42] The location in the French Riviera is not accidental. These are the places where a century earlier Picasso, Francis Scott Fitzgerald, and Ernest Hemingway led their bohemian lives, and in the close neighbourhood of Cannes, Europe's greatest film festival is annually organized.

The architecture of Eden-Olympia mockingly alludes to the tradition of art, illusion and pleasure, but the park is in fact dedicated to the hard labour of managing millions of dollars in investments. Mediated by computers, terminals, data banks, etc., most of these operations deal in the unreality of virtual money. Like in California where the Silicon Valley partly reflects Hollywood, it is the look of things that counts. To the eye Eden-Olympia resembles: "a vision of glass and titanium straight from the drawing boards of Richard Neutra and Frank Gehry, but softened by landscaped parks and artificial lakes, a humane version of Corbusier's radiant city" (Ballard 2002a: 5).

Visually alluding to utopian architecture of the International Style, Eden-

---

42. Jameson emphasizes the affiliation of architecture and economics: "Architecture is, however, of all the arts that closest constitutively to the economic, with which, in the form of commissions and land values, it has a virtually unmediated relationship: it will therefore not be surprising to find the extraordinary flowering of the new postmodern architecture grounded in the patronage of multinational business, whose expansion and development is strictly contemporaneous with it" (Jameson 1984: 57).

Olympia is nevertheless quoting, playfully recalling older stylistics in a nostalgic mode. The complex is eclectic, the common denominator of different esthetics is money: "wealth at Eden-Olympia displayed the old-money discretion of the mercantile rich". The frequent use of the adjective 'new' strikes in the descriptions of the park: it has the "neo-" quality of a conscious re-working of older styles:

> The ocean-liner windows and porthole skylights seemed to open onto the 1930s, a vanished world of Cole Porter and beach pyjamas, morphine lesbians and the swagger portraits of Tamara de Lempicka (ibid.: 21).

> [A] small single-storey building [seemed] like a general store in a mock-up of a Wild West frontier town (ibid.: 149).

> Twenty yards away was the showroom of Nostalgic Aviation, with its collection of memorabilia, ejection seats and radial engines, an Aladdin's Cave of possibilities (ibid.: 390).

> The villas and apartment houses had been designed by a latter-day Gaudi, the walls and balconies moulded into biomorfic forms that would have pleased the creator of the Sagrada Familia (ibid.: 140).

The effect is one of mirage and illusion, Eden-Olympia is no-place, and as such it constitutes a "laboratory for the new millennium", where reality is manufactured. This new reality is virtual and produced by a massive computer network. In Eden-Olympia you are continuously on-line: "every office, house and apartment cabled up to the world's major stockbrokers, the nearest Tiffany's and the emergency call-out units at the clinic" (ibid.: 16). For the inhabitants of this complex, the illusory, but extremely busy life of computer screens and endless committees is reality: transfers of data along fibre-optic cables, constant communication with all the business centres in the world, work days of sixteen hours. Moreover, when outside the park, the inhabitants have an overwhelming feeling that people in the 'normal' world are play-acting and trying to maintain the illusion of the past. "They're like actors improvising their roles, unaware that the production has moved on" (ibid.: 93).

This production is life as we—in nostalgic retrospect—knew it in the mid-twentieth century, off-line, full of lazy walks, chance meetings, manual work, discussions about politics. In Eden-Olympia representative democracy has been replaced by the surveillance camera[43] and politics and religion have outgrown

43. In *Cocaine Nights* a similar point is made even more explicitly: "Politics is over, Charles, it doesn't touch the public imagination any longer. Religions emerged too early in human evolution— they set up symbols that people took literally, and they are as dead as a line of totem poles. Religions should come later, when the human race begins to near its end. Sadly, crime is the only spur that

their use, such that people simply do not waste time on them. The exuberant "biomorfic" paradise is the place of death, hostile to biological life, which can be seen in a symbolic description of Eden-Olympia greens:

> Decorative gardens in the formal French style surrounded the pathway, refreshed by an irrigation system that left the brickwork perpetually damp. But the shrubs and flowering plants seemed pallid and defeated, the ground beneath them so crammed with electronic ducting that no roots could prosper. Together they awaited their deaths, ready to be replaced by the month's end (ibid.: 133).

At the beginning of this subchapter I mentioned *Vermilion Sands*, a book showing the near future in such an exaggerated manner that in parts it seems grotesque.[44] All the stories in this collection are set in Vermilion Sands, an imaginary luxurious costal resort and the quintessence of the affluence of Western culture. A favourite exotic village of millionaires, successful bank managers and movie stars, Vermilion Sands becomes a Mecca for all kinds of artists who try to live on the tourist trade and gullible sponsors. They create and sell such bizarre works as singing statues, photosensitive paintings, cloud-sculptures, bio-fabric clothes, psychotropic houses or mutated musical flora. Decadent, full of galleries, casinos and exhibition halls, the village suffers from beach fatigue, psycho crimes and depression. This strange milieu breeds neurosis, artists recreate half-forgotten psychic traumas, and the works of art reveal their troubled unconscious.

In this respect *Vermilion Sands* is a Freudian text, which juxtaposes the interior world of the human psyche and its exterior manifestations. Moreover, in each story different narrators seem to follow similar, compulsive patterns of behaviour, as if forced to do this by some external power. One may argue that, in fact, they become projections of the unconscious of the text (similarly to the way in each story works of art are being treated as projections of the suppressed part of the characters' minds).[45] In the cityscape of the future, deranged inhabitants indulge in re-enactment of the past—and this is how Ballard imagines the urban life to come.

---

rouses us (Ballard 1997a: 245).

44. Written decades before *Cocaine Nights* and *Super-Cannes* it is much more good-humoured: sometimes Ballard describes his ideas about social problems in the near future and sometimes he just mocks his friends, avant-garde artists in the "real" 1960s.

45. I have analyzed the influence of surrealism in *Vermilion Sands* in detail in my essay "Persistence of Memory: Surrealism in *Vermilion Sands* by J.G. Ballard" in *Acta Philologica*, Warsaw 2003, pp. 107- 118. There the reader can find more arguments and examples proving J.G. Ballard's interest in the surrealist and Dadaist art. In the present study I am going to come back to analyzing *Vermilion Sands* in the last chapter.

At the end of the previous chapter I discussed a single short story by Ballard—namely, "War Fever"—to show in miniature the most important features of his war fiction. As far as the descriptions of cityscapes are concerned, such a short story is "The Ultimate City" as in this fantastic narrative set after the decline of urban civilization Ballard signals all the most important facets of urban life. In the apparently idyllic post-industrial Garden City, and in a number of similarly small, self-sufficient villages, "the first scientifically advanced agrarian society" lives quietly on ecological energy and things they grow and manufacture themselves. Populations are not numerous, people are well-educated, peace-loving vegetarians not at the least interested in gigantic steel and concrete metropolises abandoned somewhere in a distance. Nevertheless, for some members of these communities, like the protagonist, Holloway: "the whole bucolic landscape of Garden City, this elegant but toy-like world of solar sails and flower-filled gardens, the serene windmills and gently nodding reduction gear of the tidal-power machines—all these cried for a Pearl Harbour" (Ballard 2002b: 875).

For such people deserted cities do have enormous latent power, "the scale and character of the cityscape… had all the archaic strength" (ibid.: 881). Having finally gotten to a gigantic metropolis full of cars, pieces of machinery, empty high-rises, institutions and streets, Holloway feels that he has found home, the real place humanity belongs in. Characteristically, his coming to terms with the cityscape's psychic role happens inside a derelict car he spends the night in: "a fitting womb to guard his passage from the open transits of the sky to the hard and immobile concrete" (ibid.: 881).

The story narrates Holloway's abortive attempt to revive the city: to power, people and set into motion one small district of the metropolis. With the help of a few misplaced fellow city dwellers and a group of agrarian runaway teenagers he conducts his urban experiment. Yet it ends in an outburst of disruptive aggression the city life triggered. Nevertheless, he does prove the enormous latent appeal cities have and, indirectly, the aggressive and self-immolating character of Western urban civilization, with the indulgence in violence and crime that overpopulation brings about.

The city Holloway tries to resurrect is full of cars; approximately five millions vehicles of every kind and model in surprisingly good condition are there to clean and drive fast—which is what agrarian youths have always dreamt of. Cars are objects of desire and strange obsessions. Olds, one of the characters, renovates them and creates a museum of every model of automobile ever produced: other characters heap disused cars to form gigantic monuments of the bygone twentieth century and it is from the car and by the car that people are killed and injured. Cars prompt a rediscovery of the psychopathologies of urban life: a Hell's-Angel-like Stillman, Holloway's alter ego who does all Holloway is afraid of thinking about, drives fast along empty streets and purposefully destroys and assaults shop-window mannequins resembling the long-departed inhabitants of the city. These acts of random and senseless violence, "this dream come true of the violent city" (ibid.: 910) appeal to everybody and wake latent instincts. As soon as the possibility arises Stillman forms a blood-thirsty motorized gang that the teenagers are very eager to join and, like his true uncanny double,[46] soon destroys everything Holloway has built.

The short life of this revived enclave of urban civilization shows all the problems of contemporary cityscapes and to narrate its stormy history Ballard uses his favourite intertext: William Shakespeare's *The Tempest*.[47] Stillman, the deranged murderer and the psychopath is a modern Caliban, the true inheritor of the nightmarish urban civilization, who, sentenced for murder, is set free thanks to the parole of a Prospero-like "Mr Buckmaster, Viceroy, czar, and warden of this island" (ibid.: 895), who "had been the last of the great entrepreneur-industrialists, part architect and engineer, part visionary" (ibid.: 897).

Buckmaster used to plan super-cities, "conurbation conglomerates, the mega-metropolis" and his art is strong, but after the collapse of gasoline-based civilization he had chosen to bury it. Together with his daughter Miranda they live in empty cities, he constructs elaborate shrines for them, she plants flowers trying to hasten the reclamation of cityscapes by nature. Buckmaster is helped by "an excited faun, an automobile Ariel" (ibid.: 891), Olds and, for some time, he forces Stillman to work for him: "[Stillman's] deference to the old industrialist seemed to prevent him from assaulting Miranda" (ibid.: 900). The arrival of Holloway upsets the delicate balance of power and he has to decide which party to join: the lover of violence and speed or the sage commemorating the end of the urban era. He inclines to both Stillman and Buckman, and his decision symbolically renders the dilemma our civilization has to resolve.

"The Ultimate City" shows the most important aspects of life within cityscapes: the way urban car-friendly architecture alters the countryside, the subliminal influence of life in cities on the human mind, the violence and aggression it triggers and the symbiosis of motorization and urbanism. Moreover, in discussing societies of the near future Ballard claims that idyllic high-tech villages where nothing ever happens will breed neuroses and never answer unconscious human needs.

In his novels depicting cityscapes: *High-Rise, Concrete Island, Crash* and to some extent *Super-Cannes, Cocaine Nights, The Atrocity Exhibition, Hello America* and *Vermilion Sands*, Ballard puts forward similar concerns and arrives at similar conclusions: *Grave New World* is addicted to cities because only in a nightmarish urban environment can our violent and masochistic instincts be externalized. One of the most important aspects of social life under late capitalism is the way the mass-media rule our lives and change the cityscapes into mediascapes.

---

46. By his double I mean the externalization of the drives and impulses which Holloway hides and represses. Thus in a sense Stillman is Holloway—see Freud's "The Uncanny".

47. Ballard uses the scheme taken from his play in *Concrete Island, The Drought* and also, to a certain extent in *High-Rise* (see David Pringle's interpretation of this last novel discussed earlier in this chapter).

CHAPTER FOUR:
MEDIASCAPES

"People use mental formulas that they've learned from TV. Even in ordinary conversation, if you're talking to the mechanic at the garage… you and he probably talk in a way that his equivalent thirty years ago would never have done. You use—not catch phrases, but verbal formulas. Suddenly you realize you're hearing echoes of some public-information, accident-prevention commercial. It's uncanny" (Vale 2005: 83), Ballard remarks in a recent interview showing his concern for the influence mass-media have on a contemporary subject. This problem is one of the recurrent themes in all his literary output: the *Grave New World* he describes is a land of mass culture abundant in cross-cutting messages invading the human mind: images on billboards, random fragments of TV shows, commercials and all the rest. In *Hello America*[1] mass culture and its icons are the heart of Western civilization—and after its collapse only they are remembered.

TV and other audiovisual media in Ballard's fiction not only give people models to follow, but they also shape the way people perceive reality, the result being that what is not on screen does not count. For above all TV is power in the most down-to-earth meaning of the term. In *High-Rise, Rushing to Paradise* and *Millennium People*, for example, the few who can make their way to the millions of TV screens all over the world manipulate public opinion and thus influence politics and various aspects of social life. The ever hungry TV networks hunt for interesting coverage and therefore, like in *The Day of Creation*, nothing can happen without sooner or later being televised.[2]

Being on TV is, moreover, proof of being real: only mediated images indeed exist, as our culture values simulacra so very highly. Here again Ballard's and Baudrillard's ideas converge. Being watched is being real, which in an interesting way upsets the traditional power-structure (one of the subjects of *Running Wild*). As in *Discipline and Punish* by Michel Foucault, where he describes the 18th-century idea of a panopticon, "watching" usually connotes being in control and exercising power, while "being watched" is synonymous with weakness. The Orwellian Big Brother watches you and you try to escape his gaze. But nowadays, Ballard tells us, the situation is reversed: the screens no longer watch us, we watch them and dream of becoming one of their images:

> It's as if there's a deeply masochistic strain in the population-at-large: that we want to be watched by close-circuit television cameras. It's an extension of that whole web-cam thing: we want to be observed.

> There's a very popular television program running here called *Big Brother*. Now, what is extraordinary is: the people who take part, thrive... We like exposing ourselves to the merciless all-knowing gaze of these cameras. We want to be watched. This is Orwell's "Big Brother" nightmare come true, but in an unexpected way— far from fearing Big Brother, we revel in that sort of exposure (ibid.: 27-28).

---

1. A novel which in a sense is a longer version of "The Ultimate City" with its adolescent protagonist who in the post-industrial near future re-discovers our civilization.
2. Talking about this novel Ballard says: "I was interested in the way in which the media landscape has now wrapped its umbrella around the world, and how it redefines reality as itself so that nothing can happen in the world without some TV crew arriving at the spot and immediately becoming part of the unique experience which is unfolding" (Vale 2005: 173).

This thought is elaborated upon in many of Ballard's narratives ("The Intensive Care Unit", "Report from an Obscure Planet", subplots of *The Day of Creation*, *Millennium People* and even of *The Kindness of Women* where one of the protagonist's friends is a TV celebrity). In his narratives concerned with the media and their impact on social life Ballard presents a range of commentaries and divagations elaborating on this phenomenon: from mild observations that Mickey Mouse and John Wayne are going to be all we leave behind for the next generations (*Hello America*), to alarming scenarios. In books such as *Running Wild* or *Millennium People* the unnatural conditions of life in the environment of TV screens and abortive interpersonal relations result in psychopathology and violence.

In *The Atrocity Exhibition* the best known of Ballard's novels dealing with mediascape, we see a multiplicity of images reflected in the deranged mind of the protagonist, a person who unsuccessfully but ceaselessly tries to make sense of media reality and to discover a new syntax that would structure the flow of random bits of data into a message. In this difficult text the abundance of media coverage results in the death of affect, our inability to grasp the emotive meaning of images. Here the parallel is with Frederic Jameson, who in his studies of post-modern culture discusses "the waning of affect" best depicted by Pop Art.

In my presentation of the Ballardian mediascape, apart from Baudrillard and Jameson I will also refer to Susan Sontag, who in her "Pornographic Imagination" analyzes how art renders extreme experiences.[3] Talking about obscene imagery in avant-garde texts (and *The Atrocity Exhibition* does have such instances) Sontag says: "[i]t's towards the gratifications of death, succeeding and surpassing those of eros, that every truly obscene quest tends" (Sontag 1982: 224). The extremity of death is precisely what the inhabitants of *Grave New World* crave, which introduces intertextual allusions to Sigmund Freud and his theory of the death-instinct to the Ballardian description of mediascapes.

The Land of Mass Culture

In describing our reliance on television and the results for culture that such a reliance is going to have, Ballard often alludes to his own early fiction and the disaster story tradition. The allusions are auto-ironic and have the character of a conscious intertextual game with his readers. For example, in *Hello America* (1981) an apparently catastrophic scenario and future setting serve to show mass-oriented entertainment as a crux of the cultural identity of the contemporary West. Ballard combines elements of a pastiche with a deeper reflection concerning Western society at the close of the twentieth century.

In *Hello America* the catastrophe is only a pretext to examine the cultural concept of America.[4] In the 1980s and 1990s energy resources ran out and

3. Sontag enumerates instances of extreme imagination in the contemporary world: the artist's, the erotoman's, the madman's and the leftist revolutionary's. Of all these Ballardian protagonists are not leftist revolutionaries.

4. America in Ballard's novels is synonymous with mass-culture audiovisual media. In *Empire of the*

our civilization found itself deprived of oil. Global recession and the decline of transport and industry followed, in result of which the American continent was abandoned, with its population re-emigrating to Europe and Asia. The damming of the Bering Straits warmed the Arctic Circle, and that in turn revitalized northern Europe and Siberia. Unfortunately, the consequences of such climatic engineering were calamitous for America. The entire geopolitical map changed and: "[b]y the year 2030, the American continent had been totally abandoned, its teeming cities empty and silent. The government and nation of the United States ceased to exist" (Ballard 1983: 48).

Hello America starts many years after this exodus. A group of people whose families had to leave America a few generations earlier, embark on a journey back. The *SS Apollo*—named in the memory of the space age—has the mission of checking the safety of old American nuclear plants. The journey attracts misfits who cannot stop thinking about the continent of their fathers and who dream old dreams. They manage to come back and, once in America, they are half-dazzled by the surreal landscapes of empty cities where remainders of our culture and desert wildlife mingle. They roam about absorbing the images that seem to fit their psyches and finally decide to go west, following the steps of their forefathers. Ruled by their unconscious drives, they seem inert and mannequin-like.

The book's protagonist is named Wayne (after his crazy mother's favourite actor), a boy whose alleged father, a Dr Flaming who disappeared during the previous expedition to America, is aware that "their only loyalty was to their own dreams, and to the needs of their nerve-endings" (ibid.: 57). The dreams in question are themselves echoes of American myths. Wayne dreams of finding his father, of becoming the president of the US and of reviving America. His plan to destroy the Bering Straits Dam is pure fantasy, but, as Wayne puts it in his diary, "The first settlers to cross America were driven by their fantasies too" (ibid.: 93).

Sun Shanghai in the early 1940s is a very advanced city—the city of American mass-culture. Jim grows up surrounded with numerous fictions that his peers in England never heard of. He listens to the Flash Gordon radio serial on the station XMHA and his heroes are Batman and Buck Rogers. Even before the war the cultural power of both the British Empire and Japan gives way to America. The image of England Jim has is the one of a small wet country full of rolling meadows where he will have to go to study. American goods, entertainment and comic strips have much greater appeal for him—until the war with all its excitement comes. The novel starts with Jim's dreams of wars: fed on newsreels of the European war the boy's imagination transforms the city around him and the descriptions of the life there intermingle with films, dreams, theatre and masquerades. Immense portraits of Chiang Kai-Shek in neon lights remind the boy of images from the cinema. "The whole of Shanghai was turning into a newsreel leaking from inside his head" (Ballard 1985c: 5).

Jim's attitude to reality is basically one of disbelief and the world around seems to him a gigantic show, a masquerade or a film. In Shanghai a lot of films are being made and many servants work part-time as extras, so at the moment of the attack on Pearl Harbour he "almost expected Yang to saunter in... and tell him that they were part of a technicolour epic being staged at the Shanghai film studios" (Ballard 1985c: 35). The unreal character of the city is emphasized by the gigantic screen of a street cinema showing the immense faces of the actors playing in *Gone with the Wind*, the favourite film of Chinese city-dwellers.

The American landscapes as seen by Wayne and his friends are the embodiments of dreams. The first glance upon the American shore makes them conclude that the continent is paved with gold. What later turns out to be heaps of decades-old rust resembles treasures "beyond the dreams of Columbus, Cortez and the conquistadores" (ibid.: 23). The allusions to the renaissance conquerors are not accidental. Ballard recreates the mood of hope, possibilities and ambition —which seem absurd in the situation of the *Apollo* crew, but nevertheless are psychologically plausible.

Images of the desert in the streets of New York, the empty White House, drained swimming-pools, motorways leading nowhere, colourful commercials in the middle of the forest and baboons nestling in Cadillacs, give the book a surreal quality whose major technique is that of collage. Ballard juxtaposes emblems of America known from innumerable films and iconic presentations with post-apocalyptic wildlife. The best example of such a technique is the scene when the ship sails nears the drowned Statue of Liberty:

> Lying on her back beside the ship, like its drowned bride, was the statue of an immense reclining woman. Almost as long as the Apollo she rested on a bed of concrete blocks, the ruins of an underwater plinth. Her classical features were only a few feet below the surface. Washed by the waves, her grey face reminded Wayne of his dead mother... she must be some kind of goddess... a local marine deity... (ibid.: 20).

This description, apart from placing an American icon in a new and shocking context, is in itself an allusion to mass culture. The motif of finding the destroyed Statue of Liberty comes from the popular catastrophe film *Planet of the Apes*. Similar intertextual quotes of lowbrow art show that collective memories of characters derive from popular culture. The America they remember or recognize in *déja-vu*-like illuminations, belongs in pulp fiction. Moreover, Ballard's characters are aware of the fact that their perceptions are blurred by some innate (not to say unconscious) vision of America: "Or, for that matter, what exactly we signify by the term America. It is an emotive symbol, Wayne, went out of fashion in the 1980s and 1990s, somehow lost its appeal" (ibid.: 171), one of the characters explains to Wayne. The boy starts to understand their complex relationship to the past, and to the symbol of America. In his diary he defines the real purpose of the expedition as "the attempt to find that special America inside each one of us, that golden coast..." Therefore, the continent they see is only partly material; the descriptions blend objective reality with the subjective landscapes of the mind.

The journey West in *Hello America* is a pilgrimage, and the pilgrims encounter the American icons they always dreamed of. What is significant is that American myths and dreams are translated into visual forms. The characters were fed with pictures of America all their lives and now, back on the continent, they again encounter copies and reflections of the phantoms they keep in their minds. Even before coming to America, they think about it in terms of images that they recognize later: "the illustrations of the Cape Kennedy Space Center, the Space Shuttle landing at Edwards Air Force Base after a test flight and the recovery of an *Apollo* capsule from the Pacific… the crowded streets of Washington on President Carter's Inauguration Day, long queues of holiday jets on the runways of Kennedy Airport…" (ibid.: 10-11).

America is pictorial and turns itself into pictures. The greatest dreams (one of which is the Moon conquest) are embodied in images deeply rooted in our minds. The analysis of the American landscape turns into anatomizing American dreams. In *Hello America*, Ballard concentrates on descriptions of the collages made of a post-apocalyptic wilderness, emblems, icons and inter-textual echoes of texts from popular culture. His America is a gigantic theme park covered with dust and sand. Wayne is able to understand that the quintessence of his idea of this Promised Land is a kitschy Western film; "[h]e realized that the whole secret logic of their journey across America had been leading them to this absurd and childish confrontation in a theme park frontier street, in a make-believe world already overtaken by a second arid West" (ibid.: 99).

The crew travels west surrounded by a world made of mass-cultural bric-a-brac. Anne Summers, a member of the group, is gradually becoming a Hollywood starlet or a TV celebrity. She wears heavy make-up, behaves in doll-like fashion and, later in the book, is compared either to actresses or to Jackie Kennedy. All the time we watch her from the outside, as if on the screen. Ballard writes *Hello America* in a very impersonal, descriptive style; he makes his text cinematic. Such a technique of showing rather than explaining things is, firstly, suitable for comments on a culture obsessed with screens and icons, and, secondly, convenient from the point of view of psychology. Ballard tries to reproduce dream-experiences in his dream-text; therefore, his concentrations is on awkward collages and not on psychological insights.

This surreal and impersonal technique invites associations with psychoanalysis, or to be precise, with the Freudian analysis of dreams. The basic Freudian model for the manifest and latent content of dreams very well suits Ballard's novel, in which action is scarce and monotonous, dramatic scenes read like clichés of old films, and the predominant form is description. Moreover, said descriptions are very dense, as they comprise heterogeneous symbols whose meaning needs decoding—just as in the Freudian concept of the dream-work.[5]

Images of golden cities, laser shows producing the phantoms of Mickey Mouse or Hollywood actors over the desert, huge predators in the city streets and Indians on camels camping in deserted lots—this invites us to recreate the underlying dream-world. What is implied is a potent cultural apparatus that produces such images. The dreams described by Ballard are dreamt collectively: it is not the personal experience of the characters of *Hello America* that produced them. Thrillers, Westerns, science fiction movies, adverts and newsreels infiltrated the collective imagination of the characters' predecessors

5. Compare Chapter One and the discussion of psychoanalysis.

and now haunt their dreams. Freud describes this phenomenon in *An Outline of Psychoanalysis*:

> Furthermore, dreams bring to light material which cannot have originated either from the dreamer's adult life, or from his forgotten childhood. We are obliged to regard it as part of the archaic heritage which a child brings to the world, before any experience of its own, influenced by the experience of his ancestors (Freud 1986: 399).

Ballard toys with the notion of this "heritage"—for not only does the crew carry in their minds their own dream Americas inherited from their ancestors, but there is also a small native population whose nomadic culture is rooted in the half-forgotten twentieth-century mass-culture. Torn from their original contexts, bits and pieces of mediascape messages are intermingled and used to form haphazard collages which give a transformed new vision of reality and also reveal hidden meanings of mass culture.[6]

Thus *Hello America* gives such a synthetic vision of mediascape as fulfills our unconscious needs: after the era of mass culture ends what is left is nostalgia. In the empty continent peopled by echoes and memories Wayne misses twentieth century-like mass culture: junk food and popular entertainment. He dreams about reviving the old American life style, about re-opening hamburger-bars, drug stores and drive-in-cinemas.[7] One of the most uncanny sections of the book describes his attempts to resurrect the ghosts of past fun. For instance, when the expedition reaches Las Vegas and finds the new military regime of a usurper president and his young Mexican troops Wayne decides to join them. His new job is to entertain the young Mexican soldiers. He offers them Elvis Presley, Hollywood classics and Coca-Cola, the American icons that come from his innermost dreams. The ruins, overgrown by the jungle and illuminated by neon light images of long-dead stars, seem grotesque and scary.

The psychopath president (whose name, not accidentally, is Manson) knows the uncanny appeal of popular culture with its half-forgotten images. Although his degenerate contemporaries, the Indians, do not consciously remember

6. "Collage may be seen as a practice that is programmatically indeterminate, disrupting the boundaries between the work and the frame, the conscious and the unconscious, art and life. But Breton's emphasis on combination—the attainment of two separate realities—also implies the possibility of synthesis, an overcoming of divisions into a higher sur-reality" (Gasiorek 2005: 79), writes Gasiorek. In the light of this statement Ballard's America is a synthesis of 20th-century culture, and a higher "truth" about our world is revealed. An example of such a collage is the proto-culture of the "natives". The mock-Indian tribes are named after stereotypical features of American cities. The Executives live around Manhattan, the Professors in Boston, the Gangsters in Chicago, the Gays in San Francisco, and the Divorcees in Reno. Their customs, legends, folklore and ritual costumes also refer to twentieth-century clichés, and the all prevailing presence of old billboards makes the Indians name their children after brand products, Indian names are GM, Xerox, or Pepsodent.

7. In his analysis of postmodernism, Jameson points out the affiliation of cinema and "the nostalgia mode" (Jameson 1984: 66), films popular in the end of the last century, "cannibalize" styles of the past making use of the nostalgic feelings which are in the air.

twentieth-century American icons, the revived representations invoke in their minds blurred, latent memories. Neither remembered nor fully forgotten, old pictures provoke irrational fear among the last children of the once powerful nation. Manson takes advantage of this when he wants to defend Las Vegas against nomadic tribes. His technicians prepare gigantic laser shows, in which the figures of enormous cowboys played by John Wayne, Henry Fonda and Gary Cooper are projected on the sky above the desert. An immense Mickey Mouse, coke-bottle and a space ship follow the Hollywood stars, as the whole reservoir of mass-cultural emblems is played out in a laser horror show. The Indians are awed and incorporate the images into their folklore.

A similar technique of producing horror effects by echoing and mimicking long dead stars is used once again at the moment when the expedition enters Las Vegas and in one of the luxurious casinos finds Frank Sinatra, Judy Garland and Dean Martin entertaining an affluent audience. Only later do the ghosts prove to be automata made to reproduce true American heroes.[8] Echoes and repetitions of old days and old looks form the core of Ballard's book. Images spread by mass communication infiltrate our minds and start to define our cultural identity. This is rendered metaphorically in Wayne's search for his identity and his father: "Was his obsession with America, which his unknown ancestors abandoned a century earlier, merely an attempt to find his true father?" (Ballard 1983: 14) asks Ballard in truly Freudian fashion. Therefore, we are indebted to the mediascape for our identity and this dependence has already infiltrated the collective unconscious of Western civilization: we believe and absorb images—especially on TV.

Television and the new sensitivity it introduced to our life may end in a new type of culture, whose beginnings we may already observe. The future society of the highly technological and affluent Western civilization might consist of millions of isolated individuals who never enter into any direct contact with each other. Closed in their rooms equipped with numerous screens and cameras, members of such a society communicate with the outside world via television only. In "The Intensive Care Unit" (1977) Ballard describes a future family whose children, born by artificial insemination, and parents never meet each other in person. The father is a doctor, whose practice is also mediated by cameras and computers. The mother is a masseuse meeting her clients on TV channels. Their unusual idea to meet each other in person ends in total disaster: unaccustomed to the physical presence of other human beings they attack each other.

8. It is worth noticing that the motif of automata built to replace old time American celebrities is an intertextual allusion to Philip K. Dick, the classic science fiction writer. In his novel *We Can Build You* (1972) Dick described a future paranoid USA, where ingenious technicians build replicas of old American presidents whose wisdom and honesty are the only hope for the nation. In *Hello America*, the theme of androids is further developed in the final scenes of the novel, when Wayne encounters a half-crazy engineer who lives in a deserted hall and spends his days constructing automata. His name is Dr Fleming, just like Wayne's lost father: "On the far side of the floor, Dr Fleming was drilling his Presidents. They were drawn up in four ranks and listened impassively as they each took it in turn to stand at the front and speak to the others. Lincoln presented the Gettysburg Address; FDR promised a new deal; Jack Kennedy pledged to put a man on the Moon; Nixon; rambled evasively about his missing tapes" (Ballard 1983: 172).

Human contact is dangerous. Latent and incestuous violent drives, along with the uncivilized egos of otherwise cultured people, are exposed. Television, now advanced to the status of the highest level of social development, screens people from each other and the underlying assumption is that our own biological selves may prove unacceptable. In the world pictured in Ballard's story all human perception is shaped by technology: the only intimacy possible is that of the zoom lens: people come to each other in the form of stylized TV selves, made-up and presented in a chosen guise:

> [W]e had moved from the earnestness of Bergman and the more facile mannerisms of Fellini and Hitchcock to the classical serenity and wit of René Clair and Marx Ophuls, though the children, with their love of the hand-held camera, still resembled so many budding Godards (Ballard 2002b: 950).

Living in a culture of images and of indirect contact with reality teaches people to respond to visual stimuli only. Stylized images of persons and places zoomed and cut in an interesting way replace any knowledge of the world. In "The Intensive Care Unit" and in "Motel Architecture" (1978), another story happening in a similar society, people do not recognize the real objects whose images they know so well. The protagonist of the former story is shocked by the smallness of his wife, whom he has always known from the TV screen in zooms. The character in the latter is even more alienated. Living for decades in a solarium equipped with the numerous screens, he knows the world through nature films, social documentaries and instructive programmes. His job is that of a TV critic and he spends his days analyzing frames of his favourite film *Psycho* by Hitchcock and admiring their geometrical abstractness. Culture has grown so detached from experience that the old films cease to mean anything for the viewers—new soundtracks are introduced or the frames are perceived as abstract art. Over time the protagonist grows so immersed in abstractness and so unaware of any life outside the screen that he develops a strange obsession. He believes he is being followed by an intruder whose physical presence scares him and who turns out to be his own biological body, strange and repulsive in its rhythms, smells and gravity.

It is via cameras and screens that we communicate not only with each other, but also with our own needs and desires—Ballard elaborates upon this thesis in his novels *Rushing to Paradise* (1994) and *Millennium People* (2003). In both novels television (and, to a lesser degree, other media) are the most important single factor shaping human lives. In *Rushing to Paradise* the charismatic madwoman, Dr Barbara, is from the very start camera conscious—she takes a camcorder to all the protests and demonstrations she takes part in. The novel is a story of her attempt to build a utopian society on Saint-Esprit, a nuclear test island and a unique ecological site where albatrosses nest. In fact, it is because of a video film of French soldiers shooting at her companion Neil aired on all the world's TV channels that they are allowed to plant a colony on Saint-Esprit at all.

Neil learns to understand the quasi-supernatural power of films and screens—whatever is mediated and changed into image starts to exist for real and enters the consciousness of millions of people.

Filming the ruined albatross nests trodden by soldiers' boots he already feels he is recording "a well-rehearsed scene in the theatre of protest" (Ballard 1995a: 22), while during his convalescence (the French shot him in the foot) he enjoys his five minutes of fame. The amateur films from Saint-Esprit are an enormous success in all Western countries and, during his convalescence, Neil feels like a celebrity—his life acquires a new meaning, he becomes more real. Happily enough he is aware of the illusionary power of the media and can hence detachedly observe the successes of Dr Barbara, who uses her moment of fame to gather money and enthusiasts for the sanctuary at Saint-Esprit. In her campaign the most important role is again given to the media: she knows that as long as the world is watching them with interest, the colonists will get all the help they need. Therefore, her ideological agenda is subject to the technical means of communication and, ultimately, the two become inseparable. Dr Barbara explains: "There'll be a satellite dish on board to link the film crew to the TV station here. Try to imagine it—everyone will see us reclaim that dead nuclear island and give it back to the living world" (ibid.: 42).

Dr Barbara proves a skillful manipulator of the power of the media. Once her aims are reached and she has her community of isolated colonists in her power she knows how to subjugate them by cutting off links with the outside world. No longer interested in saving the albatross she takes to her feminist plan of creating a female society and her inmates, once they are not filmed and watched all over the world, feel unreal and passive, all their ideologies evaporate when they are not on TV.

Similarly, TV and the Internet shape the world of *Millennium People*. Television spreads the news and publicizes the psychopathic murders and the bomb attacks which take place in London one summer at the turn of the millennium—even though they take place in the same city where viewers live. The Internet serves not only to provide sources of information but also functions as the "conscience" of the nation: all past sins are recorded here and may thus be found out. Television is also the moral and intellectual judge of whatever is going on. Numerous experts explain everything in all possible contexts and predict future events. The narrator (who used to be a media expert on psychology) is very critical of their opinions because he knows that in television you have to repeat clichés in order to be listened to.[9]

The characters react in their own way to the hegemonic role of the media, namely by forcibly seizing the BBC house. For more than sixty years, according

9. One cannot ultimately "tell the truth" on TV as TV jargon is not compatible with the complexity of real life problems: "As expected, the journalists had missed the point. They blamed the revolt on the deep dissatisfaction of the baby-boomer generation, a self-indulgent and over-educated class unable to hold their own against a younger age-group thrusting their way into the professions. Pundits, backbench MPs, even a Home Office junior minister offered similar pearls" (Ballard 2004: 149), says the narrator.

to them, the *BBC* had played a leading role in brainwashing the middle-class: "it imposed an ideology of passivity and self-restraint" (ibid.: 150). The impact of the media on culture and morality is shown via the example of the influential TV series, *A Neuroscientist Looks at God* (to which the narrator, who is a psychologist, had once contributed), which provided viewers with easy answers to the most difficult religious questions. Again, only a psychopath can understand the social implication of such spiritual emptiness. "The gods have died... we emerge from a void, stare back at it for a short while, and then rejoin the void" (ibid.: 261), the psychotic Dr Gould says to the narrator, explaining the popularity of televized metaphysics.

Ballard's series of stories concerned with the hegemony of audiovisual media and the growing unreality of contemporary life ends with the most extreme vision in "Report from an Obscure Planet" (1992). In this story we have a short glimpse of the Earth viewed from a cosmic distance. The planet in the early twenty-first century is empty and maintained by computer networks only. All humans have entered virtual reality, which allows them to pursue all their psychopathologies. When TV proved not good enough:

> Driven by the need for a more lifelike replica of the scenes of carnage that most entertained them, the people of this unhappy world had invented an advanced and apparently interiorised version of their TV screens, a virtual replica of reality in which they could act out their most deviant fantasies... Here they could assume any identity, create and fulfil any desire, and explore the most deviant dreams (Ballard 2002b: 1186).

The Power of the Screen

He who controls the mediascape has political power and personal charisma: a camera in the hand is for Ballardian characters often a sign of success and dominance. The big and physically strong character of *High-Rise*, Wilder (whom I have briefly discussed in the previous chapter) is additionally a TV journalist, and thus stands for the media: the aggressive power of contemporary society, which both shows and promotes violence. One of the *leitmotifs* of *High-Rise* is a TV documentary Wilder plans to shoot—his report about the hazards of life in high-rises. Wilder carries his film camera with him everywhere, even in the days of total regress and chaotic skirmishes he is always seen with this prop: broken and useless it symbolizes his status. The hegemonic position of the media in contemporary society is emphasized in the book in the way that television is omnipresent in the building (just like everywhere in the civilized world). But gradually people start watching their TVs with the sound down. Afraid not to hear what is going on in the lobbies and corridors they move in and out of each other's apartments and everywhere there are silent images on TV screens. All the channels at the same time broadcast an attempted prison breakout: everywhere to be seen are faces of inmates and police.

The parallels between the situation of the prisoners and of the people crowded in the building are apparent to everybody. Interestingly, it is when Wilder is temporarily away on location shooting scenes of prison unrest that he sees the similarities of prisons and high-rises and the idea of the high-rise documentary is born. Gradually, life inside the building grows too strange and savage for any communication with the outside world and the inhabitants switch off their TVs and the programs that "were transmissions from another planet" (Ballard 1975: 126). From this moment the power of the media is replaced by sheer physical force.

The characters of *Crash* also live surrounded by simulacra: newsreels shape their ideas about life on Earth, glossy magazines and TV shows teach them about the world, pornography and violent entertainment stir their imagination and road propaganda and commercials manipulate their desires and fears. Even a quasi-erotic fascination that Vaughan provokes in both "Ballard" and his wife can be explained by the fact that he used to be a TV celebrity, a successful presenter of scientific programs radiating with charisma. It is the memory of his face on screen that comes first: the experience of actual meeting with him is secondary.

For so many years living on images and fictions, "Ballard" has the overwhelming feeling that his initial crash was the only real experience in his whole life. Only thereafter does he experience "real" reality. "After being bombed endlessly by road-safety propaganda it was almost a relief to find myself in an actual accident" (Ballard 1977: 32). The newsreels of simulated car-crashes so often shown in television seemed to him more real than his own life and entering one of them gave his life a unique glamour and transformed all his relationships with other people. Similarly, Vaughan, many years past his TV prime, wants desperately to re-enter a hyperreal[10] world of images by violent merger with Elizabeth Taylor, a face known from thousands of photos and gigantic blow-ups presiding over the cityscape on billboards.

Vaughan cherishes mediated experience, the world seen through camera lenses. He compulsively films accidents, knows stunt drivers in TV studios, collects photos of auto-pornography, prepares in advance montage collages of future crashes where the victim's sexual organs are mutilated by car parts. Road violence is for him a potent source of entertainment—and other characters cannot help being excited by it either. In the world described in the novel, a world divorced from traditional morals, no one pretends violence is not arousing. Moreover, a popular form of entertainment is the re-enactment of collisions. Thus, Vaughan takes "Ballard" to watch the staging of "a multiple pile-up in which seven people had died on the North Circular Road during the previous summer" (ibid.: 72). They also visit a film studio where an actress is being prepared to playact in a spectacular simulation of collision. During her make-up session "she was already assuming the postures of a crash victim, her fingers weakly touching the streaks of carmine resin on her knees, thighs delicately raised from

10. "It is the generation by models of a real without origin or reality: a hyperreal" (Baudrillard 2003: 1)

the plastic seat cover as if flinching from some raw mucous membrane" (ibid.: 93). The simulated violence looks more convincing that the real thing. In the eyes of the characters it possesses some abstract beauty, similar to that of an esthetically satisfying geometrical pattern. Vaughan collects information about famous people who died in cars—Camus, Jayne Mansfield, J.F. Kennedy—and dreams about duplicating their crashes, which would become works of art far more satisfying than reality.

"Ballard" is under Vaughan's spell. Thanks to this friend and the experience of the actual crash he feels he is approaching a deeper understanding of his world, his life, and other people. One of the most revealing experiences for him is watching the film of a simulated collision whose production he witnessed in the studio. In a flash of illumination he realizes that human life can only be a blurred reflection of these simulacra.

> As we watched, our own ghostly images stood silently in the background, hands and faces unmoving while this slow-motion collision was re-enacted. The dream-like reversal of roles made us seem less real than the mannequins in the car (ibid.: 110).

As compared with the film, "Ballard's" everyday experience of his world of cars, speed, chance sexual encounters and endless travels in a confined area seems irrelevant. Violence on screen excites him and the only thing he can think of is re-enactment of the postures and gestures of this spectacle. Violence and sexuality go together as they give the illusions of real experience: the return to biological identities, the past of fear and survival instincts. Such a feeling is illusory, because sex in the novel is an abstract ritual. Immediately after watching the film he duplicates in his mind "a series of sexual postures between Vaughan and myself, Helen Remington and Gabrielle which would re-enact the death-ordeals of the mannequins and the fibreglass motorcyclist (ibid.: 111)". In her discussion of pornographic art in "The Pornographic Imagination", Susan Sontag makes a remark which sheds some light on such a propensity for having violent sexual fantasies:

> Human sexuality is... a highly questionable phenomenon, and belongs, at least potentially, among extreme rather than the ordinary experiences of humanity. Tamed as it may be, sexuality remains one of the demonic forces in human consciousness— pushing us at intervals close to taboo and dangerous desires, which range from the impulse to commit sudden arbitrary violence upon another person to the voluptuous yearning for the extinction of one's consciousness, for death itself (Sontag 1982: 222).

In the world full of images all is momentary and superficial. "Ballard" in the novel is a commercial feature-film producer. In the studios of Shepperton he creates one-minute long films advertising cars. These high-budget productions cause him to meet Hollywood stars and spend his working hours in a totally artificial world of make-believe. The commercials on television and the adverts on billboards are the most powerful medium of communication in the novel— they are omnipresent and persuade the characters that the world they live in is only a reflection of the perfect realm within the advertisement. Baudrillard writes:

> Triumph of superficial form, of the smallest common denominator of all signification, degree zero of meaning, triumph of entropy over all possible tropes. The lowest form of energy of the sign. This unarticulated, instantaneous form, without a past, without a future, without the possibility of metamorphosis, has power over all the others. All current forms of activity tend towards advertising and most exhaust themselves therein (Baudrillard 2003: 87).

In *Crash* superficial forms are the only ones left and cultural entropy is the maximum. People live surrounded by texts which invade their minds, but they cannot focus long enough to appreciate any complex messages. The characters dream about violence and excitement in their own lives, and the mediascape (ever full of aggressive imagery) makes them long for the re-enactment of atrocities: "all those scenes of pain and violence that illuminated the margins of our lives" (Ballard 1977: 30). Television shows newsreels of wars and student riots, natural disaster and police brutality—glossy magazines show photos of dead celebrities and famine victims in the Philippines: "the photograph of a swollen corpse that filled a complete page" (ibid.: 46). Baudrillard's idea of a hyperreality—the strange mixture of images that are neither true nor false and abolish both fiction and reality—is here described in detail years before *Simulacra and Simulations* was first published.[11] We see a world of simulation, death, intense sexuality (but no desire, love, fear or hatred), artificial cities, and people acting like androids in a mediascape of violent imagery. Mediated messages precede life and living becomes re-enactment, stylization and duplication devoid of any moral values. Baudrillard writes:

> *Crash* is the first great novel of the universe of stimulation, the one with which we will now be concerned—a symbolic universe, but one which, through a sort of reversal of the mass-mediated

11. Ballard tries not to create fiction (which we already have plenty of) but, paradoxically, reality. This revision makes him one of Jean Baudrillard's favorite science fiction writers. In "Simulacra and Science Fiction", an essay included in *Simulacra and Simulations*, Baudrillard writes: "There is no more double; one is already in the other world, another world which is not another, without mirrors or projection or utopias as means for reflection. The simulation is impassable, unsurpassable, checkmated, without exteriority. We can no longer move "through the mirror" to the other side, as we could during the golden age of transcendence" (Baudrillard 2003: 3). We live in a world so deeply infiltrated by reflections, copies, utopias that there is no "real" to transcend in fiction. In a way we already are inside fiction, which makes the role of a writer, especially a science fiction writer altogether problematic.

substance (neon, concrete, car, erotic machinery), appears as if traversed by an intense force of initiation (Baudrillard 2003: 119).

Interestingly, television and disaster often go together in Ballard's prose. In *The Day of Creation* (1987) he juxtaposes half-mocking allusions to the conventions of catastrophic fiction with the motif of TV as the major social and psychological mechanism at work today. It is a story of the birth and death of a river in the middle of an African desert. Dr Mallory, the protagonist, strongly believes he created the river and sets out on a journey to its source. Mallory is followed by a young black girl and a TV reporter who dreams about restoring his long defunct media career by producing a film about Mallory and his enterprise. In *The Day of Creation* the characters immediately interpret the miraculous appearance of a river according to their own obsessions. Dr Mallory calls it "the Mallory" and claims to be its creator and sole possessor. But as he cannot keep the river to himself he sets out to destroy its sources. Captain Kagwa, a local leader, interprets this as a sign of victory for his military regime and a prophecy of the future prosperity of his land. Sanger, a TV reporter, is the most extreme case—with the help of his camera he actually frames the river, creates it once again by filming its story. The only way to prevent his false representation from spreading and devouring the real river is to destroy it. The final return of dryness and the desert is at the same time the re-assertion of Mallory's control over the territory.

In *The Day of Creation* Ballard describes a contemporary postcolonial no-man's land, apparently to be found on maps, but in fact still waiting to acquire identity and recognition. Somewhere in former French East Africa lies a province "between the borders of Chad, the Sudan and the Central African Republic in the dead heart of the African continent, a land as close to nowhere as the planet could provide" (Ballard 1988: 17). As it is unknown to the global media, and thus not a part of the mediascape, it does not really exist. In order to help the country WHO and Japanese philanthropic organizations must first film it and show it on TV. Therefore the first people sent to the province are fame-seeking Sanger and his Japanese camera crew. For Ballard geography in the contemporary world is subjugated to representation; in order to exist a country has to be transformed into a media icon. Africa is therefore a construct of educational wildlife films—and what is more, to make a new African film one has to multiply already existing imagery:

> I noticed that many of the cassettes consisted of extracts from old-fashioned commercial documentaries, sequences of elephants rolling logs, warriors stamping at the coronation of a paramount chief, bare-breasted women carrying water-pitchers on their heads, and other clichés of the earliest days of the wild-life film. These, Sanger had explained, supplied a useful model for his own films, and a stream of pseudo-authentic footage consonant with the images deeply implanted in the minds of their audiences (ibid.: 175).

The vision of the world in the novel is therefore detached from material reality: what we share and believe in are TV images.[12] Boundaries between fact and fiction blur, the "objective" vision of the world is a fiction mediated and therefore shared by many people. In *The Day of Creation* Ballard pictures a contemporary mind influenced by a strange mixture of stimuli. "Dreams of rivers, like scenes from a forgotten film, drift through the night, in passage between memory and desire" (ibid.: 7), reads the very first sentence of the novel. Mallory starts his narrative by emphasizing the psychic character of his story; born in the mind it resembles images taken from a film, as films shape our perception of the world and are therefore prior to experience.

Dreams of rivers, blurred memories and fragments of self-analysis are interwoven with the events in the story and in a sense the whole narrative becomes a presentation of Mallory's mind. His personality resembles the protagonists of Ballard's previous books, especially Jim, the major character of *Empire of the Sun*, with whom he shares memories of a childhood spent in China. Fictions of different kinds subvert any stable reality presented in the book and Mallory is aware of the fact that his psyche influences the world outside; he even tends to overestimate this impact and to believe he makes things happen by a sheer exercise of will: "I felt as if I had conjured up, not just this miniature river that would irrigate the southern edge of the Sahara, but the entire consumer goods economy which would one day smother the landscape in high-rises, hypermarkets and massage parlours..." (ibid.: 51).

Ironically, this vision of some future prosperity—a modern Eden in the African wilderness—is taken straight from affluent Western civilization, a man-made cityscape. Nature in this novel cannot be approached directly; in order to domesticate it for modern people filmmakers remake it into an acceptable form. Sanger explains this to Mallory by claiming that nature has to be invented to "chime with [people's] secret hopes, their deep-held belief that the universe is a kindly place... Sooner or later everything turns into television" (ibid.: 63). Mallory's escape with the black girl Noon and his quixotic quest for the source of the river is his attempt to defend it as his own invention, a figment of his own mind. Sanger follows him with a camera, and his desperation to film the river may be seen as re-inventing and re-making the Mallory. In the documentary the uniqueness of the Mallory is gone, the river is taken away from Dr Mallory, which is further emphasized in the scenes when a delirious commentator provides an idiotic voice to the film: "his pseudo-scientific prattle assumed that television's flattering revision of nature was an act of creation as significant as the original invention of this great river and its abundant life" (ibid.: 159).

The postcolonial wasteland of a polluted desert full of rubbish needs such an imposition of fiction: it needs to be filmed to exist. Everybody in the area dreams

---

12. Paradoxically, such a process of transforming the real into the filmed is in itself egalitarian, as it concerns all places on Earth. England in this respect is not different than Chad, and the only English icon in the book is a TV celebrity, Princess Diana, after whom the local oil-company workers name a floating bordello. "The plaster goddess with yellow hair who hung below the bowsprit, crudely painted to resemble a future queen of England, dipped up and down on the shallow waves" (Ballard 1988: 59).

about television. The TV picture is prior to the reality filmed, as being on TV means being real. Sanger comes to the area with some charity rice from Japan and a camera crew who are to film the hungry in order to restore his media image. "The prime sites—Ethiopia, Chad, the Sudan—had been allocated to the most powerful television interest, the huge American networks and the British record companies" (ibid.: 35). Therefore he has to make content with a less important, virtually unknown area which is not even starving. Nevertheless, he is welcomed as "Our saviour who brings hope" (ibid.: 30) because he has a camera.

With no hungry to feed, Sanger considers making a documentary on Dr Mallory. He intends to show him as a witch-doctor who has decided to stay in Africa when everybody else was leaving, but only when Dr Mallory wills the river into existence does he see he got his story. The emergence of the Mallory gives him something to re-invent and translate into the language of television. His fiction about Africa competes with other inventions: Africa as presented in educational types played by Noon on the journey upriver which keep roaring: "tourism and bourgeois hegemony... the natural park as neo-colonist folk-lore... African wild-life and the exploitation of racist stereotypes..." (ibid.: 118).

In this postcolonial text Africa is best symbolized by the native girl Noon, who for her own reasons silently follows Dr Mallory upriver. Just like in the canonical colonial text *Heart of Darkness*, a speechless tribal queen stands for the mystery of the continent. In *The Day of Creation*, Noon, just like Africa, needs reinvention and the imposition of Western forms in order to become real. Deprived of any language apart from her incomprehensible dialect, Noon functions as an image, and thus is interpreted. Dr Mallory who is full of strange utopian ideas, sees her as a part of his make-believe paradise. Nevertheless, on the boat she discovers the twentieth century: educational cassettes and videos. Identity is born from images, and Noon acquires her modern self by adopting a role and a look offered by television:

> As a child Noon possessed almost no image of herself, and these cassettes had allowed her to describe herself for the first time. I imagined her becoming a princess of the river and the forest, ruling the leopards and the giant oaks with an authority and allure modelled entirely on the poses in Sanger's tawdry films. In many ways Noon's progress charted the future of a special kind of self-consciousness, pandered to but constrained by the limitations of this small screen. In a few moments she had stepped from the Stone Age and crossed from the spoken to the visual realm in a single stride, dispensing with language on the way (ibid.: 160).

Just like Africa, Noon is a victim of media culture and adopts a vision of herself offered on the tape.[13] It is only by the imagery from cheap Hollywood

13. In Lacanian "The Mirror Stage" (1977) we read that in recognizing and mastering one's own image in the looking glass the child learns control over its own body in relation to other persons and things and symbolically enters the symbolic order of society: "[The act of recognition] rebounds in

films that Dr Mallory can communicate with her. Visual media are far more potent than books; all the literary allusions Dr Mallory interwove into his fantasy about the river fade away when compared with the power of screen. The only moments when he uses allusions to great literary works are the mocking comparisons of Sanger to Prospero and Merlin and his camerawork to magic.

Television and other images bombarding the senses of contemporary people not only do indeed maim their perceptions but also carry ideological meanings and propagate a certain life-style. In *Running Wild* (1988) Ballard concentrates on the psychology of the mediascape and wonders what would happen if we could organize our environment according to the ideals of consumer society. The generally acknowledged ideals of today's West are affluence, education, security and pleasure, and Ballard tries to imagine the contemporary utopia as a well-protected, tasteful housing estate inhabited by enlightened and successful professionals who can afford a twenty-four hour CCTV security service.

The ideal upper-middle class family living there has a spacious, elegant house with a gym, a swimming pool, a collection of intelligent books and videos, numerous TV sets, inter-connected computers and omnipresent security cameras. They lead successful professional lives, treat their staff with politeness and understanding, and are driven each day by chauffeurs to nearby London (the ideal housing estate would be situated in the Thames valley along the M4 route).[14] They keep fit, believe in social engineering and, first and foremost, in contemporary assertive psychology and theories on child rearing. Their children (one or two per family) grow up pampered by intelligent love and care, their days are tightly planned and full of sport activities and social events in which their parents, too, participate. With a lot of small jobs to perform and interesting homework they learn to function in the society of the future and at the same time, develop their own personalities without any handicap of stress, an unhappy childhood or psychological problems.

These are the ideals which *Running Wild* challenges by describing the Pangbourne Massacre, a spectacular mass murder of all the grown up inhabitants of such a utopian estate carried out by their own children, who then escaped without a trace. Dr Greville, the narrator, is a maverick psychiatric adviser to the Metropolitan Police who investigates the case after all the detectives have failed. Slowly he learns the truth.

the case of the child in a series of gestures in which he experiences in play the relation between the movements assumed in the image and the reflected environment, and between this virtual complex and the reality it duplicates—the child's own body and the persons or things around him" (Lacan 1977: 1). In mediascape culture the true initiation into the symbolic order is to fashion oneself according to an image on screen: the image is thus first and life tries to imitate it, just like in Oscar Wilde's famous remark. Noon enters the adult world of the twentieth century culture mastering images on the screen, becoming in her mind a wildlife film heroine.

14. Compare J.G. Ballard's text on this area: "For the past 35 years I have lived in the Thames Valley town of Shepperton, a suburb not of London but of London Airport. The catchment area of Heathrow extends for at least 10 miles to its south and west, a zone of motorway intersections, dual carriageways, science parks, marinas and industrial estates, watched by police CCTV speed-check cameras, a landscape which most people affect to loathe" (www.jgballard.com, on 20 August, 2006).

In its very form this novella about clichés and the way they function in the mediascape alludes to a cliché literary genre: detective fiction. From the very start this text reproduces the well-known convention of a crime story with its stock figures, stock motifs and a recognizable story structure. Dr Greville's narrative with its sub-titled initial sections: "The Police Video", "Pangbourne Village", "The Residents", "The Murdered Staff", "The Missing Children" and "The Massacre: Various Theories" recapitulate what we would usually find in a crime story. We get to know the victims, the setting of the crime, the results of investigation and the evidence. It is interesting to note that among the many theories some come not from the police, but from the tabloid press: the investigation is a media event, important because it is televized.

The characters seem quite familiar: Greville is like a private detective, an unorthodox expert or an individualistic police officer. The authorities dislike him, but need him in the most difficult situations. The victims are also typical: rich lawyers and businesspeople with hardly any individuality. The Permanent Secretary of the Home Office who gives Greville the case is like a cliché police boss whose major problem is the mass media. The Sergeant whom Payne Greville works with is a typically sardonic, lower-class policeman who despises the rich. Nevertheless, the crime story conventions are abandoned at the moment the murderers are introduced. We no longer deal with cultured and ingenious gentlemen-criminals who pose an intellectual challenge for detectives of the Poirot or Holmes type, but with psychotic mass-killers. In turn, their antagonists the police are no longer concerned with justice and morality: the investigations are media events, just like the crimes themselves.

Dr Greville's investigation ends with conclusions that subvert cliché opinions about childhood and family and thus are unacceptable. The facts about the Pangbourne Massacre cannot be narrated within the stiff frames of media language. Public opinion demands an explanation which reinforces commonly shared beliefs. Greville is silenced and in the place of a dénouement (a detective explaining the mechanisms of the crime to all involved, followed by the imprisonment of the criminal) we get the "Postscript" set in the future.[15] In a few years time Greville learns about a group of assassins who try to murder the former Prime Minister of England and immediately connects the attempt with the lost (and now grown up) children.

In his social diagnosis of our world in this novella Ballard concentrates on films, cameras, computers and screens. Dr Greville starts his tale by referring to the mass media and, throughout the text, only TV images count: we believe what we see on the screen and our true reality is the one produced by national press, radio and TV channels. Even Greville, an independent-minded amateur detective able to ignore the ready-made assumptions of media commentaries is influenced by the media language. Some of the sentences he uses in his

15. In fact the readers know "who did it" much earlier than Greville, nearly from the very start. The annoying situation (everybody in the text puzzled by an enigma which is not enigmatic at all) makes the reader pay attention not to the resolution of mystery but to how people's minds are conditioned by media clichés.

narration sound phoney: in compiling his notes about the Pangbourne Massacre he probably unconsciously quotes fragments of texts taken from press reports and TV commentaries. The stylistic effect is very interesting—the discrepancy between Greville's inquisitive personality and the banality of some of the passages in his narration makes the reader doubt the utopian happiness of Pangbourne described in these notes.

It is important to notice that most of these linguistic clichés concern such issues as social engineering, education, or psychology. Ballard here shows the whole variety of myths that can be found in educational programmes or popular books. Also the myth of the ideal community manufactured by social engineering (if there is enough money and education) is here examined and demonstrated to be a purely linguistic concept. We all know and recognize the phrases and slogans repeated by the media and tend to consider assertive psychology right.

For his characters the unmediated reality of the senses seems unimportant and abstract, all the significant events and interesting people are on TV and the characters have learned to react to images rather than to their own mundane experience. The most traumatic event in *Running Wild*, the massacre, is described via the mediation of the screen, as at the moment when he is given the case Greville immediately asks to be shown "the police video recorded at Pangbourne within a few hours after the crime" (Ballard 1989: 6).

Watching the film Greville comments not on the crime itself, but on the nearly artistic quality of the video, something much more impressive than the documentaries about the massacre he watched on TV.[16] The police video shows first and foremost the numerous screens at Pangbourne, one of which seems to the viewers most telling: it is the image of numerous dead monitors, which introduces the element of horror and tragedy to the text. Mutilating cameras and destroying television networks is an act of vandalism, if not insanity. Without its surveillance system Pangbourne is no longer a modern utopia and a dream estate of the future. Its life was idyllic and perfect as long as it was televized. To again quote Baudrillard's essay on Ballard:

> The roll of film (like transistorized music in cars and apartments) is part of the universal film of life, hyperreal, metallic, and corporal, made up of movement and flux. The photo is no more a medium than is technology or the body—all are simultaneous in this universe where the anticipation of an event coincides with its reproduction, and even with its 'real' occurrence (Baudrillard 2003: 8).

Life at Pangbourne during the times of its greatness was constantly filmed. The computers, TVs and cameras are everywhere: children have en suite

---

16. The stupidity of the media manifests itself in the language of TV speakers, not in the fact that they record, edit and transmit reality. Greville cannot help admiring the austerity of the film. "Thankfully, there is no sound track, and one is glad that none is necessary, unlike the TV programs with their hectoring commentaries full of lurid speculation" (Ballard 1989: 7).

computer rooms, small TV sets ("ultimate adult toys", as Greville calls them) are in the parents' studies, and surveillance cameras watch everybody continuously. Sergeant Payne despises all this technology: "they were being watched every hour of every day and night. This was a warm, friendly, junior Alcatraz" (Ballard 1989: 33).

Films and camera-work are interwoven with all the important events at Pangbourne, and Greville learns about numerous films produced in the estate. Firstly, a curious home video, which seems to resemble a promotional documentary of the ideal life in the estate. Glossy and tableau-like, it was prepared by two of the children with the happy co-operation of parents and showed the inhabitants in domestic situations. The affectionate commentary and comic scenes make it a kind of parody. Greville is told that the proud parents often played the video for visitors, but he is suspicious. And soon the second, secret version of the film is discovered:

> This carried the identical jovial sound-track, but Jasper and Amanda had added some 25 seconds of footage, culled from TV news documentaries, of car crashes, electric chairs and concentration camps' mass graves. Scattered at random among the scenes of their parents, this atrocity footage transformed the film into a work of eerie and threatening prophecy (ibid.: 55-56).

This macabre video precedes the murder; the children had first watched the atrocities and later made them happen. Greville, an unorthodox psychiatrist, understands that the key to the youngsters' minds is the TV screen: life in Pangbourne has always been film-like, everything the inhabitants did was immediately transmitted onto tape, and, as a result, they have been acting around the clock. The children brought up there developed a perverted sensitivity, as they did not believe their own experience. For them the world around was false. The process of growing up and of maturation in their case meant finding true reality and true emotions different than the kind, assertive behaviour of soap-opera-like ideal families.

Greville understands that the children's rebellion is "healthy": human beings need to live in real, not manufactured surroundings. Their parents' lifestyle is a disaster. Watching the videos filmed by the surveillance cameras in the hours preceding the catastrophe Greville has a strong feeling of the unreality of these images, especially when the tape is running backwards:

> The pictures moved in reverse, showing the familiar perspectives of the estate, except for a solitary pigeon that flew tail-first down The Avenue, as if withdrawing tactfully from the tragic scene. At Pangbourne Village, I reflected, time could run backwards or forwards (ibid.: 48).

The image of the bird in the above passage is very significant—the picture, the film, and all kinds of manufactured reality are prone to manipulation. The impossible tail-first flight stands for the artificiality of the modern mediated paradise which looks good only on TV. Moreover, Greville himself thinks in film-like images: his imagination, like in the case of so many modern people, is deviated in the sense of reacting to simulacra rather than to flesh-and-blood experience.

Ballard straightforwardly juxtaposes two concepts: that of utopia and modern disaster. The media model of happy life as the *BBC* sees it becomes the model social and educational disaster: the children brought up under the cameras with a minimum of stress and a maximum of care go berserk as their TV lives are to unreal to bear.[17] Pangbourne's new-found status prompts hundreds of people who long for real experience to actually go there in a vain attempt to participate in something important. People equipped with binoculars, cine-cameras, tripods and telescopic lenses try to film Pangbourne, get themselves filmed by TV crews, or at least gaze at the houses from the surrounding lanes. Once all the inhabitants have left it, Pangbourne starts to enjoy its second media life of TV documentaries, wild theories and public charity actions.

Even before the massacre life inside Pangbourne was constantly on show, every inhabitant of the gated community was aware of being filmed and possibly being watched. "The dogs and cameras keep people out, but also keep them in, doctor" (ibid.: 26), Sergeant Payne remarks while showing Greville around the estate. And if Pangbourne is a prison, then control over the inmates is exercised by watching them. The association is with panopticon, the progressive prison devised by Jeremy Bentham and described in *Discipline and Punish* (1979) by Michel Foucault, who calls it an effective means of implementing and dispersing control.[18]

Instead of feeling apprehensive the children nevertheless cherish the cameras—they edit their own documentaries and are themselves in control of the images. Cheating the guards at the gate is no problem for them, they have mastered the CCTV technique and decide when and how to be seen on the tapes. One may risk the thesis that, just like Noon in *The Day of Creation*, in their infancy they went through "the camera stage" similar to "the mirror stage" described by Lacan. In Pangbourne a new generation was thus reared, the TV people whose true life is on the screen. The children did rebel and probably broke

17. The disastrous impact of unreality on the human psyche is best seen in the dream which one of the victims notes down on the morning of the day of the massacre: he dreamt about a holiday in Egypt in which all the temples and pyramids were replaced by film sets. The striking thing is not only the artificiality of this dream but also the very custom of writing dreams down every morning, a procedure advised by psychotherapists. Perhaps the inhabitants of Pangbourne sought psychoanalytical help, perhaps they were familiar with Freudian theory and practiced self-analysis, and anyway psychological problems were not excluded from this model utopia.

18. Bentham's ideal panopticon is a hollow circle of cells shaped like a doughnut whose inward facing wall is composed of iron bars. In the middle of the roofed central yard there is a round watching tower with a guardian who can see every single cell. The guardian cannot possibly all the time watch every prisoner, but each isolated prisoner may be watched every minute. The cells become "small theatres in which each actor is alone, perfectly individualized and constantly visible" (Foucault 1979: 201). The parallel with Pangbourne is striking, the amount of CCTV tapes make it impossible for anybody to control all footage, but the inhabitants know that they can be potentially watched every minute.

free from the tyranny of the screen, but in this story set in contemporary England Ballard created a social environment very similar to his fantastic TV societies in stories he wrote for science fiction magazines like "Motel Architecture" or "The Intensive Care Unit".

The Media and the Mind

Ballard's most extreme presentation of the late twentieth-century mediascape is *The Atrocity Exhibition*, a book dealing with social entropy, media landscape and the way it shapes human perceptions.[19] Today, this novel is usually read in the context of the post-modern writers of the sixties.[20] Pigeonholed with the books of Pynchon and Burroughs, it is considered a splendid example of the late 20th-century avant-garde.[21] The book is abundant in images, pictures, films and catalogues of exhibits. In fact, reading it is like watching a strange arrangement of items put together in some fictive space with the element of time missing. It does not tell any coherent, chronological story and instead Ballard gives you descriptions of objects and suggests their impact on the characters' minds.[22]

Composed in the Freudian manner of the free "associations" technique, it possesses the ironic character of a recurrent nightmare. A good example of such a style is the first paragraph (entitled "Apocalypse") of the novel's eponymous first chapter:

19. The following presentation of *The Atrocity Exhibition* is partly based on Chapter Four of my book *The Voices of Disaster J.G. Ballard and the Disaster Story Tradition in England*, pp.121-163.
20. With *The Atrocity Exhibition* Ballard was recognized as an experimental and ambitious writer. Moreover, though the fifteen sections that make the novel appeared singly in both science fiction and non-science fiction journals, a science fiction pulp fiction house (Doubleday) finally rejected the whole book, as the editors considered it difficult and obscene. Therefore, it was finally published by the avant-garde Grove Press, an American house which specialized in experimental fiction, among others that of de Sade, Georges Batailles and William Burroughs (Burroughs himself wrote an introduction to the book). Such circumstances of publication resulted in the critical reception of *The Atrocity Exhibition* as a non-science fiction artistic experiment.
21. Roger Luckhurst discusses it in reference to different theories of the avant-garde and juxtaposes it with modernist poetics, especially the Surrealists and post-modern esthetics—Pop Art. Colin Greenland in *The Entropy Exhibition* concentrates on how the novel compares to ambitious science fiction of the time. Greenland also carefully analyzes Ballard's fundamental Surrealism, the way in which surrealist techniques allow him to mimetically present the fragmentation of the contemporary environment. Conversely, David Punter's reading of *The Atrocity Exhibition* in his *The Hidden Script* is devoted to the way Ballard describes the influence of machines and the artificiality of contemporary civilization on the human mind. A similar point, the dehumanization of contemporary experience and the alienation of an individual presented in *The Atrocity Exhibition*, are analyzed by Michel Delville in *J.G. Ballard*.
22. Even at first glance the book seems very chaotic and strange. The text is divided into paragraphs which have their own titles and are grouped into fifteen chapters. The chapters might well function as separate short stories: they are composed of loosely connected images and situations and, moreover, certain phrases, titles and motifs are constantly repeated, ones which gives the text an obsessive character. Ballard himself used to call these chapters 'condensed novels': he claimed that they are standard novels with the redundant elements (such as traditional plot, characterization of protagonists, dialogues, digressions and descriptions) cut off. What remains is the very essence, the condensation of his meanings which are very often presented in purely visual terms.

Apocalypse. A disquieting feature of this annual exhibition—to which patients themselves were not invited—was the marked preoccupation of the paintings with the theme of world cataclysm, as if these long-incarcerated patients had sensed some seismic upheaval within the minds of their doctors and nurses. As Catherine Austin walked around the converted gymnasium, these bizarre images, with their fusion of Eniwetok and Luna Park, Freud and Elizabeth Taylor, reminded her of the slides of exposed spinal levels in Travis's office. They hung on the enamelled walls like the codes of insoluble dreams, the keys to a nightmare in which she had begun to play a more willing and calculated role... Dr Nathan approached... 'Ah, Dr Austin... What do you think of them? I see there is War in Hell' (Ballard 2001: 1).

Here, at the very beginning of his novel, Ballard signals his major themes. First of all, the patients in the lunatic asylum are in a very ambiguous relationship with their doctors. The division gradually ceases to mean much as the doctors are themselves prone to hallucinations and mental disorders, while the patients are able to sense their approaching breakdowns. The paragraph opens with the description of an exhibition, moreover, an exhibition of violent paintings that represent imagined catastrophes created in therapeutic procedures. These paintings serve to externalize the inner traumas of their authors—very much like *The Atrocity Exhibition* itself does.[23]

What is also striking is the strange juxtaposition of "Eniwetok" and "Luna Park". The former, the name of an H-bomb test-island, suggests technological violence and danger encoded in our civilization, probably one of the reasons for the patients' madness. Far more interesting is the latter name: Luna Park, "the Paris fun fair loved by the Surrealists" (ibid.: 14). By this strange pairing we get the impression that disaster in the 60s has some carnival air, that catastrophe in its surreal beauty might be considered desirable, at least by the patients and, maybe, by the doctors too.

The next shocking pair; Taylor and Freud, anticipates gigantic billboards, ones which are to preside over the landscape of *The Atrocity Exhibition*. Here we see the influence of the esthetics of the 60s (with the dominant figure of Andy Warhol and his multiplied portraits of celebrities done in a commercial manner) on the minds of mental patients. Liz Taylor is an iconic face of the

23. Travis seeks extreme experiences (he and Dr Nathan very often use the adjective "ultimate"), and persistently tries to go beyond the accepted norms of behavior, similarly *The Atrocity Exhibition* itself, to paraphrase Susan Sontag's "The Pornographic Imagination": "is making forays into and taking up positions on the frontiers of consciousness... and reporting back what's there". Sontag then describes the artist: "His job is inventing trophies of his experiences—objects and gestures that fascinate and enthrall, not merely... edify or entertain. His principal means of fascinating is to advance one step further in the dialectic of outrage. He seeks to make his work repulsive, obscure, inaccessible; in short, to give what is, or seems to be, not wanted" (Sontag 1982: 212). Although Travis is said to be a doctor, not an artist, this description fits him well and, moreover, Sontag's model artist is equally self-serious and deprived of any sense of humour.

decade, the last great star of Marilyn Monroe and Jayne Mansfield style. Her face is immediately recognizable; it becomes property in itself. By this very fact of being so well known, Taylor is in fact similar to Freud, whose image (white beard, grave eyes and inevitable cigar in hand) is also iconic.[24]

Catherine Austin, only apparently sane and detached, connects the bizarre paintings of the patients to "exposed spinal levels", in this way pointing to another important motif in the book: the blurring of the distinction between what is external and what is internal. Something as hidden and well-protected as spinal levels is here exposed: physically in Travis' office, metaphorically in the paintings. Not only are the patients able to express their innermost traumas, but Austin, too, can sense the exposure. The nervous system is on display and its workings are no longer private or restricted to singular minds. Austin herself, although cast in the role of the mad Travis' sane lover, seems in this passage to be affected by his eccentric ideas, especially his exhibitions of patent madness ingeniously in touch with the epoch's traumas.

This initial paragraph is also very telling as far as the characterization (however scarce) of the protagonists is concerned. Apart from getting to know Austin—a doctor-girl shaken a little in her sanity by Travis' outspoken madness and torn between him and the detached Dr Nathan—we learn about Travis'[25] position as a central character of the book, a patient/doctor whose experimental therapies have uncanny side-effects. The strange exhibits—objects, photographs, collages—he gathers are compared here to "codes of insoluble dreams", which fact once again emphasizes the Freudian character of *The Atrocity Exhibition*. What Travis intuitively senses to be important is in direct contact with the characters' unconscious, but nobody understands the link. Dr Nathan, the third person we get to know in this passage, is the one who tries to assess Travis' madness and examine its roots—to interpret it in the cultural context of our mediascape.

Throughout the whole book Dr Nathan is to play a superego to Travis' ego; his sane and cold voice gives explanations and reaches conclusions. Travis in all his personalities is for Dr Nathan a favourite (if not the only) object of studies, his constant care and concern. What is striking here is the degree of understanding he has for his patient/colleague. Dr Nathan is not shocked by any of Travis' behaviour—he has no difficulties in deciphering even the most bizarre of his obsessions. The ideal psychiatrist, he seems almost to share the insanity of Travis, just like the cold and detached superego belongs in the same personality as his emotional counterparts.

24. Liz Taylor's name is to recur in the book, while Freud is undoubtedly the major intellectual source of Ballard's ideas. His canonical distinction between the manifest content of dreams (short, haphazard, rife with multiple meanings) and their latent meaning (hidden in symbols, much richer but understandable only after careful deciphering) can be very well applied to the text of the novel. Reading Ballard is like interpreting a contemporary nightmare: you should identify important symbols and, via the free associations technique, connect them to the external cultural context.
25. His personality is so unstable that he is deprived even of one single identity. His personality splits into a few faces; the core personality is Traven, others, depending on the varying degree of madness are Travis, Talbot, Tallis, Trabert, Talbert, and Travers.

"There is War in Hell", Dr Nathan diagnoses at the end of passage. This remark is equally true in the context of the paintings, those externalized landscapes of deranged minds, and of *The Atrocity Exhibition* itself—a book which depicts the contemporary psyche. This visual aspect of the novel is indeed very striking. Ballard is consistent in his technique of describing mental processes by means of presenting images the mind perceives and generates. In one of the last paragraphs of the first chapter, a quite important one judging from the title (identical with the novel's title), Travis first sees physically existing "real" pictures and immediately starts to associate them with images produced by his mind.

> **The Atrocity Exhibition.** Entering the exhibition, Travis sees the atrocities of Vietnam and the Congo mimetized in the 'alternate' death of Elizabeth Taylor; he tends the dying film star, eroticizing her punctured bronchus in the over-ventilated verandas of the London Hilton; he dreams of Max Ernst, superior of the birds; 'Europe after the Rain' (ibid.: 12).

Travis watches the violence in the paintings but sees the reflection of media images, which in the mid-60s become extremely violent. Newsreels of Vietnam and the Congo spread images of war—torture, atrocities, casualties—and transform the very institution of television from static studio-centred shows to "live" reports from all over the planet that specialize in naturalistic obscenities. Pictures and snap-shots of special appeal are finding their way to billboards and various logos, thus ceasing to shock and becoming a part of the landscape.

This mediascape is an immediate source of the violence on patients' canvases and, what is more, the visual aggression of contemporary communications is not limited to reporting wars. Other media phenomena, like celebrity cults, are equally crude and obscene. Travis reacts to this by creating "alternate" (or in other chapters, "conceptual") deaths of politicians and actors who are the focus of public attention. "Alternate death" is one which did not happen (like in the case of Taylor), or happened in the wrong manner (like in the case of John Fitzgerald Kennedy) and should be enacted in a way which, in Travis' words, "makes sense" and is not random. Rather, it should reassure us in our sense of justice.[26]

The Hilton Hotel is where Elizabeth Taylor suffered from severe pneumonia, while outside the building reporters were waiting for the news of her death. "Her punctured bronchus" is "eroticized" because it is a wound that is sexual and attractive. The surreal quality of culture, which feeds on death and traumas,

---

26. Compare one of Ballard's annotations: "Alternate Deaths" occur again and again in *Atrocity*... By these I mean the re-enactment of various tragedies staged by Traven and his many selves. They take place partly in his own mind and partly in the external world, and represent his attempt to make sense of these unhappy events and attribute to them a moral dimension and even, perhaps, a measure of hope" (Ballard 2001: 90).

makes Travis "dream" of the pictures of Ernst, skeleton-like rocks, and landscapes drained of any emotions resembling the deserts of our unconscious.

In his nightmarish passage from relative sanity to terminal madness and the dissolution of ego, Talbot[27] exhibits not only paintings, but films as well. His attempts to find meaning in random images taken out of newsreels end in disappointment—violence turns into entertainment. The "Festival of Atrocity Films", something he organizes in the second chapter, features collages of real-life material: "Behind their display frames the images of Nader and JFK, napalm and air crash victims revealed the considerable ingenuity of the film makers" (ibid.: 21), notes Dr Nathan while leaving the cinema. The choice of faces mixed into the violent collages is very telling. JFK is in fact one of the major characters in the novel, though he is only present in pictures and films. In 1990 Ballard comments:

> Kennedy's assassination presides over *The Atrocity Exhibition*, and in many ways the book is directly inspired by his death, and represents a desperate attempt to make sense of the tragedy, with its huge hidden agenda. The mass media created the Kennedy we know, and his death represented a tectonic shift in the communications landscape, sending fissures deep into the popular psyche that have not yet closed (ibid.: 53).

The face of Kennedy, his widow, the Dealey Plaza where he was killed and the Zapruder film of his death (the amateur film of the assassination played over and over again on all TV channels) are refrains of *The Atrocity Exhibition*. As they were so overwhelmingly present in the decade of the 60s, their influence on Talbot and his patients is understandable, while the importance of Kennedy's death in the wider historical context makes the allusions comprehensible to us as well. Ralph Nader, the second face in the film festival, is known nowadays as a presidential candidate in the elections of 2000 and 2004, but in the 60s he was principally the author of *Unsafe at any Speed*, an enormously popular book. In that book Nader examines one of the most potent American myths, the car, and proves how dangerous it in fact is.[28] His films of test collisions with mannequin passengers and drivers getting destroyed have hugely influenced the popular imagination.

Dr Nathan, in thinking about Talbot's festival, notices that its results are disappointing: "whatever Talbot had hoped for had clearly not materialized. The violence was little more than a sophisticated entertainment" (ibid.: 21). Nathan is aware that one of the reasons for Talbot's madness is the lack of coherence in the mediascape we inhabit. Oppressed by violent and, most of all, senseless imagery, Talbot seeks escape. The represented world seems much more realistic than the world outside pictures. It is first and foremost surrealist art that appeals

27. This is his name in the second chapter.
28. *Unsafe at Any Speed* is briefly discussed in the previous chapter as an example of a book warning against automobiles.

to Talbot as expressing his own traumas. In one of the paragraphs he studies Dali's *The Persistence of Memory* and gradually the description of the picture, "an empty beach with its fused sand" (ibid.: 24) blurs, with the landscape—Talbot enters the picture and finds himself inside the image.

It is precisely on the verge of the image and the perceiving mind that the action of the novel takes place. Numerous other films—"images of neuro-surgery and organ transplants, autism and senile dementia ... landscapes of war and death" (ibid.: 111) and many, many other equally disastrous pictures blur the distinction between fact and fiction, the esthetics of film and the truth about life. In notes written in 1990 Ballard explains this visual aspect of *The Atrocity Exhibition*, referring to the 60s and the way that decade changed the Western perception of the world.

> Our TV sets provided an endless background of frightening and challenging images—the Kennedy assassination, Vietnam, the Congo civil war, the space programme—each seeming to catalyze the others, and all raising huge questions which have never been answered. Together they paved the landscape of the present day ... (ibid.: 125) a map in the search of territory. A huge volume of sensational and often toxic imagery inundates our minds, much of it fictional in content. How do we make sense of this ceaseless flow of advertising and publicity, news and entertainment, where presidential campaigns and moon voyages are presented in terms indistinguishable from the launch of a new candy bar? (ibid.: 145).

Ballard poses the same question in his 1969 novel, showing that the visual imagery of the communications landscape invalidates the human ability to tell fact from fiction.

The Atrocity Exhibition "exhibits" disasters. Violent images and collages of atrocious photographs and newsreels are the visual background of the novel, but the greatest catastrophe it describes takes place in Travis' mind. Lost in the mediascape, the protagonist perceives his environment in a disfigured manner; he projects the disasters generated by his psyche onto the urban setting. Is this catastrophe simply the result of his derangement or, similarly to some mad prophets in the past, is he—because of his very madness—able to sense the "hidden agendas", the concealed, latent meaning of reality?

> **The Concentration City.** ... *In the suburbs of Hell Travis walked in the flaring light of the petrochemical plants. The ruins of abandoned cinemas stood at the street corners, faded billboards facing them across the empty streets. In a waste lot of wrecked cars he found the burned body of the white Pontiac. He wandered through the deserted suburbs. The crashed bombers lay under the trees, grass growing through their wings* (ibid.: 10).

The very title of the paragraph from which I quote is quite striking. Combining the allusion to "concentration camps", war, an urban setting and, possibly, overpopulation, it moreover sounds familiar to devoted Ballard readers. In fact, it is taken from the title of one of his earliest science fiction stories, a dystopian picture of an overpopulated world of the future. Such a link with his early catastrophe fiction seems to show that *The Atrocity Exhibition* is a logical continuation of his intellectual concerns.[29]

We see Travis walking in the contemporary cityscape, though what he sees is not the world of the 60s, but its twin brother: the world as it would have been had it gone through disaster, perhaps the Third World War, perhaps some natural catastrophe. The suburbs of an industrial city are deserted and empty, its fleeing or dying inhabitants left behind, decomposing media symbols—cinemas and billboards. Once powerful communication channels spreading violent images, they are now turned into signs of desolation.

The white Pontiac,[30] in Travis' time a symbol of status and luxury and the most desired American commodity fit for a pop star, is burned and destroyed. Its destruction stands for the pitiful end of all the commodity culture. Travis wanders around and what he imagines to see gradually changes into an image from Max Ernst's "Garden Airplane Traps"—"a nightmare of a grounded pilot", as Ballard himself once described this painting.

What is going on in Travis' mind? What is the latent content of this manifest image of desolate suburbs juxtaposed with a surrealist painting? As the allusion to "Concentration City" suggests, there is a link between the cultural catastrophe of the 60s and the Cold War dystopias of the 50s. In the previous decade apocalyptic scenarios abundant in popular culture described H-bomb tests, nuclear war and the subsequent contamination. This clearly did not happen, but the catastrophe came (though unnoticed) and changed civilization without threatening its very existence. Travis looks at his world via traditional catastrophic imagery—he sees the alternate world coincident with our reality, whose post-apocalyptic character is easier to notice. This second world underlies ours, as we too live in the times after the end.

As we learn from other chapters of the book, years earlier Travis had been (or he imagines himself to have been) a bomber pilot. The trauma of taking part in World War II bombardments changes in his mind into anticipation of World War III and its thermonuclear Armageddon. Ballard's narrative technique here is influenced by psychoanalysis. We see the projection of Travis' troubled thoughts, memories and fears onto the outside world. Descriptions of his external environment serve to present his internal, perhaps partly unconscious mind.[31]

29. The conscious placing of this passage within a wider metafictional context of his whole oeuvre accounts for the use of italics, which is very rare in the novel as a whole.
30. Compare: "Why a white Pontiac? A British pop-star of the 1960s, Dickie Valentine, drove his daughter in a white Pontiac to the same school that my own children attended near the film studios in Shepperton. The car had a powerful iconic presence, emerging from all those American movies into the tranquil TV suburbs" (Ballard 2001: 15).
31. The same technique recurs in the novel, especially in the very condensed passages that try to compress heterogeneous material: "The Plaza. ... Talbot followed the concrete beach. Here and there

The Plaza is described as a concrete beach—the artificial landscape replacing nature. Nevertheless, Talbot sees the man-made countryside as already crumbling down, reclaimed by vegetation. Gradually details blur, colours fade—Talbot perceives only basic forms, the geometry of disaster.

Talbot's perception goes through a number of "transits", as he calls them. He reduces reality to simpler forms, and he tries to combine the outer and the inner space in a number of separate links. In a paragraph with the significant title "Journeys to an Interior" he enumerates his "transits": (1) Spinal, (2) Media, (3) Contour, (4) Astral. From the intimacy of his nervous system, through a montage of war in Asia newsreels and the geometry of his lover's body to the abstract picture of movement frozen into postures—we see the growing detachment of his mind. Each "transit" juxtaposes his psyche and external reality.

> **Spinal:** 'The Eye of Silence'—these porous rock towers, with the luminosity of exposed organs, contained an immense planetary silence. Moving across the iodine water of these corroded lagoons, Talbot followed the solitary nymph through the causeways of rock, the palaces of his own flesh and bone (ibid.: 27).

The vision of disaster described here combines another of Ernst's paintings with Talbot's deranged identification with the image: he feels as both a character pictured by Ernst and a person inside whose body the image contains. In all his "transits" Talbot swallows reality and encloses it inside himself, the world grows abstract, other persons cease to exist: finally, only pure geometry remains.

In this private, internal Universe no communication is possible. Talbot thinks in terms of geometry only. Even in the same room with his lover he cannot acknowledge her existence: "If anything, her voice formed a module with the perspectives of wall and ceiling as abstract as the design on a detergent pack" (ibid.: 94). Alone and isolated Talbot is no longer able to tolerate other people interrupting the serenity of his space. In the end of most of the chapters he commits violent deeds trying to eliminate alien factors.

As I already mentioned, *The Atrocity Exhibition*, a novel composed of fifteen seemingly separate stories-chapters, makes its readers face chaos: there is no linear action, while certain motifs and situations recur obsessively. Moreover, the initial chapters seem to be variants of the same story and towards the end of the text even the multiple-named protagonist dissolves in the abundance of loosely connected imagery. In fact, the procedure readers should adopt is the one of a therapist interpreting dreams; like in the Freudian theory of dreams, we are obliged to analyze the manifest contents of the stories and try to fathom their latent meanings.

Concentrating on the manifest contents of *The Atrocity Exhibition* and

---

sections of the banking had fallen, revealing the steel buttress below. An orchard of miniature fruit trees grew from the sutures between the concrete slabs. Three hundred yards from the helicopter he entered a sunken plaza where two convergent highways moved below an underpass. ... The geometry of the plaza exercised a unique fascination upon Talbot's mind" (Ballard 2003: 25).

attempting to find clear structure in this apparent chaos proves that the common denominator of all the events, whether real or hallucinatory, is catastrophe. Firstly let us look at the characters who appear in the stories. Apart from Travern in his many selves, Dr Nathan and Catherine Austin (both from the Institute/hospital where Travern works), the most important persons are Mrs Travern and Karen Novotny.[32] Mrs Travern is his worried and neglected wife, Novotny is an unfortunate girl whom he meets already on the run and finally attacks or murders in each story anew. These people might be called "real"; they exist in the contemporary world, which is our world in the 60s.

Koester and Vaughan are more ambiguous. In the course of the narrative these students of Travern acquire diabolical features, but the way Travern perceives them is no doubt severely disfigured. Therefore, as their descriptions are focalized by him, the picture we get is partly a product of his psychosis. About Coma, Kline and Xero there can be no mistake—they are Travern's hallucinations and avatars of, respectively, Marilyn Monroe/Mrs Kennedy, Lee Harvey Oswald and Malcolm X. They accompany Travern in his mad journey across the industrial countryside and their very existence shows the way he reacts to the mediascape.

The most mysterious persons (who appear rarely and say nothing) are: the WWII pilot and a girl with radiation burns. The pilot might be an alter ego of Travern himself (as according to Dr Nathan, he has some military past), while the girl most probably embodies his remorse (if he really did participate in bombardments) or fears of the Third World War. The list of the characters in *The Atrocity Exhibition* should be completed with the names of celebrities: Jackie Kennedy, Marilyn Monroe, Ralph Nader, Ronald Reagan and many others.

The first eight chapters of the book basically tell the same story, or rather describe images and situations that together allow us to recreate what happened. There are often differences and contradictions between them, so there is no possibility of reducing them to one coherent account. Nevertheless, we do get an impression of striking similarity.

Initially, Travern works at an Institute where he conducts a number of psychiatric tests. The participants (both mental patients and volunteer students) are exposed to violent images coming mostly from the mass media, and the conclusions are formulated. Gradually his own psychosis takes over; Dr Nathan, Travern's wife and his lover, Catherine Austin, try to help him—but all in vain. Finally, he escapes from the Institute and sets out on a journey across the country, sometimes accompanied by his hallucinatory companions. Dr Nathan followed him and keeps interpreting his behaviour and giving the readers hints.

Travern leaves behind a trail of bizarre exhibitions, collections of objects, photographs and pictures that Dr Nathan considers crucial to his diagnosis. In the meantime Travers meets Karen Novotny (at a drive-in cinema, space conference, empty resort, etc.) and they start a love affair. All ends in a burst of

---

32. Compare Roger Luckhurst: "The choice of the name must be a reference to the call-girl Marielle Novotny, allegedly a mistress of John F. Kennedy and involved in the Profumo scandal in 1963" (Luckhurst 1998: 106).

violence—Traven, who no longer is able to tell truth from hallucination, murders Novotny and Dr Nathan appears on stage too late to intervene. As the tragedy is repeated eight times in different variants and Novotny keeps coming back to life in the following chapters, perhaps some parts of the story are in themselves hallucinations of Traven and Novotny, just like Coma, is also a product of his unconscious. Whatever the case, in the ninth chapter, entitled "You and me and the continuum", the structure starts to change and the text grows more impersonal. Traven is for the first time not even named in the text. The text itself is composed of bits and pieces of "the evidence" to do with a strange Air Force pilot whose body has been washed ashore, and about whom very little is known. In an introduction to the chapter[33] we read:

> Whether in fact this man was a returning astronaut suffering from amnesia, the figment of an ill-organised advertising campaign, or, as some have suggested, the Second Coming of Christ is anyone's guess. What little evidence we have has been assembled below (ibid.: 129).

The message of the chapter, the observation that in the contemporary world full of fictions and commercial images the "real" thing, such as the alien landing or even the Second Coming, would go unnoticed, is suggested in a very subtle manner. The silent pilot around whom all the action is centered is gradually absorbed by the outside world.

In the next chapter, "Plans for the Assassination of Jacqueline Kennedy", the process of Tallis' dissolution continues. The style is scientific, very exact, and the paragraphs with apparently irrelevant titles describe the results of psychological surveys. Different groups of psychopathic patients asked to choose female victims decide on celebrities (the preferred one is Jacqueline Kennedy). Out of their faces and bodies an ideal woman is constructed and fantasies on killing her are staged. Other surveys examine the place cars have in the contemporary unconscious. Automobiles prove to be objects of desire, while catastrophes are considered outbursts of energy. The conclusion is simple: Jackie Kennedy in a car with the body of her fatally wounded husband embodies the fantasies of our epoch.

In this chapter (and all the following ones) none of the characters we already know is present: only Tallis' name appears in one of the paragraph's titles. These titles when read together form two sentences: "In his dream of Zapruder frame 235/ Tallis was increasingly preoccupied/ by the figure of the President's wife. The planes of her face, like the/ cars of the abandoned motorcade/ mediated to him the complete silence/ of the plaza, the geometry of a murder" (ibid.: 141-144). The frame of the Zapruder film is one of the images of the Kennedy

33. None of the previous chapters has any introduction. This time the text proper (images and short dialogues of Austin, Novotny and Nathan and the pilot, probably the next incarnation of Traven) is preceded by a secondary narration whose style mimics sensational journalism. The mass media seem to devour the story of Travern; he loses his individuality, dissolves.

murder played over and over again on TV. This mediated killing is generally enjoyed. Violence in the mass media turns into "geometry", and geometry in *The Atrocity Exhibition* stands for abstraction. The serene face of Jacqueline Kennedy is an icon and everybody's property. This is why it disturbs the clinically insane. Perhaps the scientific reports quoted in the story are in fact the results of the mysterious tests Traven conducted at the Institute?

A similar montage technique is used in the following chapters. In "Love and Napalm: Export U.S.A." reports on research into the latent sexual meanings of Vietnam and Congo newsreels are interrupted by paragraph titles, ones that together read: "At night, these visions of helicopters and the D.M.Z./ fused in Traven's mind with the spectre/ of his daughter's body. The lantern of her face/ hung among the corridors of sleep./ Warning him, she summoned to her side/ all the legions of the bereaved./ By day the overflights of B-52s/ crossed the drowned causeways of the delta,/ unique ciphers of violence and desire" (ibid.: 147-151). In "Crash!" the paragraphs of reports on psychopathic reactions to cars and the sexuality of death in the car are entitled: "Each afternoon in the deserted cinema/ Tallis was increasingly distressed/ by the images of the colliding cars./ Celebrations of his wife's death,/ the slow-motion newsreels/ recapitulated all his memories of childhood,/ the realisation of dreams/ which even during the safe immobility of sleep/ would develop into nightmares of anxiety" (ibid.: 153-157).

Here we can still see some connection between the research and Tallis' obsessions from the previous chapters of *The Atrocity Exhibition*. We see the serene face on billboards (he takes Jackie Kennedy for his daughter or wife, her ever-present face is intimately known to him), deserted cinemas, Ralph Nader's films of colliding cars, the images of war. The following chapter, "The Generations of America", gives only a pure abstraction of violence. The Bible-like five-page long catalogue of murder reads: "Sirhan Sirhan shot Robert F. Kennedy. And Ethel M. Kennedy shot Judith Birnbaum. And Judith Birnbaum... etc.," (ibid.: 159). The whole American heritage here is murder.

We see Tallis for the last time in the following chapter, "Why I want to fuck Ronald Reagan". The paragraph titles read: "During these assassination fantasies/ Tallis became increasingly obsessed/ with the pudenda of the Presidential contender/ mediated to him by a thousand television screens./ The motion picture studies of Ronald Reagan/ created a scenario of the conceptual orgasm,/ a unique ontology of violence and desire" (ibid.: 165-168). This text sounds like an echo of previous interrupted titles.

In this story Tallis watches another set of media imagery (Reagan's campaign) and attempts to identify its latent, abstracted meanings. Behind Reagan's right-wing propaganda he sees strong sexual undertones, and anal-sadistic imagery. [34] Reports quoted in this section are on psychiatric research into the campaign.

34. In fact the beginnings of Reagan's political career is what Ballard very vividly remembers from the American mediascape of the sixties many years later. Quite recently he said in an interview: "Reagan was a very skillful manipulator of the popular psychology of his TV and radio audiences... he had a sneering tone that he had completely lost by the time he was elected President. But he was

The disturbed and the mentally healthy alike prove to react on some subliminal level to the sexuality of Reagan's body language, grimaces and hair-dos. The language of the reports is exact and scientific, but for Tallis, as Dr Nathan once noted "Science is the ultimate pornography, analytic activity whose main aim is to isolate objects or events from their contexts in time and space" (ibid.: 49). In the annotations Ballard remembers:

> Above all, it struck me that Reagan was the first politician to exploit the fact that his TV audience would not be listening too closely, if at all, to what he was saying, and indeed might well assume from his manner and presentation that he was saying the exact opposite of the words actually emerging from his mouth (ibid.: 169).

The very last chapter of *The Atrocity Exhibition* is the completion of growing abstractions. None of the characters is present and the whole chapter, entitled "The Assassination of John Fitzgerald Kennedy considered as a downhill motor race", recapitulates the obsessively recurring motif of the Zapruder film in the most abstracted manner. The text is in intertextual dialogue with Alfred Jarry's "The Crucifixion Considered as an Uphill Bicycle Race".[35]

Ballard chooses the surrealist intertext to stress the absurdity of media fascination with the Zapruder film and the endless sensations, discovered by journalists: "The assassination of President Kennedy on November 22, 1963, raised many questions, not all of which were answered by the Report of the Warren Commission. It is suggested that a less conventional view of the events of that grim day may provide a more satisfactory explanation" (ibid.: 171), as we read in the "Author's note" to the passage. The tragedy itself became an abstracted media event and a common property to be interpreted and enacted in anyway we please. Is it Traven who spotted the similarity between Jarry and Zapruder? Is this last chapter his attempt to "kill Kennedy once again, but in away which makes sense?" The most apparent link between the chapter and the previous text is the passage at the beginning in which Koester, a diabolical student who while watching the Zapruder film remarks: "surely Christ's crucifixion could be regarded as the first traffic accident—certainly if we accept Jarry's happy piece anti-clericalism..." (ibid.: 29).

---

very skillful at manipulating the psychology, the moods and emotions of his audience—probably something he learned to do when he was a sports commentator. Schwarzenegger doesn't have any of those manipulative skills". (Vale 2005: 49-50)

35. Jarry starts:

Barabbas, slated to race, was scratched.

Pilate, the starter, pulling out his clepsydra or water clock, an operation which wet his hands unless he had merely spit on them—Pilate gave the send-off. (cit., www.jgballard.com, on 20 Aug. 2006).

Ballard echoes this text:

Oswald was the starter.

From his window above the track he opened the race by firing the starting gun. (Ballard 2001: 171)

The text continues in sentences parallel to Jarry's.

The fifteen chapters of *The Atrocity Exhibition* are followed by two more impersonal pieces in the Appendix. "Princess Margaret's Face Lift" and "Mae West Reduction Mammoplasty" are accounts of the surgeries of the two celebrities. The scientific exactness of these reports is contrasted with the names of the patients, each a popular culture icon. Celebrities, because of their popularity and the uncounted articles and photographs of them, are shown here as intimately known to everybody. The media reports each detail of their lives and physiognomies. We develop a paradoxical relationship with the pictures of them, but at the same time our lives grow de-humanized and deprived of "real" attachment. The last sentence of the whole *The Atrocity Exhibition* pessimistically reads: "The ultimate results of this operation with regard to sexual function are not known" (ibid.: 184). Mae West, a Hollywood sexual icon, is thus turned into an image and in fact deprived of both sexuality and physicality as well.

Dr Nathan, who plays the superego to Travern's ego, is given the role of an analyst who interprets the manifest contents of the mediascape and suggests its underlying meanings. Ballard does not leave his readers alone with the most complex collages of imagery, but simultaneously to its descriptions provides interpretative hypotheses. Travis himself is aware of his growing psychosis, "whose onset he had recognized during his last year at the hospital, he had welcomed this journey into a familiar land, zones of twilight" (ibid.: 4), and is even glad of its cognitive potential. Dr Nathan, his sane counterpart, is probably voicing his own opinions. Dr Nathan accompanies him in the first sections of the book. Even in the entropic "You and me and the continuum" he still tries to help and examine Travern; he disappears only when the psychosis is so severe that Travern does not have any sanity left.[36]

In the course of the narrative Dr Nathan examines the deeper and deeper layers of contemporary psychosis. As early as the very first chapter he points to the impact of wars on the modern psyche. The memories of the Second World War, the anticipation of the Third, images from wars in Vietnam and the Congo—all influence our way of thinking:

> What we are concerned with now are the implications—in particular, the complex of ideas and events represented by World War III. Not the political and military possibility, but the inner identity of such a notion. For us, perhaps, World War II is now little more than a sinister pop art display, but for [Travis] it has become an expression of the failure of his psyche to accept the fact of its own consciousness, and of his revolt against the present continuum of time and space (ibid.: 6).

The "sinister pop art display" he mentions alludes to the Cold War catastrophe novels, paperback science fiction about postapocalyptic times. After

---

36. Sometimes he is killed at the end of the chapter, but always resurrected in the next.

a disaster the few who survived (among them our protagonist) try to recreate civilization. The protagonist wanders in the empty cities, sleeps in luxurious apartments, drives a host of abandoned cars, gathers and defends food from the derelict stores. Such a vision, though it implies the slaughter of nearly all humankind, is somehow attractive: people tired of living in the overpopulated industrial world find escapist fantasies desirable. "The present continuum" is our version of modern history in which the Cold War ended and there was no thermonuclear disaster. In other continua (perhaps even more probable than ours) the war did happen. Travis sees this alternate world below ours, and tries to find in abstracted collages glimpses of the other reality.

According to Travis the war should have happened and should have ended the deviant civilization. Thus, our continuum is the wrong one. Travis' attempts to put things right correspond to our unconscious. Asked by Mrs Travis, "Was my husband a doctor, or a patient?" (ibid.: 6), Dr Nathan answers that the question is not valid any longer. He attentively watches Talbot's experiments and tests and speculates about their outcome. In his seminar Talbot and his students are preparing the scenario of the future war; students try to cast Talbot as its first victim, but he manages to regain control and create a psychodrama with more universal dimension.

Dr Nathan is able to see the interconnection between Talbot's obsessions with war, cars, Ralph Nader and President Kennedy. "These images", he says pointing to one of Talbot's collages, "constitute... a fusing device by which Talbot hopes to bring his scenario to a climax... one must remember that Talbot is here distinguishing between the manifest content of reality and its latent content. Nader's true role is clearly very different from his apparent one ... [he signifies] a conceptual auto-disaster" (ibid.: 33), explains Dr Nathan. "The scenario" is Talbot's attempt to bring about World War III,[37] "images" are violent photographs, "Nader" suggests the colliding cars and, indirectly, contemporary fascination with aggressive machines. JFK was the victim of "a conceptual auto-disaster"; his death in a car corresponded to his reader's subliminal fears and desires.

> What the patient is reacting against is, simply, the phenomenology
> of the universe, the specific and independent existence of separate
> objects and events, however trivial and inoffensive these may seem.
> ... One could say that the precise, if largely random configuration
> of the atoms in the universe at any given moment... seems to him
> to be preposterous" (ibid.: 46).

Dr Nathan notes down the above observation when he tries to diagnose Traven. His conclusions, apart from alluding to psychoanalytic theories of the death drive (which I am going to discuss in a separate subchapter), indicate Traven's ultimate dream. Tired with the world of separate phenomena, of differences and potentialities, he misses entropy—the heat death of a spent

37. In such a sense as to bring together our continuum and the parallel 'war' one.

universe. The theory of entropy fashionable in the early sixties[38] explains the inescapable end of our Universe, once all differences are obliterated, time will unwind itself and all movement will cease in total stasis. Traven's longing for the peace of this stasis reflects general cultural tendencies.

As entropy is akin to chaos, the media in spreading random and incomplete messages accelerate the end: that is why Traven is so obsessed by them. This sinister, "pornographic" discourse is for him the language of science, which isolates objects preserving their identities. The opposite of science is surrealism with its blending of all imagery: "Lautréamont, who brought together the sewing machine and an umbrella on the operating table, identifying the pudenda of the carpet with the woof of the cadaver" (ibid.: 49).

Thus, Dr Nathan explains the different peculiarities of Travern's psychosis and gives hints as to their interconnection. He even identifies the "planes" on which his patient's mind operates: "on one level the tragedies of Cape Kennedy and Vietnam serialized on billboards... On another level, the immediate personal environment... On the third level, the inner world of the psyche. Where these planes intersect, images are born" (ibid.: 72). The same is indeed true concerning the book as a whole; its collage narration juxtaposes the public sphere, which is mediated (here represented by a spaceship catastrophe and disastrous political failure—Vietnam) and the private sphere: the geometry of personal space and the phantoms bred in the psyche. Only in patchwork combinations of the three does some kind of valid reality begin to assert itself, as this is the way we perceive the world. Just before he dissolves in loose narrative, Dr Nathan formulates his final diagnoses of both Travern and reality: the death of affect:[39]

> Traver's problem is how to come to terms with the violence that has pursued his life—not merely the violence of accident... but the biomorphic horror of our own bodies. Travers has at last realized that the significance of these acts of violence lies elsewhere, in what we might term "the death of affect"... our moral freedom to pursue our own psychopathologies as a game, and in our even greater powers of abstraction (ibid.: 116).

In this world of the future, one which Travern intuitively anticipates, there is no place for immediate contact with another human being. What we are left with is violence or perversion. Within the constrains of the mediascape nothing else feels real.

38. Compare "Entropy" by Thomas Pynchon and "The Heat Death of the Universe" by Pamela Zoline.
39. According to Frederic Jameson, one of the distinctive features of postmodern art is the "waning of affect" (Jameson 1984: 61): human figures are commodified and transformed into their own image (the best example is Andy Warhol's *Marilyn Monroe*) and all feeling of emotion, and of subjectivity is excluded from the very experience of reception of a work of art and what we are left with is abstraction.

The motif of the psychological hazards of life within the contemporary mediascape recurs in most of Ballard's output; he discusses the way audiovisual media maim human perception along with many related issues from diverse vantage points. The abundance of simulacra, the emotional mutilation of contemporary image-consumers, the ontological disquiet of the Western world where nothing is real or unreal any longer[40] and the human propensity for being manipulated by the media are his main artistic and social concerns. Two of his very pessimistic short stories, "The Subliminal Man" (1963) and "The Air Disaster" (1975), show in a nutshell why the civilization which has created a planet-wide mediascape is already in decline.

The first story depicts a society where consuming goods replaces both entertainment and social and family bonds and is viewed as the moral obligation of every citizen. In order to afford massive shopping-sprees people work for over twelve hours a day (all shops are open around the clock), there are many shopping schemes and discounts—in neighbourhoods boasting big spenders prices are reduced and thus there is social pressure to buy as much as possible. TV is nothing but commercials and discount quizzes; "Spot Bargains... give you a selection of things on which you get a ninety per cent trade-in discount at the local stores" (Ballard 2002b: 416) and commercial breaks interrupt telephone conversations; "the ratio of commercial to conversation was as high as 10:1, the participants desperately trying to get a word in edgeways between the interminable interruptions" (ibid.: 422). Ballard describes the same mechanism that Alvin Toffler was later to give as a main example of the modern way of life—goods are used for an increasingly shorter period of time. In his story social pressure makes characters buy new cars and home appliances every few months, even though there is only one make of each product in the market.

In this story we see three characters representing three approaches to this reality. Dr Franklin, a psychiatrist, is intellectually capable of seeing the absurdity of his life, but he is too overworked to care and his moments of illumination are too short to do anything. Most of his time he is working or buying in a state of a semi-coma, which in his society is the norm. He thinks he controls what is going on, simply because he is not as blinded as, for instance, his wife. She is a model consumer in a buying frenzy: she spends her days in front of a TV set trying to win discounts. Together with other housewives from the neighbourhood she hunts for promotions and sales across the whole city and nags her husband to buy increasing amounts of gadgets. Only the third person, a drop-out beatnik who lives outside the social ranks, is able to see what is going on—but his weakness

---

40. In the article "Fiction of every Kind" (1971) Ballard wrote: "The role of the writer is totally changed—he is now merely one of a huge army of people filling the environment with fictions of every kind. To survive, he must become far more analytic, approaching his subject matter like a scientist or engineer" (Ballard 1997b: 206). Such an analytic approach to reality contaminated with numerous fictions is Ballard's trademark and in his novels, as Baudrillard admiringly puts it: "nothing is really invented therein, everything is hyper-functional: traffic and accidents, technology and death, sex and the camera eye. Everything is like a huge simulated and synchronous machine; an acceleration of our own models, of all the models which surround us, all mixed together and hyper-operationalized in the void" (Baudrillard 2003:3).

and status as a mental misfit make his fight with the system futile. Dr Franklin pities him, though sometimes he envies the young man a certain amount of the freedom he himself does not have.

Dr Franklin lives enclosed in an oppressive mediascape: because of the manner motorways are built he has to drive additional miles "contained within giant clover-leaves... cafes and car marts... a shanty town of shacks and filling stations sprawled away among the forest of electric signs and route indicators" (ibid. 414). This is a mediascape heavy with messages bombing his consciousness with commercials and conditioning him to behave in a desired way. The self-sacrifice of his beatnik patient who demolished mysterious "airport signs" along the expressway shows the doctor that they are all victims to subliminal advertising and to huge hypnotizing boards that order them to keep buying and prevent them from revolting:

> Then the flicker of lights cleared and steadied, blazing out continuously, and together the crowd looked up at the decks of brilliant letters. The phrases... were entirely familiar, and Franklin knew that he had been reading them for weeks as he passed up and down the motorway; BUY NOW BUY NOW BUY NOW NEW CAR NEW CAR NEW CAR YES YES YES YES YES YES (ibid.: 424).

The patient is shot down and Franklin is shocked to see the true face of the consumer regime they live in, but this moment of lucidity is short and the doctor is soon brain-washed into purchasing new items. Life within the constraints of the mediascape have deprived him of the ability to feel: the consumer culture ruled by media spectacles turns people into automata.

This last proposition is further elaborated in a story about the predatory character of our culture of simulacra, where the images are all that matters. With so much violence on screen, televized atrocities are not shocking anymore, and on the contrary, blood and dead bodies make the news, which we somehow cease to notice in our everyday lives. In "The Air Disaster" Ballard makes this point in a radical way. Not by accident does the story start at a gigantic South American film festival, one which gathers hundreds of journalists. After all, we are all conditioned to see the world via the camera eye and the film screen. The journalists abandon the festival halls when the news spreads: the biggest aircraft on Earth is said to have exploded in the air and fallen down somewhere in a gigantic catastrophe. All of the journalists rush to look for the remains with their cameras. The roads are jammed and everybody tries to outwit everybody else. The protagonist, who desperately needs to impress his boss by filming the mutilated corpses, instead of following the others along the ocean shore takes the alternate route into the Andes Mountains. He encounters poor natives whose life has not changed in hundreds of years, and the higher he goes the more miserable the people are and more inhuman their living conditions. Asked about the plane and the numerous dead bodies they gesture towards the mountaintops and only after hours of journey by car does the protagonist find the rusty wreck of an old Cessna. The natives bring to him the cadavers of their dead relatives dug up from their graves. They are willing to satisfy any of his needs if only he pays them.

What is striking in this late story is the way Ballard juxtaposes the recurrent motifs from his entire oeuvre: obsession with films, violence in the news, the hegemony of all-mighty TV networks and human indifference to mediated cruelty on screen. Violent images are worth money and in Western civilization where money is everything people are willing to film and show whatever may attract the attention of half-dozed spectators. Moreover, the "structural violence" intrinsic to the way Western civilization is spreading all over the world is something that compels other civilizations to accept its money-oriented ideology in disregard of their own cultures.[41]

At the bottom of all such displays of seemingly harmless violence there is something latent, something suppressed. In the climax of "The Air Disaster" the protagonist sees the wreck of a small, old plane, a rusty relic of the early-20th century. Dating from the days of the Great War, the plane brings up to the surface a half-forgotten reminder of the times our civilization went astray and started to cultivate aggression and self-destruction. Ballard's critique of the mediascape shows how far the Western world has gone on its way to self-destruction.

41. Compare: Jadwiga Staniszkis, *Władza globalizacji* [The Power of Globalization], Warszawa, 2003.

CHAPTER FIVE:
MINDSCAPES

Ballard's fiction depicts what I am calling *Grave New World*, a civilization in decline that disturbingly resembles our own reality, and whose days, despite its seeming affluence, are numbered. Thus, most of the stories and novels I have so far discussed describe a world we recognize, our Western civilization at the turn of the millennium. *Grave New World* in Ballard's fiction may be charted into diverse territories (for example, landscapes dominated by cities, by cars and by media) that entail various facets of essentially the same reality and can be seen as its metonymies. Their presentation is very much involved in current social and cultural issues. Ballard portrays the slow, natural process of the world's disintegration as coming from within social structures and an exhausted media culture. His vision of history and civilization is in this aspect similar to Spengler's,[1] and the late twentieth century is in his opinion the time when Western history is going to run full circle and find its conclusion in a zero point. Moreover, alluding to Freud's late theses, Ballard shows that subliminally we indeed long for the end of civilization, as its demise is in accordance with some higher logic of the Universe—an integral part of which we remain, even if intellectually we cannot explain it.

1. For the discussion of Spengler's theses—see Chapter One.

My maps of *Grave New World* that chart its external face do not yet include one very important territory, one I call "mindscapes": the inner landscape of contemporary people living in the constraints of its cityscapes and media culture. The best way to investigate the mindscapes of Ballard's characters is to study his texts that go beyond realistic discourse and belong in the tradition of disaster fiction. For although the events there are fantastic, the human psychology is not.[2] Some cases of Ballard's fiction show plausible psychological reactions to science fiction-like catastrophes in a form of, say, a gigantic drought or global warming. These catastrophes resonate in the minds of Ballard's protagonists, people who willingly embrace the said disasters. As in Freudian descriptions of the "return of the repressed",[3] inner traumas are externalized and estranged—which shows that the characters have had disasters in their minds long before catastrophe actually happens. Indeed, Ballard holds that contemporary people do dream of the end of the world. To show this I will present Ballardian mindscapes in his catastrophic trilogy *The Drowned World, The Drought, The Crystal World* and then in *The Atrocity Exhibition*, which combines the psychology of disaster and the twentieth-century mediascape.

In his charting of their mindscapes Ballard intertextually alludes to psychoanalysis, to the genre of catastrophic science fiction, and to the Surrealists, who also studied psychic responses to contemporary traumas. On the Surrealists' canvases inner hallucinatory landscapes abound in symbols that should be interpreted (with the help of Freudianism) in order to show the interplay of the latent and the patent in the human mind. Ballard employs a similar technique, though his strange disaster stories greatly depart from science fiction standards. In one of his interviews he said:

> In fact I've never thought of [my catastrophic science fiction stories] as being disaster stories because I don't see them as having unhappy endings. The hero follows the logic of his own mind; and I feel that anyone who does this is, in a sense, fulfilling himself (Linnet 1974: 4-7).

Some of Ballard's readers wish his catastrophic stories were more optimistic, with the hero surviving the catastrophe and creating anew a better civilization. They would also prefer an emphasis on adventures in the outside world, not on the broodings of the protagonists' minds. Ballard nevertheless claims that narratives describing thrilling adventures are naïve and repetitive and that today's writer should investigate mindscapes: that is, the impact of disasters on

---

2. In my book *The Voices of Disaster. J.G. Ballard and the Disaster Story Tradition in England* I give a longer presentation of the British disaster story tradition: I discuss the novels of John Wyndham, stories of other "New Wave" writers and I analyze in detail J.G. Ballard's catastrophic short stories, *The Drought, The Wind from Nowhere, The Day of Creation* and I discuss *The Atrocity Exhibition* as an example of disaster novel. In this chapter I will be using some arguments and examples developed in this book.

3. Especially, but not only, his early stories written before the nineteen-seventies.

the human psyche and the way in which external stimuli change our perception of time and space.[4]

Disasters in the Mind

In order to see how Ballard experiments with the catastrophic genre one should start with a short presentation of the British disaster story tradition. Though dating from the nineteenth century, the British disaster story flourished not until the 1950s and early 1960s during the Cold War. In that period, very much like today, science fiction was dominated by American writers and American pulp magazines such as *Astounding*. The tone of the stories published there in those decades is very pessimistic, as the recent war had left many with a feeling of despair and fear. Authors examine the implications of the nuclear bomb, political systems based on unlimited power, the Earth destroyed, culture doomed and humanity dying. T.A. Shippey writes in his essay "The cold war in science fiction, 1940-1960" (1979):[5]

> Society as a whole was adjusting gingerly to the possibility of nuclear extinction. But once again science fiction was groping for the second-order phenomena beyond the immediate horizon of reality: How would people react ...? Could anyone afford to let scientists remain at the top of the totem pole? Was there a way out of deterrents? These and other questions litter the science fiction magazines from the very start of the 1950s (Parrinder: 1979: 93).

The younger British science fiction writers who at that time were starting their literary careers were mostly readers of American magazines, and therefore the early stories of Norman Spinrad, Thomas M. Disch and Ballard are influenced by this poetics. Moreover, in England there was a strong tradition of similarly gloomy fiction of authoritarian societies: George Orwell's *1984* (1949), Evelyn Waugh's *Love among the Ruins* (1953) and Anthony Burgess' *A Clockwork Orange* (1962) and *The Wanting Seed* (1962) introduced the motif of a dystopian political future into science fiction. In fact, in the early 1960s British science fiction is very much informed by social themes. Writing about that decade in his *Billion Year Spree* (1973) Brian Aldiss observes:

> On the one side, the evolution of McLuhan's global village has involved increasing numbers of people in a forward-directed world outlook, which features SF. On the other side, the same cultural

4. This discussion concerning the future of the disaster story tradition (and of science fiction in Britain) is described in my Introduction, where Ballard's articles written for New Worlds and his guest editorial "Which Way to Inner Space?" are of crucial importance to the genesis of Ballardian mindscapes.
5. In *Science Fiction. A Critical Guide*, an influential collection of essays about science fiction edited by Patrick Parrinder.

effect has meant that SF writers and readers have become more involved with the world, less content with the old artificial patterns of SF adventure (Aldiss 1973: 293).

UK readers were prepared to enjoy a more cerebral kind of science fiction. Hence, in the years of the Cold War the late Victorian tradition of the British disaster story flourished again. At the end of the nineteenth century, when the first anti-urban, anti-civilization and anti-imperial sentiments were felt, Richard Jefferies' *After London* (1884) was published. In this novel Jefferies, a Victorian naturalist and journalist, pictures a post-apocalyptic world and describes in detail the ruin of the greatest city on Earth. Similar catastrophe narratives were written in the following decades: H.G. Well's *The War of the Worlds* (1898) and Conan Doyle's *The Poison Belt* (1913) among them. But it is in the 1930s that the genre was at last defined. Alun Llewellyn, who authored only one non-realistic fiction, to wit, *The Strange Invaders* (1934), gives the first full and complete picture of human-provoked disaster and the subsequent post-apocalyptic reality. His novel describes a future with a new ice age and the slow retrogression of humankind.[6] Other British disaster stories followed. R.C. Sherriff in *The Hopkins Manuscript* (1939) describes a planetary catastrophe—the Moon crashes down into the Atlantic and the partially destroyed Europe is raided by Asiatic races on jihad. What is important in the context of the British disaster story tradition is Sherriff's irony and sense of humour: the book parodies Victorian attitudes and telltale English mannerisms. Brian Aldiss calls this novel a paradigmatic "cosy catastrophe" of the kind written twenty years later by Wyndham:[7]

6. Joseph A. Quinn describes the novel in *Twentieth Century Science Fiction Writers*: "The story takes place in what seems to be the Gobi desert, a somewhat hostile environment, but one of the last places on Earth capable of supporting human life. The plot concerns a small group of people living in a half-destroyed town, isolated within the remains of a ruined city on the plains. There is a pseudo-medieval order to their existence: governed by a religious community of priests dedicated to the new trinity of Marx, Lenin and Stalin, and controlled by a warrior group, they manage to eke out a life of basic survival. As if their plight were not bad enough, Llewellyn has this last outpost of humanity threatened by an army of enormous lizards—huge, cold-blooded creatures that are virtually invincible. The plot is concerned with the efforts of the community to survive in the face of this new and overpowering challenge. What elevates the story above ordinary is Llewellyn's ability to show how the basic human emotions of love, hate, and jealousy survive and dominate the lives of these people" (Smith 1981: 341). The plot is worth remembering because it is partly echoed in Ballard's second book *The Drowned World* (1962).
7. The paradigm of the cosy catastrophe was set by Wyndham in *The Day of the Triffids* (1951), a novel describing an overnight end of civilization (nearly all humanity went blind) and a group of intact characters struggling to start it anew. As the material world was untouched by this catastrophe, food, automobiles and Savoys were really "free for the taking". Despite the fairytale-like atmosphere of such fictions they were in fact anxiety narratives; writers and readers were aware that civilization might indeed end overnight due to some natural disaster or, more plausibly still, because of World War III. John Christopher in his famous *Death of Grass* (1956) describes a catastrophe that is not cosy but rather horror-like. His later books such as *The World in Winter* (1962) and *Pendulum* (1968) describe even darker futures. Similarly gloomy novels followed. In Christopher Priest's *Fugue for a Darkening Island* (1972) we see England disrupted by civil war; in Robert Bateman's *When the Whites Went* the British Islands are entirely overtaken by black people.

Many heroes besides Sherriff's decided to meet the crisis in the dining room, so to speak. The essence of cosy catastrophe is the hero should have a pretty good time (a girl, free suites at the Savoy, automobiles for the taking) while everyone else is dying off. The best and most memorable example of this sub-genre is American: George Stewart's "Earth Abides", but it was the British writers—less preoccupied with aliens than their American counterparts—who specialised in Wyndham-esque comeuppances.

Among the afflictions visited on Earth by British writers are: snow (John Boland's *White August*); gales (J.G. Ballard's *The Wind from Nowhere*); insanity (Dighton Morel's *Moonlight Red*); plague (John Blackburn's *The Scent of New-Mown Hay*); disappearing oceans (Charles Eric Maine's *The Tides Went Out*); and super-beasts (J.T. McIntosh's *The Fittest*) (ibid.: 337).

What is striking is how the number of books delights in repeating a very similar disaster scheme. John Clute and Peter Nicholls in their *Encyclopedia of Science Fiction* note that disaster is what we fear, but also what we desire, at least in the overpopulated West of the twentieth century. Roger Luckhurst stresses the "Britishness" of the genre and the fact that its heyday coincides with the end of imperial England. The impossibility of a colonial future and the diminishing importance of England prepared the ground for images of destruction and death in many imagery narratives. The years 1945-1956 saw the reduction of British subjects from 475 million to 70 million and events such as the Suez crisis. Simultaneously, disaster stories were selling very well and many of them picture destruction which originates in the Far East. Their appeal was at least partly the result of the genre's repetitiveness, its schematic paradigm later parodied by Ballard. Luckhurst argues that:

The mega-textual apparatus of the genre insists on a rigorous distribution of 'iconic' scenes, plot and narrativization. The 'pleasures' of recognition begin with an identification with the… surviving narrator amidst genocidal carnage: the disaster (whatever it is) quickly assumes global proportions, offering the spectacle of cities in panic and decay. The 'veneer' of civilization and the fragility of the social order are stripped away. The genre, in other words, is propelled by a pseudo-scientific conception of 'degeneration' and the narrative moves towards the threat of remainderless destruction, the possibility that even narrative itself may not survive, before a re-generative solution is found, either inexplicably or through the machinations of an elite scientific cadre (Luckhurst 1997: 37).

These iconic scenes and motifs mentioned by Luckhurst may be found in the novels of John Wyndham, the best-known representative of the British disaster story tradition.[8] Wyndham remains a very English and a very middle-class author. His plots are fantastic, but his characters are plausible Englishmen from the fifties—intelligent, well-read, tradition-loving inhabitants of London town and its small, outlying villages. Moreover, he is a true disciple of H.G. Wells. Thus, in his books he employs both Wellsian themes (such as an invasion from another planet in the Solar System) and a Wellsian logic. Though the catastrophes he describes are imaginary, the human and social reactions to them seem probable. Moreover, all happens in the setting of the Cold War. The mutual suspicion of the Eastern and Western empires, propaganda in the media, and anti-Russian attitudes of the working class add to the vividness of his fantasies.

The beliefs and morals of Wyndham's characters reflect English middle-class standards from the 1950s. Old imperial attitudes are receding, and half-conscious fear and anxiety now prevail. England still seems the centre of the globe, where the uncanny and the dangerous should be confined to the "down below". Alas, they are not. Nevertheless, the characters are aware that their belief in their superiority is somehow dated, and thus the feelings of self-irony and distance. Traditional values and late Victorian theories (a modernized version of social Darwinism) compete with social entropy. The dominant feeling is that of uneasiness—something unknown and dangerous is lurking just behind the idyllic English countryside of green meadows.

Ballard, whose Asian background made him quite indifferent to the beauty of quaint English villages, used the British disaster story tradition to his own artistic ends. In his catastrophic stories Ballard seems to argue that we all unconsciously desire the absolute nirvana from before we were born, the quietness of inorganic matter. The way to revert to this state of no tension and no discomfort is remembering—immersing in the earliest memories. Compulsive returns and repetitions of old traumas are to take us back to pre-human and pre-biologic times, which on a genetic or molecular level we still remember. Civilization is, to paraphrase Freud, the ultimate source of discontent.

To this thesis borrowed directly from Freud, Ballard adds his own diagnosis of the historical moment we live in following World War II. Referring to the theses of Spengler, who discusses the inevitable twilight of a Western civilization that has outlived its life-span and now must vanish, Ballard depicts people unconsciously aware that their destination is extinction. Instead of mourning or trying to fight

---

8. Though his literary career started before World War II, it was only in the early 1950s, in the era of the Cold War, that Wyndham's disaster narratives became enormously popular. This popularity continued well into the last decades of the twentieth century: for example, my Penguin edition of *The Midwich Cuckoos* enumerates twenty-three reprints of the title in the twenty-year period of 1960-1980. John Clute in *The Encyclopedia of Science Fiction* argues: "[H]e wrote effectively for a specific UK market at a specific point in time—the period of recuperation that followed WWII— and he will be remembered primarily for the half decade or so during which he was able to express in telling images the hopes, fears and resurgent complacency of a readership that recognised a kindred spirit. During that period, in the UK and Australia at least, he was probably more read than any other SF author. As late as 1992, his books appeared regularly on school syllabuses in the UK" (Clute and Nicholls 1993: 1354).

the inevitable they willingly embrace disaster, which is strangely comforting for them as it resonates with scenarios we are encoded with in our inner minds. In unhappy, disintegrating societies only Ballardian protagonists sense that the time of the human race is approaching its end. Often they are prompted by their own unconscious (described with reference to Jung and the symbols he defines). Thus, we can reach the site of ancient knowledge by ignoring the outside world and immersing in our own psyche.

In "The Overloaded Man" (1961) the characters—a former lecturer who has resigned from his job, and his professionally successful wife—live in a nightmarish living estate of identical L-shaped overlapping gardens with ultra modern houses. Detached and alienated from his wife and his work, the professor learns to "switch off" the eternal reality—neither hearing nor seeing the world outside him, he travels in his mindscape. There is a strong suggestion that the man reacts to some general though elusive phenomena—the exhaustion of human society, the dead-end of civilization.

For the first time in centuries the human race is bereft of geniuses, one of the characters in the story remarks. Following the death of Einstein and Dali there is no living genius on Earth. People such as Darwin, Freud, da Vinci or Copernicus are able to single-handedly change paradigms of knowledge, step into unknown territories, understand something new about the universe and humankind and thus propel history forward. Nowadays, we are only cultivating and repeating their discoveries, there is no progress and none is possible, as we have reached the final stage of history—that of slow decay. Some people ignore this feeling and happily pursue their private ends: the need for money, prestige, and material goods (e.g., the wife of the protagonist) while others, like the professor, can find their freedom only in withdrawal from reality. His final suicide, the "switching off" of the world, is an act of self-liberation.

An even more extreme vision of the end of civilization for internal causes[9] (not any picturesque cosmic catastrophe, but via reaching the end of the natural life-span of our race) can be found in "The Impossible Man" (1966), a story apparently about transplants. Due to advanced medicine, people live long, well into their nineties and often over one hundred years but, simultaneously, the number of children decreases rapidly. The teenage protagonist of the story lives surrounded by people over sixty, the world slows down, there is no hope, no future and no reason to go on. Finally people refuse to have any transplants made, they do not want to prolong their personal lives beyond a certain natural limit. The same seems to be true for the whole of society, which simply has reached its natural end and further attempts to fight nature bring only unhappiness and trauma. The story ends with the boy's suicide, the proper response to the unconscious feeling of discomfort.

For Ballard the study of different societies, their history and culture, cannot be isolated from the unknown territory of the collective unconscious of seemingly

9. Sigmund Freud in *Beyond the Pleasure Principle* claims that all life longs to end due to internal causes (organisms try to avoid accidents and destruction, but at the same time die of old age), while Ballard's characters apply the same rules to civilization. They are not stable and eternal, but go through certain stages at the end of which lies extinction and oblivion.

dull and predictable contemporary people. Consumers of goods and commercials, boisterous holidaymakers and thoughtless tourists are nevertheless equipped with ancient primordial instincts and memories from before the dawn of humanity, which in certain situations can control them irrespectively of their civilized manners. In such moments people behave as thoughtlessly as lemmings and just as self-destructively. Following the line of the Freudian argument in *Beyond the Pleasure Principle* and applying well-known Jungian symbols (the unconscious compared to the sea, from which all life crept out billions years ago, mother as a beautiful and terrifying lamia) Ballard shows the innate irrationality of all societies.

> But I think the psychological role of the beach is much more interesting. The tide-line is a particularly significant area, a penumbral zone that is both of the sea and above it, forever half-immersed in the great time-womb. If you accept the sea as an image of the unconscious, then this beachward urge might be seen as an attempt to escape from the existential role of the ordinary life and return to the universal time-sea (Ballard 2002b: 430).

In the above quote, one of the characters of "The Reptile Enclosure" (1963), a scientist (who for reasons unknown even to himself joined the crowd rushing to the sea-side) tries to explain the strange social phenomenon of massive, instantaneous exodus to the sea. He is right as far as pointing to the innate unconscious reasons for this drive. It turns out that the launching of a new satellite and the accompanying emission of infrared light activated latent memories from the Cro-Magnon era that we all have somewhere in our unconscious selves. Following blindly the repetition-compulsion[10] drive, people repeat the movement into the sea and irrationally commit collective suicide.

Such neurotic behaviour—psychoses, repetition-compulsion, suicidal manias etc., are especially dangerous in decadent societies that are approaching the end of

---

10. The repetition-compulsion mechanism described by Freud as an automatic response of the psyche to traumas is crucial for Ballard's understanding of disasters and social reaction to natural catastrophes. In his stories and novels we very often see the regress to earlier stages of social and individual development in an attempt to master dangerous stimuli. Ballard's early fascination with psychoanalysis, and principally the repetition-compulsion mechanism, allows him to describe the neurotic behaviour of characters that live in hostile social condition. Unhappy societies, dying cultures, civilizations approaching their ends in Ballard's stories concentrate on enacting their history instead of moving on into the future. For example, virtually all the stories in his *Vermilion Sands*, a book I discuss in my presentation of Ballardian cityscapes, are based on the repetition-compulsion mechanism. *Vermilion Sands*, a beautiful decadent resort, is the home of neurotic artists and millionaires whose best days are far behind them and their principal pastime is enacting events from the past, as it is in "The Thousand Dreams of Stella Vista", a text heavily indebted to Freud's *Beyond the Pleasure Principle*. In that story the protagonist and his wife move into a once fashionable 'psychotropic' house of a film star. Psychotropic houses respond to the character and mood of its inhabitants, and this particular building years earlier was a witness of violent murder and psychic traumas, which it is now bound to repeat endlessly. As a result the protagonist and his wife have to enact the traumatic story of the film star marriage and the other people's past proves much stronger than their own present.

their life-span, as is the case (according to Ballard) with our Western world in the mid-1960s.[11] During those years in America, Philip K. Dick, one of the best science fiction writers of all times, wrote a number of books about societies (modelled upon drug-addicted California) where neuroses and basic uncertainty concerning the ontological status of the world are the norm. Alternative states of consciousness, drug-induced visions, post-mortem dreams etc., are indistinguishable from reality. In the context of Ballard's oeuvre the most important of Dick's book is *The Simulacra* (1964), which describes a society where psychiatry is prohibited and analysts have to abandon their patients, much to everybody's trauma. In his story "The Insane Ones" (1962)[12] we have a similar motif—the Mental Freedom Laws introduced by force by an ultraconservative government turn the world into a madhouse. Initially meant to reduce the mass manipulation and subliminal techniques of influence, they lead to the banishment of psychiatric practices and the imprisonment of therapists illegally giving treatment in the most severe cases. The story shows Western cities full of psychotics vainly looking for help, jumping from the rooftops etc., while the psychiatrists are either arrested or too frightened to do anything. It is worth noting that the principal reason of the epidemics of mental disorders is that of contemporary civilization itself: in a deeply unhappy and anxious society psychoses flourish.

Ballard's early novel, *The Wind from Nowhere* (1962) is written in disaster fiction poetics and upholds the standards of the genre. Nevertheless, his prose is quite idiosyncratic, and the novel has something in common with Ballard's later, more artistically ambitious catastrophes. Though it is now nearly forgotten, read in the context of the whole of Ballard's *oeuvre* it allows us to discern his gradual maturation—first he mostly repeats clichés, but some of his original ideas and thrusts are already introduced, his growing interest in mindscapes included.[13]

One day the wind starts blowing all over the globe, it is stronger near the equator and weaker near the poles, but generally speaking it has the power of a hurricane. Day after day the gales increase, tsunamis drown the shores, everything on the surface of the globe is destroyed, even the soil is carried off by the wind. No one

11. The times of hippies and beatniks, of swiftly dissolving social and sexual grouping is mentally demanding. When *The Divided Self* (1965), an extremely influential book by R.D. Laing on schizophrenia as a 'natural' response to the contemporary world, sold in the millions of copies—for details see Chapter One.
12. The story was written two years before Dick's novel, which does not necessarily imply that Dick had actually read it before conceiving of his own story (though it was published in the popular American *Amazing Stories* science fiction magazine). Schizophrenia and mental disease seem to have been at the time in the air in the whole affluent West.
13. Ballard's critics and biographers usually neglect *The Wind from Nowhere*. Colin Greenland in his *The Entropy Exhibition* suggests that the novel is artistically unsatisfying: "Written at top speed during a fortnight holiday, this was principally a commercial effort to earn Ballard enough money to leave his job and start writing full-time. The effort was successful. Ballard moved on immediately to a second novel..., which was artistically as fruitful as its predecessor had been financially" (Greenland 1983: 93). Michel Delville in *J.G. Ballard* describes this novel in a half a sentence as "a hastily written apocalypse story later disowned by its author" (Delville 1998: 7). For Roger Luckhurst it is "a conventional generic exercise... tracking the rise and fall of destructive force on the fabric of the social" (Luckhurst 1997: 38).

knows what has provoked the wind, no one is able to cope with the situation, and finally, no one knows why the wind stops to show the ruins. The novel is narrated from a number of points of view held by people in different geographical places, and, basically speaking, Ballard's aim here is to describe the catastrophe in all its colourful details. What is interesting is the fact that the book ends with the gales— Ballard is not interested in the re-building of social structures and civilization.

Attempts to explain why the wind from nowhere is blowing are weak and come exclusively from the characters; the narrator does not give the reader any hints as to the nature of this disaster. There is one stock scientist figure in the book, but his role is rather to measure the phenomenon than to discuss its aetiology. "Theoretically there are no reasons why it should not continue... indefinitely" (Ballard 1974a: 55), is all he has to say about the wind. Such a lack of fascinating pseudo-scientific explanations of natural phenomena or, even better, sinister alien civilizations that try to destroy our planet is untypical for a disaster story. What Ballard does have in common with other authors of this genre is the belief in social Darwinism. But again, in his case the conclusions are very pessimistic; the human race seems to have the times of evolutionary success far behind.

The greater part of human beings are not selected to survive, and those who are seem rather more lucky than fit (moreover, we cannot know whether they are going to survive on the destroyed, barren Earth after the wind subsides). The last sentence of the book simply states that because of certain reasons obscure to humans: "Like a cosmic carousel nearing the end of its run, the storm wind was slowly losing speed" (ibid.: 186). Given the book's pessimistic tone it is not surprising that the iconic disaster story scenes Ballard does include in his narrative are detailed descriptions of atrocities and ruins. We read about gigantic traffic jams, cities sunk by storm waves, destroyed high-rises. The fall of Nelson's column is pictured in a separate paragraph, and we see thousands of atrocities, mostly in underground stations and in the deserted streets.

In this book all social or political structures dissolve very quickly. Individuals have to cope on their own, disaster separates people and entropy prevails. Ballard's characters are made to face Armageddon and their responses to the end of their world are what interests Ballard the most. In *The Wind from Nowhere* we can see a very early stage of Ballard's experiments with mindscapes, psychology and characterization. His characters apparently derive from the reservoir of stock disaster story figures (a scientist, a general, an officer, a secretary from a governmental agency etc.), but their descriptions are far from simplicity. They are not "people next door" and they are conscious of their own conventionality:

> Physiognomically he certainly appeared to be the exact opposite of the emotionally-motivated cycloid personality. Tall, and slightly stooped, his face was thin and firm, with steady eyes and a strong jaw. If anything he was probably over-resolute, too inflexible, a victim of his own rational temperament, viewing himself with the logic he applied in his own laboratory. How far this had made him happy was hard to decide... (ibid.: 17).

Thus is one of the major characters introduced to the reader. This description is focalized by the character; sitting in a taxi he looks into the mirror and reflects upon his own face, as if seeing it for the first time. This ability to look at oneself from a distance and to juxtapose appearances ("he certainly appeared", "he was probably") with the hidden truth ("hard to decide") introduces a sense of duality: things are perhaps not what they appear to be.

This persistent emphasizing of the difference between essence and appearance, a face and a conventional mask, is not at all typical for the disaster story. Ballard describes his characters in a sketchy way and he does introduce cliché personalities, but at the same time he subverts the convention. His characters habitually analyze their own behaviour and, when the disaster comes, their reluctance for the roles they play become evident. The catastrophe is not cosy at all, as it shows what human societies really are: masses of ill-fitting individuals forcefully made to behave in a conventional manner, each closed within his own mind. There is no liberal, moral, patriotic, English or any other backbone to human reactions. In the face of real danger there is no real difference between countries and continents, all human organizations and institutions are equally impotent. Civilization is subject to cosmic hazards, and the only ideology we may find behind the chaotic actions of the people whose world is falling apart is a crude social Darwinism.

The End-of-the-World Dreams

The Drowned World (1962), written when Ballard was associated with *New Worlds*, is a catastrophic novel depicting a dying civilization and a passive, defeated human race.[14] The end of the world as we know it, is a good moment to study different human reactions to trauma. It also provides an opportunity to describe a noble but resigned protagonist whose aim is to die in the way he is destined to die. Ballard enters inter-textual dialogues with Freud, Darwin and the Surrealists; his reader is supposed to be able to decipher and interpret allusions and to be brave enough to draw the most pessimistic conclusion.

In this book the catastrophe is due to the hyperactivity of the Sun:

> The succession of gigantic geophysical upheavals which had transformed the Earth's climate...A series of violent and prolonged solar storms lasting several years caused a sudden instability in the Sun... Depleting the Earth's barrier against the full impact of solar radiation, temperatures began to climb steadily, the heated atmosphere expanding outwards into the ionosphere...mean temperatures rose by a few degrees each year...a gradual adjustment of life took place. The higher levels of radioactivity increased the rate at which mutations occurred (Ballard 1974b: 21).

14. The following analysis of *The Drowned World* is based on a paper I gave at the 11th PASE Conference in Kazimierz in 2002 which was subsequently published in *Perspectives on Literature and Culture*, eds Leszek S. Kolek, Aleksandra Kędzierska and Anna Kędra-Kardela, Lublin 2004.

Interestingly, these mutations resemble primordial organisms from archaic epochs. Gradually, as the climate and geography return to their state from millions of years ago, biological evolution is also reversed. Ferns and reptiles dominate the Earth; mammals cease to multiply while the remnants of the human race, who were earlier forced to move to the poles, now witness the end of civilization.[15] The waters of the melted icecaps flood most of the Earth and the heat is unbearable. New coastlines resemble those from the very distant past; the remains of human cities are covered with water and looted by all kinds of pirates and savages.

The action of the novel is set in tropical lagoons where London was once found, at a small station where a group of scientists are meant to prepare maps for future re-colonization of the area. This task is absurd and futile and the scientists suffer from different kinds of apathy and alienation. They are interested in neither their work, nor in self-preservation. Each of them lives separately in surreal surroundings of gigantic tropical vegetation covering luxurious hotels, looted houses and underwater streets. Dr Kerans, his former girlfriend–a millionaire's daughter, Beatrice Dahl, old Mr Bodkin, who vaguely remembers London from before the flood, and a group of soldiers, all suffer, not only from the heat, but also from strange neuroses or alternate states of consciousness. Everyone, in his own way, submerges in distant and alien memories, or rather into intuitive states connected with the world of millions of years ago. Educated and inventive scientists are aware of their condition and try to explain the reasons for their lethargy and hallucinations:

> In response to the rises of temperature, humidity and radiation levels the flora and fauna of this planet are beginning to assume once again the forms they displayed the last time such conditions were present—roughly speaking, the Triassic period... Everywhere there's been the same avalanche backwards into the past... the few complex organisms look distinctively anomalous—a handful of amphibians, the birds and Man... we have ignored the most important creature on this planet (ibid. :41).

In this conversation with Kerans, Bodkin is suggesting neither backward changes in human anatomy nor any regression to previous evolutional stages of the primate family. Their discussion, which alludes to many different branches of science, leads to the conclusion that the human race is becoming an anachronism; men are forced to live in the epoch from long before their biological time. According to Bodkin, despite our human nature and mammalian anatomy, on the cellular level, all of us retain memories of previous stages of evolution. We remember our ancestors who evolved into humans. Bodkin postulates about our

15. According to Gasiorek, in the descriptions of tropical landscapes Ballard is inspired primarily by Jung. "The terrifying jungle dreams—Jungian archetypes—experienced by the novel's characters are race memories dredged up from the unconscious and embodied in physical form by the giant, shrieking reptiles that are once again becoming the lords of creation" (Gasiorek 2005: 36). Thus these landscapes are in fact mindscapes.

innate propensity for backward movement, believing that, deep in our souls, there are traces of the passage from the most primitive protozoa to *Homo sapiens*.

As if paraphrasing late Freudian theories, he says:

> How often recently most of us have the feeling of *déjà vu*, of having seen all of this before, in fact of remembering these swamps and lagoons. However selective the conscious mind may be, most biological memories are unpleasant ones, echoes of danger and terror. Nothing endures so long as fear. Everywhere in nature one sees evidence of innate releasing mechanisms literally millions of years old, which have lain dormant through thousands of generations but retained their power undiminished (ibid.: 43).

Such genetic memory mechanisms, according to Bodkin, are responsible for the strange behaviours and abnormal psychic activities of the people at the station. He himself is the only member of the group old enough to possess his personal memories of Europe from before the disaster. All the other people were born at Camp Byrd in Northern Greenland. However, at the moment of migration, he was already six—so for him the drowned streets and looted museums are all the more dream-like as they bear resemblance to the landscape of his childhood. Bodkin closes himself in his mindscape—a vicious circle of remembrances; instead of working, he spends his days rowing around the London lagoon, and the past that he recollects devours his present. Bodkin is unable to stop thinking about the past and to concentrate on the present: when he looks at the lagoon, he sees London, seeming to him like a surreal fantasy or an artistically disfigured picture of the known landscape, and not like a new territory they are to explore and map. Bodkin's perspective is similar to ours—we too recognize the remains of the 20th-century cityscape in the descriptions of the lagoon.

Ballard purposefully gives these descriptions some surreal quality, thus suggesting the dream-like character of the setting. This setting is composed from what we remember: either from the 20th century or, on the cellular, genetic level, from the Triassic era. His allusions to the Surrealists echo André Breton, who connected the mental return to the past with the unconscious and who, in *Le Surréalism et la Peinture* (1928), suggested that the search for identity leads, via remembered images, to the things "already seen, already heard, never seen... To see, to hear is nothing. To recognise (or not to recognise) is everything. Between what I recognise and what I do not recognise is I" (Breton 1967: 26).

Surrealism in *The Drowned World* results from the oppressive heat, inertia and the apathy of the characters faced with haphazard and impossible images. These images reflect their unconscious fears and vague memories; Ballard's descriptions are stylized to resemble surreal pictures. Thus, it is not accidental that Beatrice's grandfather decorated the family residence with the works of Ernst and Delvaux. Ballard, therefore, reveals the sources of his allusions—he himself emphasizes the intertextual character in *The Drowned World*. The Jungle, the unconscious, the journey backwards and inwards, are all demonstrated to be recurrent artistic themes. At one moment, Strangman, an albino buccaneer who leads a brigade of fanatic African savages, comes to the station and starts looting the ruins.[16] The similarities to Joseph Conrad's *Heart of Darkness* are striking. Strangman's erudition, evil and presumed madness make him the embodiment of Kurtz and reflect enigmas from Conrad's text.

Ballard describes Strangman's robberies and voodoo rituals with cinematic technique, giving his reader a series of surreal images: a settee full of gigantic snakes, the dried ruins of Leicester Square overgrown with moss and fungi, a girl in the British Museum, jewellery covered with mud, etc. The logic of narration is surreal, as the order of these images is not chronological, but instead resembles a network of unconscious associations.

Some scenes or meanings are interpreted as symbolic by the characters themselves. Kerans considers Beatrice and himself to be the second Adam and Eve of the reversed creation; the last pair in the nightmarish Eden. For him the world around resembled Freud and Breton. Beatrice, on the other hand, thinks in terms of the late 60s counterculture. The overwhelming anarchy of haphazard reality composed in a patchwork manner of bric-a-brac of the old world with its various discourses makes her think about the hippie culture. Her life and perceptions blur into a slumber. Aware of this process, she comments on it, quoting Guy Debor's famous remark that: "Alcohol kills slowly, but I'm in no hurry" (Ballard 1974a: 50).

The fullest interpretation of the state of their minds is given by Bodkin, who arrives at the decision to postulate a totally new branch of science: neuronics. Based on the theories of Freud and Darwin, neuronics describes reality as a product of mindscape psychically born in the brain. Memories from the turn of the Palaeozoic and the Triassic era are coded somewhere in the hindbrain. These long-latent genetic recollections of our ancestors, the first air-breathing amphibians, are now awoken by the external stimuli resembling those from millions of years ago. Though Ballard's characters laugh at psychoanalysis, joking about "their uterine childhood" and the reality resembling Rorschach's tests, *The Drowned World* is in fact built around the Freudian motif of the dominance of the death drive over the pleasure principle; of Thanatos over Eros.

Similarities between Ballard's *The Drowned World* and Freud are striking, with the novel acquiring new meanings if read against psychoanalytical theory. *Beyond the Pleasure Principle* gives Ballard a theoretical apparatus which, together with his interests in entropy characteristic for "New Wave" writers, influence the style and the atmosphere of the novel. *The Drowned World* attempts to describe the dominance of death over life and biology over psychology in the language of fiction. Ballard alludes to Freud both in the overall philosophy of the text and in the descriptions of the particular aspects of evolutional regress.

Echoing Freudian language, Ballard's characters interpret the world around them, as well as the changes in their mindscapes:

---

16. It is possible to view Strangman as Kerans' double and an intertextual allusion to Freud's theories of the Uncanny: "An obvious Doppelganger—the despised dark side of Kerans' psyche—Strangman is also Kerans' symbolic opposite in the level of culture" (Gasiorek 2005: 38).

These are the oldest memories on Earth, the time-codes carried in every chromosome and gene. Every step we've taken in our evolution is a milestone inscribed with organic memories—... each is a record of a thousand decisions taken in the face of a sudden physico-chemical crisis. Just as psychoanalysis reconstructs the original traumatic situation in order to release the repressed material, so we are now being plunged back into the archaeopsychic past, uncovering the ancient taboos and drives that have been dormant for epochs. The brief span of an individual life is misleading. Each one of us is as old as the entire biological kingdom, and our bloodstreams are tributaries of the great sea of its total memory. The uterine odyssey of the growing foetus recapitulates the entire evolutionary past (ibid.: 43).

In these words, Bodkin tries to explain the strange behaviour of the people at the station. What strikes him is the similarity of their psychologies. Their individual features blur, as if deep inside, we all are the same and share identical memories. Bodkin calls this cellular level, "the Deep Time", thus emphasizing the timelessness of mental processes and repeating Freud's theory.

The situation at the station worsens at the moment when the characters start dreaming very special kinds of visions. One by one, beginning with the vulnerable, but eventually, the strongest, they move back in time, re-living nightmares from our common Triassic past. Gradually, their dreams and reality blur together. Even Kerans has problems distinguishing between what is real and what is imagined. The world around grows surreal, and can be explained only in the Freudian idiom: "He remembered the iguanas braying and lunging across the steps of the museum. Just as the distinction between the latent and the manifest contents of the dream had ceased to be valid, so had any division between the real and the super-real in the external world" (ibid.: 72). It is worth noticing that such a juxtaposition of phantoms and perceptions is in itself an allusion to the Surrealists, who were also very much impressed by Freud. To quote André Breton's *The Second Manifesto of Surrealism*: "Surrealism believes Freudian criticism to be the first and the only one with a really solid basis" (Breton 1929: 160).

Similar to Freud, Ballard's dreams serve to re-enact the past. All mammals retain archaic memories, returning to the inscriptions on their genes in a moment of trauma. All life longs to die and, when the right time comes, regresses to the state of inanimate matter. This regression is "evolution in reverse". Taking no short cuts, life moves backwards slowly, repeating the remembered stages. The will to die is innate and true to nature and Ballard's characters are conditioned to fulfill their destiny. Instead of saving their lives and coming back to Greenland, one by one they decide to go south when their time comes, to the places too hot for humans. Unconsciously knowing that, according to some global design, they are doomed to extinction.

Ballard comes back to similar concerns in *The Drought* (1965) where the convention of the catastrophic genre is used to chart the mindscape of the protagonist. The thesis is put forward explicitly: post-apocalyptic landscapes reflect the innermost feelings of contemporary humankind. The book only superficially belongs to science fiction—in fact it is possible to read it as a critique of catastrophic fiction, an exercise meant to prove the exhaustion of the genre. The defining elements are present: we see a global drought, panic-driven escapees, civilization in regress, etc., but the adventurous story is not convincing and our real object of interest is the human psyche and the way the outside world influences it.

The science fiction pretence of the narrative is as follows: because of pollution and some spontaneous chemical reactions in liquid refuse, the oceans are covered with a thin film of indissoluble substance that stops the process of vaporization. No clouds are formed and the climate changes rapidly. The lack of rain and the resultant slow death of the world's rivers and lakes make continents uninhabitable. People panic and try to get to the shores of the oceans. Most of them die fighting one another in the first few years, and the rest organize small communes or fishermen villages and work hard to obtain fresh water. Strange cults are born and, somewhere in the arid interiors, even stranger communities manage to survive in the ruins.

We see (or rather guess) what happens on the global scale through the eyes of the protagonist named Ransom, who is one of the last people to leave the shrinking lake and one of the first to come back from the shore after a few years. The perspective is limited to his point of view: there is very little information about the world outside Ransom's immediate surroundings as he is not much interested in it. In fact, his major interest is his own psyche, the mindscapes of half-conscious memory and obscure compulsions.

The action of the novel is set in the lakeside village of Hamilton, a suburb of Mount Royal one hundred miles away at the seashore. Although the setting is named, in fact we know neither the country nor even the continent where Mount Royal is and, moreover, all the descriptions of places emphasize Ransom's attitudes to them, not any objective characteristics. The space described by Ballard is just a reflection of the inner universe of his protagonist: "In a sense the house was a perfect model of a spatio-temporal vacuum, inserted into the continuum of his life by the private alternate universe in the household on the river" (Ballard 1985a: 31).

Ransom is aware that the world he sees is disfigured by his perception. At the moment civilization ends, its artefacts, cityscapes included, gain a surreal quality for him:

> Superficially the streets and houses resembled those of the normal world. The lines that once marked the boundaries still formed a discrete but unreal image, like the false object seen in a convex mirror (ibid.: 39).

Though the perspective in the novel is limited to Ransom we are given to understand that other characters also perceive space in their idiosyncratic manner. For Lomax, a dandy and a millionaire who refuses to leave Mount Royal in the times of the drought, human civilization regresses and the landscape resembles that of centuries earlier: "He pointed to the dusty villas along the river. 'They look like mud huts already. We're moving straight back into the past'" (ibid.: 46). The point Ballard makes is that civilization imposes its own image on landscapes and makes us perceive space in a uniform way. Once a disaster comes each separate mind works out its own image of reality and inscribes new personal meaning to apparently objective things. People in Mount Royal in the last days before the exodus create legends and make up a new half-fantastic geography. The most cherished belief is the legend of a new river full of fresh water somewhere in the desert.

The interior of the continent, along with newly created dry wastelands around Mount Royal and further inland, are places of self-discovery, surreal landscapes where the inside and the outside mingle. A reproduction of *Jours de Lenteur* by the Surrealist painter Ives Tanguy best describes Ransom's new sense of space in post-apocalyptic reality. Ransom compulsively stares at the painting seeing in it his own mindscape. This dreamy and half-real inland space is contrasted with the terrain along the sea-shore. People in panic had moved there taking with them the bric-a-brac of their former civilized lives. Slowly deteriorating, these objects form the gigantic scrap-yard of a dying culture.[17] An old but well-preserved car starts to signify the lost dream of mobility and technology, bits and pieces of machinery are composed into new, neo-primitive constructions. New religious images are painted on the walls of church huts; they feature Jesus among gigantic fish and sea monsters. The seashore is where post-apocalyptic communities start civilization anew, but in a diminished, grotesque version. Life here is an eternal regression into the past of human societies. In order to complete his internal journey of self-revelation Ransom has to return to arid Mount Royal and face his own destiny.

> At first Ransom had assumed that he... was returning to the past, to pick up the frayed ends of his previous life, but he now felt that the white deck of the river was carrying them all in the opposite direction, forward into zones of time future where the unresolved residues of the past would appear smoothed and rounded, muffled by the detritus of time, like images in a clouded mirror (ibid.: 152).

The journey back through the dry abandoned land and further away into the desert allows Ransom to regain his long lost personality and to find equilibrium

---

17. In the early 1990s Ballard gave a very interesting interview to Lynne Fox, who was then writing her master's degree thesis about surrealism in his output. Asked about what fascinates him in the art of the Surrealists he said that they—like he—were interested in creating a new mythology, different than classical myths: "most of the classical mythologies describe beginnings of things, the creation of the world, how mankind fell, the birth of gods.... These are mythologies that grapple with the starting points of human experience, whereas I'm interested in the other end of the spectrum: with where all these events are leading us. It's a classic stand of Science Fiction... So I'm concerned in most of my fiction with mythologies that draw a concluding line underneath the human experience. They represent end-points. I'm trying to suggest that there is a new psychological order awaiting us, which I'm as convinced of as an ordinary individual as I am as an imaginative writer. The twentieth century is a kind of cusp, a moving off from the old order into the new order that lies ahead" (Vale 2005: 167).

between his surroundings and his state of mind. In a way, all his life before the drought seems to be a preparation for the post-apocalyptic existence, which is psychologically more satisfying.

Instead of grieving the loss of his former life and the luxuries of affluent technological civilization, Ransom uses the drought as a means of liberation; he eagerly quits the role he played in society and enjoys the stillness and emptiness of post-apocalyptic reality. After the end all objective measures and imposed rules vanish and the only reality is psychic: "a world of volitional time where the images of the past were reflected free from the demands of memory and nostalgia" (ibid.: 176). Free from conventional confines he is ready to accept the challenge of the deserted interior. His final decision to go to the centre of the dead continent is liberating, and it means the acceptance of his true self. Many characters in the book unconsciously feel that: "we ought to accept the challenge and set off north, right into the centre of the drought... There's probably a great river waiting for us somewhere there, brown water and green lands –"(ibid.: 75). Ransom is able to follow this unconscious drive to go to the desert. He leaves behind all social relationships and all memories of his previous life—his journey is like an existential quest for identity and freedom. In this case it is the freedom to die in the way he wants to die, and in the place he feels is proper. At the moment he sets off the first rain in many years falls as if suggesting his decision is right.

Compared to, say, the disaster stories of John Wyndham, *The Drought* seems strangely abstract and detached from any real life context. We do not know where Mount Royal is—it seems not to be in England. In fact, there is no mention of England at all in the text and no suggestion that the characters are English or that they have any significant nationality. Only because of the language the book is written in and owing to the references to English literature that Ransom makes may we assume that he is English. In any case, England is not central or even important in the world described in this novel and English society, whether from the times of the Cold War or any other epoch, is not mentioned. There is in fact scarcely any information about the world, global geography or economics. The single notable exception is the paragraph right at the beginning: we learn about vain attempts to stop the drought, about the charity actions of the U.N. and ecological catastrophes in the Amazon and the White Nile areas. All this description is but a pretext to tell the story of Mount Royal and Ransom; Ballard reluctantly provides this introduction for the sake of disaster story standards, as it were, but he is not interested in working out yet another scenario for a global Armageddon.[18]

The drought destroyed the network of relationships between people. It was

---

18. His technique is to signal to his readers that he knows catastrophic clichés and is not going to elaborate on them. A good example of this method is a sentence spoken by Ransom when he finally gets to the sea-shore and sees the panic: "But what about the government evacuation plans? Those beach cards and so on..." (Ballard 1985a: 99). We never learn anything more about this government (is it a global or national one? In the sixties or in some distant future?), said plans or any other organized action. Ballard simply acknowledges the standards; in disaster stories you always read about vain attempts on the part of governments to stop the panic.

the river which bound them together: "the absence of this great moderator, which cast its bridges between all animate and inanimate objects alike, would prove of crucial importance. Each of them would soon literally be an island in an archipelago of drained time" (ibid.: 14). The disaster isolates people, everybody is confined to his own mindscape.[19] Only when they decide to fight destiny (instead of following the existential call of the desert) and organize a new life is a communal feeling born. The post-apocalyptic social structures remodel human personality. First, the escapees have to abandoned their previous selves: "Like all purgatories, the beach was a waiting ground, the endless stretches of wet salt sucking away from them all but the hardest core of themselves" (ibid.: 119). Only then could they enter a new kind of neo-primitive society with its patchwork ideology and religion made out of scraps of the previous life.

The characters of standard disaster stories are "people next door", contemporary sensible English persons who, by their typical reactions, make even the strangest events seem plausible. The people described in *The Drought* are much more difficult to classify. On the one hand they also seem "borrowings" and appeal to us because we indeed recognize them and find them familiar. But on the other hand they are certainly not real in the way our neighbours are real. First of all, as already quoted, the drought reduced them to "the hardest core of themselves", which for Ballard means the type, or even archetype of personality—and such archetypes are to be found in the literary tradition we all share. Moreover, we see all of them through Ransom's eyes and therefore through the associations he has.

At the beginning of the novel Ransom himself is compared to "a seafaring Nordic anthropologist, standing with one hand on his mast, the other on his Malinowski" (ibid.: 14). This comparison is quite important; throughout the book he behaves somewhat like a scientist, ever classifying people and pointing to the type they represent. In his eyes the millionaire Lomax is "a petulant Nero overwhelmed by the absurdity and ingratitude of the world" (ibid.: 43), and then "a grotesque pantomime dame, part amiable scoundrel and part transvestite" (ibid.: 174). Similarly, the fortune-teller Mrs Quilter is a witch. Lomax's sister Miranda, a decidedly negative female character, is in turns compared to Lamia and Medusa.

As far as Ransom himself is concerned, in order to find his 'type' we have to consider Ballard's other disaster stories. In each of them there is a Doctor figure (Dr Maitland in *The Wind from Nowhere*, Dr Kerans in *The Drowned World*, Dr Ransom in *The Drought*, Dr Sanders in *The Crystal World*, and numerous other doctors in his short stories). All these characters are withdrawn, overwhelmed by a catastrophe and willingly give up the struggle to survive in the hope of finding their true selves long since repressed by social life. In a sense we may treat them, psychologically at least, as the same person, someone whom a Ballardian reader should recognize.

---

19. "In time, the sand drifting across the dunes would reunite them on its own terms, but for the present each of them formed a self-contained and discrete world of his own" (Ballard 1985a: 102). Ransom understands the subtle relationship between people and their surrounding. Social structures and the social roles we adopt within their boundaries are far weaker that they seem; it is the psychic feeling of belonging in the outside world that our true personality emerges.

As the sources of archetypes Ballard refers to are hidden in our cultural competence, *The Drought* is abundant in literary allusions. Ballard treats culture as a reservoir of associations and *déjà vu* very much in accord with Jungian theory of the collective unconscious. The most important texts deeply rooted in our minds are those of Shakespeare, the Surrealists and the Romantics. The major intertext in the novel is the already mentioned painting by Tanguy. This painting represents the post-apocalyptic world of no time and no movement. Firstly, many years before the drought, its reproduction makes a great impression on Ransom, and some years later the vision on the picture comes true.

As for literature, the most potent source of archetypes is Shakespeare, particularly Ballard's favourite *The Tempest*, in which most of the characters have their counterparts. Thus, Ransom's young friend Philip Jordan is a "foster child of the river and its last presiding Ariel" (ibid.: 22); the idiot Quilter is "the grotesque Caliban of all his nightmares" (ibid.: 67), and Miranda Lomax is an echo of her Shakespearean namesake. The post-apocalyptic "marriage" of Miranda and Quilter makes Lomax adopt the role of "a demented Prospero examining the offspring of his violated daughter" (ibid.: 181), and recognize the text they are re-enacting: "Quilter, you obscene beast! Come here, my Caliban, show yourself to your master" (ibid.: 180). *The Drought* becomes in this way a nightmarish, catastrophic *The Tempest* gone wrong—as in the victory of Caliban, who manages to regain the island and people it with his offspring. Shakespearean plays coexist in culture: Miranda also "remind[s] Ransom of an imbecile Ophelia" (ibid.: 78), and another character, the Revered Johnstone, has "the appearance of a demented Lear" (ibid.: 130).

An equally potent source of icons is Samuel Taylor Coleridge's *The Rime of the Ancient Mariner*, especially its images of death, dryness and destruction. The deadly Lamia mentioned in the novel is like the Mariner's Life-in-Death, birds dying in the dry river "remind Ransom of a land-locked mariner and his stricken albatross, deserted by the sea" (ibid.: 24). Other references include *Arabian Nights* and the story of Ulysses—in the times of catastrophe people are reduced to their basic personality.

The eponymic drought transforms human society and each individual being alike. Social pretence, the roles we play and the masks we adopt are "sucked away by wet salt". What are left are just bare egos, outlines of personalities. Ballard was interested neither in the recreation of civilization nor in the sociological mechanisms involved in such an enterprise. There is no future for the human race as a whole: the drought marks only the beginning of the catastrophe, as the final extinction of humans will undoubtedly follow. The only thing for the characters to do is to find in the post-apocalyptic landscapes a reflection of their inner space, to embrace the catastrophe as liberating.

The Drought juxtaposes allusions to Freud and Jung in trying to chart the inner space of the human mind in the moment of disaster. A similar mechanism can be found in *The Crystal World* (1966), a novel based on Ballard's short story "The Illuminated Man" (1964), which still can be labelled disaster fiction, though the most important subject is the protagonist's search for his true latent self. The protagonist after having been rescued from the deadly zone of spontaneously crystallizing forest decides to go back: he understands the reason why his former lover stayed in the forest and finds in himself the same attitude. As Ballard explains: "for both of them the only final resolution of the imbalance within their minds, their inclination towards the dark side of the equinox, could be found within that crystal world" (Ballard 2000: 173).

"The dark part of the equinox" from the above quote stands for the unknown but wise part of the human mind, which sometimes should be given control over the conscious part. The uncanny beauty of disaster (in this case, the crystal inorganic matter) corresponds to the hidden desires and memories of the characters. Ballard seems to believe in the Jungian model of the human psyche, according to which the division into the conscious and the unconscious is painful and unnecessary. While in the Freudian system this division is structural and natural in every intelligent being, for Jung it has been caused by some evolutionary accident and is the bane of the human race. In an ideal utopian world the conscious and the unconscious should be reunited in the one Self.

This utopian unity, according to Jung's *Man and His Symbols* (1964) is best symbolized in the mandala. In Ballard's book it is shown in the perfection of crystals—dead but beautiful.[20] The unification of all the contraries—light and dark, conscious and unconscious, organic and inorganic—brings the acceptance of all the repressed material and, finally, the nirvana-like death of static beauty. It is also worth noting that though Ballard is inspired by Jung he also refers to Freudian theory, especially Freud's description of the death drive. This mixture of intertextual allusions to their oeuvres is worth discussing, as in Ballard's fiction the themes of disaster, memory, the unconscious, and the end of time go together and are expressed in psychoanalysis-inspired discourse.[21]

"The Illuminated Man" (1964) deals with the unconscious, the death instinct and the end of time. The story starts in a way similar to standard science fiction in the early 60s: a catastrophe comes and threatens life on Earth. In Ballard's story, however, the science fictional pretext is rather weak, and the catastrophe (a spontaneous crystallization of matter spreading across Earth and into the cosmos) is very implausible. Ballard is interested not in a sensational story on bravery and

---

20. Compare André Breton's *Mad Love*: "There could be no higher teaching than that of the crystal. The work of art, just like any fragment of human life considered in its deepest meaning, seems to me devoid of value if it does not offer the hardness, the rigidity, the regularity, the luster on every interior and exterior facet, of the crystal" (cit., Gasiorek 2005: 54).

21. It is worth remembering that at the time Ballard was writing his mindscapes disaster fictions, the hippie culture flourished in Britain, psychoanalysts such as R.D. Laing combined their search for the inner self of contemporary Man with the LSD cult and experimented with alternative states of consciousness. In *The Politics of Experience* (1967) R.D. Laing writes about the necessary quest for the lost inner world in a style which is characteristic for such gurus: "I am a specialist, God help me, in events in inner space and time, in experiences called thoughts, images, reveries, memories, memories of dreams, memories of visions, dreams of hallucinations, refractions of refractions of refractions of that original Alpha and Omega of experience and reality, that Reality on whose repression, denial, splitting, projection, falsification, and general desecration and profanation our civilization as much as on anything is based. We live equally out of our bodies and out of our minds. Concerned as I am with this inner world, observing day in and day out its devastation, I ask why this has happened?" (Laing 1990: 50).

survival, but in the surreal beauty of the frozen universe. Cosmic regress, the end of time symbolized by ice-like, immobile landscapes of no warmth and nothing to ever change are strangely appealing to the "dark" side of the characters' minds. The primordial state of the inorganic substance is restored, firstly in just a few enclaves—but the phenomenon will likely devour the whole Universe, which some people subliminally recognize as desirable, though consciously they try to fight for survival.

Crystallized birds, trees, objects and human beings defy the distinction between the animate and the inanimate. The narrator, a scientist whose past makes him prone to thoughts about mortality, gets into the crystallizing forests of Florida, where the jewelled extravaganza of the transparent landscape triggers his memories—firstly personal, but then those of the human species. The story starts with exclaiming the sheer beauty of the deadly phenomenon, which changes the well-known world into an esthetic image constructed by the minds of the onlookers. "By day fantastic birds flew through the petrified forest, and jewelled alligators glittered like heraldic salamanders on the banks of the crystalline rivers" (Ballard 2002b: 605). This opening sentence written in italics seems to refer to an artefact or subjective fantasy rather than to a geographical terrain and, moreover, the description of this image resembles surrealist art as it presents the unconscious reaction to the outside world.[22]

Just after the above poetic sentence the story changes into an objective, science fiction-like account of the journey to Florida interwoven with descriptions of the crystallizing disease. The story is a first person narration by a very detached introvert and it is only via his mind that we get to know what is going on and how the outside reality resonates in his unconscious:

> The beauty of the spectacle had stirred my memory, and a thousand images of childhood, forgotten for nearly forty years, now filled my mind, recalling the paradisal world of one's earliest years when everything seems illuminated by that prismatic light described so exactly by Wordsworth in his recollections of childhood. Since the death of my wife and three-year-old daughter in a car accident ten years earlier I had deliberately repressed such feelings, and the vivid magical shore before us seemed to glow like the brief spring of my marriage (ibid.: 610).

Ballard emphasizes the interaction of the landscape and the narrator's mindscape: his memory, fears, repressed thoughts. The allusion to Wordsworth introduces the idea that once the world used to be better, more beautiful and magical, and we felt united with it, belonging in nature. As in Wordsworth's poem, in Ballard's story, too, the lost splendour of reality (now regained in the beauty of crystal forests) is rendered in metaphors of light, transparency and clearness.

---

22. The use of similes is very telling here: this favourite figure of speech of the Surrealists is often repeated in the story.

In romantic poetry the lost paradise is forgotten childhood, while Ballard uses this reference to describe the psychoanalytical concept of the pre-civilized paradise of the very beginnings of time. We lost it as a race in the processes of evolution, civilization etc., but sometimes a persistent feeling of déjà-vu makes us subliminally long for ancient epochs.

The beginnings of time and its approaching end are similar. The beautiful kaleidoscopic forests are "markedly cooler, as if everything were sheathed in ice" (ibid.: 613). This coolness and the progressing stillness of the affected areas suggest the end of warmth and movement. According to the theories of entropy, the heat death of the Universe will occur at some point in the remote future, when all the energy of the universe will be spent: with no differences in temperature no more work will be possible and all space will become equally cool and motionless. Ballard's forests anticipate this state; they represent what awaits all life in the Universe—inescapable death. This death is beautiful and peaceful as it is in fact a cosmic act of restoring the long-forgotten past from before all evolution. Ballard mixes allusions to scientific theories with Biblical metaphors deeply rooted in culture. The beginning was paradise now lost and its restoration will mean the end of traumas and rejection. When the end comes we will be returned to the entropic Eden with no traumas, no meanings no divisions. Acceptance of this happy catastrophe will finally reconcile our conscious and unconscious selves into the Self—in Ballard the lay Freudian Genesis in *Beyond the Pleasure Principle* meets the Jungian concept of the united Self.

> I had a curious premonition, of intense hope and longing, as if I were some fugitive Adam chancing upon a forgotten gateway to the forbidden paradise. (Ibid.: 615)

> There is an immense reward to be found in that frozen forest. [T]he transfiguration of all living and inanimate forms occurs before our eyes, the gift of immortality a direct consequence of the surrender by each of us of our own physical and temporal identity (ibid.: 627).

The narrator's final decision to dissolve in the beauty of the entropic forest and himself become a mandala, "the illuminated man... his arms like golden cartwheels and his head like a spectral crown" (ibid.: 627) combines the idea of the end of time with esthetics. As such an end is inscribed in our natures, its coming, awaited for millions of years, possesses enormous appeal. Ballard describes the progressing crystallization in allusions to the art of different epochs, as if our idea of beauty throughout the ages was influenced by the subliminal longing to be turned into artefact. The forest is here a pre-Raphaelite dream and jewels and precious gems produce a "compression of time... [like] all baroque paintings and architecture" (ibid.: 622) in contrast to the architecture of the 20th century, which in its rectangular, unornamented simplicity suggests a longing for the end of time. The crystallization of Miami turns it into "a city of a thousand cathedral spires, like a vision of St John the Divine" (ibid.: 626)—this allusion to the Apocalypse emphasizes the anticipations of disaster people have always had.

The world as seen by the narrator seems to be glittering in the "blurred chiaroscuro, the overlapping bands of colour" (ibid.: 609), contrasts and differences dissolve in a stasis of the in-between reality where everything has a medium value. Instead of binary oppositions we have hybrid phenomena, such as "a blind snake, its eyes transformed into enormous jewels" (ibid.: 625), neither an animal nor an artefact. A human hybrid in the text is Emeralda, a young girl who sometimes seems an old woman. She is kept in the centre of the enchanted forest and is slowly dying, enlivened only by the power of precious stones—"the discharge of light from the surfaces reversed the process of crystallization" (ibid.: 622).

The crystallizing process is compared to incurable cancer, "a proliferation of the subatomic identity of things" (ibid.: 609), and as such it combines physical degeneration with the ontological crisis of the entropic universe. Trees, people and objects are turned into "Fabergé gems" and differences between categories are liquidated. "Look at the viruses with their crystalline structure, neither animate nor inanimate, and their immunity to time" (ibid.: 617), one of the characters tells the narrator, thus emphasizing the virulent and the eternal character of the process. Once started, crystallization is going to slowly affect the whole universe, liquidating all differences and therefore all movement, change and time. The disease is both physical and philosophical: "an ultimate macrocosmic zero beyond the wildest dreams of Plato and Democritus" (ibid.: 617). This "ultimate zero" is the final catastrophe in the sense of there being no possible cure and no restoration of civilization, something which usually is the theme of disaster fiction. Ballard's "The Illuminated Man" is original principally because zero here means not a sorrowful end of the wonderful human race, but a desired and comforting nirvana we all unconsciously await.

The artistic success of "The Illuminated Man" made Ballard elaborate on the story and re-write it as the novel *The Crystal World*. The book became the third part of Ballard's catastrophic trilogy, a sequel to *The Drowned World* and *The Drought*. The story is transformed in such a way as to suit the character of the entire trilogy. Its narration changes into the third person and the protagonist becomes a doctor Sanders (previous books show detached doctors who, faced with global disasters, decide to welcome—not fight—death, which they subliminally desire). Moreover, similarly to previous volumes, the action of *The Crystal World* seems to be taking place in-between catastrophes: after the disaster affected certain areas, and before its inescapable victory over the entire planet.

In his novel Ballard repeats all the key ideas of "The Illuminated Man": passages describing the Wordsworthian character of the crystal forest, its cancer-like liquidation of time and difference, and the interrelationship of unconscious memory and the inescapable future of the Universe are literally re-written. What is interesting, the setting changes: instead of Florida we see a remote part of Cameroon. Dr Sanders, a leper colony physician, is desperate to get into the centre of the crystallizing forest, to the village of Mont Royal. Ballard combines literary allusions to his own writings,[23] and once again to Joseph Conrad's *Heart of Darkness*. The latter source is prominent in the text: the action starts on a steamer and the waterway turns out to offer the only possibility of getting to the heart of the crystalline wilderness. Moreover, Ballard uses in his text a parallel symbolism of darkness, light, blackness and whiteness and the Conradian moral ambivalence of civilization juxtaposed with its dark counterpart of the primordial forest—the poetic model of the human unconscious.

The river, which leads to this forest, is in both Conrad and Ballard described as tempting but malevolent; it welcomes the characters to go back in time (and in memory) to the place of initial stasis—to the primordial mindscape from before time and change began. To go to this forbidden realm is to abandon civilization and its ethics, but some of the characters are destined to do so, and subliminally they know this. Ballard emphasizes the role of the unconscious memory prompting them to search for "a forgotten gateway to the forbidden paradise" (Ballard 2000: 79). Conrad suggests that to go there is a sin understood as a rejection of civilized ethics—and they both symbolically describe the river as a snake:

> Looking back at the river, as it turned like an immense snake into the forest, Sanders felt that it had sucked away all but a bare residue of life (ibid.: 21).

> ... the black surface of the river below spangled like the back of a sleeping snake (ibid.: 39).

> The last traces of Louise's scent dissolved in the air as he watched the dawn lift over the distant hills of Mont Royal, illuminating the serpentine course of the river as if revealing a secret pathway (ibid.: 47).
> And as I looked at the map of it in a shop window, it fascinated me as a snake would a bird—a silly little bird. ... I went on along the Fleet Street, but could not shake off the idea. The snake had charmed me (Conrad 1990: 6).

Conrad's Marlow recognizes in the accidentally spotted map a snake-river he wanted to go to as a child, and "charmed" by the image he must do so. This trip is his destiny that he has been avoiding for many years, but which is now inescapable. The same destiny in *The Crystal World* is encoded in the unconscious primordial part of the human mind, poetically rendered as "the dark side of the equinox". This phrase is very prominent in the text: used as the title of the first part of the novel,[24] which actually takes place during the equinox in Cameroon, it is then repeated to describe psychological processes. The "dark" part of the psyche is sometimes in the text the repressed Freudian double of the conscious ego—as in the scene when Sanders, because of some optic trick, sees in the mirror

23. It will be recalled that Mount Royal is a town described in *The Drought* and the protagonist of this earlier novel, Dr Ransom, tries to get back there after a few years of disastrous drought.
24. The second is called "The Illuminated Man" to show the origins of the text.

a black man, a native whom he first takes as his own reflection.[25] Otherwise, it is synonymous with the death instinct, which, albeit latent in humans, is going to determine their behaviour when the end of the Universe comes. Those like Sanders and his former girlfriend Suzanne Clair, who have the propensity for "the dark part of the equinox", recognize their destiny before other people do and are attracted by the crystalline forest where they find ecstatic death. The novel's symbolism of the Conradian ambivalence of light and dark suggests the slow blurring of traditional opposites.

Suzanne Clair, whose name literally means "bright", is the one attracted by darkness, and who prompts Sanders to come to Mont Royal. In a letter she sent him she called the forest "a house of jewels" (ibid.: 18), and to describe her own stance she wrote: "I am becoming excessively Byzantine" (ibid.: 18). She contracted leprosy, described in the text as the process of crystallizing human flesh,[26] and her face started to develop "the so-called leonine mask"(ibid.: 126)— which does not hide the true face, but rather reveals the real "crystalline" self. "You're the princess in the enchanted wood" (ibid.: 124), one of the characters tells Suzanne when her body after long walks in the forest turns into "diamonds and emeralds". Similarly Louise, the seeming contradiction of Suzanne, who tries to get Sanders out of the crystal world, is also described in comparisons to gems "beside him Louise's white body glittered in a sheath of diamonds" (ibid.: 39).

Sanders is aware of the fact that the two women are doubles of one another[27] and each appeals to one side of his psyche. Louise "a piece of the sun, a golden odalisque trapped for Pharaoh in his tomb" (ibid.: 141) is attractive to the day part of his ego, while Suzanne is the night of the unconscious, and as such must win, because the dark side of Sanders' ego is prominent. The visit to the forest, though apparently horrible, gives Sanders insight into this dark part and thus the feeling of *déjà vu*: "We've all been here before" (ibid.: 88), he is told by another character at home in the crystal world. "You aren't ready to come here yet" (ibid.: 158), the same man diagnoses towards the end of the novel. Sanders sees in the dangerous crystalline apocalypse the reflection of a forgotten ontological paradise and prismatic recollection of childhood from Wordsworth,[28] images which are strangely soothing. Rescued by Louise and returned to the "normal"

25. "Turning his attention to the reflection facing his own, Sanders noticed with surprise that among these prismatic images of himself refracted from the sun he had found one darker twin. The profile and features were obscured, but the skin was almost ebony in colour, reflecting the mottled blues and violets of the opposite end of the spectrum. Somehow menacing in this company of light, the sombre figure stood motionlessly with its head turned away from him, as if aware of its negative aspect" (Ballard 2000: 93). The passage is very telling as it suggests that firstly, the dark twin hidden among other aspects of Sanders' ego is a native of the primordial wilderness and secondly, it refers to Freud's "The Uncanny". In this essay the double represents what we repress in our personality and what is doomed to claim us.
26. One of the officers sent to isolate the affected area says to Sanders, a leprosy specialist: "It seems to me that the business here and your own speciality are very similar. In a way, one is the dark side of the other. I'm thinking of the silver scales of leprosy that gave the disease its name" (Ballard 2000: 64).
27. It is worth noticing that in the process of crystallization (at least in Ballard's book) all objects and beings acquire their crystalline doubles, in mirror-like proliferation of selves.
28. Ballard re-writes key passages from "The Illuminated Man".

world (which for a few decades may escape inevitable crystallization) he finally surrenders to "the dark side of the equinox" of himself and decides to come back to Mont Royal. Explaining his decision in a letter he formulates the major thesis of *The Crystal World*. There is an uncanny beauty in regress because the animate-inanimate hybrids of crystalline beings correspond to our mindscape and longings for the unity of space and time, in other words for the inescapable entropy which was our past and is going to be our future. Propensity for this state is innate, the human personality recognizes in it the patterns of the universe. Anticipations of the coming of the crystal world may be found in human cultures and the imagination of all previous epochs: "this illuminated forest in some way reflects an earlier period of our lives, perhaps an archaic memory we are born with of some ancestral paradise where the unity of time and space is the signature of every leaf and flower" (ibid.: 83).

The make-believe disasters described by Ballard in his early novels and short stories are simply a pretext to elaborate on contemporary civilization and the position of the individual within it. Gradually, Ballard abandons adventurous details and story structures and concentrates on the mindscape of his protagonists, whose alienation makes them embrace disaster willingly. The next step on Ballard's artistic development is to leave the make-believe worlds behind and attempt to depict our end-of-the twentieth-century Western civilization as a disaster. In his stories written towards the end of the nineteen-sixties the world as we know it is described as a catastrophe.

Our Catastrophic Civilization

> Even the stories in *The Atrocity Exhibition* are disaster stories of a kind. The book is about the communications explosion of the '60s. From my point of view the '60s started in 1963 with the assassination of President Kennedy—his death and Vietnam presided over the whole of the '60s. Those two events, transmitted through television and mass communications, overshadowed the whole decade—a sort of institutionalised disaster area (Goddard and Pringle 1976: 26).

This passage comes from an interview in which Ballard claims that there is a clear correspondence between his disaster fiction and *The Atrocity Exhibition*, which describes a catastrophe less tangible than natural disasters, but approaches it with a similar procedure. Ballard is interested in the psychology of disaster and the way the human mind functions in a disintegrating world, in this case the mediascape I discussed in the previous chapter. It is very tempting to look for a moment at *The Atrocity Exhibition* from the perspective of Ballard's disaster story poetics and to see it as a figment of the character's mindscape, the reflection of our world in which, to borrow Heidegger's famous phrase "the dreadful has already happened".

Though *The Atrocity Exhibition* is undoubtedly set in the contemporary, affluent Western world and refers to "real" cultural and political events and personages, in this book Ballard attempts to present the same fears and recreate the same atmosphere as in his catastrophe stories, for example "The Voices of Time", the story which he himself once called the best representative of his early poetics.[29] Moreover, similar motifs, situations and characters occur in all his fiction irrespective of their generic classification. This science fiction text in certain aspects anticipates *The Atrocity Exhibition*—for though the story of a declining scientist whose crisis reflects the catastrophe of his world is told in a different manner, the fears that it evokes are the same, and a short analysis of "The Voices of Time" may help to understand his views on catastrophes and human reactions to them. It seems fair to suggest that Ballard's poetics does not change: rather, it is the world that changes. Thus, in the early 60s Ballard's fiction was perceived as fantasy, and in the late 60s as culturally involved avant-garde.

The protagonist of "The Voices of Time", Dr Powers, is a famous neurologist and, as in the case of Travern, his progressing disease makes him abandon his patients:

> Initially, however, Powers was too preoccupied with completing his work at the Clinic and planning his own final withdrawal. After the first frantic weeks of panic he had managed to accept an uneasy compromise that allowed him to view his predicament with the detached fatalism he had previously reserved for his patients (Ballard 2002b: 169).

In this case the disease is different; it is not psychosis, but a half-organic, half-mental deficiency. Powers, like many other people in the society he lives in, suffers from prolonging spells of dreamless sleep, which finally lead to coma. The study of Power's reaction to his approaching end allows us to see the missing part of *The Atrocity Exhibition*, where we never have any analysis of Traven's attitude to his predicament.

Moreover, a similar set of interpersonal relationships is analyzed; Dr Anderson, the sane and somewhat patronizing colleague who stays at the Clinic, plays the role of Dr Nathan. It is significant that he advises Powers to: "read through Toynbee and Spengler again": these theoreticians of civilizational rises and falls are Ballard's gurus. Powers leaves the Clinic and already at the doorstep meets two young people: rebellious Kaldren (who plays the part of Koester and hallucinatory Kline) and his girlfriend Coma, "the girl from Mars", as the younger doctors call her.

These young people in the story have the same role as Travern's students and his hallucinatory companions Kline, Xero and Coma. They are his partners who help him to understand what is going on in the world and who accompany him to the end. Coma in particular is very significant: in *The Atrocity Exhibition* she is

29. In the author's note that preceded this story in the 1962 edition of the science fiction stories collection entitled also *The Voices of Time*.

a haunting apparition, an embodiment of remorse and longing, here a living and articulate girl. Given voice she may converse with Powers and make him express his fears and formulate his theories, ones which are defined precisely: though they refer to fictional situations, they also reflect general pessimism.

It is in the dialogue with Coma that Powers discloses the grim truth: civilization is coming to an end not because of any particular catastrophe, but because cosmic time is slowing down. Animals and plants gradually cease to multiply, the rate of metabolism is lowering, and strange mutated genes are awakening. This overwhelming slow-motion catastrophe is inescapable; most people do not realize this, but on some subliminal level they feel it coming.

In *The Atrocity Exhibition* we do not have any explanation. The moment of revelation is only suggested and it happens to Travern again in the company of Coma and her fellow hallucinations Xero and Kline:

> **Coma: the million-year girl.** Coma's arrival coincides with [Travern's] recovery from the bout of fever. At first she spends all her time writing poems on the damaged typewriter. Later, when not writing the poems, she wanders away to an old solar energy device and loses herself in the maze of mirrors. Shortly afterwards Kline appears, and sits at a chair and table in the sand twenty yards from the hut. Xero meanwhile, is moving among the oil derricks half a mile away, assembling immense Cinemascope signs that carry the reclining images of Oswald, Jackie Kennedy and Malcolm X (Ballard 2001: 45).

This later text gives us a set of images: Travern wakes up from his fever (or rather abandons his sanity and looks at the world with the new insight of his madness) and sees his hallucinatory companions in different situations. The images are out of any context. In "The Voices of Time" similar moments are incorporated into the action. Coma and Kaldren come to the place Powers lives in the moments he wakes from his spells of sleep. Their own house is a virtual maze of corridors built by a crazy architect. Kaldren decorates it with huge billboards.[30]

Not only images but also relationships recur. Coma in both *The Atrocity Exhibition* and "The Voices of Time" is a girl from a different continuum ("Mars" or the unconscious) who helps the protagonist understand his reality. Kaldren is given a more ambiguous role. This young man in "The Voices of Time" in some contexts plays Xero and Kline (while Powers has the role of Travern). Sometimes he is like vicious ex-student Koester, sometimes he takes the role of Travern himself. In this last case Powers becomes ur-Dr Nathan: "...Kaldren continues to reproach me (Powers wrote in his diary). For some reason he seems unwilling to accept his isolation, is elaborating a series of private rituals to replace the missing hours of sleep" (Ballard 2002b: 172). Kaldren, just like Travern in *The Atrocity*

---

30. Ballard commented on these recurrent characters in the notes to *The Atrocity Exhibition*: "These three figures, who are shadows projected from Traven's unconscious, had been in my mind since the end of the 1950s" (Ballard 2001: 52).

Exhibition, is the only person who really understands that the end is approaching. Even the best scientists stop at examining separate phenomena: mutations, genes, and spells of coma, but refuse to see the whole picture. Mentally unstable Kaldren sees the catastrophe as cosmic and universal, and for him what is happening on Earth is only a logical consequence of the end of the Universe. His chaotic attempts to record the twilight of humanity are quite similar to Travern's mad collages. Coma and Powers, who witness his monomania, have the role of Mrs Travern/Catherine Austin and Dr Nathan:

> Sometimes I feel I'm just another of his insane terminal documents.'
> 'What are those?'
> 'Haven't you heard? Kaldren's collection of final statements about homo sapiens. The complete works of Freud, Beethoven's blind quartets, transcripts of the Nuremberg trials, an automatic novel and so on.' She broke off (ibid.: 182).

In comparison to *The Atrocity Exhibition* the catastrophe described in "The Voices of Time" is of course very literal, and very science fiction-like. Instead of diagnosing our civilization from within Ballard sketches a whole cosmic apocalypse with alien races, dying stars, mutating flora and fauna and biological clocks slowing down. Nevertheless, even in this early story Ballard is not writing a cliché Cold War scenario: he is interested in human reactions to Armageddon and in the dual nature of catastrophe: external termination and internal, subliminal awareness. When Powers' attempts to explain biological deviations rationally fail (effects of H-bomb tests, "silent pairs" of genes activated etc.), he is obliged to accept another theory:

> Just as an individual organism's life-span is finite, or a life of a yeast colony or a given species, so the life of an entire biological kingdom is of a fixed duration. It's always been assumed that the evolutionary slope reaches forever upwards, but in fact that peak has already been reached, and the pathway now leads downwards to the common biological grave (ibid.: 181).

It is therefore not accidental that the books Powers is advised to read in his last days before coma are by Spengler and Toynbee, those theoreticians of civilization who, as Ballard understands them, claim that the end of each culture is inescapable because it is internal.[31] Each social organism has a fixed duration and an end imprinted into its structure. What is interesting is the fact that such a vision of death as internally conditioned and even subliminally desired is in accordance with Freudian theories. Powers' end merges with the end of galaxies:

31. It is important to remember that Ballard tends to conflate the theses of Spengler with those of Toynbee. In fact, though, it is in Spengler's *The Decline of the West* that the death of every civilization (ours included) is inevitable. Toynbee in *A Study of History* posits no such determinism. Indeed, he argues that there still might be some hope for us. See Chapter One.

...he felt his body gradually dissolving, its physical dimensions melting into the vast continuum of the current, which bore him out into the centre of the great channel, sweeping him onward, beyond hope but at last at rest, down the broadening reaches of the river of eternity (ibid.: 193).

In "The Voices of Time" Kaldren interprets signals received from Canes Venatici: "A countdown, as you can see... The big spirals are breaking down, they are saying goodbye... by the time this series reaches zero the universe will have just ended" (ibid.: 189). In *The Atrocity Exhibition* such a motif is shown in a much more subtle way. The decline of our culture is first of all connected to the end of the Space Age. In this book what spells the beginning of civilizational breakdown is the moment when after the assassination of Kennedy, the President ready to lead America into space, people started to gradually lose interest in space conquest (the process ends in the early 1970s). Earth is deaf to the music of the stars, but only the disturbed Travern feels this loss.

On the garage roof stood the sculpture he had laboriously built during the past month; antennae of metal aerials holding glass faces to the sun, the slides of diseased spinal levels he had taken from the laboratory. All night he watched the sky, listening to the time-music of the quasars (Ballard 2001: 20).

In his annotations Ballard explains: "Reassembling the furniture of his mind, Talbot has constructed a primitive antenna, and can now hear the night sky singing of time, the voice of the unseen powers of the cosmos" (ibid.: 37). Human civilization in losing interest in the cosmos has also lost its historical chance, and now waits for its natural end. This catastrophe is in accordance with the order of things, and unconsciously we want it to happen.

In its analysis of mindscapes *The Atrocity Exhibition* is undoubtedly a "Freudian" novel written with profound knowledge of psychoanalysis and for people who are familiar with it. Allusions to Freud function here on many levels, so that we may in fact say that Freud is one of the characters of the novel, just as John Fitzgerald Kennedy or Liz Taylor are. Freud's blown up face, which we see on one of the billboards at the beginning, presides over the whole book and watches the characters with the intense look known from his iconic photographs.

Travern as a psychiatrist knows psychoanalysis and has incorporated it into his imagination and feelings. Even when he is remembering his childhood and the war his memories are clearly influenced by Freudian theories on human development. Moreover, his collages and exhibitions are inscribed into a Freudian symbolic frame. Their interpreter, Dr Nathan, who also is a believer in psychoanalysis, deciphers their latent meanings for the sake of readers. Just like in "The Uncanny",[32] his protagonists feel safe only in a clearly defined reality.

32. For the summary of Freud's essay see Chapter One.

If the familiar and well known suddenly switches categories and proves to be strange and different than we thought it was, horror is born, just like during nightmares. In *The Atrocity Exhibition* humans and simulacra, persons and images, objects and machines are fluid categories: the advancing process of the dehumanization of life and the mechanization of communication changes the world into nightmare.

Travern's last relationship, a romance with Novotny, demonstrates this process:

> **The Sex Kit.** 'In a sense,' Dr Nathan explained to Koester, 'one may regard this as a kit, which Talbert has devised, entitled "Karen Novotny"... (1) Pad of pubic hair, (2) a latex face mask, (3) six detachable mouths, (4) a set of smiles, ... (7) photo cut-outs of a number of narrative situations—the girl doing this and that, (8) a list of dialogue samples, of inane chatter... (15) slides of vaginal smears, chiefly Ortho-Gynol jelly, (16) a set of blood pressures, systolic 120, diastolic 70 rising to 200/150 at onset of orgasm...' (ibid.: 84).

This "Picasso" conceptual woman with detachable parts is followed by other similar lists, enumerating for example the postures and gestures of Novotny. The girl (like other women in the text) becomes an object and an image indistinguishable from uncanny dolls. Travern's perception grows two-dimensional, depths change into surfaces: "These embraces of Travers' were gestures of displaced affections, a deformed marriage of Freud and Euclid" (ibid.: 118). Geometry replaces feelings, relationships are only spatial.

The most intimate of Travers' relationships—with Coma, Kline and Xero, figments of his own unconscious—are shown among mannequins, props and scenery. The world for Travers grew unreal and horror-like: together with his hallucinations he is imprisoned inside an atrocity exhibition full of machinery and simulacra:

> Coma watched him with her rune-filled eyes. Her broad cheekbones, reminiscent now of the President's widow, seemed to contain an immense glacial silence. On the roof terrace, Kline walked among the mannequins. The plaster models of Marina Oswald, Ralph Nader and the young man in the laminated suit stood by the railing (ibid.: 73).

Coma turns into an image of Jacqueline Kennedy: either an icon comes alive or a faceless hallucination takes the face which is common property. Whatever the case, Travers enters a Freudian horror where the familiar and unfamiliar are exchangeable and ghosts look like media celebrities. The physicality of contact does not exist: intimacy is devoured by abstraction. Making love to Novotny, Travers feels oppressed by gigantic images on the drive-in cinema screen. In their light Novotny disappears and is replaced by an obscene mannequin:

Love among the Mannequins. Unable to move, he lay on his back, feeling the sharp corner of the novel cut into his ribs. Her hand rested across his chest, nails holding the hair between his nipples like a lover's scalp brought back for him as a trophy... Immense fragments of Bardot's magnified body illuminated the night air (ibid.: 93).

All these dolls[33] and other simulacra serve a much more important end than the simple creation of the uncanny atmosphere. Like Freud, who while writing "The Uncanny" realized what the deeper causes of our fears and fascinations provoked by simulacra are, so too does Ballard discover the catastrophe inscribed into the mediascape.

Firstly, let us consider the arguments of Freud. Gregory Zilboorg in his edition of *Beyond the Pleasure Principle* writes:

Freud had begun working on a first draft in March, 1919, and he reported the draft as finished in the following May. During the same month he was completing his paper on "the Uncanny" (1919), which includes a paragraph setting out much of the gist of the present work in a few sentences. In this paragraph he refers to the 'compulsion to repeat'... he suggests that this compulsion is something derived from the most intimate nature of the instincts; and he declares that it is powerful enough to disregard the pleasure principle. There is, however, no allusion to the 'death instinct' (Freud 1967: 16).

Studying children at play and trying to explain why they tend to repeat even unpleasant experience over and over again Freud discovered the mechanism of repetition-compulsion.[34] This instinctual mechanism makes us come back— in traumatic dreams, during therapy, and involuntary memories to difficult, unexpected moments in the past and enact the stress. This instinct is older and more basic than the pleasure principle—natural tendencies to seek satisfaction and avoid pain—as it procures trauma.

At this point one should notice that repetition-compulsion is the most important narrative strategy in *The Atrocity Exhibition*: the titles of chapters and paragraphs repeat either one another or earlier stories and paintings by Ballard

---

33. Some of the allusions in the text refer to concrete artistic representations of dolls and figures. Compare Ballard's notes to the chapter "The Great American Nude": "'The Great American Nude' is the running title of a series of paintings by the Pop artist Tom Wesselman, which rework the iconic possibilities of the commercial nude. As much of Pop Art, the bland surface defuses the subject, making an unsettling comment on our notions of fame and celebrity... Hans Bellmer work is now totally out of fashion, hovering as it does on the edge of child pornography. Yet it is difficult to imagine any paedophile being excited by these strange dolls and dainty, Alice-like little girls with their reversed orifices and paradoxical anatomy. But his vision is too close for comfort to the truth" (Ballard 2001: 88-9). Especially the reference to Pop Art is interesting because it stresses the uncanny character of media landscape with its multiplication of copies.
34. See Chapter One, the short discussion of *Beyond the Pleasure Principle*.

and many other authors. Names and personal relationships are also repeated and, in the most general terms, each chapter is in fact a repetition of the same narrative: a story of Travern leaving the Institute and committing psycho crimes. These crimes are, at least according to Dr Nathan, in themselves the repetition of traumatic events. The stress caused by the death of JFK or Marilyn Monroe should lessen after such a conceptual enactment. "Soon the climax of the scenario would come," Travern thought, arranging an accident, "JFK would die again, his young wife raped by the conjunction of time and space" (ibid.: 34). This need to repeat the scenario is described in detail in *Beyond the Pleasure Principle*, and right at the beginning of *The Atrocity Exhibition* Dr Nathan diagnoses Travern's obsession precisely as the compulsive need to restore the earliest "symmetrical" state of both an individual life and our civilization:

> **The Lost Symmetry of the Blastosphere.** Much of Travis' thought concerns what he terms "the lost symmetry of the blastosphere"— the primitive precursor of the embryo that is the last structure to preserve perfect symmetry in all planes... In conclusion, it seems that Travis' extreme sensitivity to the volumes and geometry of the world around him, and their immediate translation into psychological terms, may reflect a belated attempt to return to a symmetrical world, one that will recapture the perfect symmetry of the blastosphere, and the acceptance of the "Mythology of Amniotic Return". In his mind World War III represents the final self-destruction and imbalance of an asymmetric world. The human organism is an atrocity exhibition at which he is an unwilling spectator... (ibid: 9).

The eponymic "atrocity exhibition" is therefore each of us, every organism disfigured by evolution and the specialization of organs. The same is true of inorganic systems, such as civilization, a major source of (to paraphrase Freud) discontents. Civilization is a mistake, its destruction—the only hope. Compulsive repetitions and returns in the novel serve to provoke, again in Freudian fashion, the final catastrophe, i.e., the blissful return to nirvana. Though described in references to the culture of the 60s, *The Atrocity Exhibition* is in itself a compulsive repetition of the most Ballardian catastrophe motif: the end of the world as final bliss, as merger with undifferentiated matter. Its contemporary setting makes it an important book within Ballard's oeuvre because it marks his growing interest in the cultural reality of the close of twentieth century. His other books continue his critique of urban life and its challenges.

Ballardian mindscapes are described in numerous texts which, although they belong to the realm of the fantastic, are a very important supplement to his presentation of *Grave New World* as they show the way the human psyche reacts to the stress of modern life. Throughout his oeuvre references to diverse theories of the mind are very important, but in the texts liberated from the constraints of realist discourse the "Jungian" or "Freudian" fantasies are directly accessible. By depicting the inner space (to borrow his own term) of the contemporary mind Ballard proves a risky point—that the days of our civilization are numbered and that we are slowly approaching its decline. Within mindscape we are in a timeless continuum from the very beginning of human history and we subliminally crave to come back to this nirvana, which sooner or later must happen, for such is the order of things. This point is made in numerous short stories written in the heyday of disaster fiction in Britain, in the catastrophic trilogy: *The Drowned World, The Drought, The Crystal World* and in *The Atrocity Exhibition*, which combines the descriptions of mindscapes with analysis of mediascapes.

Ballard's poetic tale "Prisoner of the Coral Deep" (1964), which depicts a man with a mind capable of transgressing temporal bounds by sheer intuition, subtly touches upon the interrelationship of time and the mind and in a nutshell presents the major features of Ballardian mindscapes. Its main symbol is the ocean and the primordial sea standing for the unconscious memory. Thus, enabling contemporary people to communicate with the remote past is taken straight from Jung's theory of archetypes. The sea here is the Atlantic on the Dorset coast, but the text also calls it a part of the prehistoric Poseidon Ocean, older than anything else—primordial and somehow akin to the depths of human psyche.

The narrator of the story is a young schoolmaster on a solitary vacation trip in the deserted part of Dorset, whose emptiness is to soothe his overwrought nerves. He is very knowledgeable and thinks within the boundaries of science: palaeontology, history, geology and psychoanalysis, which nevertheless do not prevent him from quite irrational fantasies, due perhaps to his nervous agitation. The rapid storm loosening the Cambrian limestone boulders, low tide and the view of the beautiful, rough shore liquidate the differences between the present and the past, imagination and reality. It is hard to say whether his strange adventure happens in the external world, or is just a figment of his unconscious reaction to the atmosphere of the place.

At one moment the narrator finds a gigantic "fossil gastropod, which had once basked in the warm Cambrian seas five hundred million years earlier" (Ballard 2002b: 569). The beauty of the corrugated shell makes him pick it up and divagate about its presumed history. In what happens then the esthetic and the scientific are interwoven, as his visions are both intellectual and sensual. He thinks he sees a strange imposing woman—Jung's lamia or a marine deity "like a Pre-Raphaelite vision of the dark-eyed Madonna of some primitive fisher community" (ibid.: 569). She speaks in a voice with "a curiously deep timbre, as if heard under water", her dress looks like a ceremonial robe and her very presence makes the narrator apprehensive. This awesome personage seems to impersonate wisdom from before the ages, serenity and, to use the Jungian term, archetypal femaleness. Beastly and human she represents the forces man fears—in the last lines of the story we see her transformed into a large lizard with empty eyes. The narrator is attracted to her and at the same time feels obliged to explain himself.

> I'm not sure why, but fossils fascinate me—they're like time capsules; if only one could unwind this spiral it would probably play back to

us a picture of all the landscapes it's ever seen—the great oceans of
the Carboniferous, the warm shadow seas of Trias...

I suppose it's just the nostalgia of one's unconscious memory. Perhaps
you understand what I mean—the sea is like memory. However lost or
forgotten, everything in it exists forever... (ibid.: 570).

The everyday language the narrator uses in the passage quoted above
(abbreviations, unfinished sentences, phatic remarks) only but superficially
disguises psychoanalytical references: Ballard gives his readers clues on how to
interpret his story. The contact with the past is then made literal, when listening
to the shell the narrator hears; "the calm measures of a different sea, a steaming
shallow lagoon through whose surface vast ferns protruded, where half-
submerged leviathans lay like sandbanks under a benign sun..." (ibid.: 571). These
moments, situations and images sent by the fossil combine the rational knowledge
of the narrator, who actually knows a lot about geology, and the uncanny feeling
of remembering pre-human times. Again like in Freud's *Beyond the Pleasure
Principle*, he is attracted by the idea of the return to the primordial wilderness.

To emphasize the fact that time goes in circles in the mind, as the remote past
from before we were born is also our inevitable future of death, in the sounds
from the Cambrian the narrator hears a human voice shouting "HELP". The
narrators imagines a future time-traveller unluckily marooned in the Cambrian
and sending message in a fossil to his contemporaries. The implications of this
image are quite clear. In the mind the past and the future are the same and they
signify mortality; we are subliminally aware of the fact that our destiny is to revert
to the state from before we were born.

CHAPTER SIX:
WASTELANDS

The charting of the contemporary *Grave New World* which I undertake in this paper results in an altogether grim picture: the various territories our civilization occupies—its cityscapes, mediascapes and even the mindscapes of its members—are realms of decadence. The prevailing feeling of an approaching end makes people indulge in diverse fantasies, the communication landscape enslaves them and the environment is hostile to mental health. For Ballard this is a sign of the inevitable, Spenglerian twilight of every civilization, as echoed in the very mechanics of an entropic universe. It is also a sign of the unconscious, Freudian yearning for a return to the inorganic, as activated in our minds following the atrocities of war.

There is thus no hope for a breakthrough or a beginning of some new chapter in the world's history. On the contrary, social and cultural situations will further deteriorate. In resonant accord with Huxley (*Brave New World*) and Fukuyama (*Our Posthuman Future*), Ballard depicts in his fiction a bleak near future. Willingly enclosed in surveillance units, people are set to live sedated by tranquilizers (at times enlivened by recreational drugs), dozing in front of their cable TV. The overwhelming inertia will be interrupted only by random outbursts of pointless violence.

Even today one can find such futuristic enclaves, small societies whose lifestyle in some years' time may be shared by a majority of the affluent countries' citizens. In this chapter I analyze Ballard's descriptions of the claustrophobic worlds these communities inhabit, pointing to two facets of their life: exhaustion and psychopathology. Though the two are interdependent, like two sides of the same coin (psychopathology both springs from the overwhelming feeling of exhaustion and enhances it), it is convenient to artificially divide the wastelands in Ballard's oeuvre into realms of exhaustion (which are escapist fantasies created by the imagination of half-crazed narrators) and realms of psychopathology (which are mimetic copies of already existent communities). The decadent resort depicted in *Vermilion Sands* and the dream-like suburb of Shepperton described in *The Unlimited Dream Company* fall into the former category, while the communities presented in *Running Wild, Cocaine Nights* and *Super-Cannes* fall into the latter. In *Rushing to Paradise* and *Millennium People* Ballard shows how psychopathology is going to spread from luxurious enclaves throughout Western civilization.

In this chapter I shall refer primarily to Rosemary Jackson's *Fantasy: The Literature of Subversion* in order to discern the ontological status of make-believe territories in the contemporary theory; to Francis Fukuyama, to place Ballard's fiction in the context of social studies; and in lesser extent to other theorists. Moreover, my discussion of wastelands will be built on the Freudian division of the mind into its conscious and unconscious counterparts, which for the whole of Ballard's oeuvre is perhaps the most important single theory.

Exhaustion

In *The Unlimited Dream Company* we see a piece of reality, the small London suburb of Shepperton, transformed by the unconscious of a megalomaniac narrator into some lush, fantastic Eden. Apparently prelapsarian, this secondary world is nevertheless a simulacrum (to borrow a Baudrillardian term) and a reflection of a reflection. That is, it is not the original Paradise regained, but a murky and cruel version of it, possibly a manifestation of the narrator's death instinct.[1] An exhausted manifestation of a narcissist ego, this wish-fulfillment world is a critique of contemporary, late capitalist society with its common sense, economy and social standards, which in the course of the narrative dissolves into entropy and nothingness.

The novel begins with the crash of the protagonist's Cessna into the Thames:

1. Critics have problems with generic classification of this novel and with placing it in Ballard's output. For Michel Delville its status as a realist account or a pure fantasy is ambivalent and it might be read as both. British science fiction fans took it to be science fiction and awarded it their prize. Sam Francis discusses it as a study of the ambivalence of imagination. Roger Luckhurst in his Ballard monograph refrains from discussing it at all, and Andrzej Gasiorek pronounces all the critical dilemmas: "How to read it? As a narration of thev inner fantasy life of a sick individual? As a dream of a dying man in the moments before his extinction? As a mystical insight into the realm of truth that glimmers behind the veil of unhallowed life? As an allegory of the transfiguring but dangerous power of the artistic imagination? (Gasiorek 2005: 134).

just as he drowns he says that he "saw a vision" (Ballard 1985b: 16), presumably a dying dream (similar to that of Maitland in *Concrete Island*) and one that provides a frame for the subsequent narrative. For Blake, the protagonist,[2] death feels like a physical split of the self: for a second he sees, as if from above, a dead body in the aircraft. He is nearly sure the cadaver belongs to some stranger, to another man whom he compulsorily tries to find in the rest of the novel. At the same time he experiences his own physicality: the imaginary self which gets out of the water and lives through magical, dream-like adventures is a corporeal, sexual being. In Blake's subjective perception the world around goes through a similar split: the oppressive and hostile twentieth-century wasteland of his memories is left behind and a new world of apparently limitless possibilities is born.

Shepperton, a Thames valley town, is transformed into a realm of bizarre birds, exotic vegetation and random strange events. All logic and coherence evaporates, time loops and natural laws are suspended, and the only truth is that of drives and emotions. This is a realm of the unconscious, generated without the reality principle's constraints. In Freudian theory: "the unconscious admits no degrees of certainty or doubt, no forms of contradiction, no logical, grammatical, or casual relations…[only] signifiers… with no relation between them" (Grosz 1990: 113). Shepperton in the novel is such a structureless never-land fulfilling Blake's innermost wishes, but also charged with his fears. Blake regains the narcissist omnipotence small infants believe themselves to have before they enter culture and understand laws and rules. He sees himself as the lord of the Universe, he magically changes the land by marking it with his semen and greets the rising sun as his equal: a primordial divinity. Like a divine impostor, he re-makes the village in seven days, claiming to have done so "in [his] own image" (Ballard 1985b: 124).

Moreover, during all this period he is kept by a strange power in the limited space of the surrounding towns,[3] thus he is liberated from the constraints of life in the *Grave New World*, but only within the village, which may stand for the liberating power of imagination/fancy limited to the inside of one's mind. Blake can do everything, but only in Shepperton: he "absorbs the whole city" (ibid.: 160) to remodel it. Symbolically, bits and pieces of the reality we share, the late capitalist affluent world, serve his mind to build an elaborate escapist fantasy he may hide in.

Blake dreams he wakes up after the accident already on the river bank. The stolen Cessna is still in the water and the details of his rescue are very obscure. Though he tries to "remember" being rescued and given artificial respiration, some part of his psyche knows he in fact is dead and in the river. This repressed knowledge tries to enter the narrative through a back door—Blake obsessively accuses people of having tried to kill him and he is vexed by the persistent intuition of an approaching end. One of the characters he meets, a young doctor

2. "[P]resumably a reference to the visionary Romantic poet and engraver William Blake, [which] signposts the way in which the novel can be interpreted as an allegory for the capacity of the imaginative writer to effect a liberation of the mind from the limitations of conventional reality" (Francis 2006a: 72).
3. Just like Maitland on his traffic island.

Miriam,[4] who embodies common sense and rationality in this imaginary realm, adds some details about the catastrophe and it is quite clear that he cannot have survived. Finally he decides to come back to the place of the accident:

> The pilot's door was open, and swung to and fro in the current.
> I was surprised by the immense span of the aircraft's wings, the outstretched fins of a huge ray... The reflected light ... lit up the cockpit, for a moment revealing the figure of a drowned man at the controls...
> Again I saw the dark figure at the controls—my own shadow cast through the water! (ibid.: 52).

Such an identification of the dead body with his own shadow (his own double, the uncanny twin brother) is in accordance with the Freudian idea of the rejection of a part of one's own psyche. Repressed and excluded from the conscious self, it comes back from the outside as a horror-like double. The awareness that the dead body is his own accompanies Blake throughout the narrative. The smell of decay attracts white vultures that appear in the town to look for carrion, finally blurring reality and imagination. Thus, imaginative powers (like these involved in any artistic creation) are shown to be uncanny as in creative activity the repressed fears and traumas return. Rosemary Jackson in *Fantasy: The Literature of Subversion* underlines the ability of fantastic literature to expose and analyze "those spaces which are hidden and cast into/as darkness":

> Themes of the fantastic in literature revolve around this problem of making visible the un-seen, or articulating the un-said. Fantasy establishes, or dis-covers, an absence of separating distinctions, violating the normal or commonsense perspective which represents reality as constituted by discrete but connected units (Jackson 1988: 48).

The world we see in the imaginative process of remodelling reality is both what we usually perceive as 'real' and what we refuse to acknowledge and repress. Jackson uses the term "paraxis" to describe such imagined but reality-based worlds "located in, or through, or beyond the mirror... behind the visible, behind the image, introducing dark areas from which anything can emerge" (ibid.: 43). In the case of Blake this "anything" is his own suicidal death, an escape from the *Grave New World* too hostile to live in.

Persistent thoughts of death make Blake incorporate an assassination motif into his fantasy. Killed by a jealous friend of Miriam, he dies once again and lies near a grave prepared for him by playing children. Nevertheless, all creatures— animals, birds and plants—give him their vital energy and he is "reborn within

4. Michel Delville calls her another of Ballard's lamias: beautiful but ambiguous women tempting male protagonists (Delville 1998: 56).

them and their love for me" (Ballard 1985b: 199). Death and resurrection are repeated and turn into a compulsion—Blake cannot master stress so he tends to repeat the experience endlessly.[5] Only at the end of the narrative, when he is ready to accept the truth, does he finally recognize his dead double and the split of the self is liquidated. He then says: "This drowned flier was my former self, left behind when I escaped from the Cessna" (ibid.: 214).

The novel sustains the feeling of uncertainty via juxtaposing the real events and places (the village, the body in the river) with imagined or surrealist accounts of Blake's miracles and his "life after life". To quote Jackson again: "The fantastic exists in the hinterland between 'real' and 'imaginary', shifting the relations between them through its indeterminacy" (Jackson 1988: 35). In Andrzej Gasiorek's opinion, Shepperton in the novel is a shadow of a shadow, an empty simulacrum of the real, and as such alludes to Plato's myth of the cave.

> But the reality [Blake] uncovers is not one of the Platonic Forms that are unreachable by the senses. On the contrary, this reality.... is corporeal and non-rational. A mutable ever-moving flux, it is a Dionysian fount of energy that flows in and through the whole of creation (Gasiorek 2005: 136).

The structure Ballard gives to this flux is Freudianism: the key concepts to understand the book are: "the double", "the uncanny", "the return of the repressed" and the "family romance"[6] which Blake tended to indulge in even before the fatal crash. A very unhappy child and adolescent, he used to view his life as a disaster and his only solace was in fantasies, compulsive role-playing and "above all dressing up as a pilot" (Ballard 1985b: 11). All his life Blake was thus escaping into the realm of imagination from the hostility of contemporary affluent society, with its disregard for the individual. Orphaned by his mother, rejected by his father and brought up by aunts, he could not communicate with his peers. His early school and professional career was no better: he failed in everything he started. From the earliest age he was compensating by creating his own make-believe version of reality: "I fantasized that my real father was one of the early American astronauts, and that I had been conceived by semen ripened in outer space" (ibid.: 120).

His short and unhappy life ended in a suicide flight in a stolen Cessna that crashed into the Thames.[7] Similar mental processes are involved in the imaginary space of his terminal fantasies. Blake finds justification for his previous life with all

5. In Chapter One, in the sub-chapter devoted to psychoanalysis, I explain how the repetition-compulsion effect serves to master unresolved psychic traumas.
6. According to Freud, children very often fantasize about their true family (usually very prominent if not royal) and construct elaborate narratives with themselves on the role of lost heirs. In these stories members of the family are cast as equally splendid characters and the more unhappy the child, the more fantastic the stories are.
7. He escapes from London airport after having tried to murder his girlfriend in what must have been a psychic fit. It is worth noticing that according to the social norms of *Grave New World* he is a misfit, a psychotic and a criminal—a model other rejected by society.

its failures and perversion in his dreamy stay in Shepperton. His past fascination with crime, murder, acts of congress with birds, animals, plants and the soil is transformed into an anticipation of his messianic all-embracing love for all the creatures in the village. Blake unites with all of them, and makes people abandon their mediocre former selves and fly away with him.

In the process of getting to know Shepperton and recognizing his mission Blake constructs an elaborate family romance giving the people he meets roles in his story. One of the first persons he sees, an elderly priest, is given the role of the father he missed all his life. It is significant that at the same time he accuses the priest of having tried to murder him: his ambivalent attitude towards his real father is reflected in his fantasy life. As Blake did crave his father's acceptance in the real world, here, in the Shepperton of his mind he does find a substitute parental love.

Similarly, the first middle-aged woman he saw, Miriam's mother, is immediately cast in the role of his own mother, lost in early childhood. The ambiguity of this love (Blake had missed his mother, but also hated her for leaving him) is here reflected in his oedipal-like attraction towards Miriam's mother. Enacting his earliest life he attacks the woman and couples with her in an act of symbolic birth, thus violating the taboo against incest. Scenes of misrule: incest, pedophilia and cannibalism are abundant in the novel—Blake tries to dissolve social structures and cultural laws, his unrestricted imagination[8] changes Shepperton into a realm of carnivalesque abandon to carnality. "The carnival life is drawn out of its usual rut, it is to a degree life turned inside out, life wrong way round" (Bakhtin, cit. Jackson 1988: 15), says Bakhtin, while Blake notes casually "Shepperton was taking on a carnival air" (Ballard 1985b: 127).

The moment of death allows Blake to meld erstwhile contraries—not only body and soul, but also the animate and the inanimate, the logical and the intuitive. In his narrative logical notions such as chronology and cause-and-effect relationships blur, time loops, "now" and "long ago" dissolve in a temporal oneness. As the unconscious is archaic, older than the civilized ego, it is in direct contact with pre-human, primordial times. Somewhere deep inside, at the level of cells and molecules, we do remember epochs much earlier than the Ice Age, the Earth inhabited by enormous reptiles, and the emergence of the first birds and mammals. Blake incorporates into his post-mortem fantasy allusions to unearthing the past and recognizing fossilized memories from bygone ages.

At the very beginning of his stay in Shepperton Blake notices a person digging in the bank of the Thames and immediately he recognizes an amateur archaeologist or geologist. The person, who later becomes his surrogate father, the priest, is fascinated with fossils and Blake learns that this part of the Thames Valley is a rich geological site. The river has preserved items dating back thousands of years, and it now takes in the Cessna and the body behind the controls—Blake finds his place among his brother creatures.

"The Thames here apparently produces the most unusual specimens.

---

8. Sam Francis points out that the novel's movement towards unrestricted imagination is also a movement towards entropy (Francis 2006: 79).

Prehistoric creatures, fossil fish—not to mention marooned pilots" (Ibid.: 62), Blake is told by Miriam's mother, and the similarity between him and prehistoric animals is marked for the first time. This motif recurs later; some creatures preserved in the Thames seem to be freaks and mistakes of nature who died out long ago and just like Blake left behind only their bodies: enigmatic, fantastic creatures embodying the impossible. The priest describes one of his finds to Blake: "A true flying fish, a precursor even of archaeopteryx, the most ancient known bird" (Ibid.: 78).

Blake is strangely fascinated by this fossil. He reconstructs the creature as half-man, half-fish and half-bird, an in-between impossible being, and one with which he identifies. The delicate "small winged man" (ibid.: 119) is for him an embodiment of the dream of flying and at the same time it is bound to earth and water, the primordial elements of life. This small skeleton of an unknown aviator is a very important object for Blake: deciphered in Freudian terms it stands for the inevitable return of every life to the inorganic world of mineral matter. Blake's persistence in comparing himself to the fossil is an instance of the return of the repressed, as he gradually accepts the fact of his own death. Additionally, the fossils comes from the times from before the differentiation of species, it symbolizes the primordial chaos to which everything will eventually return. Blake misses these ancient times, his misfortunes are partly due to the fact that he was born long after the epoch he belongs in—the archaic times before the differentiation and specialization of creatures, when nature was experimenting with the strangest forms.

> I had emerged on to the land reborn, like my amphibian forbears millions of years before me who left the sea to stride across the waiting parklands of the young earth. Like them, I carried memories of those seas in my bloodstream, memories of the deep time (ibid.: 98).

"The deep time" is not only the first epoch of life on Earth chronologically, but also a state of mind where the conscious self is in contact with its latent unconscious counterpart. Below the level of dull everyday life and the individual self there is the strange territory of biological memories all people share. Sometimes accessible in dreams, which are also timeless and illogical, this realm looks like "the young earth", a primordial garden so often described in human mythologies. In his messianic attempts to share his deeper understanding with Sheppertonians preoccupied with their mediocre pursuits, Blake decides to transform the village. Firstly, he tries to appeal to the common heritage of the human unconscious and makes everybody in the town dream of birds flying and mating in a storm. Once the unconscious is at large, the borders between fantasy and truth are obliterated, the collective vision of all Sheppertonians pours out and transforms the town.

People change into different creatures, wild animals appear in the streets turning the contemporary wasteland into a lush garden. Exuberant vegetation reclaims civilized terrain. In a chain of marvellous transformations Blake is in turn a bizarre bird, a whale, and a witch doctor. In a mystical act of identification he unites with Sheppertonians, shares their minds and bodies, and embraces all living creatures: mammals, birds and fish donate him their vital energy. There is no distinction between the real and the imagined, between the self and the external world.[9]

The world of the unconscious is peopled with the fantastic beings, hybrids of animals, humans and gods. Pre-human memories of gigantic creatures that once lived on Earth are mixed up with the images of mythical beings and demigods of shaman religions. This act of identification with non-human life gives Blake a divine status. With powerful antlers and hooves he incarnates the lord of deer, a fertility deity who spatters the town with his semen and finally is led to a grave prepared by children. The grave is surrounded by pieces of the crashed Cessna: a primitive rite of killing and burying a fertility god is symbolically staged. This ritual also seems innate, the children take it from some depths of their genetic memory, of their unconscious knowledgeable selves. Blake in his god Pan avatar is killed and resurrected with the power to renew the world, "to unify all living things by conjoining them with himself" (Gasiorek 2005: 137), and thus to restore the state of undifferentiation which is indistinguishable from entropy.

Observing the life of a contemporary commercial city—with its shops, supermarkets and massive sales—Blake plans to save it by appealing to the latent instincts of the inhabitants. The novel is a scorching criticism of the contemporary wasteland of capitalist consumption of unnecessary goods. A rich suburb with its banks and shopping centres enslaves people and severs them from their real needs and instincts. Blake leads them towards illumination by making them toss away all bank-notes and childishly play with luxurious goods. "Everyone was handing me money and credit cards, clapping delightedly as I gave them back birds and flowers, sparrows and robins... [in the shopping mall] the managers and assistants were bringing out their goods and giving them away to the passers-by" (ibid. 142). Finally, suburban housewives build a temple for Blake out of expensive merchandises. His divine or at least messianic role in the act of saving Sheppertonians is suggested in the text from the very beginning of the novel, though it is not immediately to be taken seriously.

His father figure, the priest, intuitively recognizes Blake's role and teaches him to treat his stay in the town as a preparation for entering some higher level of reality, a metaphysical, barely defined region. "For all we know, vices in this

---

9. According to Ballard such an irrational worldview is recently being re-introduced to the mainstream culture as well: "I sometimes think that in a sense we are entering a New Dark Age. The lights are full on, but there is inner darkness... because we're retreating into a sort of mind-set of our pre-rational forebears who lived in a kind of animist world where everything had a spirit—every twig, every stone in a stream... where questions of guilt and anxiety and fear and aggression ruled our reflexes. Reason is evaporating. It may well be that a Dark Age is slowly advancing over us. It's difficult to see how we're going to get out of it" (Vale 2005: 24). In the same interview he points out that subliminal fears are reflected in mass culture products, which in turn enhance insecurity: "That's the danger: when an entertainment system becomes a mental climate... and we now have a mental climate where the whole planet inhabits a kind of *Con Air-Armageddon-Independence Day* world of super-paranoid visions, with all that they summon up in the minds of the spectator" (ibid.: 70).

world may well be metaphors for virtues in the next. Perhaps you can take us all through that doorway" (ibid: 79), the priest says and introduces a metaphysical interpretation of Blake's fantasy according to which his strange sexual and violent impulses are not to be criticized, but rather considered echoes of some pagan religious rites hailing from times when we were nearer to genuine human nature. Blake's salvation of Sheppertonians, his attempts to lead them to the next world, are presented as recreating the long forgotten Eden. The next world is the prelapsarian one we have lost.

Blake starts by prompting a sexual utopia of free and guiltless coupling, but gradually he discovers that sexuality is only a means of discovering the forgotten, unconscious strengths latent in late twentieth-century people. Blake's point is that after recognizing the unlimited powers of the unconscious he should go on saving not only Shepperton, but the rest of the world as well. There is no doubt the this world does need "saving", as it is but a spiritual wasteland, is money-and-goods-oriented and hostile to individual personalities. Its "normal" inhabitants live in a semi-coma, unconscious of their real needs and instincts, and the self-aware people have to die or indulge in escapist fantasies.

Vermilion Sands offers a collection of similar escapist fantasies, this time written in a style influenced by surrealistic techniques.[10] Jackson writes: "surrealism has so much in common with fantasy, especially in its use of similar themes, such as disintegration of objects and the fluidity of discrete forms" (Jackson 1988: 36). This is true of *Vermilion Sands* and *The Unlimited Dream Company*: both narratives, the surrealist and the fantastic, depict wastelands whose exhausted inhabitants create enclaves of a make-believe extravaganza which sooner or later dissolve into despair.

Ballard shares his fascination with decadence, disintegration and overabundance with the Surrealists; like Breton or Dali he enjoys re-arranging and dislocating the elements of our world in order to obtain shocking collages. He uses as his esthetic input the nineteen-sixties culture with its love of re-cycled images and stories, and speculates about its possible mutations and its development. What is more, he shows that we cannot escape recycling, remembering and re-enactments: the stories in *Vermilion Sands* possess the haunting quality of endless repetitions: apparently different from one another, they nevertheless turn out to be a number of skillfully interwoven echoes.[11]

Despite its numerous repetitions the story, which is narrated over and over again, remains obscure and it only suggests some elusive psychological

10. As I mentioned in Chapter One, devoted to the presentations of cityscapes.
11. Reading the stories and turning the pages we over and over again face the new old story, permutations of an already known motif. In all of them there is a male artist narrator who gets acquainted with a "beautiful but quite insane" *femme fatale*. This rich and famous woman cannot stop remembering a traumatic event from her past and uses art as the way to enact it time after time. The stories are themselves memories of the narrators. What is interesting, not only can the heroines not stop re-living their past, but neither can the male narrators stop remembering their encounters with the heroines. Once the story reaches its end the narration is taken anew and we come back to the initial part—the narrator yields to an impulse of repeating everything once again. It is thus difficult to say whose compulsion we are dealing with: the narrator's or the *femme fatale*'s.

super-real (sur-realist) truth coming from the world above. To quote Jackson: "surrealism… enters a dialogue with the 'real' and incorporates that dialogue as part of its essential structure" (ibid.: 36). Thus, elements of reality—1960s culture and near-future affluent social life—serve Ballard to create an obsessive collage communicating anxiety and exhaustion. Roger Luckhurst points out that to identify a repetitive structure does not mean to understand its meaning:

> And to rely on the recognition of patterns of repetition need not in itself come to any understanding, either in one element of the series, or across it. Repetition, even with modulation, can be merely additive. Repetitions, that is, whilst being read, are also, in some senses, unreadable in that they give no access to interpretation but merely reinforce the enigmas (Luckhurst 1997: 169).

The obsessive repeating of an unresolved enigma makes *Vermilion Sands* a Freudian text, one which juxtaposes the interior world of the human psyche and its exterior manifestations. Moreover, in each story different narrators seem to follow similar, compulsive patterns of behaviour, as if forced to do this by some external power. One may argue that, in fact, they become projections of the unconscious of the text.

Repetition of plots and characters from canonical texts, e.g., intertextuality, is a very important feature of the style of *Vermilion Sands*. Describing the wasteland of the near future Ballard indicates the exhaustion of a culture obsessed with past glory.[12] In the chapter "Cry Hope, Cry Fury" the characters start consciously playing the game of intertextual allusion to literary works dealing with the strange and the uncanny. The protagonist introduces himself, and his name is, rather not by accident, Melville: the blond woman, Hope Cunard, wants to do a portrait of him reading *Maldoror*.[13] The choice of the book is very suggestive here, and the very process of producing the painting also reminds of surrealist[14] (and dadaist) tradition, namely, of automatic writing. The portrait of Melville reading *Maldoror* is produced not by the painter's hand, but by the exposure of the model to the photosensitive pigments which in few days would anneal themselves into the contours of a likeness.

Such a vision of future art as automatic repetitions of fragmented works of previous artistic schools and intertexual games apparently emphasizes the exhaustion of contemporary culture, but also shows that echoes, recycling and shocking collages are themselves a potent source of new art for the perverted world of the future. One cannot explain this strange, exhausted art away by

---

12. For more details concerning surrealism in this novel see the footnote to the discussion of *Vermilion Sands* in Chapter Two.

13. *Chants de Maldoror* and *Poésies* by Isidore Ducasse, better known by the name of Compte de Lautréamont, is the favourite text of the Surrealists. Breton many times writes about it as about the finest example of a new kind of sensitivity in praising their poetic style.

14. Compare Breton's *What Is Surrealism*, where he advocates artistic use of "thought … removed from all control exercised by the reason" (Breton 1978: 3).

simply pigeonholing it as 'avant-garde': the collages and allusions are here in order to explore the inner world of the psyche of people living in permanent unresolved stress, to describe (in Ballard's own words) their "iconography of inner space".[15]

This is precisely the feeling of paranoia which, according to the Surrealists, describes a state of artistic creativity. In "What Is Surrealism?" Breton quotes Dali's definition of paranoiac-critical activity as a "spontaneous method of *irrational knowledge* based on the critical and systematic objectification of delirious associations and interpretations" (Breton 1978: 13). Breton adds that:

> one must take into the account the property of *uninterrupted becoming* of any object of paranoiac activity, in other words of the ultra-confusing activity rising out of the obsessive idea. This uninterrupted becoming allows the paranoiac who is the witness to consider the images of the external world unstable and transitory, or suspect; and what is so disturbing is that he is able to make other people believe in the reality of his impressions (ibid.: 13).

In *Manifesto of Surrealism* Breton emphasizes the supreme role of shocking images in surreal art. Ballard's *Vermilion Sands* alludes to bygone artistic and psychological schools showing the exhaustion of a civilization unable to create anything new and doomed to repetition. The neurotic and deranged characters of the book—Ballard's ultimate inhabitants of the future—roam in the scrap-yards of the twentieth century trying to relive the past. *Grave New World* awaits us: in a few years we all are going to be its inhabitants.

Psychopathology

For Ballard the best way to describe contemporary culture is with the help of psychiatrist discourse, as the future life in affluent wastelands is going to be dominated by psychopathology. In *Running Wild*, a short novel whose setting I already discussed as an example of a *Grave New World* cityscape, Ballard proves that our ideals, our social utopias as created by skillful social engineering, breed paranoia and violence.[16] In Pangbourne, an enclave of the near future within a contemporary urban landscape, life in a gated community for the rich and privileged breeds social catastrophes that only a psychiatrist can discover. The fact that Greville, the narrator, is a psychiatrist and not a professional private

15. A quote from Ballard's article about surrealism under the title "The Coming of the Unconscious", reprinted in *A User's Guide to the Millennium* (Ballard 1997b:84).

16. Compare Ballard in a radio interview with David Gale: "mental illness is a kind of adaptation to the sort of circumstances that will arise in the future. As we move towards a more and more psychotic landscape, the psychotic traits are signs of a sort of… Darwinian adaptation… the environment today is itself so filled with pressures of every conceivable kind—the pressure to conform, the pressures to amuse oneself, the pressures to find oneself—and the constant bombardment of everyday life by advertising, the media landscape, together represent a continuing kind of challenge to one's sanity".

detective shows what it takes to understand future social problems. He starts his investigation by describing the claustrophobic atmosphere of luxury in a whole chain of such communities in Greater London:

> Secure behind their high walls and surveillance cameras, these estates in fact constitute a chain of closed communities whose lifelines run directly along the M4 to the offices and consulting rooms, restaurants and private clinics of central London. They remain completely apart... [They display] trends towards almost total self-sufficiency (Ballard 1989: 13).

In contrast to Greville, an intuitive and inquisitive intellectual who anticipates the disastrous future of our civilization, we also see psychiatrists in the novella of a second type: the Maxteds—confident and well-to-do followers of fashionable theories on child rearing. Ironically, their own son, a psycho-killer, murders them:

> By chance the Maxteds were the two murder victims whom I had actually met, at a Stockholm conference in 1986. I remembered an elegant and professional couple, almost too self-controlled with their silk suits and hand-tooled personal pagers. Their smooth, downplayed Gestalt and Human Potential jargon reminded me uncannily of the Scientologists, with the same reassuring patter concealing a hardnosed, evangelical sell (ibid.: 29).

Such a commercial approach to psychiatry, which sells ready-made pieces of advice on all subjects and which is founded on the writings of theoreticians with well-known names, results in much harm to patients' psyches. The Maxted-type of psychiatrist is friendly, nice, familiar with fashionable terms, and, in general, looks good on TV. His or her life (and their study) is for show: "none of my own books had a place on the shelves, an A-Z of once-modish names from Althusser and Barthes to Husserl and Perls" (ibid.: 29). The Maxteds rarely read the books, at least judging from the fact that they never noticed a severe mutilation of one of the volumes, not accidentally a copy of Piaget's classic text on child rearing. Their own son, Jeremy Maxted, destroyed the book in an act of revenge: for him and the other children it stood for all the 'BBC' ideology of utopian life at Pangbourne. The Piaget-like childhood turns out to harm the children and finally kills the parents who had ordained it. Greville looking at the mutilated book diagnoses the Pangbourne psycho-killers:

> The children *had* been brainwashed, by the unlimited tolerance and understanding that had erased all freedom and all trace of emotion... Altogether, the children existed in a state akin to sensory deprivation. Far from hating their parents when they killed them, the Pangbourne children probably saw them as nothing more than the last bars to be removed (ibid.: 63).

After their rebellion the children do not return to normal life in affluent society. They remain outside the social structures and probably form a terrorist or nihilist brigade. They are free and, for the first time in their lives, make decisions and experience real emotions. They are dangerous to the rest of society and it is society's fault to have reared them in this way and then to have failed to recognize them as criminals and arrest them. Greville and Payne are ignored—the authorities would never announce that innocent children may be the gruesome offenders, as society prefers not to notice the signs of the approaching *Grave New World* with its psychopathology.

The inhabitants of a gated community in *Running Wild* live their lives in a state of sensory deprivation. Fed with fiction and isolated from real experience and real emotions people go insane. In the most luxurious estates—in anticipation of the future utopian society—life grows too unreal to bear. In such societies psychopathology becomes a norm, as is the case in the two novels *Rushing to Paradise* and *Millennium People*,[17] which describe a world of radical ideologies, an all-powerful media, fringe philosophies and charismatic psychopaths whose random acts of violence punctuate the news in breakfast-time TV.

Utter boredom rules this world—the affluent West after "the end of history" as prophesied by Francis Fukuyama, when politics and religion no longer matter anymore and memories of the last "real" events—the Cold War and the 1960s social revolution—are receding into the mists of history. Contrary to all expectations, not only has global catastrophe never happened, the threat of nuclear Armageddon has disappeared. Notwithstanding this, civilization is indeed ruined (through on a spiritual, not a material level) and we live in an emotional void of informational chaos.

Rushing to Paradise is a story of a model wasteland—the French Pacific island of Saint-Esprit, which was to become a site of nuclear tests but, thanks to an environmentalist campaign led by Dr Barbara, has been turned instead into a sanctuary for endangered species. The few volunteers who stay with her on the island to tend the animals are forced to live through the traumatic experience of taking part in the cruel sociological experiment conducted by this demented woman. The book, narrated from the point of view of one of the volunteers, a teenage boy, is an intertextual echo of William Golding's *Lord of the Flies*.[18] Their stay on the island becomes an examination of the latent parts of human nature and tests the endurance of the psyche faced with the danger of such radical ideologies as pacifism, environmentalism and feminism in their most militant faces.

A similar idea—that the near future is going to be ruled by psychopaths and that the life of the affluent West is already psychopathology-oriented—is discussed in *Millennium People*, whose action takes place in London during a summer at the beginning of the new millennium, when the city is terrorized by senseless

17. The two novels depict a media-oriented society where the camera stands for power and people perceive reality via TV-enforced patterns (something I discuss in detail in Chapter Four).
18. Other intertextual echoes include *Robinson Crusoe* and *The Island of Dr Moreau* and, indirectly, Ballard's earlier attempt of 'Robinsonnade' *Concrete Island*.

violence.[19] Firstly, although the random terrorist attacks are spectacular, they are rather harmless: smoke bombs in video-stores, demonstrations protesting against cat exhibitions and parking fares, a fire in the National Film Theatre. Yet much graver acts of terror follow and there are victims.

The narrator, a middle-aged psychologist, decides to infiltrate the terrorist groups after a bomb planted at Heathrow kills his ex-wife. In the course of his narrative he gradually understands what is going on in the city. Two social phenomena coincide: the new proletariat—the London middle-class (impoverished by school fees, mortgages and rents) abandons its inbred ethics and morals and starts a revolution by spectacularly destroying such class symbols as public school uniforms, A.A. Milne's fiction and the NFT library. At the same time, however, the city witnesses acts of senseless violence inflicted by sheer psychopathology, as the psychopath is the last agent capable of real action in a world where everything has already happened.

Quite striking in both novels is the fact that the society inhabiting contemporary wastelands is primarily comprised of passive consumers of TV news and hardly anyone leaves the living room. The few who actually make the news are prompted and led by charismatic leaders. In *Rushing to Paradise* such a person is Dr Barbara Rafferty,[20] an obsessive rebel and demonstrator, a woman who compulsively fights the establishment. She loses her doctor's license after a euthanasia scandal in London hospitals and turns to saving the albatross on Pacific islands and to protesting against nuclear tests. Her enthusiasm and strong will draw international media interest to her latest crusade, to save Saint-Esprit and establish a sanctuary there. Once the colony is established she cuts off the outside world and succumbs to her private, pathological obsessions. She claims that our social structure is outdated and the only cure for overwhelming exhaustion must be radical. She starts to pursue her true ideological objectives: the elimination of all men (except a genetic minimum) and the creation of a world of women, which she believes, is going to be the future of the human race. She says:

> Men exhausted themselves building the world. Like tired children they're always fighting each other, and they can't see how they hurt themselves. It's the women's turn to take over now—we're the only ones with the strength to go on. Think of all-women cities, Neil, parks and streets filled with women... (Ballard 1995a: 224).[21]

19. The novel was written two years before the terrorist attacks in the London transport in the summer of 2005, which gives Ballard's narratives a disturbingly prophetic character. As Roger Luckhurst puts it, sometimes it is difficult not to read Ballard as anticipation of later theory and social reality.

20. In Ballard's fiction there is a long tradition of doctor protagonists: physicians, biologists, neurologists and psychiatrists, from whose point of view stories are narrated and who serve as authorial porte parole. In this book the doctor figure is for the first time female. Moreover, Dr Rafferty is the opposite of these doctors: she is active, demented and attractive, and we look at her only from the outside, via the eyes of the novel's teenage focalizer.

21. Rafferty is, despite all appearances, a complex character. Clearly inspired by Jack Kevorkian (Dr Death), the American doctor who was put on trial for numerous euthanasia cases, and ridiculed as a

Her experiment on Saint-Esprit only at the start seems rather benign—ecologists from all over the world establish a small society of nature-lovers and try to forget about the outside world. Dr Barbara is then compared to a contemporary Margaret Mead and the myth of uncivilized utopia is evoked in the text—two anthropologists from Southern California even try to get to the island on a boat in order to study social interaction in the savage colony. With time this all turns out to be a cover, and soon a more dangerous face of Dr Barbara is revealed and her dementia becomes apparent: one by one the men disappear, murdered by her out of sheer compassion. The male era, according to Dr Barbara, has ended: stained with a genetic heritage of brutality, aggression and competition men should be painlessly eliminated. The island is to be a harbinger of the future, a sanctuary not for the albatross, but for "all [of women's] threatened strengths, their fire and rage and cruelty" (Ibid.: 171).

Despite her lunacy (or because of it), Dr Barbara is a person who makes things happen. She is the opposite of passivity and consumerism, her enthusiasm has the power of attraction and though murderous she is loved by the media—just like Oswald or Kevorkian were. We in fact should be grateful to such people, as notwithstanding the price, they push life ahead and give food to the news watched in millions living rooms all over *Grave New World*. In *Millennium People* there are two characters who play a similar role: each of them represents a different aspect of Dr Barbara. Kay Churchill, a middle-class rebel and a cultural studies teacher suspended for introducing pornography to her syllabus, is an equally enthusiastic militant and is as likeable as Dr Barbara at the stage when she seems still normal. Kay rebels against the condition of culture, the suburban middle-class lifestyle, idiotic entertainment, late capitalism and globalization. She is aware that we live in a world where nothing can happen anymore and that all we do is but a simulacrum of the real thing. Just like Dr Barbara, she cannot stand passivity and does everything she can to wake people up. Planting smoke bombs in 'sacred' middle-class institutions, trying to make her students aware of the degeneration of the film industry and shocking well-to-do neighbourhoods by surveys on toilet training, she desperately tries to change the world. Her views on tourism well represent the ideology of this unstable but moral woman:

> Tourism is the great soporific. It's a huge confidence trick, and gives people the dangerous idea that there's something interesting in their lives... Today's tourism goes nowhere. All the upgrades in existence lead to the same airports and resort hotels, the same pina

representative of the extremist fringe of the feminist movement, she nevertheless often seems right. Ballard explains this paradox in an interview: "the satire on the extremist fringes of the feminist movement is more ambiguous, because I actually take the side of Dr Barbara... I can see that this is an immensely powerful, strong-willed woman who has all the ancient, ancestral power of women as creators, as controllers, as enchanters of men, as crones, as mothers—all those archetypal female images, which have so terrified and inspired men through the ages, are incarnated in a small way in this character" (Self 1995: 343).

colada bullshit. The tourists smile at their tans and their shiny teeth and think they are happy. But the suntans hide who they really are—salary slaves, with heads full of American rubbish. Travel is the last fantasy the 20th century left us, the delusion that going somewhere helps you reinvent yourself (Ballard 2004: 54-55).

Kay Churchill starts a revolution among the inhabitants of one London district fed up with contemporary city life: they set houses on fire, destroy cars and parking machines and shout slogans on the TV. Their revolution is on the news, it creates the illusion that something actually is going on in London and that changes are coming.

One more person, Dr Gould, also has the power of attracting the media (though he tries to remain anonymous) and making things happen, but by no means in a benign way—in fact he is the equivalent of the psychopathic side of Dr Barbara. In the past Dr Gould took care of handicapped children, but despite his devotion to them he was suspended for unorthodox treatment practices and now he saves the world with pointless violence. He kills people in bomb attacks at Heathrow and the Tate gallery and also shoots in cold blood a television celebrity on the doorstep to her London house, a woman whose face everybody knows, but who represents no values and no intellect either. She has millions of admirers and her death is a shock for the nation (the parallels with the death of Princess Diana are explicit), therefore her funeral changes into a media celebration. Such random acts of violence are for Dr Gould a way of facing the total vacuousness and senselessness of contemporary life: killing the presenter stirs millions of TV viewers and gives them the illusion of personal trauma. In our society the psychopath is a prophet, in that he provides the sleepy nation with the surrogate emotions they need so much.

In a very interesting interview devoted to the current social and political situation in Britain in 2003 Ballard told Graeme Revell:

> One can almost choose to indulge in a mode of psychopathic behaviour without any sort of moral inhibition at all. In fact, given the suffocating effect of the entertainment landscape, the sort of smothering flow of manufactured television programs and advertisements and all the rest of it... the only kind of fall-back position that any of us has lies with the human potential for madness... What [people] are looking for is some sort of dramatic stimulus that will penetrate the kind of bland manufactured pap that makes up most of the media landscape today (Vale 2005: 58-59).

The characters of *Millennium People* are aware that our gravest civilization problems are the overwhelming boredom and inertia that make people passive and immune to the world around. A chance meeting with Dr Gould makes the narrator realize that once an act of horror happens in front of one's eyes, the world gets more real and more meaningful—life in well-protected living-rooms with

TV sets causes the feeling of sensory depravation, as was the case with the teenage inhabitants of Pangbourne. Therefore, quite perversely, what Dr Gould is doing springs not from pure nihilism, but rather from compassion and sympathy for the people whom he terrorizes. Today we cannot do anything constructive, as in fact there is no need for us to do anything at all, so what we are left with is action with no rational motive, which carries a significance of its own.

In the context of Dr Gould's murderous campaign, everything Kay Churchill and her people are attempting is merely a sign of deep frustration and powerlessness. Dr Gould, a perceptive and highly intelligent person, is able to diagnose the social processes that are at work and he explains everything to the narrator.

> The middle-class protest is just a symptom. It's part of a much larger movement, a current running through all our lives, though most people don't realize it. There's a deep need for meaningless action, the more violent the better. People know their lives are pointless, and they realise there's nothing they can do about it. Or almost nothing (ibid.: 249).

The seemingly pampered elite of the affluent world is in the grip of a pathological boredom that can only be relieved by violence and cruelty—and it takes a psychopath to "save" the nation by introducing depravity to the world.[22] Ballard's fiction thus tries to answer a difficult historiosophical question—why has our civilization entered this cultural and moral dead-end street? What is wrong with us?

In a world of omnipresent technology and no religion—social and interpersonal bonds are loosening, people prefer to communicate via and with machines. The narrator is working on a new computerized diagnostic system—instead of talking to the consultant, the patient sits at the screen, pressing buttons in reply to pre-recorded questions from a doctor played by an actor. The success of the system is the best proof of growing social alienation—people cease to need other people. Similarly, family bonds and class bonds are slowly disintegrating. The middle-class revolt of Kay Churchill demonstrates how very feeble and outdated the British class ethos is. Once history has ended and the political institutions once dividing the world with political and economic borders were liquidated the social structures of post-Puritan society cannot survive. The end of the bourgeois economy must by followed by the disappearance of bourgeois ethics and discipline.

Both *Rushing to Paradise* and *Millennium People* show a static 'post-historical' world of no mobility and social isolation, where people are TV consumers and the media create the reality society considers true. Psychopaths and extremists alone provoke public opinion by their radical actions, ones eagerly broadcast by

---

22. In a recent interview Ballard says: "nothing disconcerts people more than an apparently meaningless act" (Vale 2005: 12).

the media, but which are devoid of any meaning other than the pure exercise of violence. People often remember and refer to the Cold War and the 1960s, because these were the last moments of the world that made sense. The characters of *Rushing to Paradise* live in the shadow of the A-bomb and their island is visited by a hippie commune from thirty years before—and in *Millennium People* the memory of 1960s London is still alive. Today's Chelsea is just a shadow of the place it used to be—with maverick scientists, drugs and never-ending parties, while contemporary psychologists miss the times of R.D. Laing and his theories of schizophrenia as a healthy response to social traumas. Those days are forever gone and, as the world which should have ended in a bang did not end at all, we have to live in a wasteland where the psychopath is a prophet as he alone can provide people with the illusion that something is still to come.

In *Super-Cannes* and in *Cocaine Nights* the psychopathology of the near future wastelands is best described. In both works the narrative strategy of *Running Wild* is used: we see a detective figure who finds himself in a totally new, hyperreal[23] place and tries to resolve a criminal enigma. They embark on a private investigation to find out not who committed the motiveless crime, but why it was committed.[24] In contrast to the protagonist of *Running Wild* they are not modern Sherlock Holmes figures specializing in enigmatic cases, but rather accidental newcomers, families of people involved in what is going on in the hyperreal enclaves. The would-be-detectives come from still 'real' places to the Mediterranean villages, which turn out to be capsules of the time future, where:

> models no longer constitute an imaginary domain with reference to the real; they are, themselves, an apprehension of the real, and thus leave no room for any fictional extrapolation—they are immanent, and therefore leave no room for any kind of transcendentalism. The stage is now set for stimulation, in the cybernetic sense of the word—that is to say, for all kinds of manipulation of these models (hypothetical scenarios, the creation of simulated situations, etc.), but now nothing distinguishes this management-manipulation from the real itself: there is no more fiction (Baudrillard 2003: 2).

23. Compare *Simulacra and Simulations*: "Simulation is no longer that of a territory, a referential being or a substance. It is the generation by models of a real without origin or reality: a hyperreal" (Baudrillard 2003: 166)

24. The narrator of *Cocaine Nights* soon finds out that: "In Estrella de Mar, like everywhere in the future, crimes have no motive. What you should look for is someone with no apparent motive for killing" (Ballard 1997a: 182). The need for senseless violence is, according to Ballard, one of the features of Western society in the near future. He explains it in an interview: "Of course, the End of Ideology means that we get apathy. Now, people hate being bored—the central nervous system needs stimulation, otherwise we become like those polar bears in zoos who restlessly walk up and down and then start hitting themselves. So after apathy comes a hunger for any kind of violent act that will break the boredom. That's the really dangerous phase... because whole nations can embrace madness deliberately, willingly, just to break the boredom" (Vale 2005: 108).

The narrators explore these unreal future realms, trying to adopt the new kind of logic, as our categories of cause-and-effect, motive, etc., prove outdated. In *Cocaine Nights* Charles Prentice, an English travelogue writer, is summoned to the British resort of Estrella de Mar, an exclusive enclave for rich retired British, centred around the thriving Club Nautico. Charles' beloved younger brother Frank Prentice, the manager of the club, pleads guilty to charges of murder. It is obvious to everybody that he could not and did not kill the five victims of arson who died in one of the luxurious villas. Charles decides to stay in Estrella de Mar and to do what Frank was doing. Gradually, just by being there, he starts to understand Frank's motives and the mechanics of "the creation of a simulated situation" (to echo the essay by Baudrillard quoted above), which rule the social life of the resort.

Similarly, in *Super-Cannes* Paul Sinclair, an invalid ex-pilot, gets to Eden-Olympia (a multinational business park on the French Riviera) in order to accompany his much younger wife, Dr Jane. She is hired to replace an English doctor at the local clinic who unexpectedly went on a homicidal shooting spree. Paul Sinclair, though too ill to work, tries to protect his wife from the dangerous people who rule Eden-Olympia and, step by step, he uncovers the criminal psychological vents that maintain the well-being of people in the park.

In both novels the detective story structure is but a pretext to address the psychological consequences of late twentieth-century technology; the private investigations of Prentice and Sinclair are soon abandoned and the narrators concentrate on describing what they see around and what is the probable future of our civilization. Though in both cases we do finally learn why the murders were committed, it is far less important than the presentation of the psychopathology of the generation who lives after the "future shock" of Alvin Toffler.

Ballard's narrators who come to the unreal domains of Estrella de Mar and Eden-Olympia from our busy world are faced with criminal enigmas. Trying to resolve the mysteries they start by adapting 'standard' detective fiction strategies—they look for motives, check alibis, talk to witnesses, visit the scenes of the crime. Though they accumulate more and more details, no conclusions appear and their investigations lead to nowhere. Only when they decide to stay and impersonate the criminals—live the lives of the communities—do they get to understand the new logic which rules there. Prentice moves to the apartments of his imprisoned brother and takes up his job at the club, Sinclair and his wife are given the villa of the psycho-killer and she, additionally, his job at the clinic.

The first striking thing about these enclaves of luxury is the very important role of psychiatrists: Sinclair in the very first paragraph of his narration emphasizes the fact that a psychiatrist was his guide to Eden-Olympia. This proves a very apt introduction to the park, which is haunted by "a kind of waiting madness, like a state of undeclared war" (Ballard 2002a: 3). The psychiatrist, Dr Penrose, not only knows more than anybody else about secrets of Eden-Olympia, but also generalizes about future psychology and the ways for maintaining mental health in totally unreal surroundings. People in Eden-Olympia are very conscious about their health—in fact, Dr Jane Sinclair is engaged in a project of permanent health monitoring. The entire estate is cabled to the medical centre: it is enough to feed the computer a drop of blood every morning to have all basic tests made for the purposes of medical prevention. But what about mental health?

> Our brains, I often told her, would soon need a false ceiling to make room for the ducting demanded by our 'intelligent' lifestyle. Before breakfast we would set ourselves a psychological test, tapping yes-or-no answers to alternative-choice questions, while a standby alarm offered an emergency package entitled 'What to do till the psychiatrist comes' (ibid.: 155).

Working sixteen hours a day and dealing with millions of dollars in transactions, the inhabitants of Eden-Olympia are very prone to psychological ailments. In fact, most of the low-grade employees: security agents, custodians etc., think them utterly mad. As Sinclair gets to know from one of the security people, minor offences ("Kiddie porn, drugs, fascist ideas...not exactly serious crimes these days", one of the characters says) help them to keep going. Such crimes in the future society are to function as psychological vents helping to maintain efficiency and dedication. The cityscape, as from Corbusier's utopian dreams, houses people who are on the verge of psychopathology. Penrose, the psychiatrist, studies this phenomenon:

> Classical psychoanalysis starts with the dream, and that was my first breakthrough. I realized that these highly disciplined professionals had very strange dreams. Fantasies filled with suppressed yearnings for violence, and ugly narratives of anger and revenge, like starvation dreams of death-camp prisoners (ibid.: 258).

This unreal life with all biological impulses suppressed makes people feel like exiles cut off from their deeper selves. Human beings have evolved to lead a real, not artificial existence, and the abundance of simulacra is harmful. Psychopathology is in a sense a "healthy" response to the artificiality of life in luxury enclaves. Violence and the fear of violence are real, just like sexuality is real, because they appeal to humans as biological beings equipped by evolution with survival instincts. In the situation where illusions and the virtual world of computer screens make people lose their sense of reality a dose of fear and aggression is all too welcome.

Places like Eden-Olympia are too clean, the servicemen work swiftly and quietly, there are no crowds, no noise, no conflicts, no social unrest. Such a smooth and painless life (whose security is granted by an army of guards with their cameras and all other technology) is, psychologically, akin to the state of sensory deprivation, which in turn leads to mental illness. People without everyday worries, unsatisfied needs or fears tend to be unhealthy, fatigued and unresponsive—they do not even wish to go out from their homes. The consumer society which produces such an elite at the same time needs constant flows of money and goods and has to do something to wake these people up and make them spend. It is in appeals to their deeper selves and biological instincts that the solution may be found. Penrose has a whole theory explaining these processes:

> Violence is spectacular and exciting, but sex has always been the main hunting ground for psychopathy. A perverse sexual act can liberate the visionary self in even the dullest soul. The consumer society hungers for the deviant and unexpected. What else can drive the bizarre shifts in the entertainment landscape that will keep us "buying"? (ibid.: 265).

Gradually, as Sinclair discovers the real nature of Eden-Olympia with its racist brigades who attack Arabian immigrants in the nearby villages, its sexual deviations, drug distribution system and child prostitution, he understands the theories of Penrose. In Eden-Olympia futuristic divagations, sociological projections and cultural prognoses are not just talk, the new ideology of more sex and violence is actually working. Psychopaths are saving the inhabitants from life in a void, and in a virtual classless community of top executives only, eruptions of aggression and violence help to maintain social structure. Penrose on the example of Eden-Olympia explains the mechanisms, which in a few years' time will be working in all affluent democracies:

> Everything is for sale now—even the human soul has a barcode. We're driven by bizarre consumer trends, weird surges in the entertainment culture, mass paranoias about new diseases that are really religious eruptions. How to get grip on all this? We may need to play on deep-rooted masochistic needs built into the human sense of hierarchy... People no longer need enemies—in this millennium their great dream is to become victims. Only their psychopathies can set them free (ibid.: 365).

In Eden-Olympia and similar business parks in the Riviera a new kind of world is being born. Superficially it is quiet, devoted to hard intellectual work and practically deprived of social life. The smooth surface of this world is, nevertheless maintained by dangerous psychological vents. Though Sinclair does everything he can to expose the racial and criminal offences of the inhabitants in order to stop the crime and let everybody in Europe know and punish the criminals it is hard to believe in *Super-Cannes'* happy ending.[25] The traditional structure of thriller fiction, with its final explanation of what happened and why, not to mention the

---

25. As one of the other characters comments: "Wilder Penrose and Delage have to be stopped, along with their lunatic scheme. Not because it's crazy, but because it's going to work. The whole world will soon be a business-park colony, run by a lot of tight-lipped men who pretend to be weekend psychos" (Ballard 2002a: 345).

final victory of justice, is no longer applicable. We do not know whether Sinclair will succeed in his plan of seizing the TV station and broadcasting his discoveries all over Europe. Perhaps he will follow the example of his predecessor the doctor, who was gunned down by a security guard and pronounced a psycho-killer on a suicidal spree. Whatever the case, sociological mechanisms at work in Eden-Olympia seem plausible, and fighting the logic of the future already descending is pointless. According to Ballard in the perfect affluent society with no tensions and no worries only psychopathology will keep us going.

Similar conclusions can be drawn from *Cocaine Nights*, the novel dealing not with hardworking future professionals (work is going to be a rare privilege soon), but with the retired. In the twenty-first century, after a decade or two of efficient professional life, people in their mid-forties are going to have to quit their careers and move to some pleasant place to spend the next fifty years on leisure. What will happen when they finally find themselves within the luxurious gated communities along the Mediterranean? Lavishly equipped with swimming pools, sport clubs, courts, courses and everything else, the enclaves may wind up being full of busy and happy permanent holidaymakers. But more probably, they will be inhabited by inert and half-asleep tranquillizer addicts who do not have the energy to do what people in the twentieth century dreamt of doing.

Cocaine Nights describes both these possibilities. In the Mediterranean enclave of Estrella de Mar the spell of unhappy inertia is broken when Bobby Crawford, a young man dedicated to saving and energizing the inhabitants, applies small dosages of crime and violence.[26] When minor crimes make them alert and invitations to slightly illegal entertainment follow, the sleepy village changes into a busy, half-bohemian resort. Of course, a price has to be paid and at the moment when certain limits are transgressed the village deteriorates and a serious crime is committed. Nevertheless, the point Ballard makes is quite clear: the future leisure society is going to face serious psychological problems. A doctor friend of Prentice, who introduces him to the life of Estrella de Mar (Prentice sees it as a hive of happy holiday activities with various clubs and societies), tells him that the present happiness is the work of Crawford:

> He's changed our lives and practically put the Clinic out of business. Before he arrived it was one huge, money-churning de-tox unit. Alcoholism, ennui and benzo-diazepine filled our beds. Bobby

26. As one of the characters explains: "A world lying on its back is vulnerable to any cunning predator. Politics are a pastime for a professional caste and fail to excite the rest of us. Religious belief demands a vast effort of imaginative and emotional commitment, difficult to muster if you are groggy from last night's sleeping pill. Only one thing is left which can rouse people ... Crime and transgressive behaviour—by which I mean all activities which aren't necessarily illegal, but provoke us and tap our need for strong emotion, quicken the nervous system and jump the synapses deadened by leisure and inaction". (Ballard 1997a: 180) And: "Everywhere you look—Britain, the States, Western Europe—people are sealing themselves off into crime-free enclaves. That's a mistake—a certain level of crime is part of the necessary roughage of life. Total security is a disease of deprivation" (ibid.: 293).

Crawford pops his head around the door and everyone sits up and rushes to the tennis courts (ibid.: 121).

In Estrella de Mar we deal with two kind of drugs. The eponymous cocaine (though illegal) and other "fun taken for fun" and distributed by villagers who role-play dealers[27] are much less harmful than legal tranquillizers.[28] The psychiatrist Dr Sanger, who ruled Estrella de Mar before Crawford kept his patients permanently sedated, claims "the whole town was Valiumed out of its mind". In *Our Posthuman Future* Francis Fukuyama describes the effect the overuse of drugs has on social life in comparison to Aldous Huxley's *Brave New World*, where citizens of the future were kept obedient thanks to massive dosages of soma.

> The second, neuropathological wave of the biotech revolution has already come crashing down around us. It has already produced a pill that looks like soma and a pill for socially controlling children, pills that appear to be far more effective than early childhood socialization and Freudian talk therapies of the twentieth century ever were. Their use has spread to millions and millions of people around the world, with much controversy over their potential long-term health consequences for the body, but almost no argument over what they imply about the conventional understanding of identity and moral behavior (Fukuyama 2002b: 52).

Fukuyama goes on to demonstrate how the spread of psychotropic drugs will alter society in the near future. Although his "wasteland" is America in a few years' time, while *Cocaine Nights* and *Super-Cannes* are about Europe, the conclusions are similar: Fukuyama prophesies an overwhelming feeling of apathy and inertia. "The desire on the part of ordinary people to medicalize as much of their behavior as possible and thereby reduce their responsibility for their own actions" (ibid. 53) is a fair way of describing what was going on in Estrella de Mar.

Fukuyama says that drugs are going to win over conventional therapies, Ballard thinks they will complement each other. In *Cocaine Nights* the psychiatrist figure, compared to Svengali and called a hypnotist, is partly playing the role of a charismatic therapist from a century before. Before Crawford comes he is the one who 'rules' Estrella de Mar, but his power is a pastiche of dangerous charisma.

He is in fact weak and pathetic, and his gift of tranquillizers lets the

---

27. Crime is treated as a game: there are amateur actresses impersonating prostitutes, people playing volunteer security forces, gangsters, etc.

28. At least to the inhabitants. Compare Francis Fukuyama: "We feel very ambivalent about substances that have no clear therapeutic purpose, and whose only effect is to make people feel good. We feel particularly ambivalent if the high produced by the drug seriously impairs the user's ability to function normally, as it is the case with heroin and cocaine. But we also find it hard to justify our ambivalence, since doing so involves making judgements as to what a person's 'normal functioning' is. How can we justify banning marijuana when alcohol and nicotine, two other drugs that make us feel good, are legal?" (Fukuyama 2002b: 56).

inhabitants survive, but deprives them of any feelings. Their life is an empty existence, a near death state of sensory deprivation. Surrounded by mock-architecture, models and pastiches of old styles, they are prone to psychosomatic diseases. In Estrella de Mar and Eden-Olympia alike (before the outburst of "healthy violence") strange colds, pains and ailments were common and Sinclair's knee inflammation is clearly psychosomatic. Of course, the diseases are not less painful because of their psychological nature—the suffering they provoke is real. In fact the distinction between 'true' and 'false', 'real' and 'imaginary' is obliterated: "Illusion is no longer possible, because the real is no longer possible" (Baudrillard 2003: 177). This thesis is elaborated on in Baudrillard's famous essay "The Precession of Simulacra" (1981), where, among other things, he discusses psychosomatic ailments. Simulated illness, where a patient produces the symptoms, is very much different from a feigned illness, where a patient goes to bed and simply pretends he is ill.

> The simulator cannot be treated objectively either as ill, or as not ill. Psychology and medicine stop at this point... For if any symptom can be "produced", and can no longer be accepted as a fact of nature, then every illness may be considered as a simulatable and simulated, and medicine loses its meaning since it only knows how to treat "true" illnesses by their objective causes. Psychosomatics evolves in a dubious way on the edge of the illness principle (ibid.: 168).

What we are dealing with in places such as Estrella de Mar or Eden-Olympia is the reversal of common sense logic. People do not suffer from symptoms because they are ill, but they are ill because they produce (unconsciously or in any other way) painful symptoms. The 'truth' is a produced thing, not the source of production. Baudrillard goes on to elaborate on these paradoxes:

> We are in a logic of simulation which has nothing to do with a logic of facts and an order of reasons. Simulation is characterised by a precession of the model, of all models around the merest fact— the models come first, and their orbital (like a bomb) circulation constitutes the genuine magnetic field of events (ibid.: 175).[29]

29. At this point it is worth remembering the fact that Ballard and Baudrillard are aware of each other's writing. As I already suggested, from the moment *Crash* was published Baudrillard has been an admirer of Ballard, and Ballard is influenced by (or enters an intertextual dialogue with) Baudrillard's theses. Roger Luckhurst, who is an admirer of both writers, even coined the term Ba(udri)llard. Therefore, *Simulacra and Simulations* seems to be the right context to discuss *Cocaine Nights* and *Super-Cannes*, as the novels are partly a response to Baudrillard's visions of the future of the West. Ballard is aware of the intertextual affiliation of *Super-Cannes* and Baudrillard's theories. "I sat down and ordered a *vin blanc* from the young French waitress, who wore jeans and a white vest printed with a quotation from Baudrillard" (Ballard 2002a: 88), as the narrator of *Super-Cannes* describes a chance visit in a cafe in the French Riviera.

The absence of truth (for both Ballard and Baudrillard) causes nostalgia for past epochs and old cultural orders. Architects try to satisfy these needs by building stylized estates—other people do so by getting involved in all sorts of 'revivals' or retro fads. The overwhelming feeling is one of spiritual void. In Estrella de Mar people prompted by Crawford try to fill the void with different pseudo-real activities.[30] The film society shoots pornographic films (sex is real as a biological activity, while stories told by 'standard' films seem senseless): when life is turned into its representation—the tape—it seems more real. Security cameras filming every moment in the estates serve as the inhabitants' memory.

Similarly, life in Eden-Olympia is much influenced by the proximity of the Cannes Festival. Film fans, street parades, premieres etc. are substitutes for reality. The fascist groups film their raids in the estate—but only watched on the screen does the violence give them satisfaction. Sinclair describes Eden-Olympia as the realm of copies, representations and models, a Baudrillardian land of simulacra. It is not accidental that the local kiddie porn society elaborated a complicated code based on a circulation of Lewis Carroll's *Alice* books.

> I wondered how the Reverend Dodgson's Alice would have coped with Eden-Olympia. She would have grown up quickly and married an elderly German banker, then become a recluse in a mansion high above Super-Cannes, with a fading facelift and a phobia about reflective surfaces (Ballard 2002a: 175).

The choice of Carroll as an intertextual allusion is very telling here, the logic of Eden-Olympia is the logic of mirror reflections: the image precedes its origins, reality is in itself a representation. Such a world is deprived of morality and indeed of choices in most spheres of life. Giant multinational corporations rule the park: they decide where the inhabitants should educate their children, how they should treat their spouses and what the sensible limits to stock market investments are. Banks decide how big a mortgage they can handle and what the right amount of insurance to buy is. "We can rely on their judgement, and that leaves us free to get on with the rest of our lives. We've achieved real freedom, the freedom from morality" (ibid.: 95), as Penrose, the psychiatrist puts it. The only obligation, the only moral duty the inhabitants have towards corporations is to keep 'buying'. Penrose holds that shopping, the ultimate social activity, is what glues the community together: "Shopping is

---

30. For Ballard the ultimate illusory place is an airport, where we have "the sense of having a real destination, the great undying illusion of travel" (Ballard 1997a: 9). This quote comes from the first pages of *Cocaine Nights*—Prentice goes on to explain that in fact everywhere the airports are identical with identical products sold in identical boutiques and shops and we only think we travel. The same point is made in one of Ballard's articles written for *The Observer*. Though this time he writes non-fiction there is hardly any difference: "Airports have become a new kind of discontinuous city, whose vast populations, measured by annual passenger throughputs, are entirely transient, purposeful and, for the most part, happy... I've long suspected that people are only truly happy and aware of a real purpose to their lives when they hand over their tickets at the check-in" (Ballard 1997b: 2).

the last folkloric ritual that helps to build a community, along with traffic jams and airport queues" (ibid.: 18).

Problems, even tiny ones, make life seem more real, which in Eden-Olympia (the Baudrillardian hyperreal estate) is very important. During his private investigation Sinclair finds videocassettes, pictures, computer data, manikins, dolls and toys: copies and records of things—not the things themselves. Smooth and luxurious Eden-Olympia seems dead and full of simulacra only:

> I circled the artificial lakes, with their eerily calm surfaces, or roamed around the vast car parks. The lines of silent vehicles might have belonged to a race who had migrated to the stars (ibid.: 37).

This luxurious estate is nevertheless a place of evil, a heart of darkness built on pain and injustice. At the end of his investigation Sinclair compares it to: "The Belgian Congo under Leopold II, very nasty and very racist" (ibid.: 320). It is not surprising, therefore, that the only busy place in the infrastructure of the neighbouring Antibes-les-Pins is the cyber-café. Bikers in metallic boots and *Mad Max* leathers sit there: "a feral presence in the hyper-modern complex, like carrion-birds on a skyscraper cornice, filling an unplanned niche in the ecology of the future" (ibid.: 324). This gloomy simile is very telling, Eden-Olympia is described as both the future and disaster.[31] The prevailing feeling that what we see in the book is going to happen everywhere in Europe and North America in a few years time goes together with a suggestion that the forthcoming epoch is a final degeneration of our culture; the end of civilization as we know it. Similar feelings are present in *Cocaine Nights* as well. The Gibraltar setting is very telling: the last outpost of the British Empire is the site of the last chapter of the history of Europe. "Here on Costa del Sol nothing would ever happen again, and the people of the pueblos were already the ghosts of themselves" (Ballard 1997a: 75).

Prentice as a travel writer knows a lot of landscapes and is able to interpret their looks. Here he senses stillness and the approaching death (or at least brain death) of the whole culture. Thus the final diagnosis that "Estrella de Mar is what the future will be like" (Ballard 2002a: 90), sounds very pessimistic indeed. Such persistent recurrence of similar opinions, images and commentaries in both Ballard's novels (and shorter fiction) seems purposeful. Ballard is relentless in emphasizing his attitude toward the present state of culture and voicing his opinions about its future development (or rather regression).[32]

In September of 2006 *Kingdom Come* was published. For a scholar interested in the way Ballard depicts contemporary culture—*Grave New World* as I call it—

31. The picture of the future in George Miller's *Mad Max* films is that of a catastrophic, post-apocalyptic Earth, a desert peopled by nomadic tribes who look like contemporary youth subcultures.
32. What is more, in interviews and his publicist work he repeats and develops such theories. In "Flight and Imagination", an interview by Chris Carter, Ballard discusses *Super-Cannes* in reference to the present cultural situation. "In order to keep us happy and spending more as consumer capitalism is going to have to tap rather more darker strains in our characters, which is of course what's been happening for a while". He defines these darker strains as "buried layers of psychopathy", such as the race hatred carried in all of us from our distant past.

this book offers a wealth of interesting insights into contemporary social life in the declining West. Firstly, the very title of the novel is ambiguous. The multiple connotations it suggests are all important to the meaning of the book. As an echo of *The Lord's Prayer* it refers to the times after the end of our profane world, when God's Kingdom comes to Earth and all civilization ceases to matter. In more everyday speech it refers to the state after death when nothing more can be done for anybody.[33] Moreover, in the context of advertising and marketing techniques (and the book's narrator is in the advertising business), "Kingdom come", as paradise on Earth, is what we are promised in commercials. Purchasing the product in question, as every ad persuades us, is to gain an entrance ticket to some better world of style and luxury—but *Kingdom Come* describes what will happen if we believe in this message. The future of the consumer world is "a kingdom where nothing was true or false" (Ballard 206: 204), made entirely from fictions manufactured by publicity people and dispersed across the mediascape.

The novel's narrator is, just like in the case of *Cocaine Nights* and *Super-Cannes*, a man in his forties who finds himself in a new strange place, a "future enclave" where people live in the way the whole West will soon live. The action of all three novels is preceded by a crime which the narrator starts to investigate once he settles down, and in each case he meets a psychiatrist, a police person, a doctor and a young woman who introduce him to the traumas of life in a *Grave New World* of psychopathology, boredom and affluence. In *Kingdom Come* Richard Pearson, an advertising man, goes to a distant London suburb after his father was killed in "a bizarre shooting accident" (ibid.: 5) in a gigantic mall called the Metro-Centre where, in trying to find out why the murder was committed, he gets involved in the local community and its problems.

"The TV ad jumped the gap between reality and illusion, creating a world where the false became real and the real false" (ibid.: 93)—this is the best description of what happened with the people living around the mall. They are the generation raised on commercials, whose life is shopping and who actually desire to be tricked by smart publicity men. Their perception of reality is commercial-based and they wait to be shocked and persuaded there is something more they should buy. The Metro-Centre, the biggest mall in the country, gives them their identity and becomes a central point of the whole district. When it was built a dull suburb changed into a battlefield with squads of middle-class people chasing and beating ethnic minorities who avoid the mall in keeping to their small shops and take-aways.

A gigantic edifice with tens of restaurants, a cable TV studio, parking lots, hotels, supermarkets, shops and parlours, the Metro-Centre satisfies the diverse subliminal needs of shoppers. Compared to the Labyrinth of the Minotaur, "a cathedral of consumerism" and to a shrine, it sustains people with a quasi-religious experience and the psychological satisfaction of infantile needs: shopping is like receiving gifts, being pampered and endlessly playing with elaborate toys and, moreover, "our main way of expressing our tribal values" (ibid.: 78).

33. As in popular, informal expressions of the kind, "they beat him to kingdom come".

The setting of *Kingdom Come* is a suburban cityscape, a "terrain of sensory deprivation" (ibid.: 6) where gigantic billboards are the only signs of cultural life and CCTV cameras outnumber people. Groups of quasi-fascist trouble-makers indulge in "willed insanity" (ibid.: 103), looting and destroying small shops of emigrants from Asia and Eastern Europe. They wear St. George shirts with England's red cross in new nationalistic pride, as within the imposing presence of the mall they feel they belong together. Some local people want to stop the riots, but a provocation they prepare to attract the attention of the authorities ends in the assassination of innocent people in a shooting accident, among them Pearson's father.

What people in this affluent "English backwater" need is a strong leader, but at the same time they are not interested in politics—or any social issues either. For the Metro-Centre mob is inert: the only ideology they have is consumerism. Richard Pearson, with his advertising man's instinct, provides them with a leader they need in the person of the Metro-Centre cable TV presenter, who appeals to people but promises them nothing, asks for nothing and has no political program. Pearson promotes him in a skillfully prepared campaign involving the way products are advertised, and thus gives an element of new hope to people in the district who, as it occurs to him during this social experiment, desperately need commercials and the empty, glossy world of commercials in all spheres of life.

The experiment ends in disaster: the assassination of the presenter by a psychic misfit on his lonely crusade against the mall ends in an outburst of violence. Some deranged publicity managers seize the mall and close themselves inside it with a group of hostages for weeks; the siege ends only when the mall is destroyed by the police. The final section of the novel describes the siege from the point of view of a hostage, as Pearson is one of them. This is the ultimate child's dream come true: being closed forever in a gallery of shops where everything is free for the taking: hotel suites, clothes, fancy foods. Towards the end of his imprisonment Pearson observes the rise of a strange consumer religion: people build temples from luxurious goods and paint barcodes on the backs of their hands "trying to resemble consumer goods they most admired" (ibid.: 268).

Once the mall is destroyed the frenzy dies down. But, as Pearson concludes, such places are sure to be re-erected in the years to come because people do need them. *Kingdom Come* is thus a study of the final stage of consumerism: people are turned into moody children who have to be humoured with gifts; suppressed emotions, once they are triggered, flare up in an outburst of senseless violence and the final social activity is shopping. The inhabitants of *Grave New World* lose contact with reality because bred on mediascape fiction they respond to the world as if it were an advertisement. Life in the spiritual void ends in bizarre quasi-religious behaviour and psychosis, society falls apart into a number of small groups whose irrational behaviour is uncontrollable and who are so bored that they desperately want to be stirred and awakened. In such milieux terrorism flourishes and people re-gain national identity in its degenerate form of racism and fascism. Thus, together with *Cocaine Nights* and *Super-Cannes*, *Kingdom Come* forms an uncannily prophetic trilogy showing what kind of life may be awaiting the affluent West—which is already becoming a *Grave New World*.

The psychological constraints of life in *Grave New World* as described in Ballard's fiction make some of its citizens indulge in solipsist fantasizing, escapes to make-believe realms of imagination. A fantastic Shepperton in *The Unlimited Dream Company* and a surrealist *Vermilion Sands* in the book of the same title are examples of such escapist never-lands of the psyche which nevertheless turn out to be wastelands contaminated with an overwhelming feeling of exhaustion. In fact, both books use imagined territories therapeutically, to examine the psyche of the narrators, and the unrestricted fantasizing ends in the repetition-compulsion of traumas and abandon to the death instinct.

A different kind of wastelands may be found in future enclaves, isolated places within the civilization of today inhabited by the privileged people of tomorrow[34] who, according to Ballard, are prone to psychopathology. Their perverted behaviour is to become a social norm in the near future and their life in too much comfort may end in the state of sensory deprivation and overuse of medication, which in turn results in psychic ailments.

Examples of such wastelands include a luxurious gated community (Pangbourne in *Running Wild*), a sun city for the retired on the Mediterranean coast (Estrella de Mar in *Cocaine Nights*), and a post-modern business park (Eden-Olympia in *Super-Cannes*). The utter boredom of these places is only interrupted by pointless outbursts of violence provided by psychopaths. In *Millennium People* and *Rushing to Paradise* Ballard describes a similar phenomenon within the boundaries of the civilization of today: he depicts the present societies of the affluent world as an inert mass of TV consumers, where only the news of psychopaths and their senseless crimes can wake them from their usual semi-coma.

The very short story "A Guide to Virtual Death" discusses these serious issues in a satirical and crude manner, showing the exhaustion of contemporary culture in one of its samples: a TV guide for one day in the near future. Starting from "6.00 am Porno-Disco. Wake yourself up with his-and-her hard-core sex images played to a disco beat" (Ballard 2002b: 1173), the TV shows are all about sex (most of it perverted and penalized in non-virtual reality), violence, utterly idiotic game shows, reality TV of the worst possible taste, and the like:

> 12.00 Newsflash. The networks promise either a new serial killer or a deadly food toxin.
>
> [...]
>
> 6.00 pm *Today's Special*. Virtual Reality TV presents "The Kennedy Assassination"... First you fire the assassin's rifle from the Book Depository window, and then you sit between Jackie and JFK in the Presidential limo as the bullet strikes. For premium subscribers

---

34. It is worth remembering that a similar distinction is made by Alvin Toffler in his *Future Shock* (which I discuss in Chapter One)—he claims that soon people will divide themselves into a privileged enclave of the future and a maladapted "rest".

only—feel the Presidential brain tissue spatter your face OR wipe Jackie's tears onto your handkerchief.

[...]

3.00 am Night-Hunter. Will the TV Rapist come through your bedroom window? (ibid. 1173-1174).

After twenty-five similar programs taking up altogether twenty-three hours there is the last item in the least favourable TV time: "5.00 am *The Charity Hour*. Game show in which Third-World contestants beg for money" (ibid. 1174). There is no comment, but the TV guide is preceded by a one-sentence introduction according to which intelligent life on Earth has become extinct and the following list of programs "offers its own intriguing insight into the origin of the disaster" (ibid.: 1173). Thus in his critique of contemporary culture Ballard explicitly refers to the disaster story tradition which has been his starting point. The process of the cultural deterioration which started with World War II is still going on, Ballard says, but soon our destiny, total disaster, will at last arrive—wiping our wastelands from the face of the Earth.

CONCLUSION

In *Future Shock* Toffler gives a telling example of the contemporary liability of the turn-over of goods. A company selling Barbie dolls announced that every girl buying a new improved model of Barbie would receive a trade-in allowance for her old doll. "What Mattel did not announce was that by trading in her old doll for a technologically improved model, the little girl of today, citizen of tomorrow's super-industrial world, would learn a fundamental lesson about the new society: that man's relationships with things are increasingly temporary" (Toffler 1980: 51).

Toffler describes the marketing techniques of American corporations in educating future consumers to renounce any sentiment towards the things that accompany people in their lives. A girl from the previous generation would probably have inherited her mother or older sister's dolls, played with them, loved them, and cherished for long years any new one gotten as a Christmas gift. She would remember the names of her dolls for years, and the accidental loss of any one of them would be a minor family tragedy. The new trade-in generation of girls, once they grow up (and the girls Toffler means are now in their forties), are a new kind of citizen with very little sentiment for any bonds with people, places, objects, fashions and ideologies alike. What they love is shopping and social conformity, they feel secure and successful among brand new things and neighbours able to afford equally new merchandise.

"Ending is better than mending"; "mending is antisocial"; and "we don't like people to be attracted by old things"—these are all examples of hypnotic suggestions in Aldous Huxley's *Brave New World*, where all babies go through obligatory conditioning in their sleep to become perfectly manageable citizens of consumer society. In Toffler's account of American life and in Huxley's dystopia people learn to become perfect shoppers subliminally, certain patterns of behaviour are imposed on them in a skillful manner. In *Brand New World*, a low-budget documentary film by Ewan Jones-Morris and Andrzej Wójcik, quotes from Huxley are juxtaposed with interviews with shopping malls clients to show the shocking similarities between the grim prophesy from 1932 and the reality of A.D. 2005. Standardized citizens are seduced to give up their freedom and do not notice their own bondage because they identify freedom with freedom to choose where and how to spend their money. In *Brand New World* we also see a modern Savage who unsuccessfully tries to show the buyers their enslavement to an oversell economy, along with some Huxley scholars who say that towards the end of his life Huxley himself was terrified to see his vision come true.

The critical opinion that Huxley's dystopia, though written over fifteen years earlier than Orwell's, has proven to be anticipatory is becoming a cliché which can be found in literary and sociological papers alike. It is central to Francis Fukuyama's *Our Posthuman Future,* a book that challenges the view that Western civilization, by giving its citizens the right to feel happy, is building a utopian society. Some contemporary social phenomena make the West uncannily resemble the social reality in *Brave New World*. One example might be the massive prescriptions of "Huxley's soma", that is, Prozac, along with other dangerous tendencies already mentioned in the chapters of the present study.

My point has been that J.G. Ballard's books should be read in the context of works of authors interested in the decline of the West such as Toffler, Fukuyama, Baudrillard, Freud, Jung, Debord, Spengler, Toynbee, Jones-Morris, Wójcik and many others.[1] His *oeuvre* is very much involved in cultural, social and psychological theories and his interests are reflected in the reality he

---

1. As well as in reference to literary conventions and intertextual influence of imaginative writers whose domain is fiction.

describes—one which I have dubbed *Grave New World*. At the beginning of this book I defined its aims: primarily to demonstrate the coherence in Ballard's output, a body of work which is seemingly very diverse; secondly to chart the territories of *Grave New World* whose description is the common denominator of Ballard's fiction.

After the initial presentation of Ballardian criticism and the works of theorists I consider important for understanding his *oeuvre*, I went on to describe the diverse territories of *Grave New World,* showing that, according to Ballard, we live in the times of the twilight of the West. Today's world and its very near future are for Ballard the end of the Age of Reason. Our civilization is slowly declining, though not evenly, as some "future enclaves" are forerunners of what is awaiting the population at large. Moreover, inhabitants of these places seem to embrace the grim future willingly.[2]

Ballard claims that World War II and the use of total weapons commenced the final phase of Western civilization: once the drives to destruction and death are set free the violent part of human nature awakes and latent aggression dominates social life. War memories and their impact on twentieth-century culture are in Ballard's *oeuvre* very important, thus the first territory I discussed is "Battlefields", whose analysis shows that the way war is remembered is influenced by war films and fictions. Real experience dissolves in an abundance of images, leaving behind the feeling of nostalgia. In the cityscapes of *Grave New World*, the next territory I map, a similar tendency may be found. Architecture becomes a pastiche of earlier styles, the urban landscape is hostile to people but car-friendly. The automobile in Ballard's books is both the most heavily advertised late-capitalist commodity and a tool of self-destruction. According to Ballard it is because of the Freudian death instinct that people organize space in a way to allow for speedy and dangerous driving, thus realizing the latent need to return to the inorganic world.

A continuous city which covers the world is full of billboards and commercials. The people who live within such mediascapes are conditioned to perceive reality in a way enforced by television and films. In the following chapter I describe mediascapes and the paradoxes they breed. Within the mediascape, experience is only real at the moment it may be watched and citizens turn into spectators. "Art thus becomes a reproduction of a reproduction" (Huyssen 1986: 146) as soon as the mimetic representation of society becomes a picture of people watching pictures. In Ballard's short story "The Greatest Television Show on Earth" such a situation is reduced to sheer nonsense, everybody watches TV so there is nothing to show on TV but TV watchers. What is still worse, the numerous fictions infiltrating reality make the citizens of the affluent West unable to tell the normal from the extraordinary.[3]

---

2. "Just as the technology has almost allowed the great utopia to take place, with a sort of informed society... the desire to go there has completely evaporated—People begin to feel that a dystopia might be more fun" (Vale 2005: 75), reads a passage from a conversation between Ballard and Graeme Revell whose subject is current social situation in the West.

3. In Ballard's short story "Answers to a Questionnaire", the Second Coming of Jesus Christ is

Traumas of life in the times of decline make people long for the peace which would follow some imaginary disaster. Thus in the chapter devoted to mindscapes I read Ballard's catastrophic fictions as examples of wish fulfilment fantasies. Building on Freud's theory that we tend to externalize inner repressed fears, Ballard writes scenarios of destruction coming from the outside, something which is recognized and willingly embraced by protagonists who subliminally know it is high time civilization ended and who behave according to instincts older and stronger than the pleasure principle.

Mindscapes are confined to the inside of people's heads—conversely, the maps of wastelands I next chart depict an external world where although nothing spectacularly fantastic has happened, it turns into a dystopia. Inertia, the overuse of tranquilizers, sensory deprivation and imagined diseases are the major social problems here, and Ballard suggests that only psychopathological behaviour may re-introduced the feeling of reality: Western society drastically needs psychopaths to keep going. It is thus not surprising that some people choose to mentally escape from the constraints of reality, but most try to adapt and the price is usually their mental health. In "Grave New World. An Interview with J.G. Ballard" broadcast in 1998 by *BBC* Radio 3 and now available on the Internet, Ballard talks about psychopathology in the contemporary mediascape as about adaptation: in the future what we today call mental illness might become a norm.

In this interview, whence I borrow the title of my book, Ballard formulates his ideas concerning social life after the End of the Age of Reason, when dreams and utopias from a century ago have to be abandoned. One of these dreams is: "the notion that science, sensibly applied to social problems, will solve most of them, and that we can all live in a kind of Corbusier world where tensions are defused by enlightened social legislation... We seem to need a certain element of sort of street level chaos in our lives." Without this element, isolated and protected by security systems we look for violence to the media and entertainment.

The final conclusion is grave—soon our simulacra-ridden experience will replace life as we know it. Let me end by quoting J.G. Ballard's description of the amoral future of *Grave New World*'s inhabitants:

> [W]hen people enter their virtual reality world, where they can play games with their own psychopathologies, where if they want to they assume, you know, the role of any character in history, or any imaginary character, if they want one day be a Nobel Prize winning physicist, and the next day, you know, play a concentration camp commandant, they'll be able to step beyond the sort of conventional bounds of morality altogether; I mean one would be morally free to play with one's own psychopathology as a game.

unnoticed by the inhabitants of the contemporary media landscape. They think the extraordinary events they are shown are simply the promotion of some kind of merchandise.

BIBLIOGRAPHY

Primary Sources

Ballard, J.G.
1974a *The Wind from Nowhere*. Harmondsworth, Ringwood: Penguin Books.
1974b *The Drowned World*. Harmondsworth, Ringwood: Penguin Books.
1975 *High-Rise*. London: Jonathan Cape.
1977 *Crash*. Frogmore: Panther Books.
1979 *Terminal Beach*. Harmondsworth, Ringwood: Penguin Books.
1982 *Myths of the Near Future*. London: Paladin.
1983 *Hello America*. Reading: Triad/Granada.
1985a *The Drought*. London: Paladin.
1985b *The Unlimited Dream Company*. London: Paladin.
1985c *Empire of the Sun*. London: Book Club Associates.
1988 *The Day of Creation*. London: Grafton Books, 1988.
1989 *Running Wild*. London: Arena.
1992a *Concrete Island*. London: Paladin.
1992b *The Disaster Area*. London: Paladin.
1992c *The Venus Hunters* (first published as *The Overloaded Man*, 1967). London: Flamingo.
1994 *The Kindness of Women*. London: Flamingo.
1995a *Rushing to Paradise*. London: Flamingo.
1995b *The Day of Forever*. London: Flamingo.
1997a *Cocaine Nights*. London: Flamingo.
1997b *A User's Guide to the Millennium*. London: Flamingo.
2000 *The Crystal World*. London: Flamingo.
2001 *The Atrocity Exhibition* (annotated version with added commentary notes by J.G. Ballard, first printed 1990). London: Flamingo.
2002a *Super-Cannes*. New York: Picador USA.
2002b *The Complete Short Stories*. London: Flamingo.
2004 *Millennium People*. London: Harper Perennial.
2006 *Kingdom Come*. London: Fourth Estate.
2008 *Miracles of Life. Shanghai to Shepperton. An Autobiography*. London: Fourth Estate.

Secondary Sources

Aldiss, Brian
Billion Years Spree. London: Corgi Books.
Barthes, Roland
1993 *Mythologies*. Trans. Annette Lavers. London, Sydney, Auckland, Parktown: Vintage.
Baudrillard, Jean
1994 *America*. Trans. Chris Turner. London, New York: Verso.
2003 *Simulacra and Simulations*. Trans. Sheila Faria Glaser. Ann Arbor: The University of Michigan Press.
Boulle, Pierre
1961 *Le Pont de la Rivière Kwai*. Julliard : Paris.
Breton, André
1929 *Manifestos of Surrealism*. Trans. Richard Seaver and Helen R. Lane. The University Of Michigan Press.
1967 "Le Surréalism et la Peinture", in : *André Breton*. J.H. Matthews (ed.). Columbia University Press.
1978 *What is Surrealism*. Trans. Richard Seaver and Helen R. Lane. The University of Michigan Press.
1988 *Mad Love*. Trans. M.A. Cows. Lincoln: University of Nebraska Press.
Breton, André and Paul Eluard
1990 *The Immaculate Conception*. Trans. Jon Graham. London: Alas.
Brown, Archie
The Gorbachev Factor. Oxford, New York: Oxford University Press.
Bürger, Peter
1980 *Theory of the Avant-Garde*. Trans. Michael Shaw. Minneapolis: University of Minnesota Press.
Burroughs, Edgar Rice
Tarzan of the Apes. Chicago: McClurg.
The Return of Tarzan. Chicago: McClurg.
Chang, Jung
2004 *Wild Swans: Three Daughters of China*. London: Harper Perennial.
Clavell, James
1999 *The Rat King*. London: Hodder and Stoughton.
Clute, John and Nicholls, Peter
1993 *The Encyclopedia of Science Fiction*. Clute, John and Nicholls, Peter (eds.), London: Orbit.
Conrad, Joseph
1990 *Heart of Darkness*. Mineola: Dover Publications.
Dali, Salvador
1994 *Diary of a Genius*. Trans. Richard Howard, London: Creation Books.
Debord, Guy
1967 *Society of the Spectacle*. London: Rebel Press/ Dark Star. (The translator and date of English edition not stated).

Delville, Michel

J.G. Ballard. Plymouth: Northcote House.

Dick, Philip K.

1969 The Simulacra. Doubleday.

1969 *Ubik*. Doubleday.

Ellison, Harlan (ed.)

Dangerous Visions. New York: Berkley Books.

Ford, Boris (ed.)

1995 *The New Pelican Guide to the English Literature, Vol. 8 From Orwell to Naipaul*. London, New York, Ringwood, Toronto, Auckland: Penguin Books.

Foucault, Michel

1979 *Discipline and Punish*. Trans. Alan Sheridan. New York: Vintage.

Francis, Sam

2006a "J.G. Ballard's The Unlimited Dream Company as Self-Reflective Fantasy". In: *Foundation*, 97, summer 2006, pp.70-85

2006b *Critical Reading of 'Inner Space' in Selected Works of J.G. Ballard*. Unpublished doctoral thesis, University of Leeds, 2006.

Frazer, James

1914 *The Golden Bough* (Third Edition). London: Macmillan.

Freud, Sigmund

1938 *The Basic Writings of Sigmund Freud*. Trans. A.A. Brill. New York: The Modern Library.

1967 *Beyond the Pleasure Principle*. Trans. James Strachey. New York, Toronto, London: Bantam Books.

1986 *Historical and Expository Works on Psychoanalysis*. Trans. James Strachey. Harmondsworth, New York, Victoria, Ontario, Auckland: Pelican Books.

1994 *The Major Works*. Trans. Joan Riviere,. "The Great Works of the Western World", ed. Mortimer J. Adler, v. 54 Freud, Chicago: Encyclopedia Britannica Inc.

Fukuyama, Francis

2002a *The End of History and the Last Man*. New York: Perennial.

2002b *Our Posthuman Future. Consequences of the Biotechnology Revolution*. London: Profile Books.

Gasiorek, Andrzej

J.G. Ballard. Manchester: Manchester University Press.

Gibbon, Edward

1905 *The History of the Decline and Fall of the Roman Empire*. London: Methuen & Co.

Goddard, James and David Pringle

1976 *J.G. Ballard: The First Twenty Years*. London: Bran's Head Books.

Golding, William

1970 *Pincher Martin*. London: Faber and Faber.

Gray, Edward (Viscount of Fallodon)
1925 *Twenty-Five Years 1892-1916*. London: Hodder and Soughton.
Greenland, Colin
The Entropy Exhibition. Michael Moorcock and the British 'New Wave' in Science Fiction. London, Boston, Melbourne, Henley: Routledge & Kegan Paul.
Grosz, Elizabeth
1996 *Jacques Lacan. A Feminist Introduction*. London and New York: Routledge.
Gunn, James (ed.)
1979 *The Road to Science Fiction, vol. 3 From Heinlein to Here*. Los Angeles: Mentor/ New American Library.
Hubert, Renée Riese
1992 *Surrealism and the Book*. Berkeley, Los Angeles, London: University of California.
Huntington, Samuel P.
The Clash of Civilizations and the Remaking of World Order. London, New York, Sydney, Tokyo, Toronto, Singapore: Touchstone Books.
Huxley, Aldous
Brave New World. Harmondsworth, Ringwood: Penguin Books.
Huyssen, Andreas
1986 *After the Great Divide. Modernism, Mass Culture, Postmodernism*. Bloomington and Indianapolis: Indiana University Press.
Jackson, Rosemary
Fantasy: The Literature of Subversion, London: Rutledge.
Jameson, Frederic
"Postmodernism and Consumer Society". In: *The Anti-Aesthetics*, Hal Foster (ed.), Port Townsend: Bay Press, pp. 111-125.
"Postmodernism, or the Cultural Logic of Late Capitalism". *New Left Review*, no. 146.
Jarry, Alfred
1965 *The Selected Works of Alfred Jarry*. London: Grove Press.
1992 *Caesar Antichrist*. Trans. Anthony Melville. London: Atlas Press.
Jung, Carl Gustav
1978 *Man and his Symbols*. London: Picador Pan Books.
Kostecki, Wojciech
1996 *Europe after the Cold War. The Security Complex Theory*. Warsaw: Instytut Studiów Politycznych PAN.
Kopaliński, Władysław
Słownik wydarzeń, pojęć i legend XX wieku. Warszawa: Wydawnictwo Naukowe PWN.
Kuhn, Anette
Alien Zone. Cultural Theory and Contemporary Science Fiction Cinema. London, New York: Verso.
LaHaye, Tim and Jerry Jenkins
2003 *Left Behind*. Brisbane: Strand Publishing.

Laing, R.D.

1965 *The Divided Self.* Harmondsworth, London: Penguin Books.

1990 *The Politics of Experience.* London: Penguin Books.

Lindley, Hal

The Late, Great Planet Earth. Grand Rapids, Michigan: Zondervan.

Linnet, Peter

1974 "Interview with J.G. Ballard". In *Corridor*, no. 5, pp. 4-7.

Lowery, Martyn

1990 *The Blessed of the Impossible Worlds. J.G. Ballard's Catastrophic
    Imagination.* Unpublished doctoral thesis, University of Exeter, 1990.

Luckhurst, Roger

'The Angle Between Two Walls'. The Fiction of J.G. Ballard. Liverpool: Liverpool
    University Press.

Materska, Dominika (See **Oramus, Dominika**)

McLuhan, Marshall

Understanding Media. London, New York: Routledge.

Merril, Judith

England Swings SF. Stories of Speculative Fiction. New York: Ace Books.

Miller, Donald

Lewis Mumford, A Life. New York: Weldenfield and Nicolson.

Oramus, Dominika (Dominika Materska)

2003 "Persistence of Memory: Surrealism in *Vermilion Sands* by J.G. Ballard". In
    Acta Philologica, eds Joanna Ugniewska-Dobrzańska et al, Warsaw, pp.
    107-118.

2004 "Realms of the Thanatos: J.G. Ballard's *The Drowned World* in the Light
    of Sigmund Freud's *Beyond the Pleasure Principle*". In: *Perspectives on
    Literature and Culture*, eds. Leszek S. Kolek, Aleksandra Kędzierska and
    Anna Kędra-Kardela: Lublin, pp. 205-214.

2005a "From the Avant-Garde to the Autobiography: The Journalism of J.G.
    Ballard" in *Anglica*, eds Andrzej Weseliński and Jerzy Wełna, Warsaw,
    pp. 39-52.

2005b "The Voices of Disaster: J.G. Ballard and the Disaster Story Tradition in
    England", Department of English Literature, Warsaw University:
    Warsaw.

2006 "In the pearl light of Nagasaki: J.G. Ballard's War Narratives", in *Anglica*,
    eds Andrzej Weseliński and Jerzy Wełna, Warsaw, pp. 11-22.

Parrinder, Patrick (ed.)

1979 *Science Fiction. A Critical Guide.* London and New York: Pearson
    Education, Longman.

2000 *Learning from Other Worlds. Estrangement, Cognition and the Politics of
    Science Fiction and Utopia.* Liverpool: Liverpool University Press.

Pringle, David

Earth is the Alien Planet. J.G. Ballard's Four-Dimensional Nightmare. San
    Bernardino: Borgo Press.

Punter, David

The Hidden Script. Writing and the Unconscious. London, Boston, Melbourne, Henley: Routledge & Kegan Paul.

1996 *The Literature of Terror.* London and New York: Longman.

Pynchon, Thomas

"Entropy". In *Slow Learner*, Boston: Little Brown and Company.

Rycroft, Charles

1995 *A Critical Dictionary of Psychoanalysis* (Second Edition). Harmondsworth: Penguin Books.

Self, Will

Junk Mail. London: Penguin Books.

Shakespeare, William

1987 *The Complete Works.* London: Henry Pordes.

Slusser, George and Westfall, Gary (eds.)

2002 *Science Fiction, Canonization, marginalization and the Academy*, Westport, Connecticut, London: Greenwood Press.

Smith, Curtis C.

Twentieth Century Science Fiction Writers. New York: St. Martin's Press.

Sontag, Susan

A Susan Sontag Reader. London: Penguin Books.

Spark, Muriel

1977 *The Hothouse by the East River.* London: Penguin Books.

Spengler, Oswald

1991 *The Decline of the West* (One-volume edition). Trans. Charles Francis Atkinson, New York, Oxford: Oxford University Press.

Staniszkis, Jadwiga

2003 *Władza globalizacji.* Warsaw: Scholar.

Sutin, Lawrance

1991 *Divine Invasions. A Life of Philip K. Dick.* New York: HarperCollins Publishers.

Todorov, Tzvetan

1975 *The Fantastic: A Structural Approach to a Literary Genre.* Trans. Richard Howard. Ithaca and London: Cornell University Press.

Toffler, Alvin

Future Shock. London, New York, Toronto: Bantham Books.

The Third Wave. London, New York, Toronto: Bantham Books.

1991 *Power Shift. Knowledge, Wealth, and Violence at the Edge of the 21st Century.* London, New York, Toronto: Bantham Books.

Toynbee, Arnold, J.

1949 *Civilisation on Trial.* London, New York, Toronto: Oxford University Press.

1987 *A Study of History.* Abridgement of Volumes I-VI by D. C. Somervell. New York, Oxford: Oxford University Press.

Vale V. and A. Juno (eds.)

RE/Search 8, 9. Special J.G. Ballard issue.

Vale V. and Mike Ryan (eds.)

2003 *Quotes J.G. Ballard*. San Francisco: RE/Search Publications.

Vale V. (ed.)

2005 *J.G. Ballard Conversations*. San Francisco: RE/Search Publications.

Wnuk-Lipiński, Edmund (ed.)

1995 *After Communism. A Multidisciplinary Approach to Radical Social Change*. Warsaw: Instytut Studiów Politycznych PAN.

Wyndham, John

1955 *Kraken Wakes*. London: Penguin Books.

The Midwich Cuckoos. London: Penguin Books.

Zilboorg, Gregory

Introduction. In: *Sigmund Freud, Beyond the Pleasure Principle*. Trans. James Strachey. New York, Toronto, London: Bantam Books, 1967.

Żiżek, Slavoy

Enjoy Your Symptom. New York, London: Routledge.

Films

Jones-Morris, Ewan and Wójcik, Andrzej

2005 *Brand New World*. Wales Arts International.

Spielberg, Steven

1987a *Empire of the Sun*. Warner Bros. Entertainment Inc.

1987b *The China Odyssey: Empire of the Sun*, a film by Steven Spielberg. Warner Bros. Entertainment Inc.

INDEX

Ingram Content Group UK Ltd.
Milton Keynes UK
UKHW022328090623
423211UK00006B/27